THE RETURN OF RAZZID

It happened without warning. A heaving line with a sling rigged at its end swished down from the top of the fore-mast. The figure sitting in the swing swung out with a broad ship's carpenter's hatchet as it sped by, and Brag-gio Ironhook lost his head. It splashed down into an open grog cask on the shore. The slayer waited as the heaving line swung back, then neatly stepped onto the prow end, kicking the headless ferret aside. Musicians ground to a halt; the drunken revelers froze, still holding up their drinks. Suddenly all that could be heard was the waves washing the sand and the fires crackling.

Mowlag's command cut the silence. "I give ye a toast. To the mighty Razzid Wearat an' his ship *Greenshroud*!"

Vermin corsairs gaped in disbelief. It was Razzid, and he was alive.

THE REDWALL BOOKS

Redwall
Mossflower
Mattimeo
Mariel of Redwall
Salamandastron
Martin the Warrior
The Bellmaker
Outcast of Redwall
Pearls of Lutra
The Long Patrol
Marlfox
The Legend of Luke
Lord Brocktree
Taggerung
Triss
Loamhedge
Rakkety Tam
High Rhulain
Eulalia!
Doomwyte
The Sable Quean
The Rogue Crew

The Great Redwall Feast (picture book)
A Redwall Winter's Tale (picture book)

OTHER BOOKS

Seven Strange and Ghostly Tales
Castaways of the Flying Dutchman
The Angel's Command
The Ribbajack and Other Curious Yarns
Voyage of Slaves

The Tale of Urso Brunov (picture book)
Urso Brunov and the White Emperor (picture book)

A tale of REDWALL

The Rogue Crew

BRIAN JACQUES

Illustrated by Sean Rubin

FIREBIRD

AN IMPRINT OF PENGUIN GROUP (USA) INC.

FIREBIRD
Published by the Penguin Group
Penguin Group (USA) Inc.
375 Hudson Street
New York, New York 10014, U.S.A.

USA / Canada / UK / Ireland / Australia / New Zealand / India / South Africa / China
Penguin Books Ltd, Registered Offices: 80 Strand, London WC2R 0RL, England

For more information about the Penguin Group visit www.penguin.com

First published in the United States of America by Philomel Books,
a division of Penguin Young Readers Group, 2011
Published by Firebird, an imprint of Penguin Group (USA) Inc., 2013

Text copyright © The Redwall Abbey Company, Ltd., 2011
Illustrations copyright © Sean Rubin, 2011

THE LIBRARY OF CONGRESS HAS CATALOGED THE PHILOMEL BOOKS EDITION AS FOLLOWS:
Jacques, Brian.
The Rogue Crew / Brian Jacques; illustrated by Sean Rubin.
p. cm.
Summary: The murderous and evil Razzid Wearat and his crew of vermin are on a mission to
seize Redwall Abbey for themselves, and Abbot Thibb and his Redwallers must defend their
home with the help of the hares of the Long Patrol and the Rogue Crew of sea otters.
ISBN 978-0-399-25416-1 (hardcover)
[1. Animals—Fiction. 2. Fantasy.] I. Rubin, Sean, 1986— ill.
II. Title. PZ7.J15317Ro 2011 [Fic]—dc22 2010013330

ISBN 978-0-14-242618-0

Printed in United States of America

13th Printing

Designed by Semadar Megged

The publisher does not have any control over and does not assume any
responsibility for author or third-party websites or their content.

For Jimmy Jacques,
a great pal who is also
an outstanding brother.

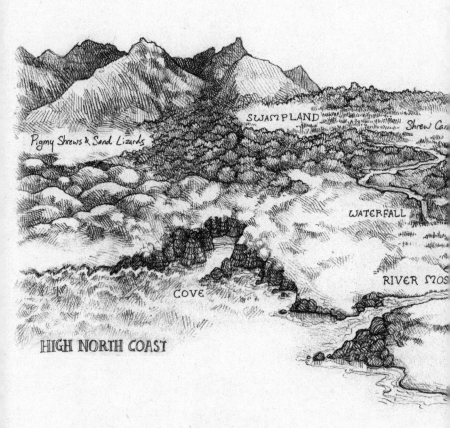

Pigmy Shrews & Sand Lizards

SWAMPLAND

Shrew Ca

WATERFALL

RIVER MOS

COVE

HIGH NORTH COAST

MOSSFLOWER COUNTRY
AND THE
HIGH·NORTH·COAST
DURING THE EVENTS OF THE ROGUE CREW

MOSSFLOWER WOOD

TUNNEL EXIT

BAT TUNNEL

FORD

REDWALL

THE WESTERN PLAINS

DUNES

Uncle Willow's Camp

SALAMANDASTRON

The Land of Dreams, that mystical realm,
where the oddest of visions appear,
come wander through scenes of joyful peace,
or stampede through nightmares of fear.
Dare we open those secret doors,
down dusty paths of mind,
in long-forgotten corners,
what memories we'll find.
Who rules o'er the Kingdom of Night,
where all is not what it seems?
'Tis I, the Weaver of Tales,
for I am the Dreamer of Dreams!

BOOK ONE

A Small Glutton's Dream

1

The face of a Wearat is a sight to instill fear and loathing in any creature. Two narrow eyes, crimson, with small green pupils, a huge, squat head sparsely coated with hair, save for the stiff mane at the back. A short, broad muzzle, with a sheen like polished leather, beneath which yellowed fangs jut in all directions. Truly a beast that should never have been born, an obscure hybrid that cannot be categorised with anybeast.

Some were of the opinion a Wearat was part weasel, part water rat. Nobeast knew. One thing was beyond doubt, however. A Wearat was the embodiment of nightmare, with a vicious nature that knew no bounds. It revelled in blood and death.

One such rare savage was Razzid Wearat, the most barbarous of all seagoing vermin. From his fortress on the Isle of Irgash in the warm southern seas, he emerged like a hurricane of destruction. His ship was the *Greenshroud*, a long, swift galley. From sailtops to hull, the entire vessel was green. It carried a single bank of oars, twoscore port and starboard. Aft of its square-sailed mainmast were two lateen sails, tall billowing triangles. The mainsail bore the Mark of the Wearat, a trident head, with two evil eyes between the forked prongs. *Greenshroud* was crewed by vermin corsairs spurred on by the promise of plunder.

The season that Razzid struck coasts and settlements both sides of Mossflower Country became known as the Winter of Slaughter. The speed with which Razzid raided helpless creatures was swift and ruthless. He left in his wake the flames of desolation and death, smouldering ruins which made his name a byword for terror.

Razzid's Seer and Soothsayer, the vixen Shekra, cast her shells, bones, feathers and stones, advising him on all his wicked enterprises. It was, therefore, his own fault when he ignored her warning to steer clear of the High North Coast. Defenceless creatures, and easy victories, made the Wearat overconfident—he laughed scornfully.

"The only trouble I have is tryin' to get somebeast that'll stand an' fight me. All I ever see is timid creatures turnin' tail an' runnin' away. Right, Mowlag?"

Greenshroud's first mate, the searat Mowlag, agreed promptly. "Ain't never seen a beast with the guts to stan' an' face ye, Razzid. Yore the terror o' land and sea, sure enough!"

Razzid kicked Shekra's collection of omen givers scornfully. "Hah—mumbo jumbo, shells'n'feathers! Set a course for the High North Coast, Mowlag!"

The decision was Razzid Wearat's greatest mistake, for he met Skor Axehound and his sea otter warriors. Expecting nobeast to stand in his way, Razzid pressed on. Reaching the High North Coast, he made a swift foray inshore, speeded by a blustering, snowy gale at his stern. The corsair crew daubed their faces with war paint, following their captain. Razzid leapt overboard into the rough grey waters, brandishing his trident, with the crew all around him roaring, "A Wearat! A Wearat! Death's on the wiiiiiind!"

Sea otters were fighters and not fools. The lookouts of

Skor Axehound had sighted *Greenshroud* as she hove into land. They were waiting in force for him. Carrying thick birchbark shields, armed from tooth to rudder with axes, spears, swords, clubs, slings and bows, they ambushed the would-be raiders. Razzid and his crew were caught waist deep in the sea, facing battle-eager beasts, the Warchief Skor and his Rogue Crew. That day the snow-flecked water of the Northern Sea was dyed crimson with vermin blood. The fury of Skor's otters was so great that the Wearat, and the remnants of his defeated crew, were forced to beat a blundering retreat. Clambering aboard *Greenshroud*, they tried to get underway. But the slingstones, spears and fire arrows of sea otters hammered their vessel.

Greenshroud finally managed to struggle off, with sails and stern gallery ablaze, lines and rigging popping as the fire took hold, and the added handicap of a damaged tiller. Skor and his warriors stood in the shallows, banging weapons on their shields, challenging the invaders to come back and fight, roaring out their victory song.

"Hoolawhey! Hoolawhey!
Hurry to the slaughter.
Hiyaree! Hiyaree!
Meet us in the water.
Come back here, do not fear,
come and grant our wishes.
Join your friends in this sea,
come and feed the fishes.
Hoolawhey! Hoolawhey!
We will meet another day.
Hiyaree! Hiyaree!
Flee, cowards, flee!"

The invitation was all in vain. *Greenshroud* headed off southwest, its vermin corsairs cursing the mothers of all sea otters for bearing such fearsome sons and daughters.

In his frantic efforts to extinguish the blaze which threatened to engulf *Greenshroud*, Razzid Wearat was badly burnt. Shekra had him wrapped in wet canvas; he was carried off screeching with pain and anger. The vixen stayed at his side, having a knowledge of healing. She stopped in the charred cabin to tend his wounds. Rain and snow helped to douse the flames. After a few running repairs, Mowlag took command, steering the vessel southwest, back to more temperate climes. Realising it was a case of stay afloat or sink, the searat mate drove the decimated crew hard, cursing, flogging, and threatening the wretched corsairs. Through endless days and wearisome nights, the damaged craft limped slowly into the far southern seas.

It took a full season until *Greenshroud* came at last to anchor in the bay at Irgash Isle. Vermin waited on the shore to greet their leader—for was not the fearsome Wearat always returning in triumph? However, this time it was different. *Greenshroud*, charred, battered and half crewed, was a chastening sight. The searats and vermin corsairs watched in silence as a party bearing a canvas-covered stretcher waded ashore through the sun-warmed shallows. Shekra had the litter well guarded by a score of heavily armed crewbeasts. There was little need for guessing. Everybeast knew who the hidden figure was by the lethal trident which had been placed on the stretcher. It was their chief, Razzid Wearat. The vixen hastened the group over the sand into the timber stockade, slamming and locking the gates as the onlookers surged forward.

There was plenty to speculate about, but everybeast held their silence. Razzid had his spies—there was always the fear of reprisal for loose talk. However, there had long been a contender for the captainship of *Greenshroud*, Braggio Ironhook. He was a big, brutal ferret, renowned as a killer, with a curved iron hook replacing his left forepaw. Braggio turned to view the damaged ship in the bay, then spoke, his voice loud and bold.

"Well, break out the grog, mates, we got us a broken craft an' a dead cap'n if'n I'm to believe me eyes, eh!"

An old searat shrugged. "Mebbe Razzid ain't dead. I saw the canvas move a bit. Wearats don't die so easy."

Braggio tripped the speaker as he turned to walk away. "Wot would yew know, ye can't even stand up proper. I say Razzid's dead—or leastways, if'n 'e ain't, well, 'e soon will be. Am I right, Crumdun?"

The small, fat stoat who was his constant shadow chuckled. "Yore right there, Bragg. Y'ain't afeared o' nobeast!"

The big ferret swaggered amongst the other corsair vermin, letting them see his lethal iron hook. "Youse 'eard Crumdun. I ain't afeared o' nobeast! Of course, if'n there's anybeast who ain't afeared o' me, all 'e has to do is challenge me by speakin' up!"

Braggio Ironhook had an enviable reputation as a fierce fighter. The corsairs looked at the ground. There was not one who fancied his chance against the ferret.

Braggio spat scornfully on the sand, watching the crew and some slaves hauling the emaciated *Greenshroud* above the tideline. "Ahoy, Crumdun, let's go an' cast an eye over that wreck."

Inside the stockade, Razzid lay in his private chamber, with Shekra attending him. The vixen had lit a fire in the centre of the floor. She tended the Wearat diligently, smoothing unguents and soothing ointments on his burns. Mowlag stood watching her in the dim light as she poured medicine into Razzid's unresponsive mouth. It spilled out. The searat mate shook his head. Perhaps his guess had been right—maybe the Wearat didn't have long to go. He looked very still. Shekra sprinkled powder upon the fire. It began giving off heavy green and yellow smoke. Now she emptied out her pouch onto the floor close to Razzid. Selecting some items from the contents—shells, stones, feathers and bones—she went into a high, croaking dirge.

Mowlag covered his mouth and nostrils, to save having

to breathe the cloying fumes of the smoke. "Well, fox, wot's the strength o' things? Is Razzid gonna live?"

The Seer cast her materials at the Wearat's footpaws, then hurried to and fro. She set the chamber door ajar, then opened a window shutter. In a short time, the chamber was completely clear of the greeny yellow smoke and fumes. Mowlag was not impressed. He repeated the question irately.

"Stow the mumbo jumbo, fox. Just tell me, will 'e live?"

Shekra studied how the omens had fallen. "Oh, yes, Razzid Wearat will live. The omens never lie. See this long shell? That is the *Greenshroud*. Three green feathers landed in it—they are the sails." She picked out a stone from the shell, explaining. "This pebble, it represents him. See how it is pitted and marked, no longer perfect—damaged but still aboard the ship? Nothing is more certain, my friend. Razzid will survive to sail his vessel again!"

Mowlag silenced her with a wave of his paw. "His lips just moved. Does he want water?"

They both leaned close to the bandaged figure as Shekra soaked some moss in water. She held it close to his mouth. He did not drink but spoke quite clearly in a low snarl. "I . . . will . . . live!"

Braggio Ironhook strolled around the beached hulk of *Greenshroud*, assessing it closely. There was a creak from the high stern deck, then the rudder moved fractionally. Braggio called out, "Wot are ye playin' at up there, picklebrain?" Owing to the number of times he had sustained head injuries whilst leading the corsair life, Crumdun was not the brightest of vermin. Popping his head between the after rails, he announced his discovery.

"She's gonna need a new tiller, Bragg!"

Braggio feigned surprise. "Well, now, who'd have thought that?"

The fat stoat seemed pleased with himself as he continued. "On me oath, she is. An' foremast, an' new sails, an' about fifteen oars, an' a whole set o' riggin'. There ain't a strand o' rope wot didn't get burnt. Good job ye brought me wid ye, eh, Bragg?"

Braggio gestured with his hook.

"Ahoy, pudden'ead, shut yore fat gob an' git down 'ere. I've got a job for ye."

Crumdun wheezed his way down the charred hull. Brushing damp black ash from his greasy vest, he grinned crookedly. "Wot job's dat, mate?"

Braggio leaned close, keeping his voice low. "Go an' round up some slaves for me, but do it nice'n'quiet. Fetch those three ole shrew wives, the ones who are good at fixin' up sailcloth. Aye, an' them vole brothers that builds carts an' such like. . . ."

Crumdun saluted and trundled off, but Braggio yanked him back by the tail. "Don't go roamin' off, mudface. I ain't finished yet. Now, lissen. Y'know those 'ogslaves Razzid uses for ship repairin'?"

The fat stoat nodded eagerly. "That'll be ole Kalstig an' 'is kinbeasts. Shall I fetch them, too?"

Braggio nodded. "Aye, bring 'em all an' make sure they've got their tools with 'em."

Crumdun wrinkled his snout in a secretive smile. "Are ye figgerin' on makin' the ole *Greenshroud* shipshape agin? Are ye, Bragg?"

The hulking ferret touched the tip of his hook to the end of Crumdun's nose, snarling savagely. "Just one word o' this to anybeast on Irgash Isle, ye middenbrained lard bucket, an' ye know wot I'll do to ye?"

"Aye, ye'll stick yore 'ook so far up me nose that it'll come outta me left ear." Crumdun grinned cheerily. Braggio released him.

"Right. Now, get goin', addlebrain!"

Braggio Ironhook had always wanted a ship of his own. The idea of being a sea captain appealed immensely to him. Razzid Wearat would soon be making the voyage to Hellgates—he wouldn't be needing this charred wreck, so why waste it if it could be made seaworthy again? Sitting down on the shore, Braggio began marking out in the sand a blue-print. This was the plan for a vessel he had long dreamed of. Many seasons of cunning and ingenuity had gone into the idea. Braggio knew it would work.

The ship was to be named *Ironhook*. It would be invincible, fast and powerful, feared both on deep sea and dry land. He pictured it sailing out of Irgash harbour, with him pacing the foredeck, a master of vermin corsairs, Braggio Ironhook. This island would become his—the day would come when Razzid Wearat would be nought but a dim memory.

Contrary to Braggio's prediction, Razzid Wearat was not dying. It took almost half a season of constant attention from the vixen Shekra before his condition began to improve. Then one morning he called Mowlag to his side. The searat mate knew his master was recovering when Razzid's claws dug sharply into his shoulder. The Wearat hauled himself almost into a sitting position.

"Did ye think I was goin' to Hellgates, Mowlag?"

The mate winced as the claws tightened their grip. "Not me, Cap'n. I knew ye'd live. I'm 'ere t'serve ye—just give the word an' I'll do as ye say!"

Razzid released Mowlag and lay back. "I know you were here night an' day, my friend, but now I want ye to go out an' be seen round the island agin. Put the word about that I'm slowly sinkin' an' won't last out the season. Then report back here t'me every evenin'."

Mowlag nodded. He could see Razzid's right eye peering from a gap in the bandaged face. "Aye, Cap'n. Anythin' special ye wants me t'look for?"

Razzid beckoned to Shekra, who helped him to sip some water. Licking blistered lips, he closed his eyes. "Tell me how that fool Ironhook is progressing with his work on my ship. Make him think you are on his side."

Mowlag rose. "I'll act as if'n Braggio was me own brother."

When Mowlag had gone, Razzid whispered to Shekra, "When will I be fit enough to move about again?"

The vixen bowed respectfully. "Why ask me when you already know, Lord?"

A faint chuckle rose from the bandaged figure.

"I would have slain you for answering falsely."

2

Brisk breezes caused the window shutters to rattle and clatter round old Redwall Abbey. It was a boisterous late spring. With no prior warning, the rain arrived. Workers left their outdoor chores, hurrying to seek warmth and comfort inside the ancient building. Leaning on the sill of his study window, Abbot Thibb watched Sister Fisk hurrying over the rainswept lawns toward the gatehouse. Fisk was the Infirmary Sister, a youngish mouse the same age as Thibb. Her habit flopped wetly about her as she held on to the hood with one paw whilst clutching her satchel in the other. Thibb was popular with the Redwallers, though some thought that the squirrel's lack of seasons was not quite appropriate in an Abbot. This did not bother him. He was normally cheerful and fair in his dealings with everybeast. However, Abbot Thibb was not a squirrel to gladly suffer fools and wrongdoers. He saw Sister Fisk stumble and fall ungracefully.

Thibb struck the sill with a clenched paw, muttering angrily, "Right, Uggo Wiltud. Let's find out what you've got to say for yourself, shall we?"

He ran from the chamber, slamming the door behind him. Taking the stairs two at a time, he descended rapidly to Great Hall, still muttering under his breath. "A full-sized hefty fruitcake, with marchpane topping as thick as an otter's rudder, and the greedy hog ate all of it!"

A burly otter stepped aside as Thibb hurried by. "Arternoon, Father Abbot, where be ye off to in such 'aste?"

Thibb nodded to old Jum Gurdy, Redwall's Cellardog. "Oh, hello, Jum. Thought I'd take a look in at the gatehouse."

A Dibbun volemaid (Dibbun is the affectionate name for all Abbeybabes) tugged at Thibb's cloak. Little Brinky chuckled with unconcealed glee at the thought of what the Abbot was about. "You goin' ta tell Uggo off? Can I come wiv ya, Farver?"

He patted the Dibbun's head. "No, no. Stop here, Brinky."

The volemaid asked that question which all little ones ask. "Why?"

Thibb's eyes twinkled momentarily, but he kept his voice stern.

"I don't think some of the things I have to say to Master Wiltud would be fitting for a little maid's ears!"

Thibb had to push hard on the door to open it against the blustering wind. The big oaken door closed with a boom which echoed round the vaulted hall.

Wide-eyed, Brinky turned to a molebabe called Murty. "Ho, my jingles, I wouldn't like t'be Uggo when Farver T'ibb has a word wiv him!"

Murty shook his small velvety head, replying in the quaint mole accent. "Boo urr, nor wudd oi, Brinky. They'm sayen Uggo stoled a gurt fruitycake, burr aye, an' 'ee etted it all boi 'isself. 'Ee never give'd uz none, so 'ee'm dissurves a gudd tellen off, so 'ee doo!" At the main gates of Redwall's high outer walls, Thibb wiped rainwater from his eyes, gave a brief knock on the small gatehouse door and entered. Sweeping off his wet cloak, he allowed Dorka Gurdy, the Cellardog's sister, to hang it on a peg.

"Well, how is the young glutton, Dorka?"

The female otter Gatekeeper nodded at the large, over-stuffed bed, which occupied almost a third of the little room.

"Ye'd best ask Fisk that, Father Abbot."

Sister Fisk was sitting by the bed, her head enveloped in a towel, scrubbing herself dry. She peeked from beneath its folds. "Oh, 'tis you, Father. Young Wiltud's still sleeping. I thought it best not to wake him just yet." Thibb looked over to the figure. Uggo Wiltud was huddled in the shadows at the far side of the bed.

"I don't know why you're mollycoddling him, Sister. He's brought all of this on his own head, the rascal!"

Dorka Gurdy explained. "Young Uggo's in some kind o' funny dream, Father. Wrigglin' an' jabberin' away, like as if he's afeared of summat. See, there he goes agin."

The young hedgehog began throwing up his paws to protect his face or to blot out some fearsome sight. He started to wail aloud, pleading shrilly, "Oooowwww! No, no, go 'way! Don't take me, please. Yaaaaah!" Uggo pulled the pillows over his face, holding them tight.

Sister Fisk tut-tutted. "Young fool, he'll smother himself."

Reaching over, she snatched the pillows from her patient. Uggo Wiltud sat up with a jerk, his eyes popping open. He was trembling all over, staring straight ahead. Abbot Thibb's stern tone caught his attention.

"So, Master Wiltud, what was all that caterwauling about, eh? Were you being chased by a monster hefty fruitcake?"

Uggo stared at Thibb, as if seeing him for the first time. "It was the ship, a big one, with a green sail!"

Dorka chuckled. "Yore stomach must still be queasy after all that cake you scoffed. Dreamin' ye were at sea, I s'pose."

Uggo's voice trembled as he fought back tears. "I wasn't at sea, marm. I were stannin' on the path outside the Abbey. . . ."

There was a touch of irony in Sister Fisk's tone. "And you saw a ship, a real sailing ship. Coming over the west flatlands, was it?"

The young hog shook his head. "No, Sister. 'Twas comin' along the path, straight at me!"

Abbot Thibb sat down on the edge of the bed. "Was it a real sailing ship chasing you? What did you do?"

Uggo waved his paws in anguish. "I ran, Father, ran for me life, but the ship came after me. I looked back an' I saw the 'orrible beastie leanin' over the side o' the ship, gnashin' 'is teeth at me." Uggo yanked the bedsheet up over his face, howling. "Owwwowowww! It was dreadful, I was so scared, I was—"

The Abbot interrupted him sternly. "You were having a nightmare after gorging on enough hefty fruitcake to feed ten creatures, and this was your reward for the deed, you stupid young rip!"

Uggo took to snuffling and weeping piteously. "Waaaha-haaah! I'm sorry, Father Abbot, I'll never do it agin, I prom-ises ye, never agin, waaahaaahaaaah!"

Sister Fisk took over then. "Stop this silly blubbering right away, d'you hear me? Now, drink this!"

She held Uggo's snout, forcing him to open his mouth whilst she poured medicine from a beaker into him. "Come on, now, drink it all down. 'Twill ease any tummy aching and help you to get some rest!"

The Abbot took a thick old blanket from the chest at the bottom of the bed. He passed one end to the Infirmary Keeper. "Come on, Sister. I'm sure Dorka can look after him now. I'll have a proper talk with Uggo when he's recov-ered. Let's go to lunch. We can use this blanket as shelter—sounds like 'tis still raining out there."

After the pair had departed, Dorka sat by the bed watch-ing Uggo. His eyelids were starting to droop as the Sister's potion took effect. The big old otter Gatekeeper spoke softly to him.

"There now, young un. I 'opes ye keep that promise ye made to Father Abbot. You go asleep now like a good lid-dle 'og an' don't dream about monsters an' ships no more. Hush now an' sleep."

It was warm and snug in the little gatehouse. Glowing embers from the log fire in the grate cast gentle rays of red light into the shadows. Dorka sat back in the old armchair, listening to the rain pattering on the window and Uggo's drowsy mutterings as he dropped into a slumber.

"Ship . . . big ship . . . green one . . . green sail, too. . . . Aye, green sail, wid a black fork top, an' two eyes marked on it. Won't rob no more cakes. Be a good 'og now. . . ."

Dorka Gurdy stood up, alarm bells going off in her head at the symbol Uggo had described on that green sail. A black fork head with two eyes.

A moment later she dashed out into the rain, running for the Abbey building. Her brother Jum Gurdy, the Cellardog, knew what the sign meant. She fervently hoped it was not what she thought.

Razzid Wearat had endured the pain of his injuries, hidden away in his fortress; he suffered for several seasons. The burns to his body would have killed a lesser creature, but not a Wearat. Eventually he regained his old strength and vigour, convalescing whilst he laid cunning plans. Now up and about, he went to an upper loft in his stronghold. Through a hole in the timbered wall, he viewed the refurbishment of his ship. Initially he had looked upon the scheme with scorn, but as time went by, Razzid's opinion changed radically. He came to realise that Braggio Ironhook was not just a loudmouthed bully. The big ferret was a clever and resourceful beast, highly inventive when it came to shipwork. Braggio had nearly all the corsairs behind him. Everybeast believed that the Wearat had died of his injuries some seasons back. That was the way Razzid wanted things—he had his spies to keep him informed.

The Wearat observed with growing wonder as Braggio supervised his slave labourers. Things he had never imagined were happening to his once-battered vessel. This irked Razzid. He began questioning himself. Why hadn't he thought of that? Why had he never envisaged a ship armed in such manner? How had Braggio thought up all these great modifications?

Razzid knew the answer. Because Braggio was more intelligent than he! The Wearat could not tolerate such a notion, yet he knew it to be true. However, Razzid also knew that the most dangerous creature was a brainy one, a thinker, and one whom others would follow. Hence, the simplest way he could rid himself of the danger was to kill Braggio.

But not right away. When *Greenshroud* was fixed up and seaworthy, that would be the time he would make his move. Meanwhile, it suited his purpose that all the vermin of Irgash Isle believed their Wearat ruler was dead. So Razzid continued to watch and wait and let his spies report back to him.

It was toward the end of winter when the vessel was shipshape and ready for sea. Braggio had selected his crew, promising everybeast a share in the plunder and loot they would be bringing back. Down on the shore that night, festivities were in full swing. Bonfires blazed on the beach, coloured lanterns had been strung amidst the ship's rigging, and there was a general air of celebration about. Slaves rolled casks of grog bearing names which denoted their ferocity. Shark's Tooth, Scorpion Sting and Old Turtlebeak were but a few of the potent brews. Laid out upon the flat rocks was a spread to delight any corsair's heart: lobster, crab, mussels, cockles, clams and a wide variety of fish which inhabited the warm southern seas. Searats and other corsair vermin reeled about in drunken hobjigs to the accompaniment of flutes, drums, fiddles and accordions played by a band of slaves, whom they had "volunteered" for the job.

Braggio Ironhook sat on the long, flat prow, beaming with pleasure as he raised his tankard and bellowed, "Drink 'earty, buckoes! Hahaarr, 'ere's to the good ship *Ironhook*! Aye, an' all 'er crew o' rakin's an' scrapin's o' land an' water. Hahaharrr! Beasts after me own 'eart, killers all!"

Crumdun dipped a large clamshell into a cask of Shark's Tooth, his speech slurred with grog. "An' I'll shecond tha', Catping. 'Appy shailin' to ye!"

Drunken vermin raised their drinking vessels, roaring, "*Iron'ook! Iron'ook!* Waves o' blood an' plenny o' plunder!"

It happened without warning. A heaving line with a sling rigged at its end swished down from the top of the foremast. The figure sitting in the sling swung out with a broad ship's carpenter's hatchet as it sped by, and Braggio Ironhook lost his head. It splashed down into an open grog cask on the shore. The slayer waited as the heaving line swung back, then neatly stepped onto the prow end, kicking the headless ferret aside. Musicians ground to a halt; the drunken revellers froze, still holding up their drinks. Suddenly all that could be heard was the waves washing the sand and the fires crackling.

Mowlag's command cut the silence. "I give ye a toast. To the mighty Razzid Wearat an' his ship *Greenshroud*!"

Vermin corsairs gaped in disbelief. It was Razzid, and he was alive. He had lost both ears, and his head was a mass of shining scar tissue, minus its fur. One of his eyes was slitted, half shut and leaking. But there was no mistaking the brutal face and the barbarous stance. It really was Razzid Wearat. Shekra attended him, passing her master a tankard of grog and his trident. He raised the tankard, his voice hoarse and rasping from a scarred throat. "Well, cullies, aren't ye goin' to take a drink with yore ole cap'n?"

Mowlag and his comrade, a weasel named Jiboree, who was one of Razzid's secret spies, shouted lustily, "Three cheers fer Razzid Wearat, the cap'n wot can't die!"

There was a moment's pause, then the cheering and shouting broke out. More so when Razzid bellowed, "*Greenshroud* sails with the mornin' tide. Who's with me?"

As dawn broke over the southern wavecrests, *Greenshroud* took the breeze, sailing out in fine style with a new crew, a Wearat as captain and the head of Braggio Ironhook impaled on the foremast top. Razzid Wearat was well and truly back in command.

3

It was cold and windy on the shores of the great western sea, near the mighty mountain fortress of Salamandastron. Scudding clouds raced across a full moon, scattering silver light patterns over the vast, heaving waters. A swelling spring tide boomed and hissed, sending foam-crested rollers at the coast. Huge waves were flung forward, dashing and breaking on the tideline. Salamandastron towered over all, a long-extinct volcano, now the rocky stronghold of Badger Lords and Warrior hares of the Long Patrol.

Colour Sergeant Nubbs Miggory leaned on the rough-hewn sill of a high window in the fortress. The old hare wiped moisture from his eyes, seared by the buffeting wind. From his lofty viewpoint, the sergeant commanded a fair view of the night panorama. Long seasons as garrison instructor in unarmed combat had sharpened Nubbs's senses. Catching the slightest of sounds behind him, he identified the approaching creature and spoke quietly.

"That ole wind's a touch nippy t'night, marm. Do I smell mulled nettle ale with a touch o' spice 'ereabouts?"

His visitor, a strikingly regal-looking young badgermaid, placed the steaming tankard close to the sergeant's paw. "My father used to say there was nought like mulled nettle ale to warm a beast on bleak nights. When I was young, I often stole a sip when he wasn't looking."

The sergeant's craggy features softened. "I recalls h'it well, Milady. But yore pa knew you was suppin' his h'ale, so 'e looked t'other way an' let ye. Steal his h'ale. Hah, you was a real liddle scamp back then, but look at ye now. Lady Violet Wildstripe, ruler o' Salamandastron an' commander of all the Western Shores!"

With her jagged cream muzzlestripe and clouded violet eyes, she looked every inch the noble Badger Lady. Violet smiled. "Happy times, those young seasons. But what of the present, Sergeant—anything to report?"

The tough old veteran paused, as if loath to speak. Then he pointed down to a patch of fireglow on the south shore. "Er . . . beggin' y'pardon, marm, but those four young uns on Seawatch—they should be carryin' out their duties from h'up 'ere, h'inside the fortress, h'instead o' sittin' round a fire down there, toastin' chestnuts h'an singin'. Who gave 'em permission t'do that, I asks meself?"

A note of concern crept into Violet's voice. "It was me, Sergeant. Forgive me—did I do something wrong?"

The colour sergeant took a sip of his mulled ale. "Well, now, h'if 'twas yore order, Milady, then that's that. Beggin' yore pardon, there h'ain't n'more t'be said."

Violet had always held Miggory in the highest regard. Disconcerted, she placed a paw on his shoulder. "My thanks to you for pointing out my error, friend. There are so many rules and traditions for me to learn."

The kindly sergeant patted the paw on his shoulder. "Ho, t'aint nothin', really, Milady. You'll soon learn. Them four rascals sittin' down there took advantage of ye. They're only second-season cadets. Salamandastron standin' h'orders states they've got t'serve four seasons afore they're qualified for nighttime Seawatch h'outdoors."

Violet nodded. "Thank you, Sergeant. Rest assured I'll consult you on all such matters in future."

The old hare shrugged. "No 'arm done, marm. Mebbe 'twill teach those young buckoes h'a lesson. Mark my words, by the time their relief watch arrives at dawn light, those cadets will be sittin' round h'a pile of ashes, chilled t'the scuts an' snifflin' away t'beat the band. That'll teach 'em not to trick ye h'into lettin' 'em disobey h'orders!"

Lady Violet chuckled. "Right you are, Sergeant. Well, I'm off to my nice, warm bed in the forge chamber. What about you?"

Miggory swilled down the last of his mulled nettle ale. "Barrack room dorm for me, marm. Long Patrol snores don't bother me on cold nights like these. Thankee for the ale, an' good night to ye, Milady."

Down on the shores, the four cadets—two bucks and two maids—drew closer to the fire. Trying to ignore the keen, cold breeze on their backs, they put a bold face on things by singing raucously.

"With the stars for me roof an' the shore for me floor,
good chums an' a roarin' hot fire,
down by the seacoast, fine ole chestnuts we'll roast,
ah, what more could us warriors desire!
With no bossy sergeant to come marchin' by,
a-bellowin' orders galore,
whilst keepin' close watch with his cold, beady eye—
Attention, left right, two three four!
We'll sleep all the day whilst the chaps drill away.
Aye, we'll snore just like hogs down a hole,
firm comrades let's stay until our dyin' day,
in the ranks of the great Long Patrol!"

Contending with the boom and hiss of breaking waves, the four young hares sang out lustily, full of the joys of life as only young ones can be. Unaware that they were being watched by evil murderous eyes.

*

Most creatures agree that whenever it is a cold, rainswept day, the best place to be is indoors. One of the Redwallers' favourite retreats is the Abbey cellars, where Jum Gurdy is Head Cellardog. The big, jovial otter never fails to make everybeast welcome. His forge constantly glows, radiating warmth from a fire of old barrel staves and charcoal lumps. Jum's two companions, Roogo Foremole and the Redwall Bellmaster, a squirrel known as Ding Toller, usually preside over the food and fun for all. An old iron battle shield is placed on the fire whilst chestnuts are piled on it to roast. Young and old are given sharpened sticks to retrieve the nuts when they are ready. Once peeled, they are dipped in a basin of cornflower honey. Jum has a fine collection of large clamshells, sent to him by his sea otter cousins. He sits by a barrel of Baggaloob, dispensing shells brimming with the delicious brew (made from a recipe known only to Jum himself).

Many a pleasant day is passed in Jum Gurdy's cellars by the Abbey community playing instruments, singing songs, solving riddles and listening to poems and stories whilst feasting on delicacies and drinking the good Baggaloob. The Foremole plays his melodeon whilst Ding Toller sings out his challenge, to begin the proceedings, thus . . .

"'Tis cold an' wet outdoors this day,
but we be snug an' dry.
So now I'll name a name to ye,
of some goodbeast who'll try,
to entertain us with a song,
a joke, a poem or dance.
Now, pay attention, one an' all,
an' give our friend a chance. . . ."

There was a hushed silence (apart from a few giggles) as Ding's paw circled the audience, suddenly stopping to point at his choice as he called out the name.

"Friar Wopple!"

The furry watervole, who was Redwall's Chief Cook, stood up amidst resounding applause, shuffling her footpaws shyly. "Dearie me, I ain't much of a singer at all, friends."

Everybeast knew Wopple was a fine singer, who always had to be coaxed. The Dibbuns were the most vocal in their pleas. "Ho goo on, Friar marm, sing us da one 'bout Dibbun Pie!"

Wopple smiled furtively whilst fidgeting with her apron tassels. Then she nodded at Foremole, who played the opening bars as she started singing.

"If any babe won't go to bed,
an' will not take a bath,
an' talks back to his elders,
Oh, that fills me with wrath.
Come right along with me, I say,
don't try to run or fly,
don't pull or tug, you'll soon be snug,
inside a Dibbun Pie!
Dibbun Pie, my oh my,
I won't tell you a lie.
If you ain't good, you surely should
end up as Dibbun Pie!
I covers him with honey 'cos
some Dibbuns do taste sour,
I stuffs a chestnut in his mouth,
then rolls him round in flour,
I shoves him in the oven,
an' sez yore time is nigh,
for with a piecrust o'er yore head,
you'll soon be Dibbun Pie!
Dibbun Pie, my oh my,
no use to weep or cry.
If you ain't good, you surely should
end up as Dibbun Pie!"

The Dibbuns sang the chorus lustily and cheered the Friar loudly, giggling and chortling at the idea of a Dibbun Pie.

Foremole Roogo shook his head with mock severity. "Burr, you'm likkle villyuns, Oi wuddent larf so loud if'n Oi wurr ee, or Froir Wopple'll make ee into pies!"

Brinky the vole Dibbun scoffed at the idea. "Hah! No likkle Dibbuns never got maked into pie!"

Old Fottlink, the ancient mouse who was Recorder to Redwall, interrupted. "That's all you know, young Brinky. I knew a very cheeky Dibbun who was once baked into a Dibbun Pie, so there!"

The little volemaid stared wide-eyed at Fottlink. "Who was it? Was 'e very naughty?"

The Recorder nodded. "Very, very naughty—it was me!"

Brinky mulled over this revelation for a moment, then said, "But if you got eated for bein' naughty, why are you still 'ere?"

Fottlink whispered knowingly, "Because I was very young."

Brinky went into some more deep thought before speaking. "Very, very young an' only a tiny likkle beast?"

The Recorder nodded solemnly. "That's right!"

Murty the molebabe enquired hopefully, "But you'm wasn't naughty again, was you'm, zurr?"

Jum Gurdy chuckled. "Oh, no. Ole Fottlink was a goodbeast from that day on. I know, 'cos 'tis true!"

The two Dibbuns stared open-mouthed at the big otter. If Jum said it was true, then it had to be so.

Dorka Gurdy, Jum's sister, entered the cellars. She looked cold and distracted.

"Jum, I've got to talk with ye!"

Jum rose, waving his sister, whom he was tremendously fond of, over to the forge fire. "Dorka, me ole tatercake, come an' sit 'ere. Ding, fetch 'er some 'ot chestnuts an' a drink o' Baggaloob." Taking off his sister's wet cloak, Jum placed a warm blanket around her shoulders. "Now, wot is it, me ole heart, is ought troublin' ye?"

Dorka leaned close, dropping her voice. "I don't wants t'say it aloud. 'Twould upset these good creatures. Could I speak with ye in private, Jum?"

The big otter gestured to a stack of empty barrels. "Right ye are, sister dear. Come over 'ere."

Once seated behind the barrels, Dorka clasped her brother's huge paw. "D'ye recall young Uggo Wiltud? Stole a hefty fruitcake an' ate the whole thing by hisself?"

Jum managed to hide a smile. "Aye, I think that ole cake must've been nearly as big as liddle Uggo. I know he's a scamp, but I can't 'elp likin' 'is boldness."

Dorka shook her head. "Well, he's sufferin' for it now, but that's not wot I wanted t'talk to ye about. It was Uggo's dream. He told Abbot Thibb that he saw a ship comin' to attack Redwall, a big green craft. Later I 'eard 'im say somethin' about a design on the ship's sail."

Jum chuckled. "A ship attackin' our Abbey? I think it was really a big cake attackin' Uggo. But why all the fuss, me ole darlin'? 'Twas only a greedy liddle 'og's dream."

Dorka gripped her brother's paw tighter. "Well may ye say, Jum Gurdy, but let me tell ye the design Uggo saw on the ship's sail. 'Twas the prongs of a trident with a pair of evil eyes starin' from the spaces atwixt 'em. You know wot that means. 'Tis the sign o' the Wearat!"

Without either of them knowing, little Brinky had been eavesdropping on the conversation. She skipped to the forge, calling out in a singsong baby chant, "A Wearat, a Wearat, Uggo see'd a Wearat!"

Every Redwaller knew what a Wearat was, though none had ever seen one. *Wearat* was a forbidden word in the Abbey. It was an unmentionable horror, a thing of nightmare. There was a moment's silence, then frightened shouts rang out from everybeast.

"A Wearat? Uggo Wiltud saw a Wearat?"

"Where did he see it—is it in our Abbey?"

"Oh, no, we'll all be murdered in our beds!"

"Lock the gates, bar the doors, it's a Wearat!"

Abbot Thibb came hurrying in to see what the alarm was about. "What Wearat? Where?"

Little Brinky was sobbing with fright. Jum came from behind the barrels and swept her up in his paws. "There now, liddle un. There's nought to fret about." Raising his voice, he silenced the panicked cries. "Calm ye down now, goodbeasts. There ain't no Wearat at all, so stop all this noise or ye'll disturb my barrels of October Ale. Nothin' worse than unseemly shoutin' for October Ale!"

Abbot Thibb confronted the Cellardog. "Then perhaps you'd best keep your voice down, sir. Mayhaps you might explain this upset to me."

Dorka curtsied respectfully to Thibb. "'Twas my fault, Father Abbot, but I didn't know the Dibbun maid was lissenin'. I was tellin' Jum that after you left my gate'ouse, Uggo was talkin' in his sleep again, describin' the marks on the sail of the green ship 'e saw in 'is dreams. 'Twas the sign o' the Wearat, weren't it, Jum?"

The big Cellardog caught the warning look in Thibb's eye, so he chose his words carefully.

"Well, that's wot Uggo said it was, but who can tell wot an overstuffed liddle 'og sees in a bad dream, eh?"

Dorka's observation slipped out before she could think. "But 'e did describe the sign right, I'm sure of it!"

Jum saw the look of dismay on his sister's face. Making light of the situation, he smiled, patting her back. "Now you lissen t'me, ole gel—an' you Redwallers, too. There ain't no Wearat within twenny sea leagues of 'ere, nor is there likely t'be. There was only one such beast I ever 'eard of. Razzid Wearat, the corsair cap'n. I know wot 'appened to that un, 'cos when I went t'the coast I saw my ole uncle Wullow, the sea otter. 'Twas Wullow that gave me a gift o' those fine clamshells wot yore usin' t'drink from. Any'ow, some seasons ago, Wullow got news from 'is kinbeast, Skor Axehound, chieftain o' the High North Coast. It seems that

27

Razzid Wearat an' 'is corsair crew came a-raidin'." Jum paused to give a wry chuckle.

"Sorriest day o' that Wearat's life, 'twas. Skor an' them wild sea otters loves battle more'n Uggo loves stolen cakes. They gave those vermin a mighty whackin'. Aye, slew most o' the corsairs an' set their cap'n back out t'sea, with decks awash in gore an' the ship in tatters an' flames. So ye can take my ole uncle Wullow's word, as give to 'im by the Axehound hisself. If there ever was a Wearat, well, 'e's lyin' on the seabed now, burnt to a soggy crisp!"

An audible sigh of relief rang through the cellars. Abbot Thibb stowed both paws in his wide sleeves, acknowledging Jum with a slight bow.

"Thank you, Mister Gurdy. Now, who was next to sing us a song—a good jolly one I think, eh?"

Foremole tootled a lively ripple on his melodeon, nodding to a pair of little moles, who immediately began singing and dancing.

"Ho round an' round an' round ee floor,
shutten ee window, close ee door,
moi likkle beauty take ee charnce,
join Oi en ee molebabe darnce!

"Clappen ee paws a-wun, two, three,
twiggle ee tail roight murrily,
moi ole granma carn't do thiz,
a-'cos she'm got ee roomatiz!

"Jump ee h'up naow gurtly 'igh,
watch thy 'ead, doan't bump ee sky,
jumpen 'igher than ee trees,
hurr, wot 'arpy childs uz bee's!

"Jumpen 'igh as trees you'm arsk,
Ho, by urr, a drefful tarsk,

you'm a h'orful silly lump,
doan't you'm know ee trees carn't jump!"

They sang it again and again. Dibbuns joined in the dance,
showing off much tail wagging and jumping. Amidst the
merriment, mention of Wearats was soon forgotten.

Jum Gurdy edged close to the Abbot, murmuring a message. "Father, can ye tell Foremole Roogo t'keep an eye on
my cellars for a few days? I'm off t'the seacoast. That ole
uncle Wullow o' mine, he's a rare ole tale teller. I think he
makes a lot of 'is stories up, so I'm just goin' t'see if'n wot
'e said about that Wearat was for true."

4

Dawn had scarcely shown its pale light over the western coast when pandemonium broke loose at Salamandastron. A bugle blasting out its brassy alarm set every hare on the mountain dashing to the call. Lady Violet Wildstripe hurried from her forge chamber, joining Colour Sergeant Miggory and Lieutenant Scutram as they rushed downstairs. From dormitory, mess hall, kitchens and barrack room, Long Patrol members charged to the main gate. They parted to make way for the Badger Lady and her officers.

A bewhiskered and monocled Major Felton Fforbes was waving his swagger stick, rapping out orders. "All ranks back off now, quick as y'like, wot! Come on, chaps, give 'em room t'jolly well breathe, if y'please!"

Two young hare cadets, Lancejack Sage and Trug Bawdsley, who formed half of the Seawatch dawn relief, were sitting slumped against a gatepost. Both were obviously in shock, shivering and moaning incoherently.

The colour sergeant twitched his ears enquiringly. "Nah, then, wot's goin' h'on 'ere, buckoes?"

Lady Violet came forward, sweeping off her warm cloak. She draped it about both the hares. Then, crouching down in front of them, she enquired in a calm low voice, "One thing at a time, young uns—easy does it now, take your time, try to speak slowly and clearly. Sage, make your report. What's upset you so?"

Lancejack Sage, normally an ebullient haremaid, stared blankly into space. She spoke in a flat, halting, monotone. "We went straight out t'the south beach, to relieve the night Seawatch. I came back straight away with Trug. We left Ferrul an' Wilbee with 'em. Not proper form, y'see, marm, leavin' 'em alone like that. . . ."

Violet took the haremaid's face in both paws, staring into her dazed eyes. "Left Ferrul and Wilbee with whom? Tell me."

Sage's companion, Trug Bawdsley, a hefty young buck, could no longer restrain himself. He shouted aloud, "Saw them in the mess yesterday, had tea with 'em. Now all four o' the poorbeasts are dead! Gilbee, Dobbs, Dunwiddy an' my sister Trey. They're dead, I tell ye!" Here the sturdy fellow broke down, sobbing uncontrollably.

Nobeast was swifter than the Badger Lady. Seizing a lance from a wall rack, she swung into action. "Sergeant Miggory, Lieutenant Scutram, bring a score of armed warriors and follow me! Major Felton, see these two are cared for. Fortify the gate and shutter all windows!"

It was a sad and shocking scene on the sands of the south shore. Four young hare cadets, the night Seawatch, lying mangled and pierced by arrows amidst the cold ashes of their fire. Ferrul and Wilbee, whom the lancejack had ordered to stay, were staring hypnotised at the ghastly tableau. Running in Lady Violet's wake, Scutram and Miggory halted the rest at the badger's command.

"Hold fast there until I can see what went on. Do you have a tracker with you, Sergeant?"

Miggory waved his paw at a lean haremaid. "Buff, go with 'er Ladyship, see wot ye can find."

Buff Redspore wore the tan-hued tunic of an expert scout and tracker. She walked with Violet to where the four slain hares lay. Beckoning Ferrul and Wilbee to remain still, Buff ran a paw through the fire ashes. "Hmmmm. Burnt out long before dawn."

She turned her attention to the dead hares.

"Look at these young uns, marm. Three of 'em crushed by somethin', then shot by an arrow apiece, one in the chest, two in the throat, as they lay there. Now, see this fourth cadet—he escaped bein' crushed an' ran. Three arrows took him in the back, first one just near the nape o' the neck."

Lady Violet studied the evidence. "How can you tell, Buff?"

The tracker explained. "He's clutchin' at the shaft in his neck—that was his reaction to the first hit. Next two in the back finished him. Wasn't crushed, though, Milady. No wheelmarks on him at all."

The Badger Ruler interrupted. "Did you say wheelmarks?"

Buff nodded. "Aye, marm, wheelmarks. Those three never had time t'run. They were ambushed by some sort o' big, heavy cart. Just mowed 'em down like reeds, pore things. Must've been archers ridin' on the cart. Note the angle these arrows are leanin' at. They were shot after bein' run down. No need for it—they were already dyin', marm."

Violet spread her paws in despair. "But why? Run over by a big cart, then shot by arrows? It doesn't make any sense, Buff."

Picking up a stray arrow, the tracker pointed with it. "Way back up there in the dunes, that's where the wheelmarks seem t'come from. Aye, straight down here at a pretty fast rate, I'd say. The young uns were on Seawatch, facin' the water. They didn't see it comin,' all except one of 'em, an' he was too late to escape."

Violet shook her head in bewilderment. "But where is this big, heavy cart? I can't see it, can you?"

Buff scratched her ear with the arrow she was holding. "No, Milady, though I can say this. It had iron-rimmed wheels, I think—look at those marks it made. Came speedin' down the dune slopes, not makin' a sound, hit the young uns from behind, then carried right on toward the sea. Left marks in the damp sand by the tideline. Passed that way just as the tide was on the turn."

Violet blinked, scanning the Western Sea. It was fairly still, and overlaid with thick mist. "And you think this big cart went into the sea?"

Buff shrugged. "That's what it jolly well looks like, marm. Who can flippin' well say? The tracks are plain, an' what don't speak don't blinkin' well lie, as my pa used t'say."

Lady Violet's paw suddenly shot out, pointing northwest. "What's that out there, off to the right, Buff? Something green, maybe—it's not too clear, but it will soon be out of the mist. . . . See? It's a ship!"

On the long prow of *Greenshroud*, Razzid Wearat, flanked by the searat Mowlag and his bosun, the mean-featured weasel called Jiboree, showed themselves in plain view. Razzid pointed his trident at the creatures onshore. "Let them take a good look an' see who killed their little rabbets!"

Mowlag sniggered. "I wagers they're wishin' we was in arrow range so they could pay us back for wot we did."

Razzid wiped at his weepy eye, judging the distance. "We ain't in their range, but they're in ours. Let's give 'em somethin' else t'think about. Jiboree, get the for'ard weapon ready!"

Razzid and Mowlag moved back behind a huge crossbow, which was set up on the prow. Two corsairs carried forward a massive bolt, a long, thick, timber arrow, iron tipped, with stiff canvas flights. The thing was half the length of *Greenshroud*'s mainmast. Laying it flat on the crossbow, they notched it against a bowstring of greased heaving line and cranked the handle which wound the bowstring taut. Razzid stood behind it, sighting with his good eye and muttering, "That big stripedog's a prime target!"

He tripped the lever with his trident pole. With a mighty

whoosh, the bolt shot off over the sea. Streaking over the shore, it missed Lady Violet by a pawlength. Whizzing on, it ended its flight buried in a duneside.

The Wearat spat into the water viciously. "Missed! Ahoy, Mowlag, sail closer in. Put the ship about an' load the back bow. I'll get 'er as we sails off!"

The vessel was brought about so it sailed landward. Now it was stern onto the shore. The few hares who were armed with firing equipment hurled slingstones, javelins and arrows, none of which reached their target.

Razzid bared his fangs as he tripped the lever. "Yaharr, stripedog, off to Hellgates with ye!"

Violet had beckoned everybeast back now. She stood boldly on the tideline, facing the stern crossbow. The huge bolt sped out, straight at her. With graceful contempt, she paced a step to her right, watching the lethal projectile rush by. It went right across the sand, smashing to splinters on the rocky fortress base.

Long Patrol warriors seized the chance, charging forward into the shallows, hurling everything they could at the big green ship. A few arrows got as far as the high-galleried stern. As they stuck into the timbers, Razzid shouted orders.

"Mowlag, get them oarbeasts workin'. Take 'er out to sea!" Moments later, the *Greenshroud* had vanished into the thinning curtain of mist.

Colour Sergeant Miggory rattled out orders at the Long Patrollers who were wading into deeper water to attack the enemy ship. "H'all ranks inna water will retreat! Fall back! Move yoreselves h'afore that ship turns round an' cuts ye off from the shore!"

As the hares waded reluctantly back to land, the sergeant turned to Lady Violet and Buff Redspore. He saluted the Badger Ruler. "Well, Milady, you nearly got yoreself slain twice there, h'if'n ye don't mind me mentionin' h'it!"

Violet watched the bright morning sun dispersing the

mist over the Western Sea. "Rest easy, friend. I knew what I was doing."

Buff Redspore nodded. "Aye, marm, you were tryin' to bring that confounded ship closer in, so you could inspect her, wot? So, did ye manage to jolly well see what I saw?"

Violet made a circular motion with one paw. "Indeed I did, Buff. I know how our hares were murdered. It wasn't a cart. It was a ship with four wheels."

Miggory's jaw dropped in disbelief. "A wot? A ship with bloomin' wheels, Milady?"

The tracker confirmed Violet's words. "Aye, Sergeant. I saw 'em m'self, four iron-rimmed wheels, two for'ard and two aft. I glimpsed them when the vermin ship turned about. The crafty scum—who'd have thought up such an idea, wot?"

Violet shrugged. "Not all vermin are stupid. It was a fiendish idea, but a good one from their point of view. The beast carrying the trident, who stood out on the prow, was that the Wearat?"

Buff Redspore answered. "That was him, marm. I've seen the blighter twice in bygone seasons. Once when I was scoutin' far down the south coast and again when that ship was in these waters. That time he sailed right by our mountain, though he didn't dare jolly well try an' land. Like most of his flippin' kind, a born coward when it comes to meetin' real warriors."

Lieutenant Scutram joined the conversation. "Be that as it may, that Wearat can do as he likes with a craft like that. Either by land or sea. Did ye see the size of the two crossbows she was carryin'? 'Pon my word, they could do some damage, I'll tell ye!"

The speculation was interrupted by young Trug Bawdsley. He marched up to Lady Violet with tears streaming down his sturdy face, then saluted her.

"Permission to form a burial detail, marm. For our fallen cadets. I don't want t'see my poor young sister Trey lyin' out on the sands like that, marm!"

His head drooped as he began weeping inconsolably. As Lady Violet pulled him gently to her, Trug buried his face in her robe, sobbing pitifully. Violet patted his back.

"You have my permission, Trug. We'll turn the regiment out at sunset and give them full honours." She nodded to the tracker and any officers present. "Make your way back to my forge chamber. We've got important business to discuss, which can't wait."

Inside Salamandastron, a late breakfast was served in the forge chamber. All senior Long Patrol officers listened intently to Lady Violet as she spoke of the day's tragic events.

"I, and no doubt you, too, friends, are deeply grieved at what took place before dawn today. You've heard Buff Redspore's report on the corsair vessel, and you are aware of the danger it threatens."

She paused to acknowledge a very old, overweight hare. "Yes, Colonel Bletgore?"

Colonel Blenkinsop Wilford Bletgore was the oldest hare on the mountain. His tunic, which could hardly be seen for medals and ribbons, was weathered from scarlet to faint pink. Huffing and puffing, he was hauled upright from his chair by two younger hares. Bletgore's profuse silver whiskers jumped up and down in time with his wobbling chins as he grunted.

"Stap me swagger stick, vermin ships attackin' this mountain fortress—stuff 'n' nonsense, marm, fiddlesticks an' hobbledehoy! Wot, wot, wot! Stand as much chance as a gnat chargin' a bloomin' oak tree!"

Lady Violet remained patient until the ancient colonel had run out of humphing and blathering. Picking up a slim rapier, she pointed to the relief map graven on the stone wall, showing all the coast, from north to south on the west side.

Politely, she explained, "Thank you, Colonel. I appreciate what you say, but it isn't just us. The entire coastline, and this part of it in Mossflower, is our responsibility. We must protect all good creatures, not just ourselves. So, my friends, I'm open to any helpful suggestions."

Old Colonel Bletgore spoke out to nobeast in particular. "Blood'n'vinegar, wot—that's all vermin understand! Shout Eulalia, charge an' leave none o' the villains alive. That's what we did in my younger seasons, eh, wot!"

Major Felton Fforbes sniffed. "Trouble is, we've never had a navy. No disrespect to you, marm, but vermin ships can commit murder, then sail off, free as flippin' larks. There ain't a bally thing us hares can do about it, wot?"

Sergeant Miggory summed up further. "Now they've got h'a ship that can sail the land, too. We're in double trouble, so wot's the h'answer? Do we get h'our own navy, marm?"

Lady Violet toyed with the rapier hilt. "There's no vermin force that could stand against our Long Patrol warriors, even in land-borne ships. Major Fforbes is right. If they can slip back into the sea, we can't pursue them. Hares have never been seabeasts, it's no good talking about us having a navy. We know little of mariners' ways. We need allies who are skilled in the ways of sailoring."

Lieutenant Scutram had a suggestion.

"What about otters, marm? I don't mean river an' stream types who dwell inland, but sea otters."

Buff Redspore spoke out in agreement. "Aye, sea otters who are fighters. I know there's a lot of 'em up on the High North Coast. They like nothin' better than a good skirmish. I'll wager they'd be willin' to jolly well help us!"

Colonel Bletgore, who had been dropping off into a doze, immediately began a diatribe at the idea. "Hah, sea otters? Confounded rogues, ye mean! Not a scrap o' manners among that flamin' lot. Skor Wotjamicallim . . . Hatchet Dog, or some other dreadful outlandish name. Hah, pish an' tosh, marm. Never!"

Lady Violet looked around the assembly. "I think I've heard him spoken of as Skor Axehound. Has anyone further knowledge of him or his tribe?"

Captain Rake Nightfur, a tall, dangerous-looking black hare, with a deep scar running from ear to chin, stepped forward, pawing the hilts of two claymores he wore across his shoulders. "Afore Ah came tae Salamandastron, Ah lived on the High North Coast. When Ah was younger, Ah fought alongside the braw Skor an' his warriors. Ye'll no' find bonnier an' no mair fearsome beasties than the Chieftain Skor—aye, an' his Rogues."

Captain Rake paused, staring around the forge chamber. "Hark tae me. Ah'll no' tolerate a slight or ill word against Skor Axehound or his crew. D'ye ken?"

Lady Violet smiled at the captain. "Oh, I think we all got the message, Cap'n Rake. This High North Coast you speak of, I take it the territory is some fair distance from here. Would you be willing to visit there as an ambassador from me?"

Rake bowed gallantly, then drew his swords, placing them in front of Violet. "Mah fealty, mah blades, mah heart an' paws are yours tae command, fair lady!"

The Badger Ruler's violet-hued eyes twinkled momentarily. "I never doubted that for an instant, Rake, thank you! Now, I wish you to start as soon as possible on this mission. Take with you a score of Long Patrollers of your own choosing, and may fortune be with you."

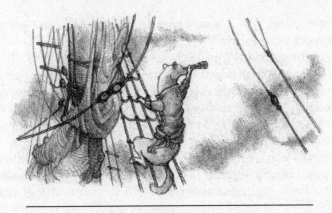

5

As dawn's rosy paws stole over the Abbey walls, Jum Gurdy was getting ready to leave for the coast, intent on questioning his old uncle Wullow. The sturdy otter chuckled as he watched Friar Wopple packing rations into his haversack.

"Go easy, marm. I ain't plannin' on bein' gone for ten seasons. That's enough vittles t'keep a regiment o' Salamandastron hares goin'."

The kind watervole waved a package of candied chestnuts at the Cellardog. "Be off with ye, Jum Gurdy. I'll not see any Redwaller starve on a journey. Besides, y'might like to give some o' these vittles to yore ole uncle Wullow."

Jum smiled as he slipped a flask in with the food. "Aye, thankee. Ole Wullow'd like that, marm. I'm takin' 'im some o' my best beetroot port as a gift."

Young Uggo Wiltud, who had got over his ill stomach and was now sentenced to three days' pot washing, looked over from his greasy chore. The gluttonous hedgehog was always interested in the subject of food or drink.

"I've never tasted beetroot port, Mister Gurdy. Wot's it like?"

Jum shouldered his loaded haversack, commenting,

"Never mind 'ow it tastes, young Wiltud. You just get on with yore pot scourin'!"

Scowling, Friar Wopple picked up one of the pots. "The whole Abbey'd be down with tummy trouble if they had to eat vittles cooked in this—it's filthy! Do it again, Uggo, an' make sure ye scrub under the rim!" She turned to Jum with a long-suffering sigh. "I've never seen a young 'og so dozy in all my seasons!"

Uggo's voice echoed hollowly as he poked his head into the pot. "I can't 'elp it if'n I ain't a champeen pot washer!"

The Friar waved a short wooden oven paddle at him. "Any more of those smart remarks an' I'll make yore tail smart with this paddle. Stealin' hefty fruitcake is about all yore good at, ye young rip!"

Still with his head in the pot, Uggo began weeping. "I said I was sorry an' wouldn't steal no more cakes. But no-beast's got a good word for me. I'm doin' me best, marm, but I just ain't a pot washer."

Jum Gurdy suddenly felt sorry for Uggo. There he was, clad in an overlong apron, standing atop a stool at the sink, with grease and supper remains sticking to his spines. The big Cellardog lifted him easily to the floor. "Smack me rudder, matey. Yore a sorry sight, an' that's for sure. Stop that blubberin', now. You ain't been a Dibbun, not for three seasons now. So, tell me, wot are ye good at, an' don't say eatin' cake!"

Uggo, managing to stem his tears, stood staring at the floorstones, as if seeking inspiration there.

"Dunno wot I'm good at, Mister Gurdy."

Jum hitched up the haversack, winking at Friar Wopple. "I think I know wot we should do to this scallywag, marm."

The Friar leaned on her oven paddle, winking back. "Oh, an' wot d'ye think you'd like t'do to Master Wiltud? Fling him in the pond, maybe?"

Uggo flinched as Jum took off the long apron. The otter walked around him, looking him up and down critically.

"Hmm, he don't look like a very fit beast t'me, Friar. Bit pale an' pudgy, prob'ly never takes any exercise, eats too much an' sleeps most o' the day. I think a good long walk, say a journey to the sea. That might knock 'im back into shape. Wot d'ye think, Friar marm?"

Wopple agreed promptly. "Aye, it might do our Uggo the world o' good, sleepin' outdoors, marchin' hard all day, puttin' up with the bad weather an' not eating too much. I think y'might have somethin' there, Jum!"

Uggo's lip began to tremble as he looked from one to the other. "Marchin' all day, sleepin' out in the open, gettin' wet'n'cold in the wind an' rain. Wot, me, Mister Gurdy?"

Jum shrugged. "As y'please, mate. There's always more pots t'wash an' floors to scrub, I shouldn't wonder, eh, marm?"

Friar Wopple narrowed her eyes, glaring at Uggo. "Oh, yes—an' ovens to clean out, veggibles to peel an' scrape, the storeroom to sweep out . . ."

Jum Gurdy began trudging from the kitchens, calling back, "Ah, well, I'll leave ye to it, Uggo mate. 'Ave fun!"

The young hedgehog scrambled after him, pleading, "No, no, I'll go with ye, Mister Gurdy. Take me along, please!"

Hiding an amused grin, Friar Wopple waved a dismissive paw. "Take him away, Jum. The rascal's neither use nor ornament around here. Go on, young Wiltud—away with ye!"

She followed them to the kitchen door as Jum strode off, commenting blithely, "Well, come on then, young sir, but ye'd best keep up, or I'll 'ave to tie ye to a tree an' pick ye up on the way back. Come on, bucko. Move lively, now!"

Uggo scurried in the big otter's wake. "I'm goin' as fast as I can, Mister Gurdy. You wouldn't leave me tied to a tree, really, would you . . . would you?"

Abbot Thibb saw the pair walking across Great Hall as he entered the kitchens. He picked up a fresh-baked scone, spread it with honey and took a bite.

"Good morning, Friar. What's going on with those two?"

The Friar poured cups of hot mint tea for them both. "Oh nothin', really. I suspect that Jum's givin' young Uggo a lesson in growing up usefully. A trek to the seacoast with our Cellardog behind him may do that hog a power o' good, Father."

Thibb blew on his tea and sipped it carefully. "Right, marm. I think Jum Gurdy's just the beast to teach that scamp a lesson or two."

In the belltower, Matthias and Methusaleh, Redwall's twin bells, boomed out into the clear spring morn, signalling breakfast at the Abbey.

Outside on the path, Uggo called out hopefully, "May'aps we'd best go back for our brekkist, Mister Gurdy?"

Jum Gurdy shook his head, pointing the way. "Already 'ad brekkist whilst you was still snoozin'. Keep goin', young un. 'Tis quite a way 'til lunch!"

By midday, *Greenshroud* was well out to sea. Razzid Wearat took a leisurely meal of grilled seabird, washed down with a beaker of seaweed grog. He watched a wobbly-legged old searat clearing the remains away, then rose from the table. He snapped out a single word.

"Cloak!"

The rat dropped what he was doing to get the green cloak, holding it as Razzid shrugged his shoulders into it.

"Trident!"

The serving rat placed the trident in his waiting paw. Without another word, the Wearat waited on his minion to open the cabin door, then strode out on deck. A corsair searat was at the tiller.

Razzid wiped moisture from his weepy eye. "What's the course?"

The corsair replied smartly, "As ye ordered, Cap'n, due east!"

Vermin were loitering near, coiling ropes and doing other

needless tasks, listening alertly for the Wearat's command as to where they would be sailing.

He did not keep them waiting, calling out loud and clear, "Take 'er in closer to shore! Lookout, keep watch for anythin' interesting onshore!"

A sharp-eyed young ferret tugged his ear in acknowledgement. "Aye aye, Cap'n!" He began climbing into the rigging.

Razzid's next words came at the crew like a thunderbolt. "Stay close to the shore, but set a course for the High North Coast!"

The word had been given. Razzid Wearat was bent on a return battle with the sea otters. An ominous silence fell over the crew. Those who had lived through the last disastrous foray knew the strength and bloodlust of Skor Axehound's warriors. None of the vermin had thought that Razzid would be foolhardy enough to try a second attack. However, none of the corsairs was so rash as to dispute their captain's decision. They returned to their tasks in sullen silence—all but one.

A muscular, tattooed ferret, who had barely escaped with his life at the first incident, was heard to mutter to the rat he was working alongside, "Huh, those wavedogs beat the livin' tar out of us. They ain't beasts t'be messed about wid."

He turned and found himself facing Razzid.

"Ye were sayin'?"

The ferret backed off nervously. "Never said nothin', Cap'n."

Like a flash the trident was a hairsbreadth from his neck. The Wearat sounded dangerously calm. "Lie to me an' I'll slay ye here an' now. What did ye say? Tell me."

The ferret was a seasoned killer and no mean fighter, but he quailed under the Wearat's piercing eye.

"I jus' said those wavedogs wasn't beasts t'be messed wid." Razzid let the trident barbs drop.

"So, that's what ye think, eh? Anyone else think that?"

The ferret looked nervously at his mates' faces, but nobeast was about to speak out. He smiled weakly and shrugged. "I didn't mean nothin', Cap'n. On me oath, I didn't!"

Razzid stared levelly at him, still calm. "Ah, but I heard you, my friend. What was it? 'Those wavedogs beat the livin' tar out of us . . .'?" He paused to wipe dampness from his bad eye. As he spoke again, his voice rose to a shout and his face became contorted with rage.

"Beat the living tar out of us? Nobeast has ever done that to Razzid Wearat and lived to tell of it. My wounds came from saving this ship—aye, and all the idiots I called a crew. You were one of them. I saved you all. And you dare to say that some foebeast beat me!"

Before the tattooed ferret could reply, Razzid lunged with his trident. Pierced through the stomach, the ferret shrieked. Like a farmer lifting hay with a pitchfork, the Wearat heaved his victim up bodily on the trident and hurled him overboard.

The crew stood shocked by the swift, vicious act.

Laughing madly, Razzid leaned over the stern gallery, bellowing at the dying corsair, "When ye get to Hellgates, tell 'em it was me that sent ye—me, Razzid Wearat!"

He turned to the crew, wielding his dripping trident. "Avast, who's next, eh? Any of you bold bullies wants to argue with me, come on, speak out!"

The silence was total. Rigging creaked, sails billowed, waves washed the sides of *Greenshroud*, but not a single corsair spoke.

Razzid laughed harshly. "The High North Coast, that's where this ship's bound. But this time we won't be ambushed up to our waists in the sea. Now I know wot my vessel can do, it'll be me dishin' out the surprises. We'll give those wavedogs the same as the rabbets got at the badger mountain."

Shekra the vixen called out. "Aye, the waves'll run red

with the blood of our foebeasts. Our cap'n's name will become a legend o' fear!"

Mowlag and Jiboree took up the cry, until all the crew were bellowing, "Wearat! Wearat! Razzid Wearat!"

Exulting in the moment, Razzid chanted with them.

Suddenly he slashed the air with his trident, silencing the noise. His anger quelled, he spoke normally again. "I am the Wearat. I cannot die—you've all seen this. Fools like that one, and that one, would not heed me." He gestured overboard to where the ferret was floating facedown in *Greenshroud*'s wake, then up to where the head of Braggio Ironhook was spiked atop the foremast. Razzid chuckled. "But believe me, there'll be no mistakes this time. The beast ain't been born who can get the better o' me, or my ship, or my crew. Right, mates?"

This triggered another wave of cheering.

Razzid beckoned to a small, fat stoat. "I remember you. Yore Crumdun, Braggio's little mate."

Crumdun saluted hastily, several times. "Er, aye, Cap'n, but I'm with yew now. On me oath, I am!" The Wearat winked his good eye at Crumdun.

"Go an' broach a barrel o' grog. Let my crew drink to a winnin' voyage. Make that two barrels."

As they sailed north, the corsairs drank greedily from both barrels, one of which was named Strong Addersting and the other Olde Lobsterclaw. The vermin swilled grog, grinning foolishly at the slightest thing.

Jiboree rapped Crumdun's tail with the flat of his cutlass. "Ahoy, wasn't you a pal o' Iron'ook?"

Crumdun giggled nervously. "Heehee . . . I was, but I ain't no more."

Jiboree leered at him, then waved his cutlass blade. "I 'eard that none o' Iron'ook's mates could sing. So, if'n yew wasn't a proper mate of 'is, then ye must be a good ole singer. Go on, lardtub, give us a song!"

With Mowlag's dagger point tickling him, the fat stoat was forced to dance a hobjig whilst warbling squeakily.

"Ho, wot a drunken ship this is,
'tis called the *Tipsy Dog*,
an' the bosun's wife is pickled for life,
in a bucket o' seaweed grog!

"Sing rum-toodle-oo, rum-toodle-'ey,
an' splice the mainbrace, matey,
roll out the grog, ye greedy hog,
'cos I ain't had none lately.

"Our cap'n was a rare ole cove,
'is name was Dandy Kipper.
He went to sea, so he told me,
in a leaky bedroom slipper!

"Sing rum-toodle-oo, rum-toodle-'ey,
this drink is awful stuff,
me stummick's off, an' I can't scoff,
this bowl o' skilly'n'duff!

"The wind came fast an' broke the mast,
an' the crew for no good reason,
dived straight into a barrel o' grog,
an' stayed there 'til next season!"

Night had fallen over the vast seas. The water was relatively calm, though a faint west breeze was drifting *Greenshroud* idly in toward the shore. Both grog barrels had been liberally punished by the vermin crew, most of whom were slumped around the deck. The tillerbeast was snoring, draped over the timber arm. He never stirred as the ship nosed lightly in, to bump softly into the shallows.

Only one crew member was wakened by the gentle collision of vessel and firm ground—the sharp-eyed young ferret lookout. It was his first encounter with the heady grog, so he had fallen asleep in the rigging. Fortunately he was low down and not up at the masthead. The light landing dislodged him from his perch. He fell into the shallows, waking instantly on contact with cold salt water. Shaking with shock, he clambered back aboard, his mind racing. Who would get the blame for allowing the vessel to beach itself? Would he be blamed?

Almost all the crew were in a drunken sleep. The ferret took a swift look overboard; it was low tide. How long would it take for *Greenshroud* to float off on the turn? Off to his right, he saw something. It was a small dwindling fire above the tideline. The lookout saw it as a chance to concoct a feasible excuse should the ship not float off before Razzid Wearat wakened himself. He slipped back ashore and crept stealthily toward the fire.

The young ferret had exceptional eyesight. Long before he reached the fire, he could see what was around it. A tumbledown lean-to, fashioned from an old coracle, with a big, fat, old bewhiskered otter sitting outside. The otter, wrapped in a sailcloth cloak, had his head bowed. He was obviously fast asleep in front of the glowing embers.

As the ferret hurried back to the ship, he saw a furtive figure jump overboard and scurry off eastward. Telling himself it was no business of his, he climbed aboard and gently wakened the searat who was slumped across the tiller. They held a swift whispered conversation, then the searat went off and roused Mowlag.

"I saw a firelight on the shore, mate, so I took the ship in to get a sight of it. The lookout saw there was an otter asleep by it. Big ole beast, 'e was. Wot d'ye think we should do?"

Mowlag tottered upright, still staggering from the grog he had downed. Patting the searat's back, he nodded at the lookout. "A waterdog, eh? Ye did well. I'll go an' tell the cap'n. There's nobeast 'e hates more'n those water-dogs. Yew stay put. Keep an eye on the waterdog in case 'e moves."

Nothing could have pleased the Wearat more than the

opportunity to revenge himself on his enemy. He stole silently from the prow of *Greenshroud*, carrying his trident. Mowlag, Jiboree, the lookout and the steersrat flanked him.

"Wot d'ye think the cap'n will do to that beast?" the young ferret lookout whispered to Jiboree.

The weasel grinned wickedly in anticipation. "Yew just watch. Cap'n Razzid don't like waterdogs. I wager 'e slays 'im good'n'slow, bit by bit!"

Jum Curdy's uncle Wullow snuffled a little. His head drooped further onto his chest, then he carried on snoring, stirring his whiskers with each breath. The coracle lean-to was sheltering his back, the fire embers were warming his front, and the tatty sailcloth cloak was keeping vagrant breezes at bay. A bundle of dead twigs and dried reed landed on the little fire, causing it to flare up. A spark stung Wullow's nosetip. He woke to find himself facing a strange, brutal-featured beast and four vermin corsairs. The flickering firelight reflected the evil glitter in the Wearat's one good eye.

"We wouldn't want yore fire goin' out on ye, friend. We'll make things nice an' warm for ye—won't we, mates?"

The other four vermin sniggered nastily. Wullow gave a deep sigh of despair as they closed in on him.

6

Trug Bawdsley unbuttoned his green uniform tunic as the column marched along a dunetop. "Funny how a chap can get so jolly hot just marchin', ain't it, Wilbee?"

Colour Sergeant Nubbs Miggory, who was flanking the column, flicked Trug's ear sharply. "Wot's h'all this, then, laddie buck? H'out on a picnic ramble, are we? Ho, 'ow nice!"

Trug grinned. "Actually, I was just sayin' how bloomin' hot it gets when one's out marchin'—"

The sergeant roared in fine parade-ground manner at the young hare. "Well, h'actually you'll find yoreself h'on a fizzer if'n ye don't git that tunic buttoned up proper, young Bawdsley. Now, gerrit fastened, ye lop-tailed, lollop-eared, doodle-eyed h'excuse for a ranker!"

Marching alongside Trug, Lancejack Sage giggled.

Miggory fixed her with a beady eye. "Nah then, missy, would ye like me t'give ye somethin' to giggle about, eh?"

The pretty young haremaid cast a doe-eyed peep at the sergeant, but she was swiftly corrected for it.

"Git yore eyes front, Sage. I h'aint some wool-'eaded cadet to flicker yore h'eyelashes at!"

Captain Rake Nightfur, striding with Buff Redspore, nodded with satisfaction. "Et'll do those young uns guid tae

49

have Sergeant Miggory keepin' 'em up tae scratch, Ah'm thinken."

The tracker smiled. "Aye, 'twill. I remember old Nubbs from my cadet seasons, though his bark's worse'n his bite."

Corporal Welkin Dabbs, a small, trim veteran hare, checked the time by glancing up at the sun. He spoke out the side of his mouth to Lieutenant Scutram. "Midday, sah. Lunchtime, wot?"

Scutram nodded, calling from the rear, "Sarn't, halt 'em for refreshments, if y'd be so kind!"

Miggory always felt slightly put out by the lieutenant's well-mannered requests. He liked orders to be orders, so he bellowed resoundingly, "H'on my command the column will 'alt! Wait for it, Wilbee. Wait for it. Column . . . haaaaalt!"

The Long Patrollers kicked up a fine cloud of sand as they halted abruptly, awaiting further orders, which the colour sergeant issued aloud.

"H'attensun! Stan' easy. Salute smartly t'the right an' fall out! Lunch detail, attend to vittles!"

It was campaign rations, simple but nourishing. Hardtack scones, cold mint tea, the previous autumn's apples and a small wedge of cheese apiece. Many of the younger hares, who were unused to long marches, rubbed their footpaws tenderly.

"Whew, wish I'd been jolly well born as a bird!"

Miggory eyed the speaker. "Well, try flappin' those pretty ears h'of yores, Miz Ferrul. Who knows, ye might jus' take h'off!"

Some of the younger hares wolfed down their lunch, lay back and closed their eyes to take a short nap. Rake Nightfur immediately upbraided them.

"Ach, whit'n the name o' seasons are ye up tae? Sergeant Miggory, will ye no' look at this sorry lot? Och, they're like a nursery full o' babbies!"

The sergeant knew what he had to do. "H'up on yore paws, ye dozy creatures. C'mon, let's be havin' ye!

Quick'n'sharp now, afore h'I starts kickin' tails. Drander, if'n ye don't move yoreself faster, then I'll move ye myself!"

Drander, who was the biggest, most powerfully built of the younger hares, stood up casually. He towered over the sergeant, dusting off sand in a leisurely manner. "Beggin' y'pardon, Sarge, but I rather think it'd take somebeast bigger'n you to jolly well move me, wot!"

A crooked grin appeared on Nubbs Miggory's battered features. His paw moved almost faster than the eye could follow. Drander was suddenly kneeling, grasping his stomach as he tried to catch his breath.

Miggory had reigned as Regimental Champion Boxing Hare since he was no more than a first-season cadet. He winked down at Drander.

"Ho, t'aint so 'ard, young sir—h'I've moved bigger buckoes than you. H'up y'come now."

Ignoring the sergeant's helping paw, the hulking young hare stood upright, his eyes hot with anger. "Caught me by surprise there, Sarge. Don't suppose you'd like t'have a second blinkin' try, now that I'm bloomin' well ready for ye, wot?"

Miggory shook his head. "Don't suppose h'I would, big feller like yoreself. Ye prob'ly carry a good wallop, Drander. Tell ye wot, though. 'Ow'd ye like to take h'a punch at me? C'mon, h'I won't raise h'a paw to ye."

The other young hares were all for it.

"Go on, Drander old lad, knock his blinkin' block off!"

"Aye, take a flippin' good whack at him, Drander!"

The big young hare shook his head. "Against regulations t'strike an officer. I'd most likely get a ten-season fizzer if I struck the sarge."

Captain Rake intervened. "Och, nae sich thing, laddie. Ah'll jist declare it as a sportin' contest. Have at him!"

Drander clenched both his huge paws, grinning confidently. "Good enough, sah. Right, are you ready, Sergeant?"

Miggory held up a paw. "No, wait!"

He scratched a short line in the sand and stood on it.

"Ready now, Private Drander. Take as many tries h'as ye like, h'I won't move h'off this 'ere line h'or strike back." Drander looked as if he could not believe his good fortune. The young hares were yelling encouragement as he judged, then sent a thunderous right haymaker at Miggory. The sergeant swayed easily, allowing the punch to whistle harmlessly past his nose.

"Nice try, young feller. 'Ow about h'a left 'ook?"

Drander swung a speedy left, hoping to catch his opponent off guard. Miggory ducked. Carried by the force of his own effort, Drander fell flat on his face. He leapt up without warning, lashing out with both clenched paws. Miggory never moved from the line, his fluid, almost careless movements causing every blow to go wide of the mark. The younger hares watched, awestruck, as Drander tried another foray, which missed. He was beginning to puff and blow.

Lieutenant Scutram spoke to Drander's hushed supporters. "'Pon me word, he'll have t'do better'n that, wot? Good job the colour sarn't ain't hittin' back, or he'd have boxed Drander's bloomin' ears off. Hawhawhaw!"

After several more fruitless attempts, Drander collapsed on all fours, gasping for breath. Sergeant Miggory moved off his line then, offering Drander his paw. This time the hulking young Patroller accepted, allowing himself to be hauled upright. Miggory shook his paw cheerily.

"No 'ard feelin's, mate?"

Drander managed a shamefaced grin, returning the pawshake. "None at all, Sarge. I've learned my flamin' lesson!"

The colour sergeant nodded modestly. "You've got the makin's of h'a good 'eavyweight, bucko. By the time this march is over, with h'a spot o' my trainin', there won't be many who'll fancy standin' agin' ye!"

When Miggory gave the order to form up and march, the younger hares obeyed with alacrity. Admiration and a new respect for the grizzled veteran shone in all their eyes.

Buff Redspore joined Captain Rake. "Patrol's marchin'

well, sah. I don't think there'll be any more complaints after the sergeant's little exhibition, wot?"

The captain agreed with her. "Aye, a lesson learned is a wee bit o' knowledge gained, Ah ken!"

Behind them, Trug Bawdsley and Wilbee started a marching song.

"These are the days, mates, these are the days,
obey the sergeant's orders, do what the officer says,
your paws'll grow much tougher, march another mile,
a stroll with the Long Patrol . . . Salamandastron style!

"One two, left right, tunics buttoned tight,
O Sergeant, dear, please lend an ear. . . .
What's for supper tonight?

"There's sand between me paws, mates, an' blowin' up
    me nose,
covered in dust'n'sweat, I ain't smellin' like a rose,
totin' a blinkin' backpack that weighs down all the
    while,
true blue, forward the buffs . . . Salamandastron style!

"Chin up, eyes front, shoulders good'n'square,
show us a scurvy vermin,
we'll knock him flat right there!

"Take me out o' barracks, march me out o' doors,
o'er hills an' mountains, across the dunes an' shores,
forget your mothers' weepin', smile, me bucko, smile,
don't look sick, that's the trick . . . Salamandastron
    style!"

The column made good time that day. Late spring weather held fair; larks wheeled and soared on the cool air. Without breaking ranks, some of the haremaids managed to pick scarlet pimpernel and crane's-bill blossoms on the march. Neither the sergeant nor Lieutenant Scutram objected to seeing them wear the dainty flowers as buttonholes. To the west, the vast sea shimmered in the noonday sun, lapping the flat golden shore sands. Small early grasshoppers chirruped, leaping to either side as the Patrol marched by. Evening fell in a blaze of carmine glory as the sun sank below the western horizon. Buff Redspore chose a sheltered campsite in a hollow between three dunes, where campfires would be hardly visible by night.

The tracker was an excellent cook, as was Lancejack Sage. Between them, they produced a fine spring vegetable stew. Flatbread was baked on slates fixed over the fire. With a beaker of dandelion cordial, it made a very appetizing supper. At one point, young Ferrul gulped, holding her throat and coughing. Corporal Welkin glanced up from his stew.

"Oh, dear, too hot for you, miss?"

Ferrul pulled a wry face. "No, Corporal. I think I've swallowed one of those small grasshopper thingies!"

Welkin held up a cautionary paw. "Hush, now, or they'll all want one, you lucky gel!"

After supper the hares dug out cloaks from their packs and lay down. There was much shoving to see who could get closest to the fire, until Captain Rake was heard to whisper loudly to Miggory, "Sergeant, tell those beasties sleepin' nearest the fire et's their duty tae keep it burnin' through the nicht. They can form a rota tae gather firewood when 'tis needed."

There followed a deal of scuffling. Suddenly there was ample room for anybeast to sleep near the flames. Miggory tapped the footpaws of two hares whom he had chosen for the task.

"Bawdsley, Wilbee, yore h'on firewood duty t'night. Lie easy, there ain't much needed for h'a while."

It was an hour or two past midnight when Wilbee nudged Trug Bawdsley.

"Er, I say, Trug old scout, d'you fancy goin' out t'get some flamin' firewood? That blaze is startin' t'get low."

Trug poked his head out of a fold in his cloak. "Go an' boil your bloomin' head, Wilb. You go—unless you're scared o' the dark."

Wilbee jumped up indignantly. "Scared? Who said I'm blinkin' well scared, wot! I'll go an' get wood, lots o' the bally stuff. You just lie there an' snooze your big head off, fatbrain!"

Wrapping the cloak about his shoulders, he swaggered off over the dunetops, muttering to himself. "Scared—what's t'be jolly well scared of, wot? I'll show that Trug that I'm the least scaredest of the entire bloomin' Patrol. Huh, scared, the very idea!"

It was then that a hasty sequence of events occurred. Young Wilbee tripped over a reedy tussock, falling ears over scut into a shallow depression. He knocked over a dark shape of a creature who was trying to sneak up on a nesting corn-crake, which was sitting on a clutch of eggs in the hollow. The bird screeched harshly as both beasts fell in on it. The creature yelled out in surprise, and Wilbee squeaked in dismay as the corn-crake's wing buffeted him in the eye and the shadowy creature kicked out at him. All three fled in a panic, the bird flapping awkwardly into the night, the strange creature kicking sand in Wilbee's eyes as it scurried off amidst the dunes. Wilbee sat in the hollow, rubbing sand from his eyes and wailing aloud as he tried gingerly to climb from the mess, with a broken bird's egg clinging to his scut.

Alerted by the noise, Buff Redspore, Sergeant Miggory, Lieutenant Scutram and Corporal Welkin Dabbs came running, with weapons at the ready.

Young Wilbee staggered up to them, jabbering, "I'm wounded! There was two o' the blighters, one with big claws, the other was some kind o' blinkin' phantom. Scrabbled with 'em, of course, but they jolly well scooted off. After woundin' me, that is."

Scutram peered at the young hare. "Wounded, laddie? Where?"

Wilbee turned around, so they could see his injury.

"Er, in the confounded tail area, I think."

Miggory took a quick look, dabbed it with his paw and sniffed. "Where did h'all this 'appen?"

Wilbee pointed over to the small depression. "There, Sarge!"

Corporal Dabbs crouched over the scene, sweeping something up in his paw. "Eggshell. It's a blinkin' bird's nest."

Scutram inspected the nest before questioning Wilbee. "There were two of 'em, y'say—one with big claws, eh? Was that the one that flew away?"

Wilbee was confused. "Flew away, sah? Er, I didn't notice."

The lieutenant was not in the best of tempers, having been awakened and hurried off over the dunes. "So, ye didn't notice, young puddenhead. It was a bird, Wilbee, a corn-crake. Can ye not see it hoverin' over yonder? As for your wound, 'twas nothin' more'n a broken egg ye sat on. Shove some sand on the stuff. It'll brush off once it's dry. Bloomin' buffoon!"

Buff Redspore interrupted. "Beg pardon, sah, but what about the otherbeast—the dark phantom thing?"

Corporal Dabbs chuckled. "Phantom beast, hah, piffle!" The tracker pointed to blurred trailmarks in the sand. She shook her head. "I think not, Corp. Hard t'say, but I'd guess that's a vermin track, too blurred t'see what sort. Went that way, north through the dunes."

Scutram peered in the direction indicated. "Hmm. Any chance of catchin' the blaggard, marm?"

Buff was expert at such things; she suggested a plan. "I'll take a good runner with me, cut down t'the shore where the sand's firm an' the goin' quicker. The rest of you give us a moment, then come across the dunetops. Make a bit o' noise—that'll get our villain lookin' back over his shoulder. He won't notice us gettin' ahead of him. That way we should cut him off. Are ye game, Sergeant?"

Despite his seasons, the sergeant was still a great sprinter. "Aye, c'mon, Buff, we'll make the pace for each other."

The fugitive vermin was none other than Crumdun, the fat stoat who had deserted from *Greenshroud*. It was he whom the lookout had spotted and ignored. Panicked by his encounter with the hare and the corn-crake, he fled willy-nilly through the dunes. The realisation that he was heading north, instead of south as he had intended, kept him away from the shore. Crumdun did not want to be spotted by any of the Wearat's crew. It was awkward going in the dunes, all hills, hollows and long ryegrass, but it was safer than travelling in the open. His pace began to slow; he stumbled, blowing sand from his lips. Hauling himself wearily to a dunetop, he stopped to pull a thistle from his footpad. Then he heard the shouts.

"Eulaliiiiaaaa! Blood'n'vinegar!"

Looking back, he saw three figures topping a hill not far away. Crumdun took to his paws then, panting, with the sound of his own heart hammering in his chest.

"Yeeeeharrr! Forward the buffs! Eulaliiiiaaaa!"

The fat stoat could not understand any of the shouts, but he knew they were coming after him. He skidded and stumbled onward, staring over his shoulder at the pursuing trio.

With jarring suddeness, he was halted by a hard punch to the stomach.

"Nah, then, scruffy 'ead, where d'ye think yore h'off to!" The hare who had struck him looked a real tough beast. Another taller female stood beside him.

Sucking in air, the fat stoat began to babble pleadingly. "I never killed no rabbets, yer 'onours, on me oath, I never—it was Razzid an' Mowlag an' that weasel Jiboree. Them was the ones wot did it, I swears it!"

Dawn broke over the Long Patrol camp as breakfast was being prepared over the replenished fire. Captain Rake stared down at the stoat lying tightly bound on the ground.

Crumdun blinked nervously at the black hare's paws, resting on the twin claymore hilts. He swallowed hard, then started to sob. "On me ole mother's life, yer lordship, I've told ye all I knows, everythin'! Like I said, I jumped ship back there, deserted. 'Twas no place fer a simple creature like meself. They was beatin' an' bullyin' me, sir. Makin' me dance, an' sing, an' fetch an' carry for 'em. Merderers, ruffians, that's all *Greenshroud's* crew are.

"An' I'll tell ye somethin' else, yer majesty. That Razzid Wearat, rot 'is tripes'n'eyes, 'e slew my best ole matey. Aye, pore Braggio. They've got 'is 'ead stickin' atop o' the ship's mainmast—'ow about that, eh?"

Rake eyed him scornfully. "Ach, shut yer mouth, ye fat whingin' slawb! Ah'm no' worried aboot yer scurvy matey, nor how they had ye dancin' an' singin'. What Ah wish tae know is where ye left yon ship—why did she pull intae shore, an' where's she headed?"

Crumdun whined, "I'll tell yer wot I knows, sir, but first could ye spare a pore beast some vittles, an' a drop to drink? I aint had nothin' for a'most two days."

Rake Nightfur drew his twin blades with alarming speed. His tone became harsh, merciless. "Have ye ever tasted yer ain blood? Well, ye will if ye dinnae answer mah questions, vermin. Now, speak!"

The fat stoat cringed away from the steel points. "I can take ye t'the spot where the ship made land an' I 'opped off. But why she berthed there I don't know. Nobeast aboard ever tole me nothin', sir. I didn't even know where we was sailin' to. On me oath, I never!"

After breaking camp, the sergeant unbound Crumdun but kept him on a rope halter. The column marched down out of the dunes onto the shore.

The stoat pointed. "That ways, straight north."

Trug Bawdsley, paw on swordhilt, kept trying to edge within blade distance of the prisoner. Lieutenant Scutram clasped his paw tightly over Trug's, stopping him from drawing his blade.

"What the deuce are ye playin' at, Bawdsley?"

Trug gritted his teeth with rage. "My sister Trey, she was slain by that vermin an' his crew. Allow me to draw my sword, sah. I mean to kill him!"

Scutram released the young hare's paw, shaking his head. "Carry on, by all means, Bawdsley. I'll write it up in my report as an act of bravery. 'Private Trug Bawdsley slays a foe in an heroic battle. The vermin, a half-starved stoat, was unarmed and held under guard on a rope halter. Bawdsley showed great courage by attacking him with a sword. The prisoner did not—beg pardon, could not—defend himself.' There, young Trug, how does that jolly well sound, wot?"

Shamefaced, the young hare did not attempt to draw steel.

"Blinkin' awful, sah. 'Twould make me sound like a coward."

The lieutenant winked broadly as he patted Trug's back. "You're no coward, young un, anybeast could tell that. Wait, watch an' learn, Bawdsley, an' one day you'll make us all proud o' ye, eh!"

Trug squared his shoulders, saluting. "Aye, sah!"

Captain Rake Nightfur gave a tug on the prisoner's halter. "We've been marchin' the best part o' the morn, ye rascal. Where are ye takin' us tae?"

Before Crumdun could answer, Buff Redspore, who had climbed back into the dunes to scout the land, called out. "North an' a point west along the shore, sah—can't make out what it is. Shall I scout ahead an' see?"

Captain Rake waved a paw. "Aye, do that, lassie. Sarn't Miggory, go with her in case o' bother."

Miggory joined the tracker as she descended out of the dunes. Together they set off at a brisk run along the tideline.

As the column followed up at normal march pace, the haremaid Ferrul looked at Wilbee, who was trudging alongside her.

"Beg pardon, did you say somethin'?"

Wilbee pointed to himself. "Who, me? No, 'twas Drander."

Drander explained mournfully, "I never said a word. It's this bloomin' belly o' mine, growlin' an' beggin' for scoff."

Flutchers, another young ranker, grinned foolishly. "Y'don't say? My tummy is, too. Listen, can ye hear it?"

He began making a noise out the side of his mouth, like a growling stomach speaking actual words. "Gwaaaawww, I want lunch! Kwuuuurrr! Gimme some grub!"

This caused general merriment amongst the young hares, who began imitating Flutchers.

"Bwuuurrr! Foooooood, I wan' foooood!"

"Kwuuurrrrk! Scoffff, I need scooooofffff!"

Corporal Welkin Dabbs was down on them sternly. "Silence in the ranks, ye bellowin' beasts! Don't think ye can start playactin' 'cos Sarn't Miggory ain't here. The next growlin' gut I hear'll be on half rations an' double guard duty tonight! D'ye hear me, wot!"

Ferrul fluttered her eyelashes prettily. "We hear you, Corporal!"

Dabbs pulled a ferocious face at her. "Then pay attention, me beauty. I may only be a corporal, but I'm an 'orrible, fearsome corporal who'll have your ears for breakfast, your scuts for snacks an' your guts for garters! Wot'll I have, Miss Ferrul?"

The pretty haremaid fluttered her eyelids again, replying in a soothing tone, "You'll have the most frightful headache if you continue bellowing like that, Corporal dear."

Welkin Dabbs glared at her, his ears a-twitch with wrath. "Watch that dressin'! Pick up your pace at the back there! Hup two, left right! Shoulders back, Wilbee. Eyes to the front, Miss Ferrul! Now march, you sloppy, straw-pawed, 'orrible, misbegotten lot!"

From the ranks, an unidentified young hare sobbed mockingly, "Oh, dear. I wish our lovely old sergeant would come and rescue us from this cruel corporal!"

The object Buff Redspore had espied from the dunetop appeared as no more than a dark smudge above the tideline.

Miggory's paws drummed time with the tracker's as they drew closer to their goal. The sergeant put on a spurt. Drawing ahead of Buff, he held up a paw, calling out a warning.

"Hold 'ard, marm. Let me take a peep first!"

Buff knew Miggory never acted without purpose. She halted but could not help querying his motive. "I say, Sarge, why do I have to stay here?"

Miggory's reply was terse. "Just smelled somethin' I don't like. Stay put, if ye please, marm."

It was a large mound of ash, black, white and grey, from a sizeable fire long gone cold. The grizzled colour sergeant stirred the debris with a swift paw. He crouched down, eyes roving over the area, shaking his head.

The tracker took a few tentative paces forward. "What is it, sah . . . ?"

Miggory whirled in her direction, his voice loud and strained. "Wot did I tell ye, Redspore? Stay back! Take yoreself off now, back t'the column. Tell Corporal Dabbs t'keep the young uns away. Send Cap'n Rake an' Lieutenant Scutram t'me, quick h'as ye like!"

Buff hesitated. "But, Sergeant, what is it?"

Miggory's bellowing sent her scurrying to obey.

"Don't argue with me—just do as yore h'ordered!"

The column stood well off downshore as Captain Rake and Scutram crouched amidst the ashes with Miggory. Rake Nightfur's eyes were blank with shock as he picked an object from the ruins.

"What manner o' monster could do sich a thing tae another creature? Ah've never seen ought like et!"

Scutram surveyed the awful scene, leaning on a lance. "Aye, this has got t'be the work of a Wearat, sah."

7

Young Uggo Wiltud soon found that Jum Gurdy's bark was not serious, and his supposed bite was nonexistent. The young hedgehog knew that the otter, despite his forbidding size and appearance, was quite easygoing. Together they trudged off along the path, cutting across the ditch and travelling west through the area of Mossflower woodlands which skirted the vast flatlands. Midmorning saw warm sun seeping through the leafy canopy of oak, beech, elm, sycamore and other big trees. Soft, loamy earth was sprouting with grass, young fern, cowslip, primrose, silverweed, milkwort and alkanet. Birdsong was everywhere, echoing through patches of sunlight and shade.

None of this was of any great interest to Uggo, whose stomach had been telling him of his need for food all morning. Jum, who had been forging doggedly ahead, turned to the young laggard in his wake. "Are ye weary already, Master Wiltud?"

The reply was loud and swift. "No, I'm 'ungry, Mister Gurdy!"

Jum nodded at the sky. "Sun ain't reached midday yet. That's when we stops for lunch. Keep goin' awhile yet." He carried on.

Uggo followed, but not without complaint. "Huh, 'tis

alright for you, Mister Gurdy. You 'ad brekkist back at the Abbey, but I never, an' I'm starvin'!"

The otter leaned on the lance he used as a travelling stave. "Ho, dearie me, pore liddle 'og. Wot a pity ye can't go sneakin' off down t'the kitchens a-stealin' vittles."

Uggo stuck out his lower lip surlily. "Wouldn't 'ave to. There's always summat t'be 'ad round Redwall. You only 'ave to ask nicely."

Jum made a sweeping gesture with his stave. "An' wot about ole Mossflower, eh? There's plenty t'be 'ad around here without even the askin'!"

Uggo chanced a scornful snort. "Hah! Like wot?"

The big otter cast swiftly about, then pulled a stem with yellow buds adorning it. "Like this. Try it."

The young hedgehog took the stem, sniffed it, then took a tentative nibble. "Tastes funny—wot is it?"

Jum shook his head pityingly. "You young uns are too used t'bein' carried round an' gettin' vittles served up on a platter. That's young dannelion, matey. I ate many a stem o' that when I was yore age. Now, try some o' these."

He gathered various pieces of early vegetation, feeding them one by one to Uggo and explaining.

"This is alkanet—taste like cucumber, don't it? Try some coltsfoot. Nice, ain't it? This one's tutsan, good for ye. Charlock, sweet Cicely. There's all manner o' vittles growin' wild in the woodlands. No need t'go 'ungry."

Uggo chewed gingerly, pulling a wry face at the bitter flavour of one particular plant.

"T'aint the same as proper food, though, is it, Mister Gurdy?"

Jum snorted at the lack of gratitude. "Maybe not to yore way o' thinkin', but 'twill keep ye goin' until lunchtime. Now stop moanin' an' git walkin'!"

When midday eventually came, Jum was secretly glad of the rest. He had aged, and he had put on weight being in charge of Redwall's Cellars. It was some while since he had undertaken a journey to the coast. Careful not to let his young companion see that he was tired, the big otter put on a springy step.

"Keep up now, Master Wiltud. Yore fallin' behind agin!"

Uggo was not in a good mood. He pointed angrily upward. "You said we was goin' t'stop for lunch when the sun reached midday. It did that some time ago, an' you ain't stopped. Wot are we waitin' for, Mister Gurdy, nighttime?"

It was the sight of a stream ahead which prompted the otter to say, "On the bank o' yon water 'neath that willow. That's the spot I was aimin' for. Would've been there afore, except for yore laggin' behind."

It was indeed a pleasant location. They soon had a small fire going and mint tea on the boil. From the haversack, Jum sorted out some cheese, scones and honey. Cooling his footpaws in the shallows, he oversaw Uggo toasting two scones with cheese on them. "That's the way, matey. Nice'n'brown underneath with bubbly cheese atop. Perfect!"

The young hog did not mind preparing lunch. "I'll need two more scones, to spread honey on for afters."

Uggo was surprised at how good food tasted outdoors.

After they had eaten, Jum spread a large dockleaf over his eyes. Lying back against the willow trunk, he settled down.

"Let's take a liddle nap. Ain't nothin' like the sound of a gentle runnin' stream at early noon."

Uggo skimmed pebbles awhile, then felt bored. "I ain't sleepy, Mister Gurdy."

The otter opened one eye. "Go 'way an' don't bother me fer a while. Do a spot o' fishin' or somethin'."

Uggo stared into the clear running stream. "But there ain't no fish t'be seen round here."

The otter gave a long sigh. "Well, go downstream. There's a small cove where the water's still. May'aps ye'll find some freshwater shrimp there, an' we'll make soup fer supper t'night."

Uggo persisted. "I'll need a rod an' line."

Jum took on a threatening tone. "Ye don't catch watershrimp with a rod'n'line. Take one o' them scone sacks an' make a net. I trust yore not so dim that ye can't make a simple fishnet, are ye?"

Uggo stumped off, muttering, "O' course I can make a net. I ain't dim, Mister Gurdy. You take yore nap. Huh, old-beasts need naps!"

It was lucky for him that Jum did not hear most of what he said. Closing his eyes, he settled down with a yawn.

Finding a long twig with a forked end, the would-be shrimpcatcher attached the ends to either side of the little cloth sack. Making his way downstream, he watched the water intently, feeling happy about his new purpose, still murmuring to himself. "Just wait, Jum Gurdy. I'll catch a whole netful o' watershrimps. Then I'll creep back an' flop them in yore lap—that'll waken ye!"

The cove was further than he had expected, but Uggo finally came across it—a small inlet, patrolled by dragon-flies skimming the still, dark water. There were no shrimp to be seen, but Uggo gave his net a speedy pull beneath the murky surface. Pulling it out, he turned the net inside out and was rewarded by the sight of two tiny, transparent-grey, wriggling things.

"Ahaah! There ye are, me liddle watershrimps! Any others swimmin' about down there? Let's see, shall we?"

A curious wasp, investigating one of Jum Gurdy's eye-lids, woke him. He brushed it off dozily and was about to continue his nap when he noticed the position of the sun through the hanging willow branches. It was past midnoon! The big otter heaved himself upright. Had he really been asleep all that time? Taking the pan of lukewarm mint tea from the ashes of the dead fire, he drank it in one draught. A quick dash of streamwater across his face brought Jum fully awake and alert.

"Where's that liddle rascal got to? He should've been back an' waked me long since!"

Wading into the shallows, the otter cupped both paws

around his mouth, shouting aloud. "Uggo! Git back 'ere right now! Uggo! Uggooooo!"

Raising a spray of water with his rudderlike tail, Jum splashed back onto the bank. He stood, looking this way and that before bellowing again.

"Uggo Wiltud, where are ye? If'n ye ain't back by the time I've counted to ten, then I'm leavin' without ye! One . . . two. . . . Can ye hear me, ye liddle rascal?"

He counted to ten, then repeated the performance, with more dire threats. All to no avail. Packing everything back into his haversack, he tried to recall his words before napping.

"The cove downstream . . . freshwater shrimp . . . that's it!"

Without further ado, he scooped water over the fire ashes and stumped off along the bank, downstream.

Every now and then, Jum paused, calling into the surrounding woodlands. He tried to be less bad tempered, not wanting to scare the young hedgehog away. "Uggo, come on, liddle mate, I ain't mad at ye. 'Twas my fault for goin' off t'sleep like that. Come on, show yoreself, there's no real 'arm done!"

Still travelling on and calling out, Jum came upon the cove. There was the improvised shrimping net, floating in the water. He pulled it out with a cold fear creeping through his stomach. Had Uggo fallen in? Could young hedgehogs swim? Swimming was no problem to otters, but what about hedgehogs—were they like moles or squirrels? He had never seen any of them showing a fondness for water. That did it. Jum Gurdy dived into the cove.

Through his frantic underwater efforts, he stirred the cove into a muddy area. Four times he dived, each time scouring the cove from end to end, side to side, with no success. Regaining his breath, the big otter swam out of the cove. He searched the stream for a great length in either direction.

The sun was setting in crimson splendour when Redwall's Cellardog sat upon the streambank, weeping. Why had he slept so long at midday? Why had he been so irate with his young friend? He would regret it for the rest of his life. Uggo Wiltud was gone, drowned and carried off downstream to the sea. Shouldering his pack, Jum plodded wearily off, following the stream out over the flatlands toward the dunes, the shore and the sea.

It was a warm, still afternoon at the Abbey as Friar Wopple settled herself down on the southeast corner of the rampart walkway. She relished a quiet afternoon tea with Sister Fisk after all the bustle and heat of the kitchens. Spreading a cloth on the worn stones, the plump watervole laid out the contents of her hamper. Two oatfarls filled with chopped hazelnut salad, a latticed apple and blackberry tart, napkins and crockery.

Seeing Sister Fisk coming up the south wallsteps, Wopple waved, hailing her friend. "Cooee, Sister!"

Redwall's Infirmary mouse came bearing a steaming kettle. The Friar rubbed her paws in anticipation as Fisk sat down beside her. "I've set all our food out. What sort of tea are we drinking today?"

Fisk poured out two dainty beakers of the hot amber liquid, passing one to her companion. "Taste and guess, then tell me if you like it."

Blowing fragrant steam from the drink, Wopple sipped. "Ooh, it's absolutely delicious, Sister. I'd never guess, so you'd best tell me."

Fisk looked both ways, as if guarding a secret, before whispering, "Rosehip and dandelion bud, with just a squeeze of crushed almond blossom!"

The female Friar sipped further, closing her eyes with ecstasy. "It's the best you've ever invented, my friend!"

Fisk took a hearty bite from her salad farl. "Not half as good as your cooking, though. I had a bit of a rush getting up here this noon. Had to put some salve on a bruised footpaw. Little Alfio again!"

The Friar chuckled. "Dearie me. Sometimes I think that poor Dibbun was born with four left paws. How many times is it that he's fallen and hurt himself, clumsy little shrew!"

The Sister shook her head in mock despair. "I've lost count of Alfio's tumbles."

She settled her back up against the sun-warmed battlements. "Ahhh, this is the life. A quiet moment of tranquillity on a peaceful noontide, away from it all!"

Wopple set a slice of tart in front of her. "Aye, until somebeast injures themselves again, or a whole Abbeyful of Redwallers wants feeding!"

A thin, reedy quaver interrupted them.

"Could you feed me, please? I don't eat much!"

Fisk turned to Wopple. "Did you say something?"

The Friar was already pulling herself upright. "'Twasn't me—sounds like somebeast outside."

Fisk joined her as they peered over the walltop.

Below, amidst the trees, was an old hedgehog. She looked very thin and tottery. Leaning against an elm, she waved. "Didn't mean t'spoil yore tea, marms. I was just wonderin' 'ow ye gets into this fine place."

Friar Wopple answered promptly. "Stay right there, marm. We'll come down and get ye!"

Opening the small east wall wickergate, they hurried to the gable where the old hogwife had seated herself. She began thanking them as they assisted her inside the grounds.

"May fortune smile on ye goodbeasts, an' may yore bowls never be empty for yore kindness t'me!"

Helping her up to the walltop, they sat her down, placing their afternoon tea before her. She immediately fell upon the food with gusto. Whilst she fed herself unstintingly, Friar Wopple studied the newcomer's face, murmuring, "Sister Fisk, who does she put you in mind of?"

Instead of answering, Fisk turned to the old hedgehog. "Do you have a name, marm?"

Their guest looked up from a slice of tart, smiling to reveal only a few snaggled teeth. "Twoggs, me name's Twoggs."

The Friar nodded knowingly. "And is your second name Wiltud?"

The old hogwife finished off a beaker of tea at a swig. "Wiltud, that's right. . . . But 'ow did ye know?"

Friar Wopple shrugged. "Oh, I just guessed."

Twoggs Wiltud turned her attention to Fisk's partially eaten salad farl. "Good guess, eh, marm? Any more o' these nice vikkles lyin' about?"

Wopple moved to help her upright. "Come along to my kitchen, and I'll see what I can find!"

Abbot Thibb joined Dorka Gurdy in the kitchens. Both were intent on viewing the new arrival. The scrawny old hogwife had seated herself on a heap of sacks in one corner, paying attention only to the food she had been given.

Friar Wopple indicated her guest to Thibb and Dorka, remarking, "Sister Fisk and I are both agreed as to who she is."

The Abbot needed only a brief inspection of the snaggle-toothed ancient, who was slopping down honeyed oatmeal as if faced with a ten-season famine. He nodded decisively. "That's a Wiltud, without a doubt, eh, Dorka?"

The otter Gatekeeper agreed readily. "Split me rudder, she couldn't be ought else but a Wiltud. Ain't shy about table manners, is she? Lookit the way she's wolfin' those vittles!"

Friar Wopple refilled the guest's bowl with oatmeal. Twoggs Wiltud gulped down a beaker of October Ale, nodding to the Friar as she turned her attention back to the oatmeal.

"Thankee, marm. I likes a drop o' 'oneyed oatmeal. Don't 'ave enough teeth left t'deal wid more solid vikkles. I tries me best, though."

Sister Fisk stifled a chuckle. "I'm sure you do, good lady.

We have another member of your clan at Redwall—young Uggo Wiltud. Though he's off travelling at the moment."

Twoggs licked the sides of her empty bowl, holding it toward the Friar for another helping. "Huggo, ye say? Hmmm, don't know no Huggo Wiltud, but that ain't no surprise. Mossflower's teemin' wid Wiltuds. We're wanderers an' foragers, y'see. Don't suppose ye've got a drop o' soup t'spare. I likes soup, y'know."

Friar Wopple commented, "Is there any food you don't like?"

Twoggs sucked at her virtually toothless gums a moment. "Er, lemme see. May'aps oysters. I've 'eard tell of 'em, though I ain't never tasted one. So I can't tell if'n I'd like 'em or not. Yew ever tasted an oyster, marm?"

The Abbot interrupted this somewhat pointless chatter. "Forget oysters—but tell me, do you have a purpose in visiting our Abbey? You're welcome, I'm sure. However, a creature of your long seasons, you must have passed our gates many times if you live in Mossflower Country. So why do you suddenly turn up here today?"

Twoggs took a sip from the bowl which the Friar had just passed to her. She wrinkled her withered snout with delight. "Oh, 'appy day—spring veggible soup, my fav'rite bestest thing inna world. Fortune smile on ye, Cook marm, an' may ye allus 'ave someplace soft to lay yore 'ead at night!"

Taking a crust of bread, she began dipping it in the soup and sucking noisily. Dorka smiled at the Abbot. "Don't look like she's up to answerin' any more questions as long as the vittles keeps comin'."

Thibb shrugged. "I think you're right, friend. Friar, I'll leave her in your care. See she gets what she wants, then let her nap in the storeroom. Mayhaps she'll talk to me when she feels like it. Oldbeasts like her aren't usually in the habit of visiting new places without a reason. Though maybe she was just hungry."

Sister Fisk watched as another bowl of soup disappeared.

"Aye, that's probably it, Father. Let's hope she soon gets enough, before she eats us out of house and home. Incidentally, how's that torn pawnail of yours?"

The Abbot held it up for Fisk's inspection. "Oh, it's not too bad. I'll take more care next time I'm trying to shut the main gates on my own."

Dorka shook her head. "Aye, wait for me. I know them gates—they can be tricky if ye don't handle 'em right."

Fisk examined the pawnail, noting that the Abbot flinched when she touched it. "Hmm, you'd best come with me to the Infirmary, Father. I think a little of my special salve and a herbal binding is what's needed to solve your problem."

The Abbot made to walk away, excusing himself. "Oh, it'll be quite alright as it is. Pray don't trouble yourself, Sister."

Fisk caught him firmly by his habit girdle. "It's no trouble at all. I won't hurt you—now, don't be such a Dibbun and come with me."

She marched him off briskly. Friar Wopple passed Twoggs Wiltud a slice of mushroom pasty, remarking to Dorka, "I think there's a bit of the Dibbun in all of us when it comes to visiting the Infirmary. One time I got a rose thorn in my footpaw when I was a Dibbun. Old Brother Mandicus had to dig it out with a needle. I've had a fear of healers ever since."

Twoggs interrupted through a mouthful of pasty. "Ain't ye got nothin' decent t'drink round 'ere?"

Friar Wopple looked slightly offended. "What d'ye mean, somethin' decent to drink? All the drinks are decent at Redwall, I'll have you know!"

The ancient hedgehog cackled. "I means summat sweet tastin'. Alls I've 'ad since I came 'ere is tea an' ale. I'm partial t'sweet drinks, cordials'n'fizzes."

Dorka Gurdy put on an expression of mock pity. "Oh, ye pore ole thing, we shall have t'get ye some strawberry fizz or dandelion an' burdock cordial."

Twoggs sensed that she was being mocked and replied

71

sharply, "Less o' yore cheek, waterdog, or I won't say a word about wot I was sent 'ere t'say!"

The big otter wagged a paw at the old hedgehog. "Who are you callin' waterdog, pricklepig?"

Friar Wopple got between them. "Now, now—no need for insults an' name-calling. I'll go and ask Foremole Roogo to fetch a jug o' damson an' pear cordial from the cellars."

Twoggs pulled herself upright, the picture of injured dignity. "Aye, an' I'll come with ye. I ain't stayin' 'ere t'be h'insulted by that imperdent creature!" She stalked off behind the Friar.

Dorka humphed. "We takes 'er in, an' that's how we gets treated for bein' 'ospitable to 'er. Scrawny ole beggar. If'n my brother Jum were 'ere, he wouldn't let 'er near his cellars. Huh, that ole 'og needs a good bath, if'n ye ask me!"

"Hurr, if'n Oi arsks ee wot, marm?" Foremole Roogo entered the kitchen from the serving hatch door. Dorka explained about Twoggs.

"One o' that Wiltud tribe turned up at our Abbey. She's eaten 'er fill an' gone down to the cellars with Friar for a jug o' cordial."

Foremole jangled the ring of keys at his side. "She'm b'aint a-gettin' nuthen. Oi locked ee door."

Dorka was about to reply when from the cellar stairs there came a hubbub of crashing, shouting, squealing and bumping. The big otter hurried off with Roogo trundling in her wake. "Good grief, what's all the commotion?"

They found Twoggs at the bottom of the spiral sandstone stairs. Friar Wopple was leaning over her, trying to sit her up against the locked door. "She pushed past me at the top of the stairs. Tripped on those old rags she was wearin', an' tumbled from top to bottom. I couldn't stop her!"

"You'm 'old on to hurr, marms, an' stan ee asoide!" Foremole produced the key, opening the door. They bore Twoggs Wiltud in between them, laying her down on a sack of straw.

Friar Wopple passed a paw in front of the old hog's nostrils. "Dorka, run and get Sister Fisk. I don't know how bad she is, but she's still breathing. Foremole, can you find a beaker of sweet cordial, please?"

Dorka arrived back with Sister Fisk and the Abbot as Friar Wopple was attempting to get some of the cordial between the patient's closed lips. The Sister immediately took charge.

"Give me that beaker, please. Hold her head up gently—it looks like she's been knocked out cold. I don't know what injuries she may have taken. Dorka says she tumbled the length of the stairs, right into the locked door."

The Friar watched anxiously as cordial dribbled over the old hedgehog's chin. "She just pushed past me—there wasn't anything I could do!"

Foremole patted the watervole's paw. "Thurr naow, marm. Et wurr no fault o' your'n!"

To everybeast's amazement, Twoggs's eyelids flickered open. She licked her lips feebly, croaking, "Hmm, that tastes nice'n'sweet. Wot is it?"

Foremole wrinkled his velvety snout secretively. "It bee's dannelion'n'burdocky corjul, marm. Thurr's ee gurt barrel-ful of et jus' for ee, when you'm feels betterer."

Twoggs gave a great rasping cough. She winced and groaned. "I 'opes I didn't break none o' yore fine stairs. . . ."

Abbot Thibb knelt beside her, wiping her chin with his kerchief. "Don't try to speak, marm. Just lie still now." He cast a sideways glance at Sister Fisk, who merely shook her head sadly, meaning there was nothing to be done for the old one.

Twoggs clutched the Abbot's sleeve, drawing him close. The onlookers watched as she whispered haltingly into Thibb's ear, pausing and nodding slightly. Then Twoggs Wiltud extended one scrawny paw as if pointing outside the Abbey. Abbot Thibb still had his ear to her lips when she emitted one last sigh, the final breath leaving her wounded body.

Friar Wopple laid her head down slowly. "She's gone, poor thing!"

Thibb spread his kerchief over Twoggs Wiltud's face. "I wish she'd lived to tell me more."

Sister Fisk looked mystified. "Why? What did she say?"

The Father Abbot of Redwall closed his eyes, remembering the message which had brought the old hedgehog to his Abbey. "This is it, word for word, it's something we can't ignore.

"Redwall has once been cautioned,
heed now what I must say,
that sail bearing eyes and a trident,
Will surely come your way.
Then if ye will not trust the word,
of a Wiltud and her kin,
believe the mouse with the shining sword,
for I was warned by him!"

In the uneasy silence which followed the pronouncement, Dorka Gurdy murmured, "That was Uggo Wiltud's dream, the sail with the eyes and the trident, the sign of the Wearat. But my brother Jum said that he'd been defeated and slain by the sea otters."

Abbot Thibb folded both paws into his wide habit sleeves. "I know, but we're waiting on Jum to return and confirm what he was told. I think it will be bad news, because I believe what old Twoggs Wiltud said. The mouse with the shining sword sent her to Redwall, and who would doubt the spirit of Martin the Warrior?"

8

Each day, as the *Greenshroud* ploughed closer to the High North Coast, Shekra the Vixen became more apprehensive. She feared the sea otters, those wild warriors of Skor Axe-hound's crew, who revelled in battling. Shekra had never seen the Wearat defeated until he encountered Skor and his creatures. The vixen was a Seer, but she was also a very shrewd thinker. No matter what refinements had been added to his vessel, she knew that corsairs, and searats, would be foolhardy to attack the sea otters on their own territory. Recalling the vermin bodies floating in a blood-stained sea and the blazing ship limping off, savagely beaten, Shekra was certain a second foray would only result in failure. Through listening to the gossip of those who had been aboard on that bumbled raid, it was obvious that they were of a like mind with her. However, it did not do to discuss such things with Razzid as captain. Moreover, Mowlag and Jiboree, the Wearat's closest aides, were ever on the alert for mutinous talk.

Shekra knew it was a dangerous situation to which a solution had to be found. Some serious thinking was called for. The answer came one evening, sitting in the galley with other crewbeasts. It was after supper as they were sipping grog when an old corsair stoat began plinking on an unidentifiable stringed instrument and singing. It was a common vermin sea song, full of self-pity induced by swigging quantities of potent grog. Shekra listened to the singer's hoarse rendition.

> "O haul away, mates, haul away, hark 'ow the north
>   wind wails.
> There's ice upon the ratlines, in the riggin' an' the sails!
>
> "When I were just a liddle snip, me mammy said t'me,
> Don't be a corsair like yore pa, 'tis no good life at sea.
> O follow not the searat's ways, or ye'll be sure to end
>   yore days,
> beneath the cold an' wintry waves, 'cos corsairs 'ave no
>   graves!
>
> "O haul away, mates, haul away, hark 'ow the
>   north wind wails.
> There's ice upon the ratlines, in the riggin' an' the sails!
>
> "I scorned wot my ole mammy said, now lookit me
>   t'day,
> aboard some vermin vessel, o'er the waves an' bound
>   away.
> The cook is mean, the cap'n's rough, I lives on
>   grog'n'skilly'n'duff
> I tell ye, mates, me life is bad, now I'm grown old an'
>   sad."

Shekra passed the singer a beaker of grog. "Aye, 'tis right, mate, but once ye follow the sea, there ain't no goin' back. I know 'tis too late now, but tell me, wot would ye have done, if'n you'd stopped ashore? Been a farmer mayhaps?"

The old stoat chuckled humorlessly. "Wot, me be a farmer? Huh, sounds too much like 'ard work. I would've liked t'live the easy life, in some sunny ole place. Aye, with others to cook me vittles, an' a nice soft bunk t'sleep in.

Where yore sheltered from storms an' cold in the winter, wid a big roarin' log fire to toast me whiskers by. Ah, that'd be wot I'd 'ave liked!"

Shekra nodded, her brain working furtively. "It sounds good t'me. Wonder if'n there is such a place."

A youngish searat offered a suggestion. "That big stripedog mountain place, where all the rabbets lives, that looked alright t'me."

The vixen sounded scornful, knowing which way she was leading the conversation. "No chance of gettin' anywhere near that mountain. Those rabbets are warriors, just like the wavedogs. Ye'd be slain afore ye knew it. Now, the Red Abbey place, that'd suit me. D'ye know it?"

The youngish searat shook his head. "Red Abbey place?"

The cook, a fat greasy weasel, dipped a tankard into the grog barrel. "Aye, I've 'eard tell of it. Ain't it rightly called the Red Abbot place?"

Shekra nodded slyly. "Right, mate. Wot've ye 'eard tell?"
The cook finished half his tankard in one swig and belched. "Somewheres in mid-country it is, with a forest growin' round. My granpa saw it once. Said it was all built o' red stones. Woodlanders, treemice, 'edgepigs, mouses an' such lives there. They ain't short o' vittles neither."

Shekra added her own embellishment to the cook's narration. "Aye, somebeast once told me there's orchards there with ripe fruit 'angin' off all the trees. Strawberries too, blackberries, enough honey to sink a ship, a big lake full of fishes, birds an' eggs, many as ye please!"

The old stoat singer shook his head wistfully. "The Red Abbot place, eh? Sounds wunnerful. Why ain't we been there? Woodlanders ain't warriors like wavedogs'n'rabbets."

The vixen shrugged. "'Cos it's in mid-country an' ships couldn't reach it. Corsairs don't go nowhere widout their ships. But wot am I talkin' about? This *Greenshroud* can go anyplace now—land or sea, it don't matter, do it?" An air of excitement suddenly pervaded the galley.

"We could go there, I'd wager we could!"

"Hah, wouldn't be no trouble slayin' a load o' woodlanders!"

"Aye, an' it'd all be ours, just for the takin', mates!"

"We'd live like cap'ns an' . . . an' . . . er, kings. I wonder if'n their grog's any good, Shekra."

Now she had sown the seed, the vixen left the galley, calling back to her shipmates, "They've prob'ly got cellars loaded with barrels o' the finest drinks, or they should 'ave, wid all that fruit juice. It might taste nice an' sweet!"

She wandered out on deck. It was a fine spring night, with a hint of summer promise on the breeze. Jiboree came down from the stern deck. "Ahoy, vixen, where've ye been? Cap'n Razzid wants ye." Wordlessly, Shekra followed him to the master cabin.

The Wearat was taking supper with Mowlag and Jiboree. Wiping moisture from his damaged eye, he glared at Shekra through his good one. It was always unnerving to be scrutinised by his cold stare.

Shekra tugged an ear in salute, unsure of why she had been summoned. "Cap'n?"

Razzid put aside the grilled herring he had been nibbling, keeping Shekra waiting as he wiped his lips and drank from a fine crystal goblet of good-quality grog. He spoke just the one word: "Well?"

Shekra swallowed hard, her paws trembling. "Did ye want me, Cap'n?"

The Wearat continued to stare, knowing the effect it had. "Well, yore my Seer, ain't ye? Tell me wot ye see."

The vixen breathed an inward sigh of relief. "I've been waitin' on ye to ask me, sire. A moment please." She shook out the jumble of stones, wood, shells, feathers and other objects from her pouch. Selecting what she required, she began murmuring.

"Voices of wind and water, say
what fate may bring this Greatbeast's way,

78

Omens of earth, of wood and stone,
is thy message for him alone?"

She cast three stones upon the table, two of common grey, one a black pebble, pitted and marked. The grey stones bounced from the table onto the deck. The black one stayed on the table, close to Razzid.

Closing her eyes, Shekra spoke. "I speak to none but you, Great One."

The Wearat dismissed his aides. "Leave us."

Both Mowlag and Jiboree shot hate-laden glances at the vixen. They left the cabin—though, once outside, they pressed their ears to the closed door in an effort to learn what the Seer had to say.

Shekra went to work with an air of mystery, which she created by sprinkling powder on the table candle. It produced green and black smoke, which swirled around both her and Razzid. The vixen picked up the black, pitted pebble from the table, showing it to the Wearat. "This stone is thee, Razzid, marked by wounds, yet still tough and hard. Watch where it falls and know thy fate, which only the omens can foretell."

She cast it back onto the table, together with a lot of other bits. Her fertile brain was racing as she studied the jumble of objects.

Razzid dabbed at his bad eye. "So, what do the omens tell ye, Seer?"

Shekra spoke out boldly, knowing what she needed to say. "Death brings death. The old one must be paid for! Look ye, the stone can go any way, but which way to choose, high north or south and east? Which path leads to death, and which to victory? Choose, O Mighty One!"

Razzid seized the vixen's paw in a cruel grip. "If yore tryin' to feed me bilgewater, I'll hang ye from a mast an' skin ye alive, fox. Do I make meself clear?" The Wearat's claws had pierced Shekra's paw, but knowing her life depended on deceiving Razzid, she tried to keep her voice calm and show no pain.

"I am but the messenger, Lord. Slay me an' the knowledge will remain unknown. 'Tis thy decision, sire."

Razzid snarled as he released his hold. "Then speak. What do the omens mean?"

She began pointing at the way her objects had fallen. "See, the black stone lies between two groups, one facing north, the other southeast. The northern group is mainly stones and shells, all signs of strength and sharp edges."

Razzid picked something from the small heap. "This is neither stone nor shell. A scrap of dried moss—explain that t'me if'n ye can."

Shekra took it from him, blowing it off into the candle flame, where it was shrivelled to ash. She responded promptly. "Nought but the vision of an old wavedog, whose life ended by fire. He was an old chieftain. His spirit must be avenged by the wavedog warriors. Hearken to what I said before. Death brings death. The old one must be paid for."

Razzid was staring hard at his Seer. "Whose death?"

"My voices say it would be those who slew the old one."

Razzid sat back in his chair, gazing at the objects on the tabletop. "Wot's that other lot for, the ones ye said were southeast?"

Shekra ran a paw over them. "Wood of trees and soft feathers, Lord. It is not clear, but I feel that is where thy time of victory lies. South, and not too far east, where the sun shines and the weather is fair."

Razzid leaned forward, his curiosity aroused. "An' where would that be? What place do ye speak of?"

The vixen looked as if she was thinking intently, looking for an answer. Then her ears drooped and she shook her head slowly. "Alas, Mighty One, my powers are not endless. The omens reveal nothing else. My spell is broken."

The Wearat leapt up, sweeping everything from the tabletop. Suddenly he was dangerous, angry.

"Play me false, an' I'll rip ye apart. A Seer who can't see is no use to me!"

Shekra fell to the floor, trying to scrabble under the table. She was blabbering, "No, no, sire, spare me. I spoke truly—the omens never lie!" She jumped with fright as the Wearat's trident thudded into the wooden deck close to her skull.

Razzid was roaring. "Where in the south an' east will my time of victory be, ye useless worm? Tell me!"

It was a stone which saved the Seer's life. One of the two grey stones she had cast to the deck. Her paw had brushed against it as she sought refuge beneath the table. Now the grey stone was smeared with blood from the deep scratches Razzid's claws had gouged into her paw. As the brain wave struck her, Shekra pointed, yelling, "The stone, Lord, the stone by thy footpaw! It has turned red, see? My omens were right—it's a place of red stones. That's what ye seek, a place of red stones!"

Mowlag and Jiboree had eavesdropped on all that went on in the captain's cabin. By morning next day it was the talk of the ship. So much so that when Razzid emerged to pace the deck, he was faced with Mowlag, hauling the greasy weasel cook along by his tattered apron.

He booted the fat weasel down on the deck, smirking at Razzid. "Ahoy, Cap'n, lissen to wot this gutbucket's got t'say." He walloped the cook's rear end with the flat of his cutlass. "Go on. Tell the cap'n wot yore mates 'eard ye sayin'. Speak out now, cooky!"

Under the Wearat's gimlet glare, the greasy weasel could hardly stop himself talking.

"Er, beggin' yer pardon, Cap'n, but my ole granpa tole me that 'e'd been t'the Red Abbot place, a long time back that was, an', an' 'e said 'twas a great bi—"

The words froze on his lips as the lethal trident slammed once more into the deck. Realisation hit the Wearat like a thunderbolt. He dismissed the cook abruptly. "Stop talking rubbish an' get back to yore galley." Razzid grabbed

Shekra, thrusting her into his cabin. Slamming the door, he hissed in excitement, "Redwall Abbey, I've heard o' that place! That's it—Redwall Abbey!"

The vixen nodded agreement eagerly. "My omens never lie. Redwall Abbey is where your victory lies, Lord."

Putting aside his trident, Razzid sat down, wiping his leaky eye as he pondered his position.

Shekra was puzzled. "What is it, sire? Is something amiss?"

The Wearat nodded. "Aye, my oath to be revenged on the wavedogs—what of that?"

The Seer shrugged. "What of it? You are the Wearat, an' ye can do what ye want, O Great One."

Razzid shook his head. "But I would lose face in front of my own crew if I turn tail from them."

Shekra spread her paws pleadingly. "But, sire, the omens have spoken—"

Irately, Razzid cut her short. "I know all about your omens. Sometimes I think they say what you want them to. D'ye think me a fool?"

Knowing she was on dangerous ground, the vixen backed off. "Oh, no, sire. I was just saying . . ."

The look from the Wearat's piercing eye silenced her. He waved in dismissal. "Tell nobeast of this. Now leave me. I must think about what to do. Go!"

When she had gone, Razzid smiled, a rare sight to see.

9

Two things were really bothering Uggo Wiltud—a headache like nothing he had ever suffered and a sharp object up his nose, which alternately tickled and irritated. He was brought back to consciousness by a shrill voice berating him.

"Wakey up, dozypig! Quick now, afore diss comes outta ya ear!"

Uggo's eyes flicked open. Instinctively he jerked his head aside, ridding himself of the probing twig. This was held in the paws of a young rat about the same age as himself. The rat had a vicious, feral face. He tried to jab the twig back up Uggo's nose, but it snapped as it missed the nostril.

Despite the banging pain in his skull, Uggo lurched at his tormentor. Not realising his paws were bound, he tripped, butting the rat full in its mouth.

The young vermin gave a stifled scream, dancing about and clasping two broken front teeth. Uggo struggled to a sitting position against the earthen wall of what he took to be an underground tunnel. There was light coming in from one end, and the sound of the not too distant sea. The rat dabbed a wad of dried grass against its injured mouth, seeing the thin trickle of blood upon it. Glaring murderously at the bound captive, the young vermin pulled an old broken knife from a waist sash.

"See wotja dun ta me, daftpig? Yirji'll 'ave ta kill ya now!" He advanced on Uggo, who wriggled about madly, kicking out with bound footpaws to keep his foe at bay. Something blocking the light from the entrance caused the rat to look around. It was a lean old fox, clad in flowing rags and carrying a carved beechwood staff to serve as a walking stick. Lashing out with the staff, the fox struck the rat's paw, knocking the knife from it.

The young rat immediately went into another dance of pain, clutching a numbed paw and screeching. "Worraya do dat for, Snaggs? 'E was tryna kill me!"

The old fox, Snaggs, advanced on him, brandishing the staff in one paw whilst covering an ear with the other. "Iffa ya don't stop dat screamin' I'll kill ya meself. Now, quit ya noise afore it drives me outta me skullbrain."

The young rat, Yirji, slumped down in sullen silence.

Snaggs turned his attention to Uggo, prodding him with the staff. "Betcha yore 'ead's 'urtin', ainnit? Ya must 'ave a t'ick skull. Ole Snaggs 'it ya 'ard enuff t'kill ya. Yerra lucky 'edgepig t'still be alive!"

Snaggs tugged on a long rope, which Uggo had not noticed before. Anchored to a stake driven deep in the clay floor, it ran outside the tunnel. The fox called out, "Posybud, bring some water fer the pris'ner ta drink!"

Uggo was surprised to see a very pretty young hedgehog carrying a pail and a scallop shell dipper shuffling toward him. Then he noticed that she was attached to the rope, a captive like himself.

Yirji stood on the rope, stopping her progress. "Gizz summa dat water. Me mouth's been 'urted!"

Snaggs poked him from the rope with his staff. "I 'opes yer mouth's been 'urted good. Might stop ya screechin' an' wailin' alla time." He pointed the staff at his newest captive. "Yew—wot's ya name?"

Uggo answered promptly. "Uggo Wiltud!"

84

Snaggs shook his head, chuckling. "Buggo Muggo Wuggo—heehee, der names some o' these young uns 'as now'days. Posybud, give Uggo a drink, there's a good liddle maid!"

Sitting alongside Uggo, the young hogmaid dipped the shell into her pail, offering it to him. "Does your head hurt very much, Uggo?"

He tried a wan smile. "Aye, Miss Posybud. Hurts like fury!"

Taking some dried moss from her apron pocket, she soaked it with water. "Lean your head forward, and I'll bathe it whilst you drink. By the way, you can call me Posy."

The water was cold and clear; it tasted good. Uggo could feel Posy pressing the wet moss firmly on his head. He relaxed, sighing as she murmured soothingly, "It's quite a bump you have there, but don't worry. It'll go down after a while. How does that feel now?"

Uggo refilled the shell from the pail.

"Ooh, much better, thank ye. I think the headache's beginning to go. How long have you been with Snaggs?"

She was about to reply when two more young rats and a hulking young ferret came strolling into the tunnel.

Snaggs questioned them. "Anythin' 'appenin' out there?"

The ferret sprawled on the floor, chewing on some wild radish he had dug up from somewhere. "Nah, nothin' much. Saw one o' those streamdogs goin' along the riverbank."

One of the young rats contradicted him. "Dat wasn't no streamdog—'twas a wavedog."

The ferret waved a wooden club at him. "Who asked yew, limpetbrain? It was a streamdog. I knows me streamdogs from me wavedogs. Unless ya wants ter step outside an' argue about it?"

The ferret twirled his club in the air skilfully.

Snaggs caught it, then passed it back. "No need fer dat sorta talk, Wigga me darlin'. Blawd didn't mean nothin'. So, why didn't ya catcher the streamdog, eh?"

The ferret, Wigga, scoffed. "Yew never seen the size of

'im. Huh, dat was one big beast, an' 'e was carryin' a lance. Why don't yew track 'im down an' catcher 'im yerself, Snaggs me darlin'?"

The fox shook his head at the burly young vermin. "Nah. I'm too old fer that kinda thing. That'n is more suited ter me. Guess wot 'is name is. Uggo! Heehee—wot sorta name's dat fer an 'edgepig? Uggo!"

Blawd, one of the two young rats, took out a thin-bladed knife and tested its edge by licking it. He stared pointedly at Uggo. "Worra ya gonna do wid 'im, Snaggs, gut 'im an' kill 'im? Dat's wot I'd do, aye—roast 'im fer supper."

Snaggs could move quickly for a fox of his long seasons. He tripped Blawd, kicked the knife away and pinned him down with his staff. "Ho, ya would, would ya? Well, yew lissen t'me, slime nose. I'm the chief round 'ere, an' I sez wot we do. So if'n ya wants ter eat a roasted 'edgepig, go an' git one o' yer own. I catchered 'im while 'e was fishin', so 'e could be useful." Snaggs turned to Uggo. "Are ya any good at fishin', 'og?"

The young hedgehog was frightened. He nodded several times. "Oh, yes, sir. I'm a good fisher, fished all my life, I have!"

Another two young vermin had wandered in, a stoat and a weasel. Snaggs beckoned Posybud. "Go an' see wot's left o' dat soup an' serve it out."

It was a thin broth of seaweed, a few herbs and some cockles and whelks, cooked in a cauldron on a fire outside the tunnel. The hogmaid dished it out to the vermin. There was about half a bowlful over, which she shared with Uggo. Snaggs sucked his broth noisily, chewing the shellfish. Wiping a paw over his mouth, he addressed Uggo.

"Ain't a bad liddle cook, is she? From now on yew can be fisher. There's a whole sea fulla fish out der. So, yew catch the fishes, an' she cooks 'em. If'n yew doesn't catch no fishes, then we'll try Blawd's idea, we'll slay ya an' roast ya . . . both!"

Snaggs and his gang settled down then for their nap.

Posy continued treating Uggo's headache with the wet moss, talking quietly with him. "Don't worry, they're always threatening evil things, but none of it comes to anything, usually. Is it true—are you a good fisherbeast?"

Uggo shrugged. "I don't know. I've always done my fishing in Redwall Abbey's pond. I suppose the fox wants me to fish in the sea, but I've never done that before. You're a good cook, Posy. I know because I thought your broth was delicious."

The pretty hogmaid smiled at the compliment. "Oh, it ain't that good, though I like to cook, an' if I'm given the right ingredients, I could suprise you."

Uggo dropped his voice to a whisper. "There'll be plenty o' time to surprise me after we've escaped this fox an' his bullies."

Posy pressed down hard on his headbump with the wet moss. "Hush! Don't even think about it, Uggo. Snaggs and his vermin are wicked beasts. They'd enjoy recapturing us an' roastin' us for supper. I know, 'cos they've done it before. I've heard them jokin' about it, an' I've seen the bones scattered in the sand. Forget escape, friend. It's a sure way to get us slain."

The young hedgehog straightened his head, flexing his neck back and forth. "By the seasons, Posy, y'must have healin' paws. I feel much better, an' the headache's gone. Listen, if'n we stay here, they'll kill us both sooner or later. We've got to escape, but we need a plan. I'm not goin' to let 'em track us down an' catch us again. Don't say any more for now, Posy. I need to think."

The pretty hogmaid saw the determination in his eyes. She nodded. "Right, we'll both do some thinking and keep our eyes an' ears alert for any chances."

Uggo pretended he was dozing, but he watched the activities within the tunnel through half-closed eyes. Several more young vermin returned to Snaggs's lair, mainly rats, but one or two stoats and ferrets. By the light filtering in from outside, Uggo guessed it was early evening.

Snaggs woke and stumped about with his staff, questioning the gang. "Any of ya see'd the big streamdog wot Wigga'n'Blawd saw this mornin'?"

There had been no further sightings of Jum Gurdy. The fox nudged a young stoat, who was armed with a long sling. "Worrabout yew, Jonder? Catch anythin'?"

The stoat made a throwing gesture with his sling. "Aye, Snaggs, I kil't a big seagill wid one stone. Caught 'im swoopin' down an' slung me best pebble—smacko! Gorrim right in the eye. I left it outside."

Snaggs waved the staff at Uggo and Posy. "Yew two, gerrout there an' git the seagill in the pot. Pluck all its fedders off first, though. Jonder, Vilty, go an' keep an eye on 'em. Make sure they don't get itchy paws an' try ta run."

Yirji, the rat Uggo had butted, pulled out his knife. "I'll go, Chief. If'n dat 'edgepig tries ta run, I'll cut 'is paws off!"

Snaggs tripped Yirji as he rose, pinning him down with the staff. "Yew'll stay where ye are. If'n there's any paw cuttin' round 'ere, I'm the one wot'll be doin it. Startin' wid yew!"

Vilty was a young ratmaid. She untied Uggo's paws, roping him by his neck to the line around Posy. Having been marched outside, they were confronted by the body of a black-headed gull lying by the fire next to the cauldron.

Jonder lifted its limp head. "See? Right in the eye—blatt!"

Vilty saw the look of sadness on Posy's face. She matched it with a similar expression, mockingly. "Ah, dearie me, a pore dead bird, ain't dat a shame!" She flicked a knotted piece of rope at the hogmaid, her tone hardening. "Move yaself, snoutpig. Get dem feathers pulled off it!"

The distasteful task was difficult. Starting on a wing, they both found the feathers hard to pull out.

Jonder stood twirling his sling, watching them impatiently. "Didn't ya never pluck fedders off a bird afore? The way youse are shapin', it'll be winter season by the time yer finished. Gerrout the way!"

He kicked them both away from the dead gull.

"Vilty, move dat cauldron off the fire. This is the best way ta git the job done!"

Grunting and shoving, Jonder managed to get the gull halfway into the flames. He dusted off his paws. "Dat's der best way to git fedders off'n a bird!"

After a short while, the acrid stench of burning plumage filled the air. A breeze coming in from the sea blew the fumes into the tunnel. Hawking and coughing, Snaggs came staggering out, followed by the others. He yelled angrily at the hedgehogs. "Wot'n blazin' are ya doin'? We're gettin' choked in there by that stink!"

He raised the staff to hit Uggo, but Posy placed herself between them, shouting, "It wasn't us—it was Jonder, he did it!"

A heated argument broke out between Snaggs and Jonder. The other vermin began taking sides and were soon involved. Blows were struck as they yelled at one another.

For a moment, Uggo and Posy were forgotten. They found themselves backed up by the side of a dune.

Uggo murmured to his friend, "Wish I had a blade. If'n there was somethin' to cut this rope with, we could make a run for it!"

"Don't try anythin', young Wiltud. If ye run they'll catch ye. Stay where ye are for now."

Posy stared at Uggo. "What was that you said?"

Uggo was mystified. "I never said anythin'."

The voice, which seemed to come from the grassy dunetop, continued. "I said, don't try to run. Try to get t'the sea tomorrow. Look out for a log!"

Yirji, who had been hopping about on the edge of the fray, came running toward them, waving his rusty knife.

"Worra yew two yappin' about? Tryin' ter escape, eh? I been waitin' fer sumthin' like this!"

Before he ever got to them with the knife, Snaggs felled him with a hard blow from his staff. The fox stood over Yirji, breathing heavily. "I warned ya t'stay away from my pris'ners!"

The affray had ceased. Now everybeast was watching Snaggs. Sensing he was back in command, the fox bawled out orders. "Git that bird offa the fire afore we're all suffercated! No more fightin', or I'll give yez wot I gave 'im." He tapped Yirji with the staff but saw that he had knocked him out cold with the first blow.

"Jonder, Wigga, carry this idjit back inter the den. Vilty, Blawd, cover that bird wid sand—it'll keep the smell down! The rest of ya, back inside. Cummon, yew two." He gave the rope a sharp tug, muttering as he hauled the captives along. "Blood'n'guts, dat's brekkist tomorrer spoiled. I couldn't eat gull after sniffin' those fedders!"

The idea came to Uggo in a flash. "I'll get fish for ye, Chief—me'n'Posy, early in the mornin'. Round about dawn's the best time for fish."

Snaggs eyed Uggo suspiciously. "Wot do ya wanna gerrup earlier an' go fishin' for, eh?"

Uggo smiled hopefully. "'Cos if me'n'Posy catches enough fish, there might be some for us, too."

Posy nodded enthusiastically. "Aye, sir. I'll spit the fish on fresh reeds an' roast them nice for ye!"

The fox smiled. "Aye, I likes roasted fish fer me brekkist. Wot'll ye need?"

Uggo scratched his headspikes. "Er, two rods, some line, few stones for weights an' a few hooks."

Snaggs ushered them into the tunnel, leaving Uggo's paws unbound, though he was still attached to Posy's rope. The fox snuffled distastefully. "I kin still smell burnt fedders in 'ere. Jonder, no more birds fer a while. Yew an' Wigga take the two 'ogs fishin' at dawn. Keep an eye on 'em—they'll be gittin' fish fer brekkist."

Seated back in their former position, Uggo squeezed Posy's paw. "Now we'll get to the sea an' look out for the log. At least it's a chance."

10

Between them, Lieutenant Scutram, Captain Rake and Sergeant Miggory buried the remains of the old sea otter. They worked swiftly, marking the sandy grave with a charred piece of timber, which had served Jum Gurdy's uncle Wullow as a paddle. The stoat Crumdun was standing nearby, guarded by Corporal Welkin. Captain Rake beckoned him forward.

"Ye say ye seen nought of what happened here?"

The former corsair shook his head vigorously. "Nay, sir, an' by the look of wot was left o' that pore creature, I'm glad I didn't. On me oath, sir!"

The captain looked to Scutram, who nodded. "I'm inclined to believe the rascal, sah, 'pon me word. Though I can't believe that a livin' thing, vermin or not, could do such a cruel deed to another, wot!"

Crumdun stared at the grave, still shaking his head. "I'll tell ye, gentlebeasts. Razzid Wearat enjoyed doin' things like that. I've 'eard stories about that un as'd make yore fur curl. My ole mate, Braggio—d'ye know wot the Wearat did to 'im? Wait'll I tell ye—"

Captain Rake cut him off sharply. "No, ye won't, mah friend. Ah don't want tae hear another word about the mur-

91

ders done by yore Wearat master. An' mind, Ah forbid ye tae speak o' it tae any o' mah young Patrollers, d'ye ken?"

The stoat tugged his snout. "Aye, sir!"

The tall captain saluted the grave. "'Tis a sad end tae anybeast, but rest easy, mah laddie, an' know that your death'll be avenged by us. We'll make yon Wearat weep tears o' bluid, Ah swear et on these blades!"

Touching his lips to the blades of the twin claymores, which he had drawn to salute the fallen otter, Rake Nightfur sheathed them, turning smartly. "Sarn't Miggory, get the Patrol underway, if ye please!"

They marched off along the shore into the sunlit spring day, though gossip was rife throughout the ranks about what they had missed seeing.

"I say, why d'you suppose we weren't allowed one bally peek?"

"Search me. We've all seen deadbeasts before, haven't we?"

"Speak for y'self, Wilbee, I jolly well haven't!"

"Huh, must've been somethin' pretty dreadful, wot!"

The stern voice of Sergeant Miggory warned the speaker. "Somethin' pretty dreadful will 'appen t'you h'if ye keep on blatherin' h'in the ranks, laddie buck. H'an that goes for you, too, Miss Ferrul. Eyes front, now, an' pick up the pace. Left right, left right!"

Corporal Welkin called out to Miggory, "Only one thing t'keep 'em marchin' smartlike an' stop the blighters talkin', Sarn't!"

Miggory bellowed back to him. "Ho, an' wot's that, Corp?"

Welkin's reply came back equally loud. "Get 'em singin' an' slap anybeast who ain't singin' out 'early enough on a fizzer, wot!"

The colour sergeant performed a maneuver which amazed the young hares. Twirling about, he began marching backward without breaking pace, keeping up with the column and roaring cheerfully at them. "H'I say, wot a spiffin' h'idea! Right, you 'orrible lot, h'I wants to 'ear you singin' like flippin' larks. H'every verse o' that liddle dittie h'entitled 'The Barracks Bunfight'! An' woe betide h'anybeast whose tonsils h'I can't see wagglin' like the clappers. Corporal Welkin, will you lead off? The rest of ye, join in smartly now h'in yore best voices!"

The marching ballad Miggory had chosen was one to cheer their spirits and drown any curiosity and speculation about former incidents. Everybeast sang lustily, with even the officers joining in.

"One two three four, tell me, Sergeant, tell me more!
The bloomin' barracks bunfight's a sight you ought to
    see,
we went along last winter, old Tubby Dobbs an' me,
with brushed an' curled moustaches, an' buttons
    polished bright,
the gels were flutterin' lashes at both of us that night.

"Five six seven eight, on the dot an' don't be late!
Stap me flippin' vitals, the barracks did look bright,
all spiffed up with lanterns, an' glitt'rin' candlelight.
Two buffet tables groanin' 'neath scads o' lovely stuff,
pudden'n'pie'n'trifle, an' pots o' skilly'n'duff.

"One two three four, off we jigged across the floor!
The band was tootlin' gaily, when Tubby gave a wail,
he'd backed into a candle, which set fire to his tail,
he bumped into the colonel, who was wolfin' down his
    grub,
they both went staggerin' headlong, into the port wine
    tub.

"Five six seven eight, Wiggy cried, 'Look out, mate!'
The cook was servin' duff, which went flyin' off his
    spoon,
it splattered an old fiddler, scrapin' out a tune,

his bow shot like an arrow, an' hit the major's niece,
she wasn't afraid to speak her mind, so she gave him a
  piece.

"Nine ten eleven, sah, give 'em blood an' vinegah!
Hurrah for barracks bunfight, I leapt into the fray,
I meant to hit the fiddler, but his pal got in the way,
a regimental bandbeast, a hefty chap, by gum,
this ain't a hat I'm wearin', it's . . . a euphonium!"

Captain Nightfur chuckled, stepping out jauntily. "Och,
that's the stuff tae give 'em, Sergeant. Can ye no' sing 'Hares
o' the Highlands'? That's a braw ditty—an' 'Long Patrol
Laddies,' too. There's nought like a wee spot o' singin' tae
keep the spirit up, the noo!"

They made good progress throughout the morning.
Lunchtime found the column halted in the lee of some
dunes. Last autumn's russet apples, cheese, oat bannocks
and pennycloud cordial was the fare. There was no more
talk of the early morning's events.

Lieutenant Scutram winked at the sergeant. "They seem
jolly cheerful now, wot!"

Miggory brushed crumbs from his tunic. "Aye, that's as
'ow h'it should be. Look out, 'ere comes the for'ard tracker,
back from scoutin' ahead."

Buff Redspore came loping in, throwing a hasty salute.
She ignored the food which was passed to her and went
straight to the captain. "Wish to report, sah. Spears ahead,
'bout half a league."

Rake Nightfur gave a quizzical glance at her. "Ah think
ye'd best explain. What spears?"

The tracker clarified her report. "Further north, sah, from
the tideline t'the dunes, line o' spears, about twoscore.
Stickin' up in the sand, with skulls an' tails decoratin'
'em. Looks like some kind o' warnin', sah. Couldn't see
anybeast about but felt I was bein' watched. So I did a jolly

94

quick about-paws an' came straight back to inform you, sah!"

The tall, dark hare snapped out orders. "Sergeant Miggory, Scutram, Lancejack Sage, come with me. We'll stick tae the dunes until we see how the land lies. Corporal Welkin, whilst we're awa' get them tae clean an' ready their weapons, an' stay on the alert."

With Buff Redspore leading them as pathfinder, the four hares set off at a lope through the dunes. The rest of the column relaxed, seeing as the officers were not there. Corporal Welkin berated them in real parade-ground manner. "Nah, then, you idle lot, you heard the offisah. Get them blades clean an' sharp, no slackin' now, an' that means you, young Drander!"

The hulking Drander spat on his sabre blade, rubbing it moodily with sand. "Not much flamin' point sharpenin' weapons if a chap doesn't get the chance to use the bally things, is there, wot!"

Corporal Welkin treated him to a stern glare. "Yore here t'do as you're jolly well ordered, Master Drander, not what ye bloomin' well please!"

Ferrul pouted as she tugged a knot from her sling. "T'ain't blinkin' fair though, is it, Corp? Why don't we ever get to join in the fun?"

Welkin roared at her. "Stannup, miss. Attention! Chin in, shoulders square, straighten that back!"

He paced around her in a tight circle. "Join in the fun, did I hear ye say, m'gel? Go chargin' into a row o' spears full o' skulls'n'tails an' get slain by a band of savage vermin? Stop talkin' tosh an' look to your weapons! Aye, an' be grateful that there's gallant offisahs goin' out to face up to the foe just for your benefit. Now get t'work, the whole idle, shiftless, scroungin' lot of ye!"

Buff Redspore crouched in the reeds on a dunetop, nodding at the shore below. "Looks scary, don't it, Cap'n, wot?"

Captain Rake took in the line of spears at a glance. "Och, weel, Ah dinnae think those things were placed there tae welcome travellers, lassie. Ye were right, though. Ah feel as though we're bein' watched!"

Boom boom boom!

"Yikaaaheeeee!"

The sound of drums and bloodcurdling cries rent the noontide air. Scutram drew his sword.

"Can't see 'em, sah, but it sounds as if there's a horde o' the blighters, wot?"

Rake Nightfur drew both his claymores, setting off at a leisurely pace. "Fine braw warriors we'd be if we let noises frighten us awa'. Let's gang doon an' take a closer look. Mayhap they'll show themselves."

They followed the captain's easy advance. Sergeant Miggory, guarding their rear, noticed that Lancejack Sage, the youngest of the party, could hardly hold her javelin for shaking. The drumming and screeching rang out louder. Sage half turned to run, but the craggy-featured sergeant placed a firm paw on her back, murmuring softly, "Nah, then, missy, put h'a bold face on things an' don't be afeared. Vermin are only vermin, no matter 'ow they paints their mugs an' yells!"

Sage took a deep breath, smiling nervously. "I know, Sarge. It's not bein' able to see the blighters that worries me. Where in the name o' sufferin' seasons are they?"

A hollow booming voice rang out. "Death awaits all those who venture into the Bloodrippers' territory! Yaaaaah!"

Lieutenant Scutram chuckled grimly. "Well, at least they're speakin' to us, wot!"

"Waaaah, look!" The cry came from Buff Redspore, who was pointing to a low hillock.

A skull, probably that of some vermin, ferret or weasel, was moving over the crest of the low rise. It halted, gave a despairing screech and tumbled down onto the shore not far from them. It lay there, bleached white, grinning through socketless eyes at them. The drums pounded out, increasing their intensity.

Early eventide saw the galley *Greenshroud* in sight of the High North Coast. She drifted far offshore on Razzid Wearat's orders. He no longer desired to avenge himself on sea otters, knowing they were too warlike and on the alert for battle. Redwall Abbey was Razzid's current desire—his crew were not relishing any coming conflict with Skor Axehound's warriors. Neither, for that matter, was Razzid, but he could not afford to lose face in front of his vermin. In the light of this, he had planned craftily to gain his aims. Knowing that even from this distance, his ship had been sighted by the sea otters, he acted. Pacing the deck with trident in paw, he scowled landward, calling up to the lookout, "Ahoy, what goes on ashore, Splitears?"

The lookout, a weasel with both ears torn from tip to base, called back from the masthead, "Lights on the point nor'east, Cap'n. Looks like alarm beacons t'me!"

Razzid nodded to Mowlag. "Muster my crew—all paws on deck!"

Searats and vermin corsairs trooped onto the welldeck, glancing up at their captain, who stared down at them from the stern gallery rail. He pointed slightly south. "See yonder lights—look hard or ye'll miss them. Well, do ye see?"

Shekra, who stood with the crew, replied dutifully, "Aye, Cap'n, I see the lights. They glint now an' then. Ha, there's one, just flashed."

Razzid wiped at his bad eye, the good one transfixing the crew. "That's sea otters, flashin' the last o' the sunlight off their swords an' axeheads. We've been spotted sailing into these waters. They'll be gatherin' round those fires on the headland. Ain't that right, lookout?"

Splitears was not about to contradict a Wearat. He called back, "Aye, Cap'n, right ye are. There's fires all over that 'eadland. That's where they'll be waitin'."

Razzid made a sweep from the south to the far point with his trident, dropping his voice to a rasping growl. "Aye, that's the enemy, waitin' on us, an' we're headin' in straight to war with 'em. I don't care a barnacle's blister how many fightin' beasts their chief can face us with. I couldn't care less how many axes, spears, swords, slings an' fire arrows they've got. I'm Razzid Wearat, an' I'll fight 'em down to my last crewbeast, aye, an' go down battlin' myself. I tell ye, mates, the name o' *Greenshroud* will be a name t'be remembered on the High North Coast. Haharr, that it will! Well, are ye with me?"

What he had hoped for happened then. There was silence from the crew. He banged the gallery rail with his trident haft. "Well, are ye?" The only sound was a shuffling of footpaws. Avoiding his eyes, searats and corsairs stared at the deck planking.

Razzid shook his head. He no longer sounded confident. "Does none of ye want to fight the wavedogs?"

Still no reply was forthcoming. He slammed his trident points down into the deck, scorn dripping from his voice. "I've been lissenin' t'the talk aboard this ship. What ye want is to find the Abbey o' Redwall an' loot it."

A few murmurs arose from the welldeck, but Razzid silenced them with a wave of his claws.

"Harr, ye can't fool me, ye cringin' seascum. Right, then, so be it, let's have a show o' paws. All those wantin' to invade the Abbey place?"

There was an immediate mass show of paws—all but three. Razzid drew in a breath, which sounded like a sigh of despair. "Now, all those who wants to fight the wavedogs?" Mowlag, Jiboree and Shekra held up their paws.

Apart from the sound of waves and the creak of rigging, there was silence aboard the *Greenshroud*.

Razzid let them wait awhile, then wiped at his bad eye and grunted, "Mowlag, take the tiller an' turn this vessel about. Set a course south an' east."

Turning abruptly, he stumped off to his cabin, slamming the door after him. Though nobeast cheered aloud, there was subdued chuckling from the crew.

Jiboree cut it short, hissing sharply, "Don't start enjoyin' yoreselves too soon, or the cap'n might want to make a few examples. It ain't pleasin' 'im too much, bein' outvoted by 'is own crew."

As they dispersed silently, he winked at Mowlag and Shekra. "Looks like we're 'eaded for the easy life, mates."

Mowlag grinned. "Aye, 'twas a close-run vote, though."

Shekra added a word of caution. "We're not home an' dry yet, friends. Does either of ye know how to get to this Redwall Abbey?"

They shrugged wordlessly.

The vixen spoke. "An' neither do I!"

Uggo and Posy were kicked into wakefulness. It was just after dawn. The stoat Jonder and his ferret companion, Wigga, were still sleepy and irritable at having to rise early. Jonder showed them his long sling.

"Ya see diss? Well, I'm a dead shot wid it. Got a seagull right through the eye, killed it first go. So one funny move outta yew two spikepigs an' it'll be ya last, understand?"

Wigga produced a short rope halter and tied Uggo's left footpaw to Posy's right.

The pretty hogmaid protested, "Isn't it enough that we're both tied together by the waist already?"

The young ferret ushered them out into the open at spearpoint. "Shut ya mouth an' move!"

In other circumstances it would have been a pleasant day. The sea was releasing small wavelets as it ebbed, and the rising sun warmed their backs as it slowly evaporated the mist from the calm waters. Uggo took the two lines, which he had prepared the night before. They were already baited with fragments of mussel and weighted by pebbles. He passed one to Posy, pretending to sound experienced.

"Now just stand on the edge of the water. Keep a tight hold of your line with one paw, an' chuck it out with the other, like this."

He cast his line, which fell miserably short, plopping into the shallows not far from their footpaws. As he was doing this, Uggo was peering anxiously into the misted sea for a sign of a log, but there was none.

Wigga prodded him with his spear. "Are ya sure ye've done this afore, pin'ead?"

Jonder also appeared scornful. "Hah, there ain't no fishes round 'ere. I kin see inta dat water, an' there's nuthin' there!"

Posy tried to help with a suggestion. "I think the fish must be farther out. We'll have to wade in a bit. Might be mackerel or herring if we go deeper."

At that moment, Uggo caught sight of a dark, blurred shape off to their right in the mist. He tried hard to act casual. "Er, right, let's head outward this way."

They had taken only a few paces into the sea when Jonder called after them, "Where do ya think yer goin'?"

Putting a bold face on, Uggo retorted, "Where d'ye think? We're goin' after fish!"

Wigga leaned on his spear. "Wot, all the way out there?"

Uggo could see the object. It was a log, still some distance away—an old pine trunk, with branches sticking from it. He nudged Posy, but she could already see the log.

Jonder waded into the water, shouting at them. "Don't ya go no deeper—dat's far enough!" He struggled quickly back ashore, shaking himself. "Brr, dat water's blinkin' well freezin'. I ain't goin' after 'em, are yew?"

Wigga spat into the ebbing tide ripples. "Who, me? I ain't gittin' drownded fer a couple o' 'edgepigs. Leave 'em ta fish. They can't go nowhere, it's only sea out there."

Posy chanced a backward glance at the vermin guards. "They're not following. Must be afraid of the cold sea."

Uggo drew in a deep breath as they forged deeper into the water. "About time we made a break for that log, Posy. Can you swim?"

She shook her head. "No."

Uggo shrugged. "Neither can I. Come on, let's try!" Dropping the fishing lines, they splashed off toward the log.

Now the vermin had spotted it. Jonder set a stone in his sling, yelling, "Git back 'ere, or I'll slay ya. Git back!"

His stone fell short.

Wigga kicked him angrily. "I thought yew was supposed ter be a dead shot wid dat thing. Snaggs'll skin us both if'n we go back widout those 'ogs. Cummon!"

He waded in, holding the spear above his head, forging after the captives as fast as he could. Jonder slung more stones, until Wigga roared at him.

"Stop slingin', ya idjit, afore I gets 'it by a stone!"

Now the sea was too deep for wading. Uggo and Posy tried their best, but they kept sinking. Posy spat out salt water.

"Phwoo—that one with the spear's after us now!" Uggo shouted. "Ahoy, the log, we're sinkin' an' the vermin are comin' for us. Heeeeelp!"

Then things developed swiftly. Four dark shapes sped past them, straight for Wigga. Two huge, strong paws lifted their heads clear of the sea. It was Jum Gurdy. He bore them both across to the log, lifting them onto the floating pine trunk. The Redwall Cellardog's homely face beamed at them. "Hold on tight, young uns. Yore safe!"

Wigga was not a bad swimmer. He struck out after Uggo and Posy, his teeth clenched around his spear. That was when the four dark shapes hit him like flying missiles. He sank limply beneath the waters, leaving a broken spear floating on the surface. At the tideline, Jonder was puzzled at the turn of events. Why had Wigga vanished from sight like that?

Swinging his sling, he ventured into the shallows, crying, "Wigga, where are ya, mate? They're gittin' away!"

The four dark shapes came speeding at him through the sea. Jonder dashed back to dry land, yelling in terror.

"Snaggs, the fish monsters 'ave got Wigga! 'Elp, Snaaaggggs!"

The fox and his young vermin gang came rushing to the tideline. One of the monsters shoved its sleek head above the surface. It made a defiant honking sound, as if challenging the vermin.

Snaggs snatched the sling from Jonder. "I ain't afeared o' no fish monster—'ere, take this!" He slung the stone at the sleek-headed beast, but the thing caught the missile in its mouth. Spitting it back at him, it flapped a pair of webbed flippers, encouraging Snaggs to have another try.

The rat Blawd threw his club at the fish monster. This time it caught it skilfully in its mouth, tossed it in the air and began balancing it expertly on its nosetip. The beast's three companions surfaced, clapping their flippers in applause.

As Uggo and Posy perched on the log, watching the performance, Jum Gurdy floated beside them, holding on to the log. He explained, "They're seals. That big un doin' all the clever tricks is a bull seal. They've been with me ever since they came across me waitin' offshore with this log. I don't know wot t'make of 'em, really. That big ole bull seal just popped up alongside an' nudged me hard with his snout. Prob'ly warnin' me away from his wives. They never said a word, even though I tried to talk with 'em. They kept me company, swimmin' easy-like an' keepin' an eye on me. Then those vermin showed up. Did ye see the way they slew the ferret? I tell ye, young Wiltud, those seals are big dangerous beasts, an' they don't seem t'take kindly to vermin.

"Anyhow, whilst they're keepin' the fox an' his cronies busy, we'll get out of here. Snap off a few o' those branches an' get paddlin'. I'll rest awhile. I'm bone tired after pushin' this thing around half the night in cold seawater. Oh, er, who's yore pretty liddle friend?"

The hogmaid shook Jum's paw. "I'm Posybud, sir, but you can call me Posy. I was captured in early spring by the vermin. They murdered my pore ma an' pa."

Jum caught the desolate look on Posy's face, so he quickly changed the subject. "Well, 'tis a pleasure t'meet ye, Posy—

an' you, young Uggo. I thought for certain you was dead, drowned in that woodland pool back there, then washed out t'sea on the stream. So I followed the stream awhile, then I saw the smoke from the vermin fire an' spotted their den. I could see this log driftin' round in the shallows. So, figurin' there was too many o' those rascals to fight with, I thought up my plan."

They were a fair distance from the seals and vermin now. Uggo smiled as he looked back at the scene. "I don't know wot would've become of us without you, Mister Gurdy, an' the seals, too."

Posy was watching the performance of the big bull and his three mates. "See, the seals are tormenting the vermin, but Snaggs is afraid of taking them on in the sea. He must be furious that we've escaped."

Jum continued helping to propel the log along. "Well, let's not give 'em a second chance, young un. Let's get out o' the way o' vermin, an' seals, too. We'll stay on this course until I see someplace to land. Mebbe I'll spot ole Uncle Wullow, then we'll get vittles, a fire an' a place to rest our heads in peace. Wouldn't that be nice!"

Uggo pointed to a dark cloudbank rolling in from the western horizon. "Looks like rain!"

There was a flash and a distant boom.

Posy nodded. "Aye, rain, and a lot more, if I'm not mistaken. It sounds like we're in for a storm!"

11

The bleached skull, which had rolled down the hillock, sat rocking gently in the sand, facing the hares with its hollow grin. Buff Redspore was trembling with fear.

"Did ye see that, sah? This Bloodripper territory must be haunted. Ooooh, I don't like it one little bit!"

Captain Rake Nightfur, however, was made of sterner stuff. He made straight for the skull. "Och, fiddlesticks, lassie. There's nought tae be fear't frae an auld vermin skull!"

Thrusting a claymore point through one of the eyeholes, he flicked the thing in the air. With a squeak of dismay, a small greeny-brown sand lizard fell out. It scrabbled about, looking for somewhere to hide.

Sergeant Miggory leapt smartly forward, trapping it neatly under his footpaw. He addressed it in a very sergeant-major voice. "Nah then, young bucko, stay still h'an I won't 'ave to squelch ye. That's the ticket, laddie, stand easy!"

The warning voice boomed out once more. "If ye slay a Bloodripper, ye will not live to see the sun set on this day. Be warned and fear the Mighty Bonecrusher. Aaaaaiiiiieeeee!"

Lieutenant Scutram's ears began twitching. He took a hasty look around, then whispered to Captain Rake, "Keep the blighter talkin', sah. I've an idea where he is. Chat to the rascal an' buy me a bit o' time, wot!"

Nightfur began a harangue with the unknown Bloodripper as Scutram crept off into the dunes.

"Ach, Ah'm nae scair't o' anybeast. Who d'ye think ye are, talkin' tae me in that uncouth manner?"

The mystery voice retorted angrily, "Fool, you would do well to fear the Bloodrippers. We will make you curse the mother who gave birth to you!"

The captain continued baiting the speaker. "Leave mah mother oot o' this, or mah blade'll find your gizzard. Aye, an' don't dare tae call me fool!"

Now the voice sounded truly wrathful. "Enough! The boldness of your tongue has brought down doom on ye— yeeeeeek! Gerroff! Lemmego!"

Lieutenant Scutram came marching out of the dunes with his prisoner.

Sergeant Miggory fell about laughing. "Hahaha. Where'd ye get that liddle maggot, sah?"

Scutram had a pygmy shrew by the scruff of its neck. It wriggled and kicked furiously, striking out at him with a huge megaphone fashioned from birchbark. Captain Rake brought a halt to its struggles by placing a claymore point to its tubby little stomach.

"Be still, ye wee ruffian, or Ah'll carve a bit o' the blubber from ye. Be still, Ah say!"

Scutram placed the pygmy shrew next to the small sand lizard. He upturned the megaphone and slammed it down, imprisoning both creatures beneath it.

Buff Redspore smiled sheepishly. "So that's all it jolly well was—a couple o' bloomin' runts, eh, wot!"

Always on the alert, Miggory spoke out the side of his mouth to the tracker. "There's more'n h'a couple o' runts marm, look around ye."

The dunes were crowded from top to bottom with sand lizards and pygmy shrews, who seemed to have appeared from nowhere. The shrews were armed with bundles of what seemed to be reed javelins. Most of the lizards carried thin slings or spears tipped with pieces of broken shell.

Buff Redspore inched closer to Sergeant Miggory, gazing fearfully around. "There must be a horde of the blinkin' little fiends. What do we jolly well do now?"

Rake Nightfur sheathed both claymores, spreading his paws wide in a gesture of peace. He addressed the lizards and shrews in a cordial tone. "Mah friends, we mean ye no harm. Och, we're only passin' through here, on the way tae the north."

An aged pygmy shrew came forth to speak. He was dressed in a woven grass tabard and carried a carved driftwood stick. His manner was terse.

"Ye have no permission to pass through that barrier of spears. Why did ye not make a request?"

Scutram could tell by Rake's erect ears that he was not about to put up with the old one's attitude. Sidling past the tall, dark captain, he remarked casually, "Sah, if you'll allow me, a touch of the jolly old diplomacy mightn't be out o' place, wot?"

Rake stepped aside. "Aye, carry on, Lieutenant. Buff, Sage, retreat guid an' slow now, then get ye back tae the column an' bring them here on the double, ye ken."

As Buff and Sage backed slowly away, Scutram smiled disarmingly. "Apologies for our clumsiness, sire, but there didn't seem t'be any of your chaps about to, ah, put in our request to pass through your domain."

A sharp little voice rang out from a dunetop. "It's my domain, not his! Me, Empraking Dibby Drampik! Hah, you should've asked me!"

A half dozen sand lizards scuttled to his side. They were towing a moss-cushioned chair, which slid along on broad, flat runners. The empraking sat on it, waving the lizards to proceed. They set the chair in motion downhill, jumping hastily onto the runners and standing to attention. Despite the comical idea of an armchair sliding down the duneside, the empraking retained his regal dignity. His retainers steered the chair-cum-sled to a smooth halt in front of the hares. He did not alight until several attendants dressed him in a colourful woven cloak and a ridiculously tall crown adorned with seashells, dried flowers and small bird feathers. A ceremonial mace, topped with a polished agate, completed the ensemble. He peered shortsightedly up at Scutram.

"I'm the one you ask! I'm emperor round here—king, too, an' ruling Bloodripper! So, what d'ye want? Speak out."

Lieutenant Scutram saluted courteously. "Permission to pass through your territory, sah!"

The pompous little creature scratched his rotund stomach, paced up and down once, then sat back on his chair, waving a dismissive paw.

"Not today. Tomorrow maybe, I don't know."

Colour Sergeant Miggory planted himself in the path of the chair, his jaw jutting aggressively. "Then ye'd better git t'know, bucko. Y'don't talk like that to h'officers of the Long Patrol!"

He was suddenly dragged down by a score of pygmy shrews, who were making stabbing gestures with their javelins.

Rake Nightfur sprang into action. With a bound, he was at the empraking's throat with both claymores, roaring, "Touch mah sergeant, an' Ah'll slay this wee braggart. Stan' ye clear o' him—Ah mean it!"

Through the centre of the melee came a pygmy shrew wearing a coronet. This was the empraking's queen, Dukwina, a dumpy little figure in regal garb, with a voice of earsplitting volume. "What's all this, what's all this? Gerroff that ole rabbet this instant! An' you, big black un, stow them swords or I'll make ye eat 'em!"

Everything stopped. Shrews and lizards threw themselves facedown on the ground in homage to the one who was the real power in Bloodripper territory. She stumped up to the empraking and seized him by the ear, twisting savagely as she gave him a public dressing-down.

"You're nought but trouble, Dibby Drampik. Now wot've you been up to, eh? No good, I'll be bound!"

She had the little empraking out of his chair doing an agonised dance as she tweaked his ear fiercely. He was squeaking pitifully.

"Owyeek, leggo! I wasn't up to nothin', Dukky darling. Those rabbets were tryin' to cross through our lands. Yaaaargh! Ooh! Yeek! You'll pull my ear off!"

Captain Rake noticed that though the shrews and lizards were still facedown in front of royalty, there was a good deal of giggling and mirth at the empraking's dilemma. His dumpy little wife was still berating him.

"Silence or I'll pull both your ears off! Huh, you never listen to what I say anyway. Is that wot all the fuss was, a few travellers passin' through?"

The older pygmy shrew with the carved driftwood stick spoke out hesitantly. "But, Majesty, they were intruders, trespassing on Bloodripper ground!"

"Shuttup, you dodderin' ole fool. Who asked you, eh?" She turned upon her unfortunate husband again. "I put that rule there for vermin—foxes, rats an' such like. Have ye got mud in yore eyes as well as yore ears? Do they look like vermin? Well, do they?"

With tears streaming down his face, her husband wailed, "No, no, my sweet Dukky dear. Owowow, my poor ear!"

She released him with a shove that sent him flat on his tail. Instantly her demeanour changed. The queen put on a polite smile, offering Lieutenant Scutram her paw.

"Sorry 'bout that. I'm Her Majesty Queen Dukwina Drampik, an' you are . . . ?"

Scutram flourished an elegant bow, kissing her paw. "Lieutenant Algernon Scutram of the Long Patrol at Salamandastron, at y'service, marm. These other hares"—he stressed the word *hares*—"are Captain Rake Nightfur an' Colour Sergeant Miggory."

A female lizard attendant whispered something to Duk-wina, pointing up at the sky. She nodded.

"Captain, as you can see, a rainstorm is due. May I offer you an' your friends our hospitality?"

Rake saluted gallantly. "Och, we'd be obliged tae ye, marm!"

The Bloodrippers' communal home came as a revelation. A short way into the dunes, it had been built in a clearing between four of the high sandhills, connecting them under a huge roof. Scutram was mightily impressed at the construction.

"Beggin' pardon, marm, but how's this all been made, wot?"

She called a shrew who was wearing an apron. He had thick crystal spectacles and a charcoal drawing stick behind one ear. "Burmboss, tell our friend what you do."

Burmboss smiled over the rim of his glasses. "Mats, that's the thing, sir. Mats made out o' thick woven dune-grass, aye, big mats made by scores o' weavers. Sand then, good, sharp shoresand, limestone, ground down to powder, white wood ash an' fresh water. My workers makes it into a paste—cement, ye might say. Then 'tis plastered o'er the mats an' erected."

He took Scutram to a section that reached the ground. Knocking his paw against the surface of the wall, he proclaimed proudly, "See? Tougher'n a hazelnut shell, but light. Warm in winter, cool in summer, an' 'twill last forever. Providin' the dunes stay where they are, supportin' it. Oh, an' with a final outer coat o' sand, it's invisible from the outside. Just looks like part of the dunes to those as don't know."

There was a firepit at the centre of the dwelling, and there were several clay ovens. Queen Dukwina bade the guests sit on soft woven mats. They were given drinks.

Miggory sipped approvingly. "Hmm, tastes like wild fennel an' coltsfoot 'erbs—very nice!"

The old tabard-clad shrew took a message from a sand

lizard and communicated it to Dukwina. "Majesty, there's almost a score o' rabbet—er, hares—proceeding along the dunetops toward us."

Dukwina scowled at the empraking's counsellor, who was obviously in her disfavour. "Proceeding, ye say, Vigbil? Aren't they marching, walking or running, like any normal creature? Well, don't stand there thinkin' up more fancy terms. Go out an' meet them. *Proceed* them in here, if y'please, so our cooks can feed 'em."

With the arrival of the column, there was consternation amongst the shrews and lizards at the sight of Crumdun, the captive stoat, being led on a rope. Empraking Dibby was first to complain.

"Vermin, vermin—take it out an' slay it!"

Dukwina twitched a paw at him. "Dibby, dearest, d'ye want me to treat your ear again? No? Then hold your tongue an' go an' help the cooks." The king went off nursing his ear, muttering sulkily, "S'not fair. It's Vigbil's turn. I did it yesterday!"

Dukwina ignored him, beckoning to the hares of the column who had newly arrived. "Come in, sit ye down—you two, sit by me!"

Ferrul and Buff Redspore, whom she had indicated, did as they were bade. There was an immediate hurry to serve them with drinks before the rest.

Rake Nightfur murmured aside to Miggory, "Looks like the lassies rule the roost here, mah friend."

The craggy-featured sergeant shrugged. "Ye could be right, sah, but h'I ain't sayin' nothin' 'cos h'I don't want t'get me h'ear twisted."

Lancejack Sage, whom the queen had not previously noticed, called out eagerly at the arrival of the food, "I say, chaps, that scoff looks jolly scrumptious!"

Dukwina waved a paw at the haremaid. "Then we shall have to see that you get lots of it. Come and sit over here with us, missy."

The food was excellent. There was a savoury cress and

seaweed soup, as well as dishes of chopped acorn, hazelnut and wild celery garnished with a fresh late-spring salad. The bread was warm and crusty, with a hint of sorrel to it. Apart from hawthorn and buttercup cheese, there was a steaming whortleberry pudding with sweet arrowroot sauce. Cool mint tea was served constantly.

Drander, the biggest of the young hares, proclaimed after his second helping of pudding, "Oh, whacko! This is the stuff t'give a chap, eh wot?"

Flutchers, who was tucking in with a will, agreed. "Rather, better'n the flippin' mess vittles at Salamandastron, I'd say, old lad!"

Seated beside the queen, Ferrul called to Flutchers, "I heard that! Did ye know that Mess Cook Sergeant Frawler is my uncle? Shall I tell him what you said when we get back, old lad?"

Dukwina smiled at Ferrul's quick reply. She patted the haremaid's paw. "Well done, my dear. Just look at the face on your friend now. . . ."

Still smiling, she turned her attention to the captain. "What clever young maids you have in your patrol. Perhaps you could spare them to join me at my court for a season. It would please me greatly."

Rake Nightfur returned her smile, assuming that her request was merely a joke. He countered politely, "Och, Ah'm sure it'd please mah lassies, too, marm, but we're on a mission, ye ken, an' they've their duties tae attend."

Dukwina's eyes hardened momentarily, then she chuckled. "I understand, Captain."

She waved an imperious paw at her minions.

"Some music, singin' an' dancing for our guests. Dibby, bring out my special wine for them—quickly, now!"

Drums began a slow, muffled beat as an octet of young crested newts danced sinuously. In the background, a pygmy shrewmaid choir hummed soft harmonies.

Corporal Welkin, who was seated behind Scutram and the captain, leaned forward, keeping his voice low. "I've noticed somethin' since I h'arrived 'ere. The chaps are the ones who does all the runnin' an' servin', bowin' an' scrapin', y'might say. But the ladies, they just sits about enjoyin' theirselves h'an givin' out h'orders."

Lieutenant Scutram put aside his platter. "Top marks. I've noticed that meself, doncha know. What d'ye think, Cap'n?"

The tall hare answered without taking his eyes off the dancers. "Aye, Ah think the same mahsel'. Yon wee queen's a force tae be reckoned with. Weel, now. Here comes a dram o' the special wine, an' will ye look who's servin' et!"

Empraking Dibby waddled up bearing a tray with a crystal decanter surrounded by an array of beautifully crafted cherrywood goblets. Pouring out the first, he passed the goblet of purple-tinted liquid to the captain.

Leaning close, Dibby whispered, "Drink that an' ye won't waken for a day or two, rabbet, be warned. She's out to steal your maids!"

Smiling cordially, Rake raised his drink, calling across to the queen, "A toast tae yer very guid health, Majesty!"

He murmured a swift aside to Miggory. "Dinnae drink this wine—pass the word on."

Scutram lifted the goblet, watching keenly over its rim. "I say, look! There's a shrewmaid servin' the queen an' her cronies from another tray!"

Corporal Welkin was equally vigilant. "Aye, an' that queen's servin' our gels from ole Dibby's tray. Oh, corks, h'an they're suppin' it, too, sah!"

Miggory made a pretence of drinking from his goblet. "H'aint nothin' t'be done about that fer now, Corp. We'll just 'ave to 'ope for the best!"

The choir began singing a tranquil song that was almost a lullaby, soothing and melodious.

"Hushed golden sand covers the land,
lazily swirling, by warm breezes fanned,
still summer noontide 'neath tranquil blue sky,

far, far away now, I hear seabirds cry.
Live without fear, shed not a tear,
a vale of quiet shadows awaits thee, my dear.

"Sleep now in peace, list' whilst I sing,
nightshade falls dark as the black raven's wing,
tired eyelids close as weary day dies,
flutt'ring and drooping like small butterflies.
Feel cares drift away in slumber's broad wake,
fading as ripples o'er some moonlit lake."

The drums beat softer, the choir subsided to a muted hum, the dancers folded gracefully into recumbent positions.

From beneath partially closed eyes, Captain Rake saw Buff, Sage and Ferrul curled up on the woven mats, fast asleep. Covering his lips with a paw, he spoke in an undertone to those closest to him. "Watch me. Follow mah lead."

Stretching his paws, he blinked. Simulating a cavernous yawn, he apologised to Queen Dukwina. "Och, ye'll have tae pardon me, marm. Ah'm fair wearied an' feelin' the need tae sleep."

Scutram put on a similar act in agreement. "D'ye know, sah, I think we're all ready for a jolly good old nap. Must be with trampin' through the sand all day, then tuckin' in to all that scrumptious fodder, wot!"

Dukwina gestured magnanimously. "Why not sleep right here? It's warm and the floor mats are easy enough to lie upon. I'll have some rugs brought for you all. Dibby, you and Vigbil get some rugs for our guests. Come on, stir yourselves. Can't you see they're tired?" The little empraking and his aide hurried to obey their overbearing queen.

The two pygmy shrews were covering the supposedly sleeping hares over with soft rugs when Wilbee whispered to the sergeant, "I say, Sarge, I think big Drander must've drunk that bloomin' stuff. He's snorin' away like a flippin' hog!"

Miggory muttered sternly as he peeked over at Drander.

"The great wallopin' lump'ead. I'll deal with him later. Keep yore 'ead down, Master Wilbee, an' be quiet!"

The empraking knelt alongside Captain Rake, making a pretence of tucking him in as he spoke quietly. "As soon as the queen thinks you rabbets are unconscious, she'll have your maids moved out of here."

Rake Nightfur spoke out the side of his mouth. "Where'll she take the lassies?"

Empraking Dibby moved close to Rake's ear. "Outside, to the left, it looks like an ordinary dune, but it's been built like this place. It's got a secret entrance which only Dukwina an' her cronies know about."

Corporal Welkin had sharp ears. He had caught all the conversation, so he joined in. "Beg pardon, ole Majesty, but how'll she explain their disappearance, wot?"

Empraking Dibby fussed with the rug as he replied. "She doesn't need to. Once they're hidden away, she'll just come back in here an' sleep where she is now. She'll act as surprised as you when you see the maids are gone. I know her well. She'll say that they've probably gone on alone, an' the best course is for you to follow them. I must go now, before she gets suspicious. Good luck, Captain."

After some moments had passed, Captain Rake felt a footpaw nudge him a few times. He lay inert, not moving a muscle. One of Dukwina's courtiers called out, "If they're all flat out like this one, Majesty, then there's no need to bother with any of these rabbets."

The queen and a group of her helpers bundled the three haremaids, Sage, Ferrul and Buff Redspore, in rugs, rolling them up and dragging them off.

Through half-closed eyes, Miggory watched until they left the dwelling. "They're gone, sah. Wot's the next move?"

The tall, black-furred captain outlined a swift plan.

Young Trug Bawdsley, who was lying at the back of the others, hissed a warning. "Silence, chaps—be still now. They're comin' back!"

Dukwina strode in with her attendants in tow. She noticed the empraking and some other males settling down. "An' what, pray, are you idle beasts up to?"

Her husband answered meekly, "Just goin' to sleep, Dukky darling."

She bustled over to him, paw jabbing the air. "Never mind Dukky darling. Have you cleaned all the dishes an' pots an' tidied up? No, you haven't! Don't you, or any of your idle good-for-nothing friends, even think of sleep until all the chores are done!"

The empraking and his little following scuttled off quickly.

Dukwina chuckled grimly as she and her ladies settled close to the ovens, wrapped in their rugs. "Keep them on their paws an' give them lots to do. Empraking, indeed! All Dibby an' his friends are good for is fetching, carrying, mopping an' dusting. Make them know their place, that's what I say!"

In the warmth and comfort of the dwelling, it would have been easy to relax and sleep. However, apart from big Drander, who was snoring gently, the hares of the Long Patrol lay awake, listening and watching Queen Dukwina and her retinue of pygmy shrews and sand lizards intently.

After what seemed a long while, Captain Rake moved into a crouch, issuing whispered orders. "They've all gone off tae sleep now. Flutchers, go an' keep that wee stoat quiet. Sergeant Miggory, collect up all the rugs. Scutram, Welkin, watch our backs. The rest o' ye follow me, wi' nae clankin' o' weapons, ye ken!"

Drawing both his claymores, the dark-furred captain crept like a night shadow toward the queen and her companions.

12

Earlier that day, whilst Captain Rake and his column were inside the Pygmy shrew dwelling being entertained, the storm broke out over the sea. Heralded by dull thunder and some forked lightning flashes, the purple-grey cloudbanks released a veritable deluge of rainwater. With winds prevailing westerly, the face of the deep became a scene of chaos. Foam-crested waves were lashed into a fury of mountains and troughs, battered by the incessant downpour.

Without sail, rudder or any means of propulsion other than branches broken from the pine trunk, the escapers were in real trouble.

Jum Gurdy was half in, half out of the water, trying to stop the log rolling over. Spitting seawater, he shouted above the din of the gale. "Throw those branches away, young uns. Try to stay in the middle of this thing, an' 'old on for dear life!"

Uggo and Posy were terror-stricken. They clutched each other and the pine bark, sobbing with fear. Never in their wildest imaginings had they ever witnessed the awesome force of a storm on the high seas. There was no controlling the log as it was swept further out from sight of land. Drenched and sodden to the spikes, the two young hedgehogs were sickened to their stomachs by the seesaw motion—first up on the high crest of a wave, then dropping swiftly down into a deep watery vale. Sometimes they would glance up from the trough to find themselves facing a wall of translucent blue-green water. Next moment would find them riding a foam-lathered wavecrest with nothing above them save an angry, purple-bruised sky.

It was at the top of such a wave that the log began to topple from end to end. Uggo and Posy screamed as they hung in midair for a brief moment, grabbing at the underside of the rolling pine. Trying to hold one end of the log from an underwater position, Jum saw them both slip into the sea. He struck out toward them with the dull, boiling boom of breaking waves above him.

Uggo and Posy had gone under, still hanging on to one another. The big old otter grabbed them both, hurling them back onto the log, which was just descending from another wavetop. They scrabbled onto the pine trunk, but Jum Gurdy was not so lucky. He was struck over the head by the log end.

The pine trunk careered wildly off to the northwest, skidding between the serried lines of rollers. Uggo and Posy clung to the branches, half crouching, half standing as they yelled, "Jum! Jum Gurdy! Juuuuuuummmmm!"

Though they shouted until they were hoarse, there was no sign of their otter friend anywhere amidst the wild world of trackless heaving sea.

Aboard the *Greenshroud* Razzid Wearat and Mowlag fought to master the swivelling tiller arm to hold the vessel on some kind of course. Rigging sang, and drenched sails ballooned out tightly as the corsair galley flew through the storm-wrenched seas like a great green-plumed bird.

Blowing spume from his muzzle, Razzid snarled orders at his crew. "Set up those pawlines runnin' fore to aft— make fast every sheet an' sprit. We'll keep her out to sea an' ride this storm out, 'tis the only way!" Shielding his good eye, he peered up to the mainmast head. "Ahoy, what d'ye see up there? Is there any break ahead?"

Jiboree had lashed himself into the crow's nest. Dashing spray from his eyes, he peered about, then his paw shot out. "Ahoy, the tiller, south an' east! I can spy the edge o' the gale. See, there!"

Razzid passed his hold on the tiller to a searat. Making his way for'ard, he limped out onto the long prow. Clinging to the rigging, he stood upright, staring southeast. There it was, the end of the cloudbanks. Long rays of early evening sunlight shafted down, like golden slides from sky to sea.

He laughed triumphantly. "Take 'er on a tack, port an' ahead as she goes!"

Shekra the vixen looked distinctly wan; she was no lover of storms. A grizzled searat clapped her on the back.

"Haharr, we'll be outta this by nightfall, fox. There ain't a ship on the seas like ole *Greenshroud*, aye an' not another master to 'andle 'er so well as Cap'n Razzid!"

Shekra leaned over the starboard rail gloomily. "Aye, an' nobeast has any idea where Redwall Abbey is. I've a feeling we'd be better off taking to the land."

The ship dipped suddenly into a trough. Shekra floundered halfway over the rail before she was yanked back by the grinning Searat. "Haharr, the only land ye'll find down there'll be the seabed. Ain't no Abbey down there!"

The vixen smiled weakly. "You're right. I'd better stay amidships."

The seas calmed as night fell. True to the searat's prediction, *Greenshroud* had weathered the storm. Razzid and his crew were so fatigued from fighting the elements that they did nothing further that day. A sounding line was lowered, and the water was found to be of a suitable depth for a kedge-anchor. This was an anchor on a long hawser, which stopped the vessel drifting too far in any direction.

It was past midnight when Shekra, still feeling queasy, could no longer abide the muggy surroundings of the galley. Leaving the grog fumes, the smell of cooking fish and stodgy skilly'n'duff, she wandered out on deck. Being Razzid's Seer, the vixen did not want to go to the captain's cabin. It would only mean a further round of questions as to the location of the fabled Redwall. Razzid would want her to start casting spells and reading omens, a dangerous thing to do if they did not agree with his ideas.

She was leaning over the stern gallery, staring into the dark waters, when something hit the starboard side close to the stern. It was not a great impact, merely a gentle thud. Unhooking a lantern, Shekra moved around to locate the object.

There it was, rocking against the hull—a battered pine trunk, with two senseless little hedgehogs draped over it. Shekra quickly got a boathook, a long, pikelike implement. Using the point and the hook, she maneuvered the log easily along, until it was amidships.

The searat she had spoken to previously lurched out onto the deck. "Still a touch wobbly on the ole paws, are ye, fox? 'Ere, take a swig o' this grog, that'll set ye right!"

Shekra declined the offer. "Put that stuff aside and help me to get these two creatures aboard."

Razzid Wearat sat at his cabin table, staring at the two bedraggled young ones. They lay on the decking in a pool of water, still senseless. He touched Posy with his footpaw.

"Ye say ye found them adrift on a log? Now I wonder what two liddle 'edgepigs would be doin' out at sea alone. They're still breathin'—see to them, Shekra. If they come around, maybe they've got a tale to tell."

The vixen had Uggo and Posy carried to the galley, where it was warm. She laid them on a worn rope fender in a corner. The cook cackled as he honed his skinning knife. "Brought 'em for the pot, 'ave ye, fox? I never peeled one o' those spikybeasts afore. Still there's always a first time, eh. Wot say ye, shipmates?"

The crewbeasts guffawed coarsely, commenting, "'Tis a while since we 'ad some fresh meat!"

"Huh, they'll make skinny pickin's, I'll wager!"

Shekra stood over her charges, snarling, "Git back, ye seascum. These two ain't t'be touched or hurt—cap'n's orders, so stay yore distance!" She whipped out a thin, keen-edged blade, menacing them.

A slobbering weasel gave her a look of mock alarm. "Ho, deary me, ye've got us all frightened, marm!"

The vixen jabbed her blade, making him stagger back. "Better t'be frightened than dead, grogsnout. Then cooky would have t'cook you. Anybeast fancy weasel stew?"

Her remark appealed to the corsairs' macabre humour and made the atmosphere more cordial. They began bantering.

"Ahoy, mate, 'ave ye ever tasted weasel stew?"

The fat greasy cook, himself a weasel, shook his head. "Nah, us weasels don't taste nice. I bit me tongue once, an' I tasted 'orrible!"

Even Shekra had to smile at that. Taking down a wheezy and tattered concertina, the greasy cook sang in a raucous tone a ditty he had composed.

"Yoho, me hearties, hark t'me,
pay 'eed now whilst I sing,
I'm a salty cove, give me a stove,
an' I'll cook anything!

"When I first went to sea,
'twas a long long time ago,
as second cook to an ole searat,
who taught me all I know.
An' many's the fox we fried,
an' ferrets we flambéed,
'til I slew the cook wid a rusty 'ook,
wot a tasty dish 'e made!

"Yoho, me hearties, hark t'me,
pay 'eed now whilst I sing,

I'm a salty cove, give me a stove,
an' I'll cook anything!

"But I'll tell ye, shipmates,
there's nought like roasted rat,
an' not a skinny, weedy one,
just roast 'im to a turn,
an' serve wid skilly'n'duff,
all pipin' 'ot, right out the pot
haharr, mates, that's the stuff!

"Yoho, me hearties, hark t'me,
the fact is pretty plain,
once you've chewed at a roasted rat,
y'll be back for more again!"

Several irate searats whipped out their blades. The cook hopped out of the galley smartly, shouting, "Wot's the matter, mates—can't ye take a joke?"

Uggo opened his eyes. Spitting seawater, he sat up gingerly, gazing around. "Where am I? Wot happened? Posy, are you alright?"

The pretty hogmaid attempted to rise but fell back. "Oh, my head. I feel awful, Uggo!"

Shekra hauled them both up. "Come on, you two. Now yore awake, the cap'n will want a word with ye. Come on, 'tis not good to keep him waitin'."

The vixen shoved them out onto the deck, still half dazed and bewildered. Uggo was looking up at the mainsail when Shekra chivvied him along. "Stop gawpin' about an' move yoreself, 'edgepig!"

Posy heard Uggo murmur to himself, "That sign on the sail—where've I seen it before?"

They were bundled roughly into the captain's cabin. Razzid had his back to them but turned at the sound of their entry. The truth hit Uggo Wiltud like a thunderbolt. Before he could think properly, he blurted out, "I've seen you before, an' that sign on the sail—a big fork with evil eyes starin' through it!"

The Wearat hooked a claw about Uggo's neck, drawing him close. "Where was it ye saw all this?"

The young hedgehog quailed as he gazed at Razzid. The burn-scarred features, the weeping half-closed eye and the other one, which bored into him like a gimlet.

He answered in a faltering stammer. "I—I don't mean I really saw you, like now. It was in a dream I had at Redwall Abbey, sir."

Owing to his facial wounds, Razzid's smile was more of a wicked grimace. He pulled the young hedgehog closer. "Redwall Abbey, eh? I like the sound o' that. We've got a lot to talk about, my friend!"

Queen Dukwina was sleeping soundly when she was ambushed by Captain Rake and his hares. She was immediately smothered by rugs, a lot of them, cutting off her muffled cries. The queen's retinue slumbered soundly on, unaware of the incident. Silently, the hares carried her out of the dwelling. The empraking followed them, hopping excitedly alongside Miggory.

"I hope you're going to take her far away so she won't find her way back here. Promise me you will."

The sergeant chuckled quietly. "Keep yore voice down, Majesty. Now, could ye point out this place where they've taken our maids?"

Empraking Dibby skipped eagerly along in front of them. "I'll show you, follow me. Though I don't know the way in—it's a secret, you see!"

He led them to another dome, virtually unnoticeable to the casual observer. It looked like a solid wall connecting two dunes, much smaller than the main construction. Corporal Welkin, Flutchers and the captive stoat Crumdun staggered up, bearing the hulking form of Drander between them.

Welkin let Drander's footpaws drop to the floor. "Whew,

stripe me, that big buffoon weighs more'n three of us put t'gether! Is this where they've got our maids locked up, sah? How do we get into the confounded place? Can't see any doors as such, wot!"

The little empraking kicked the bundle of rugs lightly. "She knows. Make her tell you—stick things in her that'll loosen her tongue!"

Scutram chuckled. "My word, Dibby, you're a proper little savage. Fancy doin' that to your beloved!"

Captain Rake began undoing the rug bundle.

"Och, Ah've nae doubt the wee lad's had plenty o' provocation. Ah'd no' like her tae be mah queen. The auld biddy has a tongue like an adder!"

He hauled the kicking Dukwina out of the rugs.

"Now, marm, will ye no' open this thing for us?"

The queen straightened her wrinkled finery, then let out a piercing yell. "Guards! Heeeeeeelp meeeeeee!"

The empraking remarked wistfully, "I told you sticking things in her would've been best."

Sergeant Miggory poked his head around the main dwelling entrance. "Sah, we'd best do somethin' sharpish. They're comin, h'armed t'the teeth an' lookin' like business!"

Captain Rake acted swiftly. "Lieutenant Scutram, hauld ontae the queen! Sergeant Miggory, take the column an' keep them off! Young Bawdsley, stay by me. Ah'm goin' tae force an entrance tae this place!"

The horde of shrews and lizards advanced, waving their weapons and hissing viciously. However, they halted short of the Long Patrol hares, who stood resolutely, ready for trouble. Dukwina's army danced, bared their teeth and threatened, but they did not seem disposed to charge the young warriors.

Trug Bawdsley ran his paws over the smooth sand-cemented surface in front of them. "Not havin' much luck, sah. Can't even find a flamin' crack!"

Dukwina smirked. "Hah, an' you won't find a crack, either!"

Captain Rake replied coolly, "So we won't find a crack, marm? Och, then Ah'll just have tae make one!" Drawing both his claymores, he attacked the wall, striking it repeatedly in the same spot using the butt of his left blade as a hammer and the point of the right as a gouge. It produced a curious sound on the hardened shell.

Thock! Thock! Babbong! Thock!

Wilbee came from the entrance to report, saluting smartly. "Beg pardon, sah, but the sarn't told me t'tell you that we can't hold the foebeast off much longer. They're gettin' rather jolly close to us now. Sah!"

Rake left off his assault to spit on his paws. "Is that a spear you're carryin', young Wilbee?"

The young hare hefted it. "Rather, sah. Jolly heavy one, too—belonged to my pa, wot!"

Captain Rake took the weapon from Wilbee. "Aye, so 'tis, a braw, hefty spear, Ah'd say."

The captain paced back a few steps, then launched himself at the wall, gripping the spear with both paws. "Eulaliiiiaaaa!"

Rake's mighty blow sent the point right through the wall, almost a third of the length of its shaft. He winked at Wilbee. "Nought like a guid spear, tell yore pa. Now give it a sidelong push wi' me!"

As they pulled it sharply to one side, there was a rending crack. The wall split from top to bottom. Another two solid thwacks with the spear, and a big triangular piece of the structure fell away.

Rake pointed to the entrance he had made, bowing mockingly to Queen Dukwina. "After you, marm!"

As the column filed in, the captain kept Dukwina at spearpoint, in view of her army. He called out harshly to them, "Ah'd stay back if'n I were you, or ye'll get yer queen back wi' an awful hole through her, ye ken?"

The queen sneered. "You're an officer and a creature of honour. You wouldn't dare harm me!"

The captain jabbed her lightly with the spearpoint. "Marm, Ah'd dare anythin' tae preserve the hares o' mah platoon. Now, call yer beasties off!"

Dukwina squeaked hastily at her army, "Stay back, all of you—that is a command!"

The lizards and shrews were still hissing and wielding their weapons, but they made no move to charge.

Scutram picked up the large, triangular fragment of broken wall. It was surprisingly light. He blocked the aperture with it.

"Corporal Welkin, Bawdsley, hold this bloomin' thing in place. It'll give us some protection, wot!"

Trug Bawdsley placed his shoulder against the impromptu barrier. "Aye, sah, an' 'twill save us havin' to look at their flamin' ugly mugs!"

The three haremaids were lying in a corner, sedated by the drugged wine. Scutram waggled his ears reflectively.

"That's four of our lot out for the count now. Confound Drander, the big greedy lout. Well, what's t'be done, eh?"

Sergeant Miggory lifted Drander's limp paw, then dropped it. "H'I wonder 'ow long those knockout drops'll last."

The little empraking replied, "Dukwina's special wine can lay a shrew or a lizard out for a full day. I know, 'cos I've seen her use it."

The pygmy shrew queen snarled at him.

"You shut up, blabbymouth!"

The empraking poked his tongue out at her. "Shan't, an' you can't make me, bossytail!"

She made as if to run at him but was halted by Captain Rake. The empraking scurried behind young Flutchers. "Keep her away from me—she's vicious!"

Rake Nightfur silenced him with a glare. "Och, quit yer grievin' now. But if what ye say is right, shrews an' lizards are nought but wee beasties. That stuff shouldn't work for long on anything as big as a hare, eh?"

Miggory nodded. "Yore right, sah. Let's get 'em up on their paws an' march 'em h'around a bit. That might bring 'em round."

The captain allowed a hint of a smile to play on his lips. "Aye, we'll do that. Oh, an' Sergeant Miggory, you take young Drander. An' ye have mah permission tae box his ears a bit. Just tae speed his recovery, ye ken?"

Miggory's craggy face broke into a big grin. "Aye, sah. Just to speed the pore young beast's recovery, as ye say!"

Queen Dukwina plumped herself down on some rugs, looking quite smug. "Do what you like, you're all still prisoners in here. There's no way out, an' sooner or later, my creatures will rescue me."

Scutram and Rake were supporting Buff Redspore around the floor. Keeping his voice low, Scutram spoke to Rake. "She's right, y'know, sah. Seems we're in a bloomin' fix, wot!"

The captain patted Buff's cheeks as she began moaning softly. "Och, Ah wouldnae say that, friend. There's nought tae stop us breakin' through this place at the far wall. Ah trust there'll be no foebeasts waitin' for us there."

Suddenly the entire structure seemed to echo with a rattling noise. Miggory's ears stood up straight.

"Wot'n the name o' vinegar's that?"

"It's those flippin' nuisances outside, sah!"

Young Trug Bawdsley pushed his back hard against the barricade. Corporal Welkin was spread-eagled flat on it, his body reverberating with the noise.

"Ain't too much to fret over, Sarn't. They're beatin' the outside o' the wall with those long reed javelins. Hah, they won't git past me'n'young Trug 'ere!"

Their captive, the stoat Crumdun, gnawed at a grimy pawnail. "I 'ope they don't! By the sound o' that racket, there must be enuff o' them out there to eat us alive!"

Under the sergeant's none-too-gentle ministrations, big Drander was beginning to come around, though he still sounded groggy. "Ooh, me head! What's all the noise for . . . eat who alive? What's goin' on, chaps?"

Captain Rake tweaked the big young hare's ear. "Aha, so ye've finally decided tae join us, Drander!"

"Och, yer in braw trouble, laddie buck. Allowin' yersel' tae be drugged by the enemy, sleepin' whilst on duty an' Ah don't know what else!"

Drander groaned. "Beg pardon, sah, but it wasn't my fault, really. I was thirsty, y'see—"

"Silence!" Miggory roared in fine parade-ground style. "Yew lop-eared, lollop-faced h'excuse for a Long Patroller, 'ow dare yew h'interrupt a h'officer! Yew was sayin', Cap'n?"

Rake fixed the culprit with a gimlet eye. "Yer a sair disgrace tae the column, Drander, an' as your captain, Ah'll have tae consider your servin' with us!"

Tears sprang to Drander's eyes; his sturdy frame shook. "Cap'n, sah, don't say that, I blinkin' well beg ye! Put me on a fizzer, lock me in the guardhouse, feed me on weeds'n'water, anythin' but chuckin' me out o' the Patrol. 'Tis my whole life, sah!"

Rake Nightfur's attitude took on an unexpected change. He winked at Drander and smote his back heartily.

"Och, yer a great gormless galoot, but ye have a guid heart, laddie. Now, how are ye at breakin' doon walls?"

Drander sniffed, wiped his eyes and saluted smartly. "Sah! Just show me the flamin' wall an' I'll break it, sah!"

Rake nodded toward the far section of wall. "Take Wilbee's spear an' let's see ye do a wee bit o' damage tae that. Smartly, now!"

Big Drander grabbed the spear and charged the wall, his bellows ringing out over the din of javelin rattling. Everybeast leapt aside as he stampeded past. "Eulaliiiiaaaa! Blood'n'vinegaaaaar!"

He hit the composition of sand, limestone and reed grass so hard that he went clear through it.

Captain Rake stepped through the huge, ragged gap and shook his paw. "Well done, bucko! All charges dropped, Ah think, eh!"

Drander's face lit up like a summer sunset. From flat on his back, where he had landed, he saluted.

"No more sleepin' on duty for me, sah. Thank ye, Cap'n!"

With the crash of the broken wall, the rattling of weapons died away. There was an ominous silence from outside.

Queen Dukwina sniggered maliciously. "Get ready to die. My warriors are coming soon now, rabbets!"

The little empraking waved his paws in agitation. "She's right, Cap'n. They're goin' to charge!"

The tall, dark-furred hare nodded. "Ah've nae doubt she is, mah friend. Right, Drander, Flutchers, lead off wi' the lassies, if they're fit tae go."

Lancejack Sage took the paws of Buff Redspore and Ferrul.

"We're all correct an' ready for duty. Sah!"

Rake drew his twin blades. "Guid—then off ye go! Lieutenant Scutram, you follow 'em wi' the stoat an' they two wee shrews. No arguments now, Scutram, go!" He allowed both parties a few moments to get clear, then turned to Miggory. "Sarn't, take the remainder o' the column an' back us up."

Joining Corporal Welkin and Trug Bawdsley, Rake Nightfur gave final instructions. "Now, when Ah give the word, we three will fling this piece o' stuff in their faces an' get oot o' here smartish. Are ye right? One . . . two . . . heave!"

Seizing the large, triangular fragment between them, the three hares hurled the thing into the foremost rank of the foebeast, yelling, "Eulaliiiiaaaaa!"

BOOK TWO

Enter the Rogue Crew!

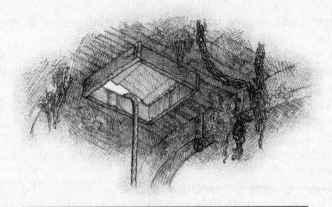

13

Rigid with fear, Uggo Wiltud quailed under Razzid Wearat's evil eye. He could feel the vermin's foul breath on his face as Razzid hissed, "So, yore a Redwall creature. Don't be afraid, I won't harm ye. Tell me yore name an' the name of yore liddle friend. She's a pretty one, ain't she?"

Uggo opened his mouth, but no sound came forth. The Wearat turned to his companions, chuckling. "Pore liddle 'og's lost his tongue."

Jiboree slid out a curved dagger. "Shall I find it for 'im, Cap'n?"

From some untapped well, courage sprang up in Posy. She leapt up, shouting angrily at Jiboree, "You leave him alone! I'm called Posy, an' his name's Uggo!"

Razzid signalled the weasel to stow his blade. He seemed amused by the hogmaid's outburst.

"Posy, eh? Ain't that a pretty name. So, yore the one who does the talkin', Posy. Then you tell me about this place they calls Redwall Abbey."

She shook her head. "I'm not from there, so I can't tell you anything, Captain."

Mowlag pointed at Uggo. "No, but I wager 'e can."

Shekra joined in encouragingly. "But of course ye can,

Uggo. Look at yore friend Posy—she ain't scared to speak to us."

Uggo found his voice then. He blurted out, "I'm not scared. Aye, I'm from the Abbey o' Redwall, but Posy isn't, she's never even seen the place."

The vixen gently moved Uggo away from Razzid. She whispered casually to the Wearat, "Uggo fears you, Lord, but I think he'll talk t'me." She turned back to Uggo. "I've heard wonderful tales about Redwall. Wot's it like, liddle friend?"

Uggo caught a warning glance from Posy, so he went back to being silent. Shekra did not seem unduly bothered. She smiled in a friendly manner.

"Let me tell you about Redwall, then, though I can only say wot I've heard, 'cos I'm like Posy—I've never been there. They say 'tis a beautiful place, all built from good red stone, very big an' old. There's everything there a creature could want, orchards full of ripe fruit an' berries, an' a pond, too, teemin' with fish."

Uggo could not contain himself from correcting Shekra. "The pond doesn't teem with fishes. Friar Wopple says there's a few trout an' mebbe a greylin' or two. But they don't catch one, unless it's an Abbot's feast. An' we don't eat birds, or their eggs, or any livin' creature—er, 'cept watershrimp for otters' hotroot soup."

Mowlag pulled a face. "If'n ye can't eat eggs'n'birds, an' fishes, it don't sound like much of a place fer vittles. Don't think I'd like ter live there!"

Uggo spoke eagerly in his Abbey's defence. "But you'd love the vittles, an' there ain't no better cook in all Mossflower than Friar Wopple. She makes pies an' soups, an' pasties, an' cakes, an' trifles, an' tarts, an' deeper'n'ever turnip'n'tater'n'beetroot pie for the moles. Best food you've ever tasted. . . ." His voice trailed off as he saw Posy's shaking head, telling him that he was talking too much.

Razzid dabbed at his leaking eye, surprising Uggo by agreeing with him. "Pay no 'eed to Mowlag. Yore Friar's vittles sounds good t'me, Uggo. Aye, Redwall, eh? All that fruit, a nice pond fer a dip on a summer's day. D'ye know, that's why I'd like to visit there, just t'see it all!"

Uggo merely nodded. All the talk of his home had brought a lump to his throat.

Shekra took up the thread in a wheedling tone. "That's right. We just want to pay a visit to Redwall Abbey. Mebbe you could show us the way?"

The young hedgehog sighed deeply. "But I don't know the way. Mister Gurdy did, but he got drownded in the storm, I think. He knew the way."

Razzid rose from his seat. He hauled on an iron ring set into the cabin deck. It opened a trapdoor to an ill-smelling rope locker. All the friendly manner gone from him, he pointed down. "Get in there, both of ye!"

Assisted by kicks from the corsairs, Uggo and Posy tumbled down into the locker. Holding the lid up, Razzid bared his teeth at them.

"I'll leave ye to think. If'n ye still don't give me an answer I like tomorrow, Uggo, then ye can bid goodbye to yer liddle friend Posy!"

The door above their heads slammed, leaving the pair in total darkness. Uggo felt as though he were in the pits of despair. A sob crept into his voice. "Oh, Posy, what're we goin' t'do? I don't know the way to the Abbey. When I left there with Mister Gurdy 'twas the first time I could remember bein' outside in Mossflower. I'm lost without 'im."

The pretty hogmaid reached out in the darkness, finding Uggo's paw. "Then we'll have to think of something to tell this vermin Razzid."

Uggo muttered hopelessly. "Huh, like wot?"

He winced as Posy tweaked his nose. She berated him angrily. "Like something that'll save my life! Look, I know you're frightened of the vermin—I am, too. But it's no good sitting and moaning here. We've got to do something. Make a plan, try some sort of escape, anything except wait here to be slain!"

Her defiant spirit boosted Uggo's nerve.

"Yore right, Posy. Wait, I've got an idea. Suppose I tell them I know the way to Redwall? That'd give us time to plan an escape from here."

Posy considered it. "Hmm, sounds good, but how long could you keep fooling Razzid? He doesn't seem a stupid vermin to me. As for escaping, there's not much chance of getting out of here. It's nought but a big cupboard, or that's what it feels like." She felt around. "We're sitting on a heap of old rope. Wait, let's get a better look."

Standing up in the dark, she touched the trapdoor lid. "Get a piece of rope, not too thick. I'll lift this door a touch, and you jam the rope in. Then we'll try to get an idea of what this place is like. Let's hope they're not watching too closely."

Thankfully, the door did not creak as Posy opened it a touch. Uggo fed the bit of rope between the tiny gap. It worked, allowing a small shaft of light to shine through from the cabin lanterns. Standing on tippaw, Uggo strained his head to one side, reporting what he could see.

"There's only two of 'em there now. One lyin' on the bunk, the other—the fox, I think—snoozin' in a chair."

Posy was exploring the rope locker. She replied in a whisper, "That must be the Razzid vermin on the bunk. This place is just a mess of old rope ends. Oh, just a moment, what's this?"

Uggo was at her side swiftly. "Have ye found somethin'?"

Posy scratched the bulkhead with her pawnails. "Look, there's been a fire here at some time. This wall hasn't been fixed. . . . Great seasons, it's a door!"

Uggo could see only a sliver of the bulkhead in the light. "How can ye tell it's a door?"

There was a dull, metallic clunk, followed by the hogmaid's explanation. "Because I've found the latch. It won't open outward. We'll have to shift some of this rope. Come on."

They heaved frayed coils of sea-rotted ropes, cables, hawsers and rigging, piling them up to one side until a space was cleared. Uggo opened the door inward, holding his breath each time it made a creak or a scrape.

"Hope the vermin didn't hear anythin'. What d'ye think?"

"Ssshhh, wait a while, just in case," Posy cautioned him.

Moments ticked by as they stared through the open door into the darkness beyond. At last, Uggo relaxed. "They're still asleep. Where d'ye suppose it leads to?"

Posy felt around the door. "I don't know. . . .What's this?" Moving back into the slim shaft of lantern light, she held up a sharp but well-worn wood chisel.

"The workbeasts must've left this behind when they were repairing the burn damage. It'll do as a weapon, eh?" Bending his head, Uggo crawled through the doorspace. "Let's see where this leads."

Posy took a long piece of tough heaving line. "Wait—this should buy us a bit of time!"

There was a ring on the underside of the trapdoor flap. She doubled the rope to it and tied it tight to the latch hasp on the bulkhead door.

"There. They won't open that in a hurry. Come!"

Uggo led the way, holding on to Posy with one paw and the chisel with the other. They went slowly and carefully, feeling their way with each step. Without a lamp, or any other illumination, it was difficult.

The way narrowed, then Uggo felt cold water washing around his footpaws. Not knowing they were in the bilges, he muttered fearfully, "Hope we're not sinkin'. I can hear the waves from outside. Wish I knew wot way we're goin'—it's so flippin' dark down here, an' wet, too."

His companion had been working things out.

"When we were taken to the captain's cabin, I could see the water from the back window. I think we must be going toward the front of the ship, least I hope we are."

Uggo raised his paw, scraping the woodwork over their heads with the chisel. He wiped ash from his eye. "More burnt wood, though this board feels a bit loose. Wot d'ye think, shall I try to lift it?"

Posy was in agreement. "Have a go, but be careful in case there's anybeast nearby. Here, I'll lend a paw. Gently now, Uggo. . . . Easy, easy."

The board creaked slightly under their pressure, but the noise seemed to blend in with the usual sounds of a vessel at sea. When it was lifted enough, Uggo boosted Posy to take a view of their surroundings. After a quick peep, she dropped back down with some news.

"It's open deck above us, near the front end of the boat—the bow, I think they call it. But there's a vermin, one of those searats, about two paces from where we'll come up. You take a look, see what you think."

She assisted Uggo to peer out. He watched the searat for some time before dropping down.

"I think he's supposed t'be on watch, but he's leanin' o'er the rail. From the sloppy way he's loungin', 'tis my wager that he's fallen asleep on duty. Let's try sneakin' quietly out an' hope he don't notice us."

The board groaned ominously as they pushed at it. Then it came loose suddenly, clattering over onto the deck. Uggo levered himself up, getting scratched by the scupper edge as he emerged to face a half-awake searat, turning to stare at him in bewilderment.

"Worra yew doin' round 'ere, mate?"

Uggo swung hard, with the chisel clenched in his paw. The shock ran through him as his fist belted the vermin square on its chin. The searat collapsed to the deck, totally knocked out.

Posy was holding out a paw. "Hurry, Uggo, help me!"

He had to use one paw, the other being numbed by the force of the blow he had dealt. He was massaging the paw when the hogmaid hissed at him, "Never mind that now—

we need someway to get off this ship. Take a good look around. . . . Here, what are these?"

Uggo shrugged. "I dunno—some kind o' big arrows?"

Posy, all business now, ordered him briskly, "Get me some rope—hurry!"

Uggo cast around, coming up with a sounding line. She grabbed it and began binding the four thick shafts together. "This'll have to do as a raft. Take one end, and we'll throw it overboard. Move, Uggo!"

Grunting, he took an end of the thick bundle. "Which side do we chuck it o'er? I mean, which way is it to the land—I can't see any, can you?"

Posy hesitated briefly, then decided. "Left, I think. Aye, left. One . . . two . . . heave!"

The bound arrow bundle hit the water with a splash that was followed by two lesser splashes as the young hedge-hogs plunged into the sea after it.

There was a shout from the deck as the sleeping corsair at the tiller was wakened by the noise.

"Ahoy, wot's goin' on there?"

Holding on to the spearshafts in the sea, the two friends heard the crewbeast shuffling for'ard.

Uggo grabbed a matted fender hanging from the ship's side. "If'n we push off for shore now, we'll be spotted. I'll hold us in here, under the bow!"

They clung under the hull's curve, scarcely daring to breathe. On deck, the pawpads of the tillerbeast got closer to the prow. Posy heard the corsair, a weasel, speaking aloud to himself.

"Nah, then, wot's goin' on 'ere? Is dat you, Dirgo? Huh, yew've bin at the grog agin, aincha? Cap'n Razzid'll feed yer guts t'the fishes if'n 'e catches yer rotten drunk an' snoozin' on watch. Cummon, mate, up ye come, I'll git yer back t'the galley, out o' the way."

There followed some heaving and cursing, then the sound of the weasel staggering off under his senseless burden. Posy set her footpaws against *Greenshroud*'s hull. "Let's push off and see if we can't get a good distance away by daybreak."

It was not as easy as they had first thought, hanging on to the bundle whilst kicking with their footpaws.

Uggo gritted his teeth in exasperation. "We've been paddlin' for a bloomin' age, an' we don't seem t'be goin' anywhere. Look 'ow close the ship still is. We're goin' t'get caught soon."

They drifted slightly further on a rising swell. Posy patted her friend's paw reassuringly. "It feels like the tide's turned. We'll move quicker now."

However, Uggo continued to pose problems. "If we're travellin' with the tide, it's still no 'elp, Posy. The ship'll follow us."

The pretty hogmaid shook her head. "See that thick rope hanging from the back of the ship? It's an anchor, to stop it drifting. Now paddle, mate!"

Posy was right. In the first streaks of grey dawn, they had gone a good distance. Uggo laid his head upon the arrowshafts.

"I'm dead tired. Got to 'ave a little sleep—just a doze, eh?"

But his companion would have none of it. "Now's not the time to be sleeping. Keep going. We've got to get ashore, before those vermin find us missing!"

Uggo opened one eye, staring at the way ahead. "There ain't no sign o' land anywhere. We could be goin' the wrong way—out t'sea, for all you know."

Posy was beginning to lose her temper with Uggo. "We're going the right way, I'm sure of it. Now, stop complaining and start paddling. Honestly, you really are the limit, Uggo Wiltud. Yeek, what's that?"

The sea rose around them as something huge and black displaced the water. It had four shiny humps, and several fins. Moreover, it made the most awful noise.

14

The army of pygmy shrews and sand lizards was taken completely by surprise. A huge piece of the wall smacked down on their front rank. In that same instant, Captain Rake Nightfur and Colour Sergeant Miggory came at them, leading over a halfscore of Long Patrol hares, all of them bellowing and roaring fearsome war cries.

"Eulaliiiiaaaa!"

"Give 'em blood'n'vinegar!"

"Forward the buffs an' lay on 'em!"

"Eulaliiiiaaaa!"

Demoralised by the speedy assault and deafening battle shouts, Queen Dukwina's horde fled in disarray. They left eight of their number stunned flat by the section of wall.

Miggory came smartly to attention, saluting Rake. "H'all runts defeated, sah! Tootled h'off like billyoh h'at the sight o' proper warriors, sah. H'any further ordahs, Cap'n?"

The tall, dark hare sheathed his claymores. "Ah cannae see us pursuin' 'em, Sarn't. Form the column up, an' let's follow the others, at the double!"

The young Patrollers were jubilant at such a quick victory.

"I say, chaps, see how those blighters took off, wot!"

"Shouldn't wonder if they're still jolly well runnin', eh!"

"I say, we should've pursued the little scoundrels an' kicked a few tails, wot wot!"

It was Sergeant Miggory who brought them back to reality. "Nah, then, young gennelbeasts, h'I'll be kickin' h'a few tails if'n yore not back in line smartish. Follow yore offisah's h'orders now, lead h'off by the left!"

The main party had come out amidst the dunelands. Buff Redspore was sufficiently recovered to use her pathfinding skills; she led them as her instinct directed.

"Let's get to the flat coastland so I can get a bearin' on our position."

Lieutenant Scutram was feeling his temper sorely tried by Queen Dukwina. She stamped her paws in the sand, trying to intimidate him with her imperious manner.

"I'm not moving from here, d'you hear me, rabbet! I'm a queen, being dragged off from my own domain! Well, I won't have it, you ruffian. I'm not going another step!"

Scutram favoured her with a small stiff bow. "Apologies, marm, but I've got my orders, an' you've got to accompany us. 'T'aint your decision, d'ye see!"

With that, Dukwina plumped her backside on the ground. "Hah! Well, I'm not going, an' you can't make me—so there!"

The empraking tugged at Scutram's tunic. "Stick things in her—that'll shift her!"

Dukwina spat at him, in a most unqueenlike manner, "Shut up, you little worm!"

The little empraking twitched his snout and stuck his tongue out at her. "Yah, yah, ole bossy bum!"

Scutram had taken enough. Grabbing a rope, he looped it around Dukwina, pulling it tight.

"Drander, tow her along if she won't walk!"

The empraking found himself a thick twig. "Please, can I beat her if she slows down?"

Big Drander turned aside, stifling a laugh. "As ye wish, Majesty."

The queen was forced to comply, but that did not stop

her screeching the direst threats and insults upon the heads of her captors.

Scutram winced, commenting to Drander, "'Strewth, what flippin' language. It's enough t'make a stricken toad blench, wot!"

Crumdun, the corsair stoat, climbed a small rise and peered behind. "Ahoy, 'ere's yore cap'n an' 'is mates comin' through, an' they ain't 'angin' round!"

When Rake Nightfur and his party caught up with Scutram and the rest, the captain was a bit breathy.

"We routed 'em back there, an' they retreated, but Ah'm bound tae tell ye, Lieutenant, nae sooner were we in the clear than the wee villains came back in greater numbers than afore. There's a great, braw assemblage o' wee beasties hot on our tails. Like leaves in an autumn gale, ye ken. Och, there's far tae many for a score o' Long Patrollers!"

Scutram nodded. "I see, sah. Then we'd best put a bit o' jolly fair space betwixt us'n'em. Young Redspore's takin' us out o' these confounded dunes—t'the shore, she says, wot?"

Behind them the sandhills resounded with the yipping and hissing of countless pygmy shrews and sand lizards. Captain Rake signalled the column.

"Forward at the double, mah buckoes. Once we're on flat shoreland, we'll leave them a guid league in our wake. There's nae a creature livin' can outrun Long Patrol hares!"

Speed was imperative, even though it was heavy going through the soft, deep dune sand. Sergeant Miggory, bringing up the rear with another young ranker named Bribbs, could feel the enemy gaining on them. He jollied the young hare along, noting the look of fear on his face. "C'mon, young Bribbs, make a shape. Yore pa was battalion sprint champion. Let's see ye do h'as good h'as 'im. Those shrews'n'lizards are lighter'n us, so 'tis h'easy goin' for 'em. They don't sink h'in the sand like h'us, y'see."

Miggory dropped back slightly, allowing Bribbs to take the lead. "That's the ticket, laddie buck, make 'em h'eat yore pawdust. We'll show the blighters, eh?"

Bribbs managed a tight smile. "Indeed, Sarn't, we certainly will!"

The column broke out onto the shoreline, setting a flock of gulls, who had been resting on the sand, wheeling into the air, crying harshly. Rake called a brief halt and issued further orders.

"Corporal Welkin, Lancejack Sage, take left an' right point! Redspore, front an' centre. Head north along the tideline. Scutram, ye an' Ah'll drop back tae the rear. Sarn't Miggory may need us, Ah'm thinkin'."

As they ran back toward the rear, scores of foebeasts could be seen, sweeping over the dunes in massed waves. Scutram spotted Miggory, who appeared to have been slowed down. He was supporting Bribbs. They hastened to join him, relieving him of the burden as they shouldered Bribbs between them.

Miggory ran alongside, explaining. "Young Bribbs was 'it by somethin', sah—a dart, h'I think. Couple h'of 'em just missed me, but 'e was unlucky. One or mebbe two of 'em got 'im h'in the back, sah."

Bribbs winced, then blinked, his footpaws hardly touching the sand as he was rushed along. "Sorry about that, sah. Silly little things, never hurt much, just slowed me down a flippin' bit."

Scutram peered across his shoulders at the two tiny spikes tufted with downy feathers. They were buried right in the centre of Bribbs's back.

"Slowed ye down, eh? Don't fret—we won't tell your pa. Get 'em out for ye once we've outdistanced this little lot, eh!"

As they rounded the final dune, Captain Rake was nonplussed when he saw the column waiting on their arrival. "Corporal Welkin, Ah thought Ah told ye tae take them north along the shore. What are ye doin' stannin' roond here?"

Welkin waved a lance in a sweeping gesture along the dunes. Both sides of the sandy hilltops, north and south, were teeming with the foebeast horde, ready to charge down on them. It looked like a hopeless position.

Scutram frowned. "Ye did well t'keep the column here, Corporal. If they'd have caught us runnin' north, strung out along the shore, it would've been a flamin' massacre, wot!"

Rake weighed the situation swiftly. Silence had fallen on the dunetops. A whole army of shrews and lizards were watching the hares, waiting for them to make the next move.

Queen Dukwina squeaked scornfully, "It's over, rabbets—surrender or die!"

Buff Redspore glared at the queen. "Nobeast asked for your comments, marm!"

Rake moved casually, flicking the sand with a footpaw as he spoke with Scutram and Miggory. "There's no way out o' this, mah friends. If we fled, they'd pick us off one by one, eh, Lieutenant?"

Scutram smiled grimly. "Fled, sah? Fled, did ye say? Sorry, but we ain't much good at fleein', doncha know."

The tall, dark captain nodded. "Ah'm obliged tae ye for sayin' that. So how d'ye feel about stannin' an' fightin'?"

Scutram held out his paw. "Thought ye'd never ask, old lad!"

As they shook paws, Miggory's paw closed over theirs. "Pardon me sayin', but h'a quick dash down t'the tideline. Keep the sea at our backs, dig into the wet sand, make ourselves a trench an' make a barrier, a fort. May as well do h'it proper, sahs!"

Scutram smiled approvingly. "Jolly good, Sarn't—a tiptop plan. How'd ye think of it, wot?"

Miggory saluted both officers respectfully. "Put it this way, sah, h'I was fightin' vermin while you chaps was waitin' t'be h'enrolled as cadets."

Captain Rake winked admiringly. "Och, there's a deal tae be said for experience. Thank ye, mah old friend. Ah, weel, we'd best be aboot our business!"

143

None of the horde on the dunetops was expecting the next move. Without a word or sign, the Long Patrol column broke away, going pell-mell for the sea, carrying their wounded and captives along with them. The departure was so sudden, it took their foes a few moments to realise what was going on and mobilise themselves. Some of their leaders, who seemed to be female shrews, began to scream and brandish their thin reed lances, urging the main body forward. The horde took up their cries and charged down the dunesides.

Big Drander had hauled the queen onto his back; the empraking was hurried along between Lancejack Sage and Ferrul; Crumdun, though fat, was quite fleet on his paws, running with the column. Bribbs had totally lost the use of his limbs, so Buff Redspore, Wilbee and Flutchers bore him between them. Captain Rake, Miggory and Scutram guarded the rear of the column. They made it to below the tideline just as the first of their pursuers landed on the flat beach.

Digging like madbeasts, young hares scrabbled in the wet sand, piling it up in front of them. Captain Rake was last to leap over the barrier, into the soggy trench. He gave rapid orders. "Dinnae hurl any lances, hauld on to 'em. Those wi' bows an' slings, load up an' stand ready for mah command! How's young Bribbs farin', Wilbee?"

The young hare saluted, choking back tears. "Bribbs's dead, sah. We left him a moment so we could dig the trench. When I went back to him, he was lyin' there all limp, lookin' up at the sun, poor chap!"

Sergeant Miggory, seeing Wilbee's distress, stepped in. "Loss of h'a young life—we're h'all very sorry, Wilbee. But stand ready for action now, h'or you'll be next. Time for grievin' later. Steady in the ranks, there!"

Corporal Welkin took a hasty look at Bribbs. "Cap'n, sah, they're usin' poisoned darts—otherwise, Bribbs would've been just wounded."

Sergeant Miggory bellowed out an order. "Off tunics, wet 'em in the seawater an' use 'em as shields. Darts won't git through wet cloth!"

Then the charge came like a breaking wave.

There were three bows and ten slings in the column. They launched a salvo at the attackers. All the hares were bellowing war cries, loud and wild. The strike of missiles, and the fierce shouts, seemed to drastically slow the enemy onslaught.

Captain Rake decided that it was time to utilise the queen once more. Holding her in front of him, he roared stridently, "Back, all o' ye, or Ah'll fling her intae the sea—take mah word for it, she'll drown!"

The empraking leapt about, assuring them eagerly, "He will, y'know, just you watch! The rabbets have lost one of their young uns, so they're out for revenge!"

Wriggling furiously in Rake's iron grip, Queen Dukwina shouted, "Hold! Keep back—don't charge 'til I give the command!"

The empraking whispered to Lancejack Sage, "That did the trick. She's terrified of the big sea. All of us are, really, an' the lizards can't abide salt water."

Sage watched the horde shuffling back. "Jolly well seems to have worked, wot!"

Corporal Welkin lowered his wet tunic. "It'll work for a while, but the chaps at the back don't really know what's goin' on. They'll start pushin' those in front of 'em, right, Sarge?"

Miggory nodded. "Right enough, Corp. Sooner or later, the front rankers'll 'ave nothin' t'do but be pushed flat or shoved for'ard—that'll be the charge. I've seen h'it 'appen afore."

An uneasy deadlock fell over both sides. The trench which the hares had dug in the damp sand below the tide-line began to fill up. However, they stayed put, peering over the small barricade of sand.

A short distance from them, some of the queen's supporters were beginning to chant, waving their venomous blowpipes and lances. It was a highly charged situation.

Lieutenant Scutram conferred with the captain. "Won't be long now, sah, by the flippin' look of it. Seems like we're up the jolly old creek without a blinkin' paddle, wot!"

Rake twitched his dark furred ears grimly. "Aye, they'd have charged long since, if only they knew Ah wouldnae drown their queen in the sea. Yer right, mah friend. There's little left for us tae do but stan' an' go doon fightin'."

Big Drander brandished his sabre. "Take as many o' the blighters with us as we bloomin' well can, sah—what d'ye say?"

Rake Nightfur gave the sturdy young hare a smile. "Ah, weel, laddie, we've got a braw day for it. Ah'm thinkin' we may's well open the ball!"

Drawing both claymores, the tall captain was about to launch into a war cry when a piercing scream rent the air. "Yeeeeeggh!"

This was followed by another, and yet a third scream. Pygmy shrews and sand lizards began scurrying hither and thither. A long red-fletched arrow with a fishbone tip came soaring over the enemy ranks, thudding into the sand barricade.

Buff Redspore climbed onto the sandy rampart, pointing toward the dunes. "Otters, sah—they're bein' set upon by otters!"

Queen Dukwina threw herself flat into the flooded trench, moaning, "Axehound's beasts, the Rogue Crew!"

There were only six of the sea otters, and a seventh one who did not seem to be one of them. Their leader, a burly young beast, armed with a longbow, quiver and battleaxe, came running forward, giving a long ululating call. "Hoolawhey! Hiyareeeee! Fall down or be slain! Hoolawhey!"

The effect of this was astonishing to see. Pygmy shrews and sand lizards dropped their weapons, flinging themselves flat on the shore and covering their heads with their paws. The lead otter strode boldly up to the barricade, treading purposefully on the foebeasts' prostrate bodies. He was a barbaric sight, wearing a woven bark kilt, carrying a round shield across his back and sporting a chunky coronet of amber pieces strung through with silver.

He pointed a battleaxe at the hares in the trench. His voice bore no sign of welcome. "Who are ye, an' where come ye from? Speak!"

Rake mounted the barricade, matching him eye to eye. "Ah know you, mah bucko. Ye'll be Ruggan Axehound, son o' Skor, the bigbeast hissel'. Last time I saw ye, y'were nought but a wee bairn huntin' crabs. Ah'm Captain Rake Nightfur o' the Long Patrol. Did yer daddy never talk o' me?"

The faintest hint of a smile crossed Ruggan's fierce face. "I recall he did. We'll talk of this soon—give me but a moment, Nightfur."

He turned to scan the shrews and lizards, none of whom dared look up at him. Ruggan spoke out, harsh and loud. "Who gave ye right to war upon the lands o' my father? Ye live here only by the grace of Skor Axehound, mighty Warchief of the High North Coast! Ye skulking shorescum, where are your rulers? Send them here to stand before me!"

Trug Bawdsley pushed the queen forward. "C'mon, old gel. I think he wants a word with you, wot!" Lancejack Sage collared the empraking, who was trying to hide himself behind Drander.

"Up ye come. I think this jolly well includes you, sah!"

Drawing his battleaxe, Ruggan tested its edge. "Now, speak truly. How came all this to be?"

Captain Rake interrupted courteously. "Ah think it'd be mahsel' should explain. Y'see, in a manner o' speakin', 'twas us who were the cause o' the ruckus."

Ruggan nodded to a female sea otter. "Endar Feyblade, guard these two, hold them here. I will talk with them later. Nightfur, we will rest and dine in drier sand, by the dunes."

One of the other sea otters turned to the vanquished army. "Did ye not hear my lord? Go you and bring the best of food an' drink for his guests. Then stay in your dwelling until he comes to speak with ye!"

The seventh otter, who did not seem to be one of Ruggan's warriors, came across to Miggory and pounded his back cordially. "D'ye remember when ye visited Redwall, we sat drinkin' good October Ale in my cellars one evenin'? Sergeant Miggory, ain't it?"

The sergeant shook the otter's paw warmly. "By me scut, h'I do believe 'tis ole Jum Gurdy! Wot are ye doin' h'around 'ere, mate?"

Jum slumped down in the warm sand at the foot of a dune. "Oh 'tis a long story, Sarge, a long story!"

Bread, cheese, pasties, soup and cordial were served to them by a group of grovelling shrews and lizards. They rested and ate in the early noon sun whilst Rake narrated what had happened since he saw the line of skulls and hair strung out on spears. Ruggan listened intently to every word, then sent for Dukwina and the empraking to be brought before him.

He frowned at the pair. "So, ye disobeyed the Axehound's rules an'—I make mention—not for the first time. What have ye to say?"

Dukwina and the empraking immediately fell to bickering.

"It was her—she wouldn't listen to a word I'd say!"

"Hah, look at who's talkin'. That's all you ever did. Talk talk talk talk!"

"Wot, me? I wasn't allowed t'get a word in once you started!"

Thwack! The battleaxe head buried itself in the sand between them. Ruggan's eyes glittered dangerously.

"Silence—enough! One more word, and you'll both be deadbeasts. I do all the talking from henceforward. When my father gave you settlement on his land, it was to rule jointly in peace. You, Dukwina, this is not the first time you have tried to seize all power for yourself, and you, Dibby, cowardly little worm, allowing yourself to be bullied. Hah, I think I shall slay ye both an' put an end to all this argument. Endar, find me a log to use as a chopping block!"

The empraking and Dukwina threw themselves down, kissing Ruggan's footpaws and sobbing pitifully.

"Oh, no, noble Ruggan, spare me, I beg you!"

"No, spare me—I was the one who helped the rabbets!"

Across their bowed heads, Ruggan winked at Rake. "What think ye, Captain Nightfur? Do they deserve to die?"

Rake returned the wink. "Och, Ah'll leave the decision tae you, mah friend, though they are an awful wee pair."

Ruggan beckoned to a serving shrew. "What name do they call you?"

The shrew tugged her forelock. "Wuzgo, sire."

Ruggan nodded. "An' have ye a mate, Wuzgo?"

She shook her head. "No, Lord. My mate died a long time ago. I've only got a friend, Luggi. That lizard over there."

Ruggan looked from one to the other. "An' what's your position in this tribe?"

The little sand lizard, Luggi, flattened his tail in salute. "We serve an' carry, sire, sweep floors an' scrub pots."

Ruggan pondered this briefly, then gave a pronouncement. "From henceforth, you, Wuzgo, an' you, Luggi, are the rulers here, over all this tribe. Dukwina, Dibby, I spare your lives."

The queen and the empraking were sobbing, this time with relief. Ruggan kicked them loose from his footpaws.

"Give all your finery to Wuzgo and Luggi—you can do their jobs now. I give your rulers permission to beat you both harshly if you are idle or talkative. That is my command, and any who disobey it are breaking the law of me and my father, Skor Axehound, Warchief of the High North Coast!"

Lieutenant Scutram murmured to Sergeant Miggory, "Well, now, there's a chap doesn't mince his flippin' words, wot. He certainly laid the law down to 'em there!"

Ruggan, who had overheard the remark, replied pointedly. "Life on the High North Coast is hard. My father's word is law, with little room for disobedience or rebellion. I see that one of your hares was slain by these shrews and reptiles. If your captain so wishes, I will slay ten of them in reprisal for that death."

Captain Rake shook his head. "Och, no thank ye, mah friend. The Long Patrol does its own slayin', ye ken. We don't need others tae do it for us!"

Skor Axehound's son bowed his head deferentially. "My apologies, sir, I meant no offence. Tomorrow I will take ye to see my father."

He beckoned to Wuzgo and Luggi.

"We will stay as your guests tonight. Make provision for us. Tell some of your creatures to bury that slain hare."

Sergeant Miggory snapped to attention. "Beg pardon, sah, but we buries fallen comrades h'ourselves."

The sea otter nodded. "Again, I must apologise. Might my warriors and I attend?"

Lieutenant Scutram smiled. "Indeed, sah, 'twould be an honour to have your company. Jolly decent, wot!"

A solemn procession of hares and otters bore the body of young Bribbs to the summit of the highest dune available. He was carried shoulder high on sea otter shields, a hare one side and an otter the other side of each shield. The burial was accomplished smoothly, after which Lieutenant Scutram spoke a brief poem.

"Here, far from his mountain home,
our fallen comrade must lie,
whilst we go on together,
'til our time comes to die.
His spirit will march alongside us,
we'll honour his memory and say
he died for truth and freedom,
aye, an' that's the warrior's way!"

Corporal Welkin laid a flat stone, engraved with Bribbs's name, on the grave. Everybeast raised a weapon in silent salute, then they turned and walked away. The otters began beating their shields with their axe, sword and spear blades in a dirge, chanting.

"Heyla ho! Heyla hay!
Night must conquer weary day.
Hiyarooh! Hayaree!
Bloodred sun sinks into sea.
O, bravebeast who fell, fare thee well.
Fare . . . theeeeeee wellllllllll!"

The eerie sound echoed around the dunes and shoreline. Lancejack Sage blinked away a tear, remarking to the warrior sea ottermaid she was walking alongside, "By the scut'n'paw, when the fur on the back o' my neck stops standin' straight up, I'll thank ye for that. 'Twas jolly well done. My name's Sage, like the herb. What's yours, friend?"

Her tough-looking companion replied, "Kite the Slayer, Kite like the bird, and Slayer because of the number of vermin I've slain."

It was said so coolly that Sage felt bound to enquire, "Oh, an' how many vermin have you slain?"

The ottermaid showed Sage her shield, which was scored around its rim with a circular pattern of nicks. "Can't remember the exact count—have to start on my axeshaft soon, though. Just call me Kite, they all do."

Big Drander, who was walking behind them, chuckled. "No flippin' wonder our Badger Lady wants to talk with your warlord. Wonder how many bloomin' vermin he's slain."

Kite replied without turning to face him. "Never knew anybeast who made so bold as to ask him."

A late spring wind chilled the night air, chasing sand along the shore and drifting up the dunesides as it swept in from the sea. None of this affected the Long Patrol hares or the sea otters, who were spending the night inside the ingenious structure created by pygmy shrews and sand lizards. Wrapped in blankets, they basked in the glow of oven fires as Rake Nightfur explained to Ruggan Axehound the purpose of the column's mission.

As soon as he mentioned the name Wearat, Ruggan interrupted. "Surely not! We thought he had been slain when he tried to invade our territory. His ship left our coast in flames, the sea was red with vermin blood. My father was sure that Razzid Wearat was either burnt to death or feeding the fishes beneath the water!"

Lieutenant Scutram spoke. "Sorry to disappoint ye, old lad, but the villain's back. Er, by the bye, we are talkin' about the same foul beast, ain't we? Captains a ship called *Greenshroud,* long galley with green sails an' the Wearat corsair sign on one, eh?"

Ruggan nodded. "There's only one Wearat we've ever heard of, and that's him, the master of the green ship. You say he's back again. Tell me more, friend."

Scutram went on to explain the incident at Salamandastron, which had resulted in the murder of the young cadets. Then he revealed how the ship had been refitted, this time with wheels, so it could also sail the land, and the addition of two giant bows, fore and aft.

Ruggan's fierce eyes hardened. "Which way did the ship sail after it left your shores?"

Captain Rake took up the report. "'Twas headed north, an' we've had evidence o' that since. Mah hares captured a wee vermin who'd deserted from the *Greenshroud* a day an' a half ago, south o' here. Aye, an' we found a poor auld deadbeast, an otter like yersel'. He'd been tortured tae death by the vermin, 'twas a grievous sight, ye ken. We buried him an' marked the grave wi' a paddle from his boat, which the scum had burnt."

Jum Gurdy looked stricken. "This ole otter, a bigbeast, was he? An' his boat—could it 'ave been a coracle, Cap'n?"

Buff Redspore replied, "I was first to find the poor chap.

He'd been a fine big otter, an' though the boat was in ashes, it could well have been a coracle. Did ye know him?"

Jum Gurdy blinked through his tears, staring at the oven fire fixedly. "Aye, I knowed him a'right. He was my ole uncle Wullow, who never did harm to anybeast."

The ottermaid Kite echoed the name. "Old Wullow, he often visited our holt."

Ruggan agreed. "Aye, Wullow an' my father were great friends. This captive ye took, Captain—is that him?" He pointed to Crumdun, who was sitting hobbled between Wilbee and Flutchers.

Rake glanced at the fat little stoat. "Aye, that's him, but Ah reckon he's told us all he knows."

Ruggan rose and went to Crumdun, seizing him by the neck. "So, ye told him all ye know, eh? Have ye anything more to tell me, vermin?"

Crumdun was terrified, gasping hoarsely in the viselike grip. "On me mother's 'eart an' me family's honour, Lord, I told the rabbets everythin' I knows. I'm only a simple crewbeast!"

Ruggan hauled him up on his paws, smiling coldly. "Garrent, Bartuk, take this piece of slime outside and get the truth out of him."

As the corsair stoat was dragged off kicking and screaming, Ruggan remarked flatly to Rake, "Vermin were ever liars. He'll talk once those two get to questioning him."

Young Ferrul could not stop herself protesting. "Beg pardon, sah, but do your chaps mean to harm him in any way? T'ain't the sort o' thing we'd ever do!"

The ottermaid Kite stared at Ferrul oddly. "No, an' 'tis not the sort o' thing that old Wullow would have done. Look what happened to him."

Ruggan Axehound addressed Ferrul. "Life's harder up here on the High North Coast, miss. Codes of honour are different toward searats, corsairs and vermin murderers. That's how my father's Rogue Crew has always survived and been victorious, you'll learn."

Captain Rake sighed ruefully. "Aye, Ah've nae doubt she will, mah friend, but Ah'd be pleased if ye'd keep in mind that these are mainly young uns who've never been in real war before." Wrapping the blanket about him, Rake lay back. "Sergeant Miggory, post two sentries an' relief through the night. The rest of ye can sleep now. We'll be marchin' on the morrow."

The oven fires glowed as they took their rest, each wondering how their encounter with the legendary Skor Axehound would be.

15

Uggo and Posy hung grimly on to their makeshift raft, squeaking fearfully as the four shining black shapes whooshed up out of the sea about them. Uggo gasped with shock as he came face-to-face with four seals.

The largest seal raised its head and bellowed, "Aaah hooooom! Haukahuuuuurm!"

Hoping the four big creatures meant them no harm, Posy took the initiative. Reaching out, she stroked the head of one, speaking gently to it. "We must get to shore. Help us, please."

The seal dived underneath her and, with a shrug of its smooth, mobile body, flipped her up onto the arrowshaft raft, calling plaintively, "Aaaah hoooooommmm!"

Posy grabbed hold of Uggo, pulling him aboard. "I don't know what they're saying, but I think they want to help us. Whoops, hold tight!"

The raft took off through the water like a stone from a sling, spray drenching the two hedgehogs as they clung on tightly. Almost playfully, the four seals wafted their charges swiftly toward the shoreline.

Laughing with exhilaration, Uggo looked back at the *Greenshroud*. The merriment died on his lips when he realised the corsair galley was coming in pursuit of them. He yelled, "The vermin must've found we've escaped, look!"

Sure enough, the green vessel was bow on in their wake. Without warning, one of the huge arrows was shot from the bow mounted on the prow. However, it fell far short of them.

Posy saw the huge arrow splash into the waves behind them. "They'll hit us if we don't get to land soon!" She called urgently to the seals. "Oh, hurry, please hurry!" They seemed to sense the concern in her voice and sped the pair along even faster. As the shoreline loomed up, Uggo launched himself into the water, which was only up to his middle. Quickly he helped Posy into the sea.

"Come on, we can fend for ourselves now. These great beasts must get out of the way. I wouldn't want to see them injured, or even slain."

He splashed water at the seals, shouting, "Go now, friends, an' thankee. Go quickly!"

The largest seal raised itself from the water, flapping its flippers noisily. "Wahoooommmm! Muuuurhaaaaawm!" The four sleek beasts vanished beneath the sea.

Razzid Wearat scanned ahead, watching the two small figures wading ashore. "How in the name o' thunder did they get to land so fast? Even under full sail we couldn't catch 'em!"

The vermin crew stayed for'ard, fearful of any reprisals his wrath would bring on them. Somebeast was going to pay for letting the prisoners escape.

Mowlag, looking up from the bow, signalled for another arrow. "The closer we get, the more chance I got of slayin' 'em!"

Razzid's trident struck the bow, knocking it aside. "We ain't got arrows to waste on two liddle pinhogs. Hold the ship dead ahead an' we'll run 'em down if'n we're fast enough! Jiboree, set some good runners up here, an' let me know when we're in the shallows."

Posy was first ashore. She glanced back at the rapidly closing galley as she took Uggo's paw. "They'll be right on our tails soon. We need to run and hide amongst those dunes!"

It was easy going on the firm sand below the tideline, but once they crossed the debris of seaweed and driftwood, things became difficult. Their paws sank into the dry sand, which slowed their progress considerably.

Uggo, never the fleetest of runners, tripped, sprawling headlong. He spat sand. "Phtooh! I ain't much good at bein' chased, Posy. You go on, leave me here. . . ."

The young hogmaid pulled him upright. "I'm not leaving you for those dirty vermin. Come on now, let's get going—show me what you can do!"

Razzid sized up the four searats whom Jiboree brought for'ard. Two of them had the long, lean limbs of runners; the other two looked young but capable. He positioned them either side of the bowsprit.

"See if ye can make it to land afore this ship does an' run those two escaped prisoners down. I want them back aboard alive, understood?"

The four nodded, bracing themselves to jump the moment some shallows showed. Razzid pointed at the two little figures stumbling toward the dunes.

"A keg of best Addersting grog to the one that lays paws on 'em first!"

The searats needed no further encouragement. With shouts of joy, they leapt into the sea. However, only two surfaced.

Razzid called to Mowlag and Jiboree, "Where've those two gone?"

Mowlag pointed at two rats breaking the waves, only to sink back beneath them. "There they are, Cap'n!"

The Wearat snarled at him. "Fool! I mean the other two—maybe they got washed under the hull?"

Jiboree was gesticulating furiously. "Yaaah—look, Cap'n, look look!"

157

One of the tall, rangy searats was practically standing up on the water's surface, rushing toward the ship. Nearing the port side, he suddenly shot up out of the sea, striking Mowlag as he flopped to the deck.

Jiboree dashed to the fallen vermin's side. "Blood'n'thunder—'e's dead!"

"Hoohoohooh! Howooooooommmmm!"

Almost a score of sleek black seals popped up, flapping their fins and honking mockingly. A moment later, the limp forms of the other three searats were tossed up onto the deck.

Razzid Wearat stamped up and down on the prow with rage. "Wot the . . . ? Kill 'em, slay those things. Now!"

The seals were too close to focus the giant arrows on, but corsairs flocked to the *Greenshroud*'s midship deck, flinging anything that came to paw at the circling seals. Still hooting and honking derisively, the skilful mammals seemed to treat the corsairs' efforts as a joke. They playfully ducked any weapons, then, using their snouts, bounced them back at the vermin crew, two of whom were badly wounded by spears. A few of the seals discovered a rope hanging from the vessel's stern. A group of them seized it in their teeth and began twirling the ship, towing it in circles and submerging anytime something was thrown at them.

Razzid Wearat was in a towering rage, but the more he cursed, kicked or swore at his hapless crew, the worse the situation became. He could see that the seals were actually relishing his discomfort, honking merrily and clapping their flippers in scornful applause.

Stamping off to his cabin, he snarled at Shekra, "I need to rest. Call me when those stupid beasts tire of their silly games an' leave us alone!"

The vixen was about to reply when a bunch of wet kelp slapped her in the face. The seals were enjoying their game.

"Hoohoohoo! Haaaawuuurrr!"

The two runaways made it to the foot of the dunes,

whereupon Uggo slumped down on the warm, shifting sand, gasping wearily. "Can't go no further, mate, don't care wot 'appens!"

Hiding her own fatigue, the pretty hogmaid sat down beside him. "We can rest awhile, but not for long. Once those seals stop tormenting them, the vermin will come after us again. Our best plan is to find somewhere to hide."

A shrill voice rang out from the dunetop. "Wiggles, git back 'ere—you'll fall!"

A cascade of sand from the duneside almost enveloped Posy and Uggo. A tiny hedgehog babe emerged blinking from the sand. She pulled tongues at them, then began dancing, and squeaking back up the sandhill.

"Yah, yah! I didn't never felled, see? I jumpered!"

A moment later, a squirrelmaid of about the same age as Posy and Uggo slid gracefully down from the summit. She nodded briefly to them.

"'Scuse me, be witcha soon!"

She went after the babe Wiggles, who evaded her grasp at every turn, giggling as she did an elusive dance.

As the tiny hog was passing, Posy stuck out a paw and tripped her. Uggo grasped Wiggles, holding her still. This gave the squirrelmaid time to grab the little hog, then wrap her tightly in a shawl as she squeaked angrily, "Yew lemmee go, Foober—y'ain't my mammy!"

The squirrelmaid, Foober, tweaked Wiggles's snout. "I wudden be yore mammy, not fer a barrel o' nuts. Wait'll I tells 'er 'ow you've been behavin!"

She nodded to Uggo and Posy. "Y'ain't from round 'ere, are yer? Whereja come from, then?"

Posy pointed to the *Greenshroud* out at sea. "We were prisoners on that ship, but we escaped, an' now we need to hide somewhere before the vermin come after us."

Foober passed Wiggles to Uggo. "Ye keep ahold o' that liddle snit—yore an 'edge'og. Someplace to 'ide, eh? Foller me!"

She started back uphill; they followed her hurriedly. Living up to her name, Wiggles wriggled wildly in Uggo's grip.

He shook her, though not too hard. "Be still, baby, or you'll fall. Yowch!"

Posy turned to see what was happening. "What now?"

Uggo ducked his head out of the little one's way. "She bit me on the nose, the liddle savage!"

Foober chuckled. "Then bite 'er back—go on!"

Uggo bared his teeth menacingly, though he had no intention of biting Wiggles, who began wailing, "Waaahaaa-haaah! It not fair, yew got big sharp teef, ya bully. I'm on'y likkel."

The threat had worked. Uggo gnashed his teeth for better effect. "Then be still or I'll bite yore nose clean off!"

They followed Foober almost out of the dunes, where the heathland was dotted with scrubby hummocks. Smoke from cooking fires rose from behind a large patch of gorse bushes. Foober yelled, "Comin' in! Open d'gate, Freepaws."

A section of the yellow-flowered spiked branches was drawn back by two hairy voles with hooked staffs. They escorted the small party through to a fire, where a big old silver-tailed squirrel was roasting parsnips in the embers.

He waved to Uggo and Posy. "Hah, two young 'ogs, eh? I likes 'ogs, affable beasts they usually are. Are ye affable?"

Not knowing what the word meant, Posy nodded. "Oh, we're affable, sir, very affable. I'm Posy, and he's Uggo. We've escaped from a vermin ship."

For his length of seasons, the silver-tailed squirrel had a fine set of teeth. He grinned widely at them. "Name ain't sir—'tis Rekaby. Excaped, eh? 'Ard work, excapin'. Y'must be 'ungry, come an' eat."

Scraping ash from two roasted parsnips, he gave them one apiece. They tasted very good. Uggo looked around at the others within the gorse compound. They were a diverse bunch: squirrels, moles, voles, hedgehogs and various types of mice.

Foober helped herself to a parsnip, winking at the silver-tailed patriarch. "Nobeast kin roast parsnippers like yew, Granpa. Wot are yew starin' at, Uggo?"

The young hog explained. "Sorry, but I couldn't help noticin' yore certainly a mixed bunch."

Rekaby shrugged. "That's 'cos we're the Fortunate Freepaws, y'see. We do no 'arm to anybeast, go where we like an' do wot we please. Even the Axehound's Crew leave us be. Good name that, ain't it, Fortunate Freepaws? I thought it up meself. I like big words—d'you know any?"

Posy scratched her headspikes thoughtfully. "Er, how about *curmudgeon*, or *lackadaisical*?"

Rekaby repeated the words, relishing their sounds. "*Curmudgeon, lackadaisical*. . . . I likes them. Wot do they mean?"

Posy explained, "Well, a curmudgeon is a beast who's moody and sulky. Lackadaisical, I'm not quite sure, but I think it means some creature who is idle and couldn't care less about things."

Rekaby scraped off another parsnip, nodding sagely. "Good new words, I'll remember them. Thankee, Miz Posy." He gave the parsnip to Wiggle. "So then, ye liddle curmudgeon, 'ave yew bin behavin' yoreself, or 'ave ye bin givin' pore Foober the runabout?"

Wiggle climbed up on the oldster's lap, giggling. "Ho, Wiggle gived 'er the runabouts. I'm a real 'mudgeon!"

Rekaby kissed the babe's soft headspikes fondly. "See that? Ye've nearly learned my new word. Go on, now, off with ye an' torment yore mammy for a while."

Uggo gained Rekaby's attention. "Ain't you worried about the vermin we escaped from? They'll be comin' ashore an' huntin' for us. There's a lot of 'em, y'know, an' they're pirates an' murderers."

The old squirrel laid an earthenware pot in front of Uggo and Posy. "Try dippin' yore parsnips in this. 'Tis gorse-flower honey—we gets it from the bees here."

Both hedgehogs did as Rekaby suggested, with Posy

pursuing Uggo's enquiry. "Mmm, it tastes quite pleasant, but you haven't answered my friend's question, Rekaby."

The old squirrel gestured with his parsnip. "I think I hear your answer comin' now. Open the gates for Swiffo, will ye?"

Hooking back the spiny gorse, the two hairy voles admitted a lithe young sea otter. Rekaby called him to the fire. "Now then, ye young curmudgeon, I've roasted a parsnip or two for ye. So, what news?"

Swiffo winked at Uggo and Posy as he helped himself to the food. "You two were lucky to escape that ole vermin ship. Ye wouldn't have made it 'cept for the Whoomers. Hah, I likes Whoomers—they're good fun!"

Rekaby tweaked Swiffo's rudder. "Beg y'pardon, but yore supposed t'be reporting t'me, not chattin' away to them two. Now, tell me all that went on, an' any good new words ye've heard."

Swiffo took a great gulp from a gourd of pennycloud cordial, then took up the tale.

"Big ship out to sea. Saw our friends here make their dive from it. Great ole green-sailed tub it is, packed with searats an' corsairs. I thought these two weren't goin' t'make the shore, 'specially when somebeast aboard fired a big arrow at 'em. Coloshuss it was, like a pine tree with flights, but it missed 'em. So, next thing the Whoomers comes t'the rescue, puts the 'edgehogs on land, safe'n'sound. Then after slayin' a few vermin, those Whoomers starts tormentin' the big ship, haulin' it to'n'fro, hurlin' the vermins' weapons back at 'em. I tell ye, Whoomers knows 'ow to enjoy theirselves!"

Swiffo broke off to dip another parsnip into the honey, but Rekaby chivvied him on.

"So, what happened then—an' did ye hear any new words?"

The young otter munched away reflectively. "I heard those vermin usin' lots o' new words when they was shoutin' at the Whoomers, but I ain't about to repeat 'em with maids present. Though there was two—*bottlenosed* an' *pestilential*. 'Ow do they sound to ye?"

Rekaby repeated them slowly, then nodded. "Better'n nothin', I suppose. Well, is that all, ye lackadaisical rip?"

Swiffo licked honey from his paws, winking at the old one. "Oh, no. I was savin' the best for last. Here's wot 'appened. The Whoomers left off playin' with the ship an' went off after a herrin' shoal. Then a one-eyed ugly-mugged beast came on deck an' ordered the ship t'sail for shore."

Uggo interrupted. "That'll be Razzid Wearat. He's the cap'n."

Swiffo prodded him with a sticky parsnip. "Ahoy, d'ye mind? I'm tellin' this story. Anyhow, ye'll never guess wot 'appened next!"

Rekaby gave the young otter a long-suffering glance. "No, Swiffo, I'll never guess what 'appened next, but I'd be pleased to hear it from ye."

Swiffo covered his mouth, emitting a muffled giggle. "I wouldn't 'ave believed it if I didn't see it with me own two eyes, but that ship came sailin' right up t'the beach, then rolled out o' the sea an' along the shore like a big wagon with sails—"

Rekaby's paw shot up. "Stop right there, young un! The ship came out o' the sea an' went along the shore. How?"

Swiffo shrugged. "It's got wheels, y'see, four of 'em. If'n ye don't believe me, then go an' take a look!"

For an old squirrel, Rekaby rose nimbly. "Foober, you an' Laka gather up the babes! The rest of ye, douse the fire, pack up camp an' make ready to travel. Uggo, Posy, Swiffo, Fiddy an' Frudd, come with me!"

Swiffo led the way as the others followed. Posy trotted alongside Fiddy and Frudd, two hairy vole brothers. She could not help noticing they were unarmed.

"Don't you carry weapons?"

Fiddy shook his head. "None of us Fortunate Freepaw tribe do. We avoid violence an' offer it to none."

Leading them along a tortuous path through the dunes, Swiffo came to his former vantage point on a high, reeded sandhill. He pointed upshore triumphantly.

"See for yoreselves!"

16

Mowlag judged the distance between the flat shoreline and the dunetops. "Don't see 'ow we'll catch 'em if'n they've gone up there, Cap'n."

Razzid wiped at his weeping eye, answering caustically, "I didn't think ye would. D'ye recall who got us atop o' the dunes by the stripedog mountain?"

Jiboree wagged his head admiringly. "That was you, Cap'n!"

The Wearat nodded. "Right, an' here's how ye do it. First we find the easiest of these dunes, the smallest. Then 'tis just like steerin' a ship at sea. Get the wind behind ye, then tack an' weave from a distance away. Get the crew standin' by to punt with the oars on both sides. We gets up speed on the flat, then goes full sail at the smallest hill. Soon as we hit it, the crew start helpin' her up by pushin' with the oars. Remember now, mudbrain?"

Mowlag tugged his snout meekly. "Aye, Cap'n, 'twas yore idea. Once we're up, it's like sailin' up an' down the waves."

Swiffo and the others watched *Greenshroud* from where they crouched in the dunetop reeds.

Frudd scratched his bushy head. "Wot are they up to? Maybe they're goin' back to sea, eh?"

Rekaby, who had been eyeing the vessel keenly, shook his head. "I don't think so. Look, she's caught the breeze on the turn to get up a fair lick along the hard sand."

Swiffo gasped. "Lookit the speed it's goin' now, good gosh!"

With a stiff breeze bellying out all sails, *Greenshroud* really whipped along below the tideline. Suddenly the big craft changed course, thundering at an angle toward the lowest dune. Excited shouts could be heard from the vermin as their ship hit the reeded slope. Oarpoles shot out, port and starboard, digging into the sand to keep up the momentum. The wheels scarce had time to settle on the duneside. It was an amazing sight.

Gaining the dunetop, *Greenshroud* careered off across the hilly summits, skilfully steered by corsairs heaving and slacking the rigging and ratlines under Razzid Wearat's command.

Rekaby kept his head low, muttering to his companions, "I think 'tis time we weren't here!" The small party made a hasty retreat, though as they surmounted the next dune, a hoarse cry rang out from *Greenshroud*'s lookout at the main-mast peak.

"Ahoy, Cap'n, there they go, the two 'ogs an' four other-beasts. Straight ahead, an' a point starboard. See 'em, Cap'n? Atop o' that dune, crouchin' down!"

Old Rekaby shook his head woefully. "D'ye hear that, the bottlenosed curs have spotted us. I wonder how they managed that."

Young Swiffo knew. "It's that ole tail o' your'n. Sticks up like a curly silver flag. We'd best make ourselves scarce!"

Rekaby sighed. "Aye, but don't take the trail back to our Fortunate Freepaws, or they'll be huntin' us all down."

Fiddy pointed northeast. "We'll lead 'em away from our tribe first. Then try to lose the villains somehow."

Posy looked doubtfully at the suggested route. "But we'll

be leaving the dunes for the heathland. Surely they'll overtake us easily on the flat."

Swiffo grinned mischievously. "Hah, but you don't know this country like we do, miz!"

Greenshroud was rolling along smoothly under Razzid's command. Driven by the breeze under full sail, the ship glided uphill and down dale without a hitch.

The Wearat yelled up to his lookout, "Where away are they now, Redtail?"

The keen-sighted stoat laughed aloud, pointing. "Haharrharr! The fools are makin' fer the flatlands, Cap'n. We'll run 'em down wid no trouble!"

Jiboree grinned wickedly. "We kin keep the liddle 'ogs 'til they tell us where Redwall is. But wot d'ye say we does wid the rest, Cap'n?"

Razzid twirled his trident, imitating a spit. "Been a while since we 'ad somethin' that wasn't bird or fish. Some roast red meat would cheer us all up, eh!"

Now the fugitives were on the heathland, which apart from some scrub, was level ground. Uggo managed to run up front with Swiffo.

"I hope ye know wot yore doin', mate."

The young otter glanced back over his shoulder. "Save yore breath, friend. That wheely boat'll soon be out o' the dunes. Lissen, wot can ye hear?"

Uggo listened carefully. "Nothin' much. Wot d'ye want me to hear, Swiffo?"

Breaking stride, Swiffo caught something in his paw. He showed it to Uggo before it leapt away. "Grasshoppers, big fellers—the sort we calls marsh hoppers. Now look, there's dragonflies, an' black darters. Wot does that tell ye?"

The young hedgehog looked blank; he shrugged. "Wot?"

Swiffo called to Posy, who was running behind them, "D'you know, Miz Posy?"

"Dragonflies are usually flying near water—streams, riverbanks an' such. Is there a river round here?"

Rekaby spotted *Greenshroud* coming down the last dune-side. "Looks like we'll soon have company. How far now to the marsh, Swiffo?"

The otter scout replied, "We're already on the start of it. Single line, now, an' follow in my trail."

Uggo looked nonplussed. "Wot is all this about—" Running to one side of Swiffo, Uggo's footpaw suddenly sank.

The young otter grabbed him back on track. "Told ya to stay in my trail. I knows the track through this marsh like the back o' me own paw, so stick close."

Uggo's paw had made a hole in the crust of the marsh, which was only a thin cover of soil and dead vegetation. The paw made a sucking noise as he pulled it from the foul-smelling, dark green ooze.

Posy covered her mouth against the fetid odour. "Phwaaah! Stinks like cabbage boiled last summer and bad eggs. Don't come near me 'til you've cleaned it off!"

Grabbing a pawful of moss, Uggo began scrubbing at his footpaw. However, he was brought up sharply by a kick on the bottom from Rekaby.

"No time t'be lackadaisical, young un. We've got a ship-load o' vermin on our tails. Now, get ye goin', an' keep in line with Swiffo. Ye can get cleaned off later!"

Greenshroud had made a speedy descent out of the dunes, and a lively breeze was astern. Corsairs and searats crowded her for'ard deck, leaning over the sides and shouting at their quarry, which was looming up in clear view.

"Hoho, supper's ahead, mates—we'll 'ave 'em soon!"

"I wants first go at those fat, 'airy mouses!"

"Makes no diff'rence t'me. They'll all taste the same once they're roasted!"

"Ahoy there, friends, don't run, it'll only tire ye out. Come up 'ere an' ride with us, we'll take care o' ye!"

Mowlag began distributing boat hooks and pikes. "Git up on the prow an' 'ook them aboard once they're within reach. Look sharpish!"

Jiboree's face was one huge smirk. "Shall I tell that greasy ole cook to stoke up 'is galley fires, Cap'n?"

Razzid frowned. To him this all seemed a bit too easy; he was beginning to feel suspicious.

"Slack off sail, Mowlag. I think there's somethin' we don't know about this place that those beasts do—"

Greenshroud suddenly lurched head down as its weight burst the marsh crust. Two corsairs standing out on the bowsprit with pikes at the ready were hurled from the ship. Razzid's intuition had worked, but too late.

Fiddy and Frudd, who were bringing up the rear, heard the noise and turned to look back. Both hairy voles began leaping jubilantly.

"It worked, it worked! Look at the fools!"

"Haharr, that's wot ye get for chasin' Fortunate Freepaws!" Swiffo shouted at them. "Their ship's stuck, but they can still track an' hunt us. Come on, we ain't got time t'waste. Once nightfall comes, even I could git lost in this marsh!"

Back at *Greenshroud*, it was a scene of chaos, and incredible stench. The big vessel was almost bow deep in the dark soup, with its front two wheels buried up to their rims. Razzid Wearat laid about at everybeast with his trident haft, bawling furiously, "Get aft, all paws aft! Mowlag, we need ropes, hawsers, lines, anything. Lash 'em to the stern an' back wheels. Get off the ship—see if'n ye can find trees or rocks an' tie up to them. We've got t'stop 'er sinkin' further!"

Pushing, kicking and shoving crewbeasts, Mowlag and Jiboree ran about in a frenzy, bellowing, "Yew 'eard the cap'n, empty the rope locker! Shekra, git a shore party an' scout out rocks or trees. Move!"

A slimy paw reached out of the mess, clutching at the bowsprit, where it clung for a moment before slipping back into the gurgling marsh. That was all there was to be seen of the two crewbeasts who had fallen in.

Razzid came gingerly from the stern onto the gently heaving marsh crust. Swiftly making his way to safer ground, he encountered the fat, greasy cook. "You, get a fire goin' here, an' don't go pokin' that peg leg of yores through the floor."

The cook, a peg-legged weasel named Badtooth, saluted. "Aye, Cap'n, a fire might drive the smell away, eh?" As he spoke, his wooden peg punctured the crust, sending up a jet of odorous liquid.

Razzid was about to hurl his trident at the unlucky Badtooth when the searat Dirgo came creeping carefully up to make a report.

"Cap'n, the vixenfox says to tell ye she's found a big ole tree. 'Tis close enough to haul yore ship out."

The Wearat almost thrust his trident into the quaking ground, but thinking better of it, he waved it at Dirgo. "Show me this tree. I'd best take charge o' gettin' the ship free, rather'n trust yew idiots!"

As the runaways forged onward, shades of evening began to fall. Posy looked fearfully at Uggo. "Hope we don't get lost here once it goes dark. It's a vile, stinky place!"

Rekaby silenced her with an upraised paw. "Hush, listen!"

From somewhere not too far off, a harsh, challenging cry rang out. The old squirrel smiled.

"We'll be alright now. Sircolo's here. Wait, I'll call him." Rekaby shouted in an equally aggressive manner, "Ahoy, old raggedy tail, if'n you eat me, I'll poison ye, just for spite!"

There was a whistling noise, and Rekaby was almost knocked flat by Sircolo's huge wings as the big bird came out of nowhere to land in their midst.

Uggo and Posy ran back several paces, awestruck at the appearance of the visitor. Sircolo was a fully grown male marsh harrier, with slate grey back and tail, cream and white underwing plumage and reddish feathered legs. The harrier had the curved beak common to hunting hawks and eyes that were frightening to look at. Sircolo held forth a lethal yellow-scaled talon, which Rekaby shook cordially.

The harrier blinked at him. "Yirrrk! Who would eat you, old gristlebag!"

Rekaby chuckled. "Well, there's a crew of vermin on our tails who ain't too particular what they eat."

Swiffo boldly came up and rubbed his back under Sircolo's neck. The harrier obviously liked this and made a hoarse chuckling sound.

Swiffo spoke soothingly. "Just think of it, mate. Fat, juicy searats, plump stoats, nice easy pickings, eh!"

Sircolo eyed the present company so hungrily that Posy wondered if the savage bird was really joking.

"Vermin make good eating, much better than you scrawny lot. I suppose you want me to get ye back to firm ground before nightfall?"

Swiffo stroked under the harrier's beak. "Aye, if'n ye'll be so good. The vermin can wait 'til later. They won't be goin' far—their ship's bogged down."

Sircolo seemed to ponder things for a moment, then he rapped his beak lightly on the young otter's head.

"Well, alright, but this is the last time I help you cumbersome beasts. Next time I'll eat ye all. Agreed?"

Uggo noticed that Sircolo's eyes were twinkling; so were Rekaby's as he twitched his tail in agreement. "Cumbersome, eh? That's a good new word. What's it mean?"

The harrier snapped his savage beak close to Rekaby's nose. "It means you're a nuisance, but better than nothing to a hungry bird!"

The ancient squirrel wrinkled his snout at Sircolo. "Fair enough. This is the last time we'll bother ye, friend. Next time we do, we won't do it again. Right?"

The harrier held up a taloned foot. "Enough! Just follow me. I'll put ye off at the start of the woodlands. Ye can rest safely there. By the way, just how many vermin are there?"

The hairy vole, Fiddy, spread his paws wide. "Lots'n'lots o' the scum. Far too many for you to scoff."

Sircolo stared down his beak at Fiddy, then sniffed. "Don't fret, little furbag. I'll give it a good try!"

Back at *Greenshroud,* Razzid supervised the rescue of his vessel from the marsh. The tree, which had been found, was an old grey alder, which had long since seen its best seasons. Razzid gave the trunk a whack with his trident; it emitted a hollow sound.

Shekra kept well out of his reach. "There's not much else around here, Mighty One. It's the best of a poor lot."

The Wearat rudely interrupted her. "'Twill have to do. You lot, smear that grease around the trunk. Jiboree, set that tackle up. Come on, the longer ye hang about, the deeper she'll drop. Shake a paw!"

Between them, Jiboree and Mowlag reeved several stout ropes around the trunk, which was thickly greased. The ropes were attached at one end to the ship's stern. The other ends were tied to long oars, six of them. Four crewbeasts were yoked to each oar. The rest of the vermin, armed with pikes and pieces of wood, stood almost waist deep in the marsh, ready to push at the hull as the haulers pulled on the ropes.

Razzid paced up and down. Checking that all was ready, he roared, "Right, now. When I gives the orders, ye heave an' haul! Ahoy, you, wot are ye jumpin' about for?"

The weasel corsair in question stopped jumping but continued slapping at his neck and back. "I'm bein' bitten, Cap'n, by gnats, I think. Yowch!"

Razzid wielded his trident. "Pay attention to my orders, or ye'll get bitten by this. Now . . . heave . . . haul!" The entire crew went at it, straining and shoving. The hauling ropes moved slightly around the alder trunk, but the vermin in the swamp slipped, slid and fell as they tried to get a purchase with their implements. *Greenshroud* moved out of the marsh a fraction, then settled back to her former position.

Razzid stabbed his trident angrily into the ground. Corded sinews stood out on his neck as he bellowed at the unhappy vermin. "Idiots! Oafs! The ship was movin' an' ye stopped! Why? Has the stink gone to yore brains? Are ye so stupid that ye can't obey my orders? Mowlag! Shekra! Jiboree! Get heavin' on those oars with me. We'll show these wooden'eads how to do it!"

Pushing his way into position on an oarshaft, Razzid waited until Shekra, Mowlag and Jiboree joined crew-beasts on the other shafts. He glared at them all, snarling harshly, "If'n the ship don't start movin', here's wot I'll do. I'll choose one who ain't pullin' his weight, an' I'll sink 'im in that swamp, with rocks tied round 'is neck. Then if'n she still ain't movin', I'll pick another idle beast an' do it agin! Are ye ready? Right . . . heave!"

The knowledge that Razzid would carry out his threat was enough. Searats and corsairs hauled with an energy fuelled by fear. *Greenshroud* emerged to the accompaniment of the sucking gurgle of marsh slime.

No sooner were the stern wheels showing than an enterprising weasel, who had been pushing from the after end, waded from the mud. Grabbing a pike, he leapt in behind a wheel, yelling, "Leave 'er stern end, mates. Git pikes'n'paddles under 'er wheels—we'll lever 'er out!"

Others joined him, calling out in triumph, "Haharr, 'ere she comes, mateys. Keep 'er goin'!"

With the combined hauling and leverage, *Greenshroud* rolled out, back onto solid ground.

Razzid left off hauling to bellow orders. "Don't stop for anythin'. Keep 'er movin'! Pull! Shove! Pull! Shove! Don't stop fer nothin'!"

Mowlag protested, "But Cap'n, she'll hit the tree!"

Razzid bawled frantically, "Never mind the tree, it's an old un. It won't stand in the way of my big ship!"

He was right. The old grey alder snapped at its base as the prow struck it head-on. *Greenshroud* rolled over the stump as the trunk fell to one side.

The weasel who had come up with the idea of levering the wheels slid in the mud, falling flat. As the for'ard wheels rolled over him, snapping his spine, he screamed, wailing to the Wearat, "Aaaargh! Cap'n, 'elp me!"

Razzid, however, had problems of his own, which beset both himself and the crew. A colony of mosquitoes, formerly housed in the fork of the tree, had been dislodged. They fell upon the vermin in an angry horde. *Greenshroud* rolled on alone, ropes, mud, marshweed and paddles trailing alongside.

Cavorting and leaping about like madbeasts, the vermin crew waved their limbs about wildly, trying to fend off the vengeful insects as they wailed aloud.

"Yaaah, I'm bein' et alive!"

"Gerremoff, I 'ates skeeters!"

"Yirkk! One's gone down me ear!"

"Owchyowch! There's millions o' the liddle 'orrors!"

Spitting out a mosquito and pawing one from his bad eye, Razzid picked up his trident and took off after the runaway vessel. "Come on, move yoreselves! All paws aboard—'tis the only way we'll git away from these things!"

Hastily they followed their captain's command. It resembled some sort of crazy travelling dance. Still beating at themselves, the crew hopskipped alongside the moving vessel. Clumsily seizing the trailing ropes, they stumbled aboard.

A grizzled searat pointed back to the marsh, addressing Razzid. "Beggin' yer pardon, Cap'n, but wot about Buppler?"

The Wearat smeared a mosquito underpaw. "Buppler? Who's 'e?"

The searat sniffed. "Buppler's me matey, Cap'n. 'E was the one who fell under the wheels. Must've been bad injured, pore Buppler—'e was still alive an' callin' for 'elp when you ordered us outta there."

Razzid cast a jaundiced eye over the searat. "Anybeast stupid enough t'get hisself run over like that deserves wot 'e gets. Don't bother me, I got a ship to run. If'n yore mate's 'urt bad, then he'll die, an' that's all there is to it."

Jiboree slapped an insect flat upon his cheek. "Wot's yer orders, Cap'n?"

Razzid tested the breeze on a damp claw. "Make all sail. Let's get back t'sea. We needs to careen the muck off'n this ship o' mine an' clean it up. Good salt water'll rid us of any mosquitoes still with us. Now, I needs two good trackers t'do me a service."

Jiboree volunteered a pair. Ricker, a shifty-eyed searat, and Voogal, a lanky ferret, did not seem overpleased to be selected, but they could not refuse Razzid's wishes.

He explained what he wanted. "Those beasts we were after, I want ye to trail 'em. Wot I needs is the two liddle 'ogs, Posy an' Uggo. Catch 'em an' bring 'em back t'me if'n ye can. Take a couple o' lanterns an' tell the cook t'give ye enough vittles an' grog to last ye. We'll be somewheres south along the coast, prob'ly lyin' at anchor 'til she's ship-shape agin. Any questions?"

Ricker saluted. "Wot about the other lot, those 'airy mouses an' some squirrels? D'ye want them, Cap'n?"

Razzid waved his trident dismissively. "Slay 'em, roast 'em, do wot ye want, just fetch me the 'ogs."

It sounded like a task very suitable to the pair. They saluted eagerly. "Aye aye, Cap'n. Leave it to us!"

When they had departed, Razzid called Shekra to him. "The 'og called Uggo knows where Redwall is, I'm sure of it. If'n 'e won't talk I'll make his liddle friend weep a few tears—that'll loosen 'is tongue. I ain't givin' up on findin' that place, an' you mark my words, vixen, it better be as good as ye say 'tis. I don't like my Seer disappointin' me. Unnerstood?"

Shekra nodded vigorously. "Trust me, Mighty One, 'twill be all ye desire an' more. The omens never lie!"

17

It had turned midnight when Sircolo led them out of the marsh. A short stretch of heathland stood between the Fortunate Freepaws and the woodland fringe. The marsh harrier seemed anxious to be off.

"Yonder's the trees, that way is south, t'other way north. So then, old silvertail, have ye got yore bearin's now? I don't want to eat any of ye, but I've got a hunger, so I must hunt for meat."

Rekaby pointed back to the marsh. "Then don't let me stop ye, y'ole savage. There's vermin aplenty back there. I bid ye good night an' good huntin'!"

As Sircolo swooped off, he called to Rekaby, "Find the stream. There's Guosim camped there."

Uggo watched the big bird vanish into the night. "Wot a good friend—an' helpful, too, eh!"

Swiffo chuckled. "Aye, an' 'twas a good thing we were with ye when he appeared. If'n he'd caught ye both alone . . ."

Posy shuddered. "Don't even mention it. Sircolo looks capable of anything. Let's find the stream and those shrews. I've heard them called Guosim before. Funny name, ain't it?"

Swiffo replied, "Nothin' funny about it. Guosim—the Guerilla Union of Shrews in Mossflower. First letter of each word. They live in logboats on streams an' rivers."

Uggo aired his knowledge proudly. "Oh, I knew that. They visit Redwall Abbey sometimes. Their leader's called Log a Log."

The shrews were not difficult to find. After a short walk amidst the trees, they saw the glow of fires and heard a deep, gruff voice singing to the beat of two drums, a flute and a fiddle.

"Ho, rum-tum-toodle-oh, pardon me sayin' so,
but I'll dance anywhere.
Round a boat from fore to aft, even all around a raft,
well, I can cause a stir.
I could dance on floatin' logs, in my good ole dandy
    clogs, they're the best uns ever made.
Call me an' I'll answer, I'm a champion ole dancer,
bright'n'sharp as any blade.
I always gets top marks, when I kick up lots of sparks
I'm the Log a Log whose name is Dandy Clogs,
the Guosim Chieftain
that good ole Log a Log called Dandy Clogs!"

The source of the sound was a dancing, singing shrew. In the light of the campfires on a streambank where six logboats were moored, a quartet of musicians was playing, whilst an entire tribe of Guosim shrews were clapping and paw tapping. A handsome, athletic shrew was singing and dancing with breathtaking skill.

This was Dandy Clogs, the tribe leader; he was a sight to behold. From beneath a blue cap, decked with green lapwing feathers, he beamed a constantly twinkling smile through neatly waxed and curled moustachios. He wore a scarlet tunic and kilt belted with a broad brass buckle, which glinted in the firelight. However, it was his clogs which really caught the eye. Fashioned from highly polished golden bark, they were set with patterns of shiny steel sprig nails.

On spotting the visitors to his camp, he executed a dizzying whirl, ending in a display of sparks as he ground to a halt on a rocky slab. Seizing Rekaby's paw, he pumped it vigorously.

"Welcome, welcome, welcome, on a fine spring night! Are ye friend or foe or just plain slow? Don't answer that question. Ye ain't too slow, an' ye must be friend, 'cos if ye were foe, we'd have slain ye long ago!"

The old squirrel managed to free his paw, interrupting. "I beg yore pardon, but could I get a word in here edgeways?"

The garrulous shrew waved them to seats by one of the fires. "Of course you can, O weary but wise one. Here, bring vittles an' drink for our guests. And now, good sir, kindly put in yore word—edgeways, I think you said!"

Rekaby was looking tired after the trek through the marshes, so Posy replied for him. "Sir . . ."

The shrew pointed at himself. "I'm not sir, O maiden fair. I'm Log a Log Dandy Clogs. Pray speak on, pretty one!"

Posy could not help but smile at his courtly poetic manner. She matched him with a pretty curtsy before continuing. "My friend Uggo and I escaped from a vermin ship. These good creatures helped us to escape; Sircolo guided us through the marsh and directed us to you."

Rekaby added, "We are of the Fortunate Freepaws tribe."

The Log a Log laughed. "Oh, that lot. We've seen you from time to time. Aren't you the bunch who don't believe in fightin' an' don't bear arms?"

Swiffo defended his tribe stoutly. "Aye, that's us, an' how we choose t'live is our own business. Besides, I don't see you carryin' any weapons."

A nearby shrew murmured in the young otter's ear, "Our Log a Log don't need swords or such. He could slay ye with a single kick o' those Dandy Clogs, believe me."

The shrew Chieftain clicked his deadly clogs together

sharply. "Enough talk o' slayin'. Try some of our shrew-beer an' fried fruit flapjacks. Yore safe here with us. Oh, by the way, I don't go in for longfalutin' titles, so just call me Dandy, an' that'll be fine an' handy!"

The fried fruit flapjacks were delicious, though the shrewbeer tasted rather strong. As they ate, Dandy discussed his plans for them. "Tomorrow we'll get you back to yore Freepaw tribe. I'm sure they're not far south of here."

He looked pointedly at Uggo.

"As for you, young un, yore a long way from Redwall, ain't ye?"

Uggo was surprised. "How'd you know I'm from Redwall?"

Dandy shrugged. "There was just somethin' about ye, I suppose—a good guess, eh?"

The young hog nodded. "It certainly was. I came from the Abbey with an otter called Jum Gurdy, but we got separated. I don't know whether old Jum's alive or dead."

Dandy winked at a tough-faced shrew. "Tell him, Dobble."

Dobble was a typical Guosim warrior, spiky furred, with a coloured headband, kilt and broad-buckled belt with a short rapier thrust into it. He drew the rapier and began sketching in the bank sand.

"This is where we are—there's the marsh, the dunes, shore an' sea. I spotted yore mate Jum two days back, in company with a score of fightin' hares an' six Rogue Crew sea otters. They're headin' up to the High North Coast. Ole Skor Axehound rules the roost up there. So Jum's alive an' safe, though I don't know when ye'll meet agin."

Uggo felt immensely relieved to hear the news of Jum Gurdy, though he could feel himself blinking back tears as he stared into the fire. "Without Mister Gurdy to guide me back to Redwall, I'm lost good'n'proper. I might never see my home, ever!"

Posy patted her friend's back gently. "Don't fret, Uggo, I'll help you. We'll find it together, you'll see."

Dandy stretched and yawned. "Oh, well, not tonight ye won't. You two get a good night's sleep an' stop worryin'. I suppose I'll have to take you back to Redwall Abbey meself."

Uggo wiped a paw across his eyes. "You will, Mister Dandy, are ye sure? Do ye know the way?"

The Log a Log scoffed. "Do ye think I'd be chieftain o' Guosim if'n I couldn't find me tail with both paws? O' course I knows the way to Redwall. Went there when I was nought but a liddle shaver. My pa was Log a Log then. I remember the vittles was prime, best I ever tasted. Now, you lot get some sleep. Dandy'll take care o' ye!"

The entire party settled down on the mossy streambank. After the heady shrewbeer, it did not take them long to drift off. Uggo lay watching the reflected campfires in the broad stream, listening to mothers lullabying baby shrews and warriors readying their weapons for the journey. He fell asleep, feeling safer than he had in a long while.

Midafternoon on a still, sunny day saw a small gathering of Dibbuns at the Abbey pond. Fottlink, the mouse Recorder of Redwall, was giving them the benefit of some seasonal advice. He peered over the top of his rock crystal glasses at them.

"Now, who can tell me what day it is today, eh?"

The shrewbabe Alfio held up a chubby paw. "It a nice sunny day, I fink."

Fottlink ruffled Alfio's ears. "Right, it is a nice sunny day, but it's a very special time. Who knows?"

Brinky, the tiny volemaid, smiled shyly. "A speshilly noice, sunny day, sir!"

Fottlink returned her smile, murmuring to himself, "Aye, well, we're getting nowhere fast." He moved to the placid water's edge. "See, if I'd stood here a few days back, I'd have got my paws wet. What do you make of that?"

Brinky's friend, Murty, scratched his velvety head. "Ee pond is gone likkler!"

The Recorder encouraged him. "Very good. Now, feel this stone. Move over, Guggle, and let Murty feel the stone you're sitting on. Go on, move, shoo!"

The Dibbun squirrelmaid moved, protesting, "But it's nice'n'warm ta sit on!"

Fottlink's paw shot up. "Exactly! The pond has shrunk, and the stones are warm—it's a sign, you see? The first day of summer!"

A tiny dot of a mousebabe looked at Fottlink blankly. "Summa, wot's dat?"

It suddenly dawned on the Recorder that this was probably the first summer most of them had seen, or could recall.

He sighed wistfully and was about to launch into an explanation about changing seasons when a charming young volemaid came from the direction of the Abbey.

"Brother Fottlink, Abbot says to tell you the meeting's about to start in Cavern Hole, an' you should attend."

The Recorder took her paw gratefully. "I'll go right away, thank you, Milda. Er, would you mind looking after the little uns? Take them to the orchard, away from this water, please."

Milda curtsied. "Yes, Brother. Come on, mates, who wants to learn how to make daisy chains?"

They dashed off with her, shrilling, "Us goin' ta make daisies chains wiv Mildee!"

Most of the senior Redwallers were gathered in Cavern Hole, with Abbot Thibb presiding. "Help yourselves to the lunch table and take a seat, friends."

Fottlink piled a platter with salad, cheese and a thick slice of nut and honey roly-poly pudding. Taking a beaker of cool mint tea, he seated himself next to Sister Fisk.

When everybeast was settled, Thibb addressed them. "There's three things we have to discuss. Uggo Wiltud's dream, Twoggs Wiltud's final words and the fact that they came in some way from Martin the Warrior. Any thoughts?"

Roogo Foremole raised a digging claw. "Aye, zurr, we'm bounded to 'eed ee warnens."

Friar Wopple was in agreement. "My feelin's exactly, Father, but you never told us fully about what young Uggo's dream was. Can you explain?"

Thibb deferred to his Gatekeeper. "Dorka Gurdy was the one who recognised Uggo's dream for what it was. Dorka?"

The otter Gatekeeper explained simply. "Uggo dreamed a ship was comin' to attack our Abbey—he saw it in his dream. I would've said 'twas only the ravin's of a liddle 'og who'd eaten enough cake t'give 'im nightmares. But then he described the ship, a green-sailed craft with the Wearat sign on its mainsail. Said he saw a beast aboard it, so ugly it could've been the Wearat hisself. I think 'twas a true vision."

Abbot Thibb nodded. "Aye, so did your brother Jum. That's why he went off with Uggo, to find your old uncle Wullow. Jum said Wullow had told him the Wearat was slain by sea otters, and his ship sank after being fired. He went to find if Wullow was telling the truth."

Sister Fisk stood up to be heard. "Added to that, there's the message we received from that old Wiltud hog Twoggs. What was it she said?"

Here Fottlink took out a piece of bark parchment. "I recorded our Father Abbot's exact words—listen."

"Redwall has once been cautioned,
heed now what I must say,
that sail bearing eyes and a trident,
will surely come your way.
Then if ye will not trust the word,
of a Wiltud and her kin,
believe the mouse with the shining sword,
for I was warned by him!"

Fottlink held up the parchment for all to see. "So said Twoggs Wiltud, a wretched old hogwife who had neither skill to read nor write. Those words could only have been put in her mind by our Abbey's guiding spirit, Martin the

Warrior. To me, this can mean only one thing—we are in danger of being attacked by a Wearat. I know it sounds unlikely, but this beast is coming to Redwall in a green-sailed ship! Who amongst us would doubt the word of Martin?"

An uneasy silence fell over the assembly. It was soon broken by Foremole Roogo with practical mole sense. "Hurr, nobeast be doubten et, zurr. Point bee's, wot'n be us'ns agoen to do abowt et?"

Abbot Thibb shook the Foremole's paw. "Thank you, Roogo. There's nought to beat mole logic. So, what are we going to do, friends?"

Ding Toller, the Abbey's squirrel Bellringer, spoke. "Say nought to the young uns. No point in scarin' 'em. I say let's not go jumpin' to rash decisions. We need to go away an' think deeply about this problem. Abbot?"

Thibb settled both paws in his wide habit sleeves. "What Ding says is right. Hard, sensible thinking may well provide a solution. However, I have an immediate proposal. We need to have lookouts on all four walltops, night and day. Foremole, will you see to it? Two guards to each wall, with volunteers to relieve them four times a day. Bring any news of sightings straight to me. In the meantime, friends, let's go about our duties calmly."

The meeting broke up then as Redwallers set about their everyday chores. The remainder of the day passed without incident. Things grew quiet, even at supper that night, when conversation usually flowed back and forth, spiced with banter and good humour.

Abbot Thibb noticed this. Sitting next to Fottlink at the head of the main table, he mentioned it. "Our friends seem taken up with their thoughts tonight."

The Recorder nibbled at a mushroom and carrot pasty. "Hmm, but they're only doing what Ding Toller suggested. What about you, Thibb, have you had any thoughts?"

The Abbot sipped at his blackberry cordial. "Yes, I have. What about if you and I go to Martin's tapestry? After they've all gone to their dormitories, of course. In the silence of the small hours, maybe our Warrior's spirit will send us a message, some words of wisdom perhaps."

Fottlink brushed pasty crumbs from his habit front. "A splendid idea. I'll bring charcoal sticks and parchment, to record anything which may occur."

Thibb dropped his voice to a secretive whisper. "Give it a while after they've all gone up, then knock on my chamber door."

It was sometime after midnight. Thibb had not gone to bed; he stood at his small window. From there, he could see the west walltop. Two moles were patrolling up and down, alert but unhurried. The Father Abbot of Redwall felt a surge of pride in his faithful friends. Redwallers could always be relied upon for whatever he wished. He was distracted by a faint tap on the door. It was Fottlink, carrying a satchel containing his recording materials. He grinned furtively.

"Are you ready, Thibb?"

Silently the pair tippawed downstairs and started to cross Great Hall, in which areas of dark shadow alternated with soft golden lantern light. A cold draught of air caused them to halt—they heard the creak of the main door opening.

Thibb pulled Fottlink behind one of the huge sandstone columns, whispering, "I thought there'd be nobeast about at this hour, but someone's just come in the Abbey. Hush, now, let's find out who could be wandering about."

A moment later, Dorka Gurdy drifted past them. Looking neither left nor right, the otter Gatekeeper moved slowly and smoothly through the hall.

Fottlink watched her intently. "Hmm, sleepwalking, would you say, Thibb?"

The Abbot noted her trancelike stare as she passed them. "Sleepwalking definitely, I'd say. Best not wake her, though. Come on, let's follow her quietly."

Dorka went to the alcove by the hall's west wall. She

halted in front of the legendary tapestry depicting the Redwall hero. Soft candlelight and ruby-tinted lanterns illuminated the noble figure of Martin the Warrior. Fully armoured and leaning on his great sword, he stood at the centre of the depiction as embroidered vermin foebeasts fled from all about him. In the lantern light, his eyes seemed to twinkle as he faced out into the Abbey. To one side, held by two iron brackets, the sword itself hung beside the tapestry. Thibb and Fottlink stood back in the shadows, curious to see what would happen next.

Dorka reached up, taking the sword from its mounts. She laid the weapon flat on the worn stone floor and spun it. Fottlink already had his writing equipment out, recording her every move. The mighty blade was still spinning as Dorka spoke in a clear, unhurried tone.

"Look to the blade, my point ye must take,
to whence winds will bring evil in their wake,
for goodbeasts arriving, I bid ye wait,
they bring aid on the day thy need is great.
Two warriors that day will answer the call.
The most unlikely creatures of all!"

When the sword ceased spinning, Dorka curled calmly up at the base of the tapestry, sound asleep.

Abbot Thibb shook his head in amazement. "Well, my friend, what did you make of that?"

Scribbling away earnestly, Fottlink replied, "Hush . . . wait. The most unlikely creatures of all. Good, I got it all, every word!" The scribe pointed dramatically with his charcoal stick. "See, the sword lies still now. Which way is the tip pointing finally?"

Thibb answered quietly. "North. No doubt that's the direction the Wearat's ship will come from."

Gently they both helped Dorka Gurdy upright. She blinked owlishly at them.

"I came from the Gatehouse to ask Martin to bring Jum and Uggo safe back to Redwall."

The Father Abbot patted her reassuringly. "Of course you did, marm. Now you must go back to your Gatehouse. I wager your bed's more comfortable than a stone floor. Come on, friend, you need a proper rest."

Dorka reached down, taking the sword and replacing it on the iron mounts, remarking, "Martin's sword belongs up there. I wonder who took it down and put it on the floor. That wasn't very nice, now, was it?"

Fottlink the Recorder and Abbot Thibb escorted Dorka Gurdy back through the first summer night to her Gatehouse. As they made their way back to the Abbey, a mole called from the west walltop to them.

"Hurr, all peaceable oop yurr, zurrs. Goo' noight to ee!"

18

Dawn had already released summer's first fine day over the North Coast. Captain Rake Nightfur woke in the cleverly constructed pigmy shrew dome to find Colour Sergeant Miggory placing a welcome beaker of dandelion and comfrey tea before him.

The gnarled veteran hare saluted smartly. "Mornin', sah, an' a good sunny one 'tis. H'I brewed a drink—thought ye might like a sup."

Rake glimpsed sunlight beaming through the entrance. Blowing on the steaming drink, he chanced a sip, noting that their captive stoat, Crumdun, was attached to Miggory by a line.

"Mah thanks tae ye, Sergeant. What are ye doin' wi' that wee fat vermin? Ah thought the otters had taken him for questioning."

Miggory drew Crumdun closer to him. "So they 'ad, sah, but rememberin' that this un was h'our captive, h'an not theirs, I took charge of 'im. Just as well I did, sah. Those two h'otters, Garrent an' Bartuk, couldn't get h'anythin' from 'im, so they was h'about to slay 'im. They objected, so h'I 'ad to give 'em both h'a liddle boxin' lesson, sah. . . . H'I won!"

Rake rose and finished his drink. "Ye did right, Sarn't. We

cannae have otherbeasts slayin' our prisoners. Och, weel, we'd best get ready tae march. We're seein' the Great Axehound hissel' taeday, Ah'm thinkin'.''

Corporal Welkin, who had just come in from guard duty, interrupted. "Beg pardon, sah, but we've no need to march any flippin' further, wot. Skor Axehound has been sighted comin' this way with a crew of his warriors. We should be meetin' them anon."

Rake turned to see Skor's son Ruggan approaching. The sea otter was scowling wrathfully. He was accompanied by Garrent and Bartuk, each of whom were missing a few teeth. Ruggan halted in front of the Long Patrol captain, bellowing in his face, "What right has your sergeant to take that vermin scum away from my warriors? They say he beat them up to do it. Let me tell you, Captain. Nobeast strikes any of my crew and gets away with it. I demand satisfaction, d'ye hear!"

Rake did not seem at all put out as he replied, "Hauld yer wheesht, laddie, an' let's get a few things straight. For a start, the vermin was our captive an' not yours. Mah sergeant stopped those two bonnie buckoes frae killin' the wee stoatie. So they fell intae disputin' his right, an' Miggory disputed back an' taught 'em a lesson. Nae real harm done, Ah think. As tae satisfaction, mah friend, ye'd have tae face mah sergeant unarmed. Ah think ye'd come out on the losin' side against him."

Ruggan immediately shed his weapons and shield; he was quivering with temper. "We'll see, shall we? Defend yourself, Sergeant!"

Instantly he swung a fierce kick at Miggory, who casually sidestepped it as he conversed with Rake. "Beg pardon, sah, but h'I don't like strikin' 'igh-rankin' h'otters. This young buck's h'a chieftain's son."

Enraged by the fact that he was being ignored whilst attacking his opponent, Ruggan threw a volley of blows at Miggory's face. The sergeant evaded every one with slight flicks of his head, coaching Ruggan as though he was a

188

novice. "Keep yore left up, sah. Clench those paws only when ye strike—h'otherwise, ye'll soon be tired h'out."

Ruggan's eyes were red with temper. He swung, kicked, scratched, punched, butted, but all to no avail. Miggory seemed to sway and float, ducking and dancing with eye-blurring speed whilst continuing his instructions to the infuriated otter.

"Ye shape up better'n most, young sah, but don't leave yore chin h'open like that. 'Tain't proper form, y'see!"

Now Ruggan was puffing and panting. His paws had begun sagging when a gruff voice nearby addressed Rake.

"He's my son, but a courageous fool. The lesson will do him good."

Skor Axehound had arrived whilst the contest was on.

Rake Nightfur called out to all the hares present. "Attenshun, High Chieftain present!"

Members of the Long Patrol, who had been watching the spectacle, came swiftly to attention, including Sergeant Miggory, who took a sudden punch on the chin from Ruggan.

The veteran hare smiled crookedly, waggling his jaw from side to side. "Good shot, young sah, but ye should've hit my bread basket to double me h'over first, like this."

Miggory's right whacked into the otter's midriff. Ruggan doubled up, going down on all fours as he fought for breath.

The sergeant lifted him upright, massaging his back. "You alright, sah? H'I tried not to 'it ye too 'ard."

Skor Axehound was all that a sea otter Chieftain should be. Garbed in a chain-mail vest, with a cloak of vermin hide down to his footpaws, he had a long shield tied by a thong to his shoulder. In one paw he carried a huge double-headed battleaxe, which any normal beast would have trouble lifting. Above his grey-streaked beard, which bushed out over a barrel-like chest, Skor's eyeteeth stuck out like fangs. He had two of the brightest barbaric green eyes.

Captain Rake Nightfur felt himself enveloped in the massive sea otter's embrace. Skor laughed boomingly. "Ho ho! Still the same old longears, eh? Slim as a rake an' dark as thunder. How are ye, my friend? Ye look as if ye haven't aged a day since we last met long ago!"

Rake returned the hug, extricating himself neatly. He held the huge beast off by grasping his paws.

"Och, Skor Axehound, ye bonnie old wardog. How d'ye manage tae stay so young lookin'?"

Skor patted his bulging but rock-hard middle, chuckling. "Hah! Young lookin'. Me? I leave bein' young to beasts like my son there, Ruggan. Hoho, ye never met a boxin' hare afore, have ye, son? Come on, now. Shake paws with an ole warrior who could've slain ye with a real blow."

Ruggan gasped Miggory's paw, managing a weak smile. "My thanks for the lesson, friend. Mayhaps one day I could show ye a few tricks with sword or bow?"

The tough sergeant grinned. "H'I've no doubt ye could, sah, an' I'll look forward to it!"

A sizeable breakfast was served out on the sunwashed beach by their hosts, the pigmy shrews and sand lizards. Otters and hares dined on soft cheeses and flatbreads, fresh fruit and a honeyed coltsfoot cordial. Rake explained the mission that Lady Violet Wildstripe had sent him on, telling Skor all that had taken place to date. The chieftain listened intently.

When Rake had ended his narrative, Skor scratched his beard reflectively. "What ye tell me makes sense, my friend. I rue the day I never finished Razzid Wearat off for good, but I swear to you that I'll put that right before I'm much older. I saw the villain when he returned to seek vengeance on me. Hah, Wearat, he's the same as any coward or bully. Took one look at me an' my Rogue Crew, then turned tail an' fled."

Lieutenant Scutram, who was party to the conversation, enquired, "We knew he was sailin' north, sah. Trouble is, where'n the name o' seasons has he jolly well gone to after turnin'? We've not caught sight of his vessel."

Ruggan had a suggestion. "Mayhaps he's gone back to attack your fortress, Captain Rake."

The dark hare chuckled briefly. "Ah think not, laddie. Since he was last at Salamandastron, our Badger Lady is on the alert. Yon Wearat'll no' get a chance tae sneak in an' murder our young cadets. Razzid isnae a fool. He would-nae try tae attack the mountain."

Sergeant Miggory posed a question. "Beg pardon, sah, but if'n 'e ain't h'interested in meetin' Lord Axe'ound agin h'an' 'e won't be h'attackin' our mountain, where does 'e h'intend going to? Sailin' h'off 'ome to his den, maybe?"

Scutram shrugged. "Who jolly well knows. Where else could the blighter go to, wot?"

Skor winked knowingly. "We'll know in a short while. I've had two o' my best trackers shadow the vermin ship since it turned away from the High North Coast. Kite, Endar Feyblade, go an' see if there's any sign o' Gil an' Dreel returnin'."

Rake stood up, pacing about and scanning the sea. "Ah hope yore scouts have found where the green-sailed ship is. Bear in mind what I told ye—yon craft has wheels now. It can go by land or sea, which has me sair bothered, ye ken?"

Skor nodded in agreement. "Aye, it worries me, too. In a way I feel guilty. We've never had need o' ships—'twas enough just to defend our coast against enemies. I know your Badger Lady was hopin' sea otters had vessels. I want to help her, and I will, truly. Argh! But a ship that can sail on land or sea, that's somethin' I never reckoned with. Any sign o' those trackers yet, Ruggan?"

Skor's son scanned the beach both ways. "Not yet. We'll just have to wait, sir."

And wait they did. It was late afternoon before the scouts returned. During the intervening time, Long Patrol hares and sea otters had a chance to be acquainted with each other. It turned out they were not so different, both being warriors. Sea otters, though, had a more ruthless code. Anybeast even resembling a foe or vermin was slain without question or pity. But like the hares, they greatly valued courage and honour. In the matter of weaponry, the Long Patrol were better skilled with swords, but sea otters were far superior archers, each otter being equipped with a bow and a quiver of arrows. Both sides were showing off their skills when the scouts returned. All activity stopped as they gathered to listen to the reports.

Gil and Dreel were sisters, slim and keen eyed. They had quite a story to tell, which they did bit by bit, one at a time. Rake and Skor listened in silence, questioning only when the report had been given in full.

However, it was Jum Gurdy who spoke first. "You say two liddle 'ogs escaped from the vermin ship?"

Dreel smiled. "Aye, sir, but they wouldn't have made it without help from the Whoomers. They were funny, I can tell ye, haulin' that ship around an' throwin' weapons back at the vermin."

Jum seemed puzzled. "Wot's a Whoomer?"

Skor explained, "They're seals, bigbeasts, who don't like vermin. I rule the coasts hereabouts, but 'tis the Whoomers who rule the seas, really. That's why we don't need ships."

Jum continued, "The two liddle 'ogs—they'll be Uggo an' Posy, I'm sure of it. Did they get away safe?"

Gil nodded. "Oh, they're safe enough, sir. They were found by the Freepaws tribe. Freepaws are goodbeasts. They'll keep the young uns from harm."

Skor Axehound looked to Dreel. "Did ye see my youngest son, Swiffo?"

The scout answered respectfully. "We saw him, Lord. He is a tracker and scout for the Freepaws, an' still carries no weapons."

The burly chieftain rested his chin on a big paw, sighing. "A son o' mine, an' he goes unarmed, along with that gatherin' of travellin' ragbags. I tell ye, Rake, it brings shame upon the name of Axehound."

The dark hare captain tried to make light of it. "Och, away with ye. Your son's young—he's likely goin' through a wee phase. Did ye never have sich a time in your spring seasons, Skor?"

The huge sea otter Chieftain nodded reflectively. "Aye, I recall likin' flowers. Daisies, roses, bluebells an' buttercups. I carved 'em all over my shield, on my sword scabbard an' axe haft, sketched some on my arrow quiver, too. But no-beast seemed t'make fun o' me. Strange that, wasn't it?"

With much effort, Rake kept a serious face. "Aye, 'twas that, mah friend. So mayhaps ye might go easy on your young laddie for his odd habits, ye ken?"

Skor raised his shaggy eyebrows. "Yore prob'ly right. Swiffo will outgrow 'em, just like I did. Ahoy, Gil, where d'ye reckon this vermin ship is now?"

The ottermaid pointed south. "Someplace down yonder, Lord. She went landward for a while, then came back to sea, all muddied up an' stinkin' o' marsh muck. She headed out to deep water, but then veered south. Maybe she'll put in somewhere sheltered to careen the dirt off. Caked mud can slow a vessel down, y'know."

Skor rose, hefting his massive battleaxe. "So, what think ye, Nightfur? We number three an' a half score—that's mine an' Ruggan's crew with yore Long Patrol warriors. Are ye game t'go up agin' a shipload o' vermin?"

Rake needed no second invitation. "Ye have mah paw, mah blades an' mah heart on it, Skor. Taegether we'll find 'em. 'Tis guid tae be with a Rogue Crew again. Sergeant, form up the column tae march!"

Ruggan smiled coldly at Sergeant Miggory. "When we find 'em there'll be blood on the wind, friend!"

The veteran hare returned the smile. "H'or as we says at Salamandastron, sah, we'll let 'em taste blood'n'vinegar. Form up, column, we're goin' for a little walk, buckoes!"

Greenshroud had rounded a hilly point. She lay at anchor in a pleasant little bay. Razzid Wearat would not abide idle paws aboard his vessel, so whilst he awaited the return of his trackers, he set the crew to work. Good silver sand showed through the clear shallow water, ideal for hull scouring. Teams of corsairs and searats waded almost chest deep, rubbing the malodorous slime from the marsh off the woodwork. Mowlag and Jiboree patrolled for'ard and aft, each swinging a knotted rope's end to chastise any slackers. Razzid had retired to his cabin in a foul humour. The entire craft seemed to be permeated with the smell of green mud.

Staying clear of her ill-tempered captain, Shekra went ashore on the pretext of looking for medicinal herbs. The vixen enjoyed the early summer day, paddling awhile in the shallows, then wandering farther along the beach. Tiring of the walk, she eased herself down behind a small sandhill, grateful for the chance of taking a short nap. She had just closed her eyes when scuffling sounds disturbed her. The noise came from somewhere behind where she was sitting.

Easing gently to the hilltop, she spied out the land. The intruder was a ragged-spined old hedgehog foraging for food. He was using a crude spearhead to probe the rocky base of the main hill, which isolated the cove to the north. Shekra watched him; he had a woven reed sack slung over one shoulder, which contained any edible finds. As he rummaged, the old hog muttered and giggled to himself.

"Heeheehee, limpets. Drogbuk likes limpets. Ye can boil up a good soup wid limpets. Come on, ye shellbound rascal. No good ye hangin' on. I'll git ye off'n there!"

He pried a big limpet from the rockface, throwing it into his sack. "Aye aye, wot's this? A good ole nipclaw. Heehee, you'll go nice in Drogbuk's soup, matey. Cummere!"

The crab tried to dig in twixt sand and rock, but the hedgehog's spear stabbed it right through its shell. Still writhing and nipping, it was tossed into the sack.

Shekra stole up on the unsuspecting hunter, commenting in a honeyed tone, "By the seasons, yore good at that. 'Tis a pleasure to watch a beast who knows wot he's doin'."

The old hedgehog appeared startled for a moment, then snapped, "Well, yew ain't gittin' none o' my vittles. Go an' git yore own, bushtail. Go on, be off wid yer!"

The vixen continued chatting in a friendly manner. "Oh, I wouldn't dream of askin' to share your food. It must be hard enough, trying to scrape a livin' on this part of the coast. I admire your efforts, Drogbuk."

The ragged oldster squinted suspiciously at the fox. "Who told ye my name, needlenose?"

Shekra shrugged. "Just guessed it, I suppose. My name's Shekra. I'm with that big green ship over yonder."

Drogbuk carried on prising periwinkles from the base of the moss-clad rock. He sniffed scornfully. "I seen it afore— big clumsy lump o' wood! Makes no diff'rence t'me. I'll be movin' on by nightfall."

Shekra picked up a few fallen periwinkles, dropping them in Drogbuk's sack. "Moving on? But I thought you lived here on the coast."

The scraggy old hedgehog thrust out his chin aggressively. "I'm a Wiltud, an' us Wiltuds goes where we pleases, see? Hither'n'yon, shore or shingle, field or forest!"

At the mention of the name Wiltud, the vixen's memory jogged, remembering young Uggo. Choosing her words carefully, Shekra appeared still friendly and casual. "I've heard of Wiltuds, great travellers I believe. I'll wager you've been to many places, Drogbuk?"

Throwing the sack higher on his shoulder, the ancient Wiltud hog smirked. "Many, many places. You name 'em, an' I've been there. Nobeast knows these lands like me!"

Shekra smiled craftily. "I wager you've never been to Redwall."

Drogbuk wagged his rusty spearpoint at the fox. "Hee-heehee! Well, that'd be a bet ye'd lose. I been to that ole Abbey a few times in my seasons."

Shekra nodded. "Is it a nice place?"

The old Wiltud gnawed a grimy pawnail. "No better'n'no worser than some places I've been, though I never tasted anythin' so fine as Redwall vittles." He paused, narrowing his eyes at Shekra. "Why d'ye want to know about Redwall, eh?"

Shekra's mind was racing as she thought up a plausible answer. "Well, it's like this, friend. There's to be a great midsummer feast at Redwall, so the captain of that ship has decided to bring gifts for the Redwall beasts. We'll probably be invited to attend the feast. That's why I asked you about the place."

Drogbuk nodded. "But ye don't know 'ow t'get there, do ye?"

The vixen shook her head ruefully. "Alas, no. Our ship was blown off course in a big storm at sea, and we're completely lost. Do you know the way to Redwall, friend?"

Drogbuk wrinkled his scaly nose. "Wot's in it fer me if'n I shows ye the way? Wot do I get?"

Shekra spread her paws, smiling broadly. "Well, for a start, you get to ride in comfort all the way. Also, I'm sure my captain would include you in the invitation to the midsummer feast."

Drogbuk thrust the spearhead into the rope tied about his waist. "Come on, then. Take me to yore cap'n!"

Shekra paused, as if considering the request. "Listen, my friend. You wait here whilst I go and tell him yore comin'. He'll want to lay a table for ye. My captain is quite choosy about who he lets aboard the *Greenshroud*. So I'll run ahead an' tell him of yore kind offer. Alright?"

Drogbuk was eager, but he feigned indifference. "Aye, sounds fair enuff, but don't leave me hangin' round 'ere too long, fox. I ain't got all day."

Razzid Wearat listened to Shekra's report. "Ye did well. I'll send Mowlag an' Jiboree ashore to fetch the ole hog."

The vixen objected. "No, Cap'n, 'tis best I do that. Those two might be a bit rough on him. Let's play this softly. There's more ways of makin' a duck sleep than beltin' it over the head with a rock. I'm sure if we let Drogbuk think we're his friends an' treat him kindly, he'll show us the way to Redwall willingly."

It was an idea that was foreign to the Wearat's nature, but seeing the possibilities, he agreed. "Right. You go an' fetch him, an' I'll have vittles laid out for him. But I warn ye, fox—yore scheme had better work, or 'twill be the worse for ye."

The crew had been told about Drogbuk Wiltud. They avoided talking to him as he came aboard with Shekra. Entering the captain's cabin, he ignored everything else, making straight for the meal of grilled fish and gull's eggs. The ragged hog set about the food with all the appetite of a true Wiltud.

Shekra poured him a beaker of Strong Addersting grog, enquiring, "Is the food to your liking, my friend?"

Drogbuk spat out a herring bone and slopped down some grog. He sniffed. "I've tasted worse. Who's that un?"

Razzid remained silent as the vixen answered, "That's our captain."

Drogbuk refilled his tankard with the fiery grog. Draining it, he smacked his lips, giggling. "Heeheehee, ugly-lookin' ole toad, ain't 'e?"

Shekra held her breath in horror as Razzid stayed the ragged guest's paw from reaching for more grog.

"I'm told ye know the way to Redwall. Tell me."

Drogbuk stared into the leaky eye as if he did not care. "Ain't sayin nought 'til I've 'ad me fill!"

Razzid was fuming inwardly, but he allowed the meal to continue. Drogbuk wolfed down fish and eggs, and drained the tankard three times. Then he sat back, picking with a fishbone at his stained teeth. Staring at Razzid's good eye this time, he belched aloud.

"Good drop o' grog, that. Ain't 'ad no grog fer a season. Pour us a drop more there, Cap'n."

Nodding toward a keg in the corner, Razzid spoke, trying not to grit his teeth as his ire rose. "Not so fast, friend. You can drink as much as you like from that little barrel once you tell us how to get to the Redwall place."

Owing to the amount he had already supped, the old Wiltud hog's speech was becoming slurred.

"S'awright, Cap'n. I knows 'sactly where 'tis. Jusht sail

south downa coast 'til ye comes to a river wot runsh over the shore. S'called der River Moss, y'cant mish it. Ye goes up there t'the easht!"

Drogbuk's chin dropped onto his chest, grog dribbling out of his lips. He hiccuped, belched, then began snoring.

Jiboree curled his mouth in disgust as he drew his knife. "Slobberin' ole sot. 'Ere, Cap'n, lemme tickle 'im up a bit wid me blade. I'll make 'im sing like a finch at a feast!"

A kick from Razzid sent the weasel sprawling.

Razzid's voice was heavy with authority. "Anybeast puts a paw near this 'og will drown in 'is own blood. We'll do this my way. Leave the drunken fool to sleep it off. He'll do anythin' for a noggin o' grog. When I needs more information, I'll just let 'im take a liddle sip—that'll loosen 'is tongue. Right, Shekra?"

The Seer saluted. "Aye, Cap'n, a good plan!"

The Wearat dismissed Jiboree and Mowlag. "Git all paws onboard an' hoist sail. Take 'er south along the coast an' keep an eye out for this River Moss." Mowlag reminded him of the trackers he had sent out over the marshes on Posy and Uggo's trail.

"Ain't we waitin' fer Ricker'n'Voogal, Cap'n?"

Razzid sneered. "No we ain't. I've got wot we need, a beast who knows the way to Redwall. Those two idiots might be drowned in that swamp, an' if'n they ain't, well, they should've been back aboard long since, wid the two liddle 'ogs. Now, get my ship underway, quick!"

He lifted Drogbuk's head and let it drop again. The old hedgehog snuffled briefly, then resumed snoring.

Razzid took up his trident, giving orders to Shekra. "Lock this cabin after me. Let nobeast in 'ere. Watch 'im an' let me know when 'e comes round."

The vixen settled down with a small beaker of grog when Razzid had departed. She felt quite pleased with the way things were working out. Redwall Abbey, in sunny countryside, peace and plenty. What more could a fox want?

19

It was a moonless night out on the marsh. The two trackers, Ricker the searat, and Voogal the ferret, had not gone far. The supply of food and grog they had taken from *Greenshroud*'s galley interested them more than what seemed like a pointless task. Finding a relatively safe spot, they made camp and lit a small fire. Sitting with their backs against a fallen alder trunk, they broke out the rations.

Ricker sampled a stodgy mess, then, pulling a wry face, spat it out. "Yurk! Wot's this supposed ter be?"

Voogal sampled the lumpy mass, seeming to like it. "Skilly'n'duff, wot'd dried up inna pan. It's good stuff, mate. Yore too fussy, that's yore trouble!"

Ricker uncorked a large earthenware flask. He drank from it, then put it aside, making the same pained expression. "This is Strong Addersting grog. Why didn't ye take some o' the good stuff, like Blistery Barnacle?"

Voogal took a swig, nodding approval. "Nothin' wrong wid Strong Addersting, it's me favourite. Now, is there anythin' else to complain about, fussbucket?"

The searat scowled. "Less o' the fussbucket, ye great slopbin. Yew'd shove anythin' down yore face!"

His ferret shipmate put some of the cold skilly'n'duff on the fire to warm. He watched it sizzle. "I'm glad I'm a slopbin an' not a fussbucket like yew. Complainin' an' moanin', that's all yore good for!"

Ricker pointed indignantly to himself. "Wot me, a moaner an' complainer? Hah, wot've I got ter moan an' complain about, eh? Sent off on an idjit's errand, wanderin' round inna dark, covered in stinkin' marsh slop, an' all because the cap'n wants ter git 'is paws on two stoopid liddle 'ogs. Ho, no, bucko, I ain't complainin'. Lookit me—I'm 'avin' the time o' me life!"

Voogal prodded the mass on the fire with a twig. "Then whilst yore enjoyin' yerself so much, ye'd best start thinkin' of wot we're gonna tell Razzid when we gits back t'the ship widout any 'edge'og prisoners, 'cos I can't see 'ow we're supposed t'find 'em in this neighbour'ood, kin yew?"

Ricker stood up. Shielding his eyes, he tried to peer beyond the fire into the darkness, calling mockingly, "Ahoy there, me darlin' liddle 'ogs! Come on out 'ere. Me'n nice ole Uncle Voogal 'ave got vittles an' grog for ye. Don't be shy, now, come on out—graaaagh!"

He was tossed over backward as a huge, dark shape swooped on him, ripping the left ear from his head. It was Sircolo the marsh harrier.

Voogal had not fully comprehended what was going on. Hearing Ricker's agonised yell, he leapt up, drawing his blade. "Ricker, are ye alright, mate? Wot was it?"

Apart from another screech of pain, that was as far as the searat got. Peeved that he had missed his quarry, Sircolo made a lightning turn, striking Ricker with both sets of talons and a savage beak.

From where he crouched on the other side of the alder trunk, the ferret watched in frozen horror as the feathered hunter despatched Ricker with swift savagery. The mighty bird lifted his prey bodily, launching off into the night air. Blood spattered Voogal as he stared upward. The mighty wings flapped, and both Sircolo and Ricker vanished into the darkness.

The ferret gave an unearthly yell. Taking to his paws, he left food, drink and the campfire deserted. Hurtling off willy-nilly into the marshy scrubland, Voogal ran as he had never run before. Brush and gorse scratched at him like attacking claws. He stumbled, breaking through the marsh crust several times, but scrabbling swiftly free, he continued his flight. Completely panicked, he blundered on, unknowingly following the path of the very beasts he had set out to pursue. The ferret's only thought was to get out of the range of the giant winged predator.

Back at the Guosim streambank camp, a sentry was knocked flat by Voogal stampeding through the camp boundary. The shrew jumped up, calling the alarm.

"Logalogalogaloooog!"

The ferret was almost at the stream's edge when Dandy Clogs, who was never a heavy sleeper, came sailing sideways through the air. *Clakk!* The shrew Chieftain's clogged footpaws connected with Voogal's jaw, knocking him senseless.

Immediately the camp sprang to life. Dandy bellowed orders. "Vermin! Arm up, Guosim, an' check the area!"

It did not take long until shrew warriors began calling back, "All clear here, Dandy!"

"Ain't no more of 'em—must've been only one o' the scum!"

Uggo and Posy hurried to where Dandy was standing over the unconscious Voogal. Brushing off the side of one clog, Dandy commented coolly, "Just nicked the villain. He's out cold, but he'll live. Do either of ye know him?"

Kneeling, Uggo studied the ferret's face. "Aye. I saw this un aboard the ship. I warned ye they'd come after us!"

Rekaby chuckled drily. "Lucky we met friend Dandy, isn't it? I'll wager he could lay a whole crew o' those curmudgeons flat with those clogs o' his!"

Dandy nodded. "Good job there wasn't a full crew with him. Rawkin, sluice this rascal down with water 'til he comes round. The rest of ye, go back to sleepin'—we've got an early start in the morn."

Posy spoke for herself and Uggo. "Can we stay and watch him, Dandy, please?"

The Guosim Chieftain shrugged. "As y'please, missy."

Voogal spat water, wincing, trying slowly to rise. An ornate clog landed on his narrow chest, thrusting him back down. Dandy leaned over him, his eyes glinting like chips of flint in the firelight. He addressed the vermin in a flat, dangerous tone.

"Stay where ye are, muckface. I've got questions for ye."

Seeing the big bird was nowhere about boosted Voogal's courage. He snarled his reply. "Questions, eh? Wot makes ye think I'm goin' to answer 'em, watermouse?"

Dandy smiled at Posy. "Listen to him. He don't know the difference twixt mouse or shrew. A real thick un, eh?" He turned back to Voogal, still smiling. "You'll answer, thick'ead, an' they'd better be answers I like, or things might get a bit hot for ye. Rawkin, shove yore rapier blade in the fire, will ye?"

Posy put a paw to her mouth. "You're not going to . . . ?"

Dandy turned away from Voogal, tipping Posy a huge wink. "Better stay out the way, me darlin'. This won't be fit for a young maid t'see. Rawkin, tell me when that blade gets to glowin' red."

Voogal sighed deeply. "Alright. I'll answer any of yore questions, shrew. I ain't takin' any punishment fer a cap'n who don't care if'n I lives or dies. Ask away."

Playing along with Dandy, Posy scowled fiercely. "If'n I was you, I'd tickle the scum up with that hot blade first, show him ye means business!"

Voogal gulped visibly. "No, don't! I'll tell ye all ye wants ter know, on me affydavit I will!"

Dandy nodded. "Oh, I think this un'll sing just fine without me havin' to dirty a good blade on his hide, missy."

The Guosim Log a Log's eyes twinkled as he whispered to Posy, "Away with ye, bloodthirsty liddle snip!" He turned his attention back to the ferret. "Now, me snot-nosed ole vermin, tell us yore story."

Voogal was readily blurting out the name of his ship and captain when Dandy held up a paw. "I already know all that from young Posy an' Uggo. So tell me, why were ye ordered to hunt 'em down?"

The ferret replied promptly. "'Cos the one called Uggo comes from a place named Redwall, an' my cap'n wants ter find out where 'tis."

The shrew Chieftain glared sternly at Uggo. "Why didn't ye tell me this?"

Uggo shrugged. "Er, didn't have time to. . . . We were tired'n'hungry when Rekaby brought us here. I forgot."

Dandy shook his head in disbelief. "Razzid the Wearat has a shipload of vermin murderers aboard of a vessel that can travel land or water, an' he wants t'go to Redwall Abbey. What for, d'ye suppose? To take tea wid Abbot Thibb, eh?"

All Uggo could do was to murmur lamely, "Wasn't my fault, all I did was forget. Sorry."

Dandy struck his clogs on a stone, sending sparks flying. "Sorry! Is that all ye've got t'say, sorry? Rawkin, Dobble, Banktail! Ready the logboats! Guosim, break camp an' ship yore gear. We're leavin' now!"

The fat Guosim called Banktail scratched his ear in bewilderment. "Now, Chief?"

Dandy roared at the hapless shrew, "Aye, now! We've got t'get to Redwall afore the Wearat an' his vermin do. We got to warn 'em there's goin' t'be an attack, so come on, shift yore fat tail!"

Dandy pushed past Uggo, berating him coldly, "An' you, make yoreself useful an' lend a paw. But if'n ye can't do that, then stay out of me way!"

Feeling completely crushed, Uggo hung his head, staring at the ground.

Old Rekaby patted his back. "Don't fret, young un, we all make mistakes. Dandy'll be in a better mood once the logboats are on the move. Us Fortunate Freepaws won't be goin' with ye. We've got t'join the rest of our tribe. It's been good meetin' ye an' you, too, Posy. Good fortune go with ye, friends!"

Posy hugged the ancient silver squirrel. "Thanks for everything, Rekaby. You're a kind creature."

Without warning, young Swiffo also embraced Rekaby. "Aye, yore one o' the best I ever travelled with. I'll miss ye, too, ole silvertail!"

Rekaby merely smiled ruefully at the sea otter. "So you're off, too, ye young ripscarum. I wondered how long 'twould be afore ye grew tired of our peaceable ways."

Swiffo grinned roguishly. "I've got t'go with Posy an' Uggo, 'cos I'd hate to miss out on an adventure an' mayhaps a slice of action. Ahoy, Dandy, got room for another one?"

The Guosim Chieftain laughed. "Hop aboard, I wouldn't refuse a son o' Skor Axehound!"

They boarded the logboats, which Guosim paddlers steered skilfully out into midstream. Rekaby and his followers waved them off from the bank.

"Safe journey, hope ye make it to Redwall in time!"

Swiffo nodded toward Voogal. "D'ye want us to ship that vermin aboard with us?"

Rekaby considered the request briefly.

"No, thankee. We'll dress his wounds an' keep him with us. Maybe teach him not t'be such a bottlenosed curmudgeon!"

From the prow of the lead logboat, Dandy called out orders to his Guosim. "Keep 'em head down an' centre current. Stay in line, slipstream the boat in front of ye. No sails, there ain't a puff o' wind to fill 'em tonight. Hark, now, I wants t'see those paddles double strokin' good'n'deep. We got a long way t'go an' a short time t'do it in, so dig deep, me buckoes!"

Uggo and Posy sat with Swiffo in the stern of the back logboat. They felt a surge as their craft lurched forward under the power of double stroking. With their gruff bass voices, the Guosim shrews struck up a stream shanty, keeping the pace fast and smooth.

"Raise that paddle, dip it now,
an' don't miss yore turn.
With a bow, wave at each prow,
trailin' a wake astern.
Down the waters Guosim travel. On on on!
One day here, an' on the morrow gone gone gone!

"O you pilot in the lead,
ply yore paddle down now.
Watch for rocks an' beds o' weed,
or overhanging' tree bow.
Smoothly send yore blade a dippin' deep deep deep!
Stay alert and don't dare think of sleep sleep sleep!

"Dark an' swift we're headin',
keep both banks in sight.
See the ripples spreadin',
twinklin' with starlight.
Hold her in midstream, me buckoes. Stroke stroke
    stroke!
Bend yore backs until ye think they're broke broke
    broke!"

It was such a catchy tune that Posy found herself bumping a footpaw to keep time.

Swiffo cautioned her, "Don't do that, pretty one—ye'll put the rowers off."

Uggo snorted. "No, she won't. Posy's just helpin' 'em along." He tapped the back of the Guosim rower sitting in front of him. "Ahoy, mate, you Guosim certainly knows how to row. D'ye mind if'n I borrow yore paddle an' have a try?"

The oar shrew was big and tough. He spat into the stream, turning scornfully to Uggo. "Lissen, daftspikes. Try puttin' a paw near my paddle an' I'll belt ye right inta next season with it!"

Uggo's voice sounded small and apologetic. "Sorry, sir. I was only tryin' to 'elp."

The Guosim, a hard-faced warrior, curled his lip. "Only tryin' to 'elp, eh? Gettin' us to lose a full night's sleep, an' paddlin' like madbeasts round these streams. You've done enuff as 'tis, fool. So belt up, or get belted!"

Swiffo clouted the back of the shrew's head sharply. "Lissen, mudsnout, if'n ye feel like beltin' anybeast, then why not try me fer size, eh? Go on, I'll belt ye into that stream afore ye can raise a paw. So just shut yore trap an' row!"

Without a word, the Guosim went straight back to paddling.

Swiffo whispered to his two hedgehog friends, "An' you two stop bumpin' the side o' the boat. Don't argue wid Guosim beasts, an' grab some sleep whilst ye can!" The young sea otter grinned broadly, winking at them both.

They drifted into sleep on the dark night-shaded stream, cheered up by the fact that they had a good companion, and a real tough one, to boot.

Despite the fact that they were eager to exact retribution on Razzid Wearat and his crew, the march in search of the vessel *Greenshroud* was both long and arduous. This was mainly owing to the scorching pace set up by both hares and otters trying to outmarch each other. It became a question of regimental pride on the Long Patrol's side, opposed by a display of Rogue Crew toughness and stamina. Neither side was prepared to concede a fraction to the other. Skor Axehound, bringing up the rear with Captain Rake Nightfur, began to fall some way behind. Neither had spoken a word thus far, merely pressing onward, spitting dust and fine sand.

The big sea otter finally halted, nodding toward the

marchers. "This has gone far enough, Rake. They're goin' to run themselves into the ground if'n they keep on like that!"

The hare captain caught his breath, nodding. "Aye, Ah'm with ye there, mah friend. D'ye ken they'd hear ye if ye called a halt?"

"Let me give it a try, eh!" Skor spat on his paws, cupping them about his mouth. His massive chest swelled as he sucked in air. Then he let out a bellow which had Rake covering both ears. "On my command . . . haaaaaaaalt!"

Surveying the dust cloud which arose over the marchers, Skor chuckled. "Haven't lost my touch, it'd seem!"

Both sides sat in the sand, heads down, fighting for breath but still defiant.

"By the left, what've we jolly well stopped for, wot?"

"Search me, I was just gettin' warmed up!"

Neither side would admit tiredness. They carried on thus until Sergeant Miggory (one of the few who was still breathing normally) sprang up to attention. "Silence h'in the ranks. Offisahs'n'chieftains present!"

Skor strode up and down, shaking his big bearded head. "If we met up with those vermin now, wot good would any of ye be, eh? I order ye to stop this foolishness. Captain Rake, would you like to say a word?"

His companion fixed them all with a reproving glare. "This is nae a race, ye ken. Skor Axehound's right, an' Ah'm surprised at the behaviour of mah Long Patrol officers. Whit were ye thinkin' of, eh? Right now, let's do things proper. Take a rest for a while, but no food, just a small drink each, tae quench the dust. Then we'll be up an' marchin' again in good order. Lieutenant Scutram, ye'll do us the honour o' a marchin' song, an' I mean a proper saucy air, not a stampede scramble. Understood?"

Scutram threw him a smart salute. "As y'say, Cap'n, I'll keep it to a brisk march, sah!"

When the march resumed, things went a lot better, progressing at an even pace. Much to everybeast's amusement, Skor strode at the head of the parade, hurling his battleaxe high and catching it deftly as Scutram's tuneful tones rang out.

"Chest out! Chin in! Left right together!
Eyes front! Back straight! Can ye smell that heather?

"Derry down the fields of clover,
see the gold sun dawning,
ain't it grand to be a rover?

"Chest out! Chin in! Left right together!
Eyes front! Back straight! Can ye smell that heather?

"O'er the deep sea gulls a-wheeling,
larks are soaring inland
on we go, behind us leaving,
pawprints in the sand.

"Chest out! Chin in! Left right together!
Eyes front! Back straight! Can ye smell that heather?

"Hope my love will wait for me,
with a fond heart yearning,
aye, she'll smile with joy to see,
her warrior returning.

"Chest out! Chin in! Left right together!
Eyes front! Back straight! Can ye smell that heather?"

After the song, one of the sea otters, Garrent, chuckled as he chatted to Big Drander. "Wot sort o' marchin' song is that? Bit sissy, ain't it?"

Drander kept his eyes front, muttering out the side of his mouth, "Tell that to Cap'n Rake. He wrote it."

Kite Slayer, the tough ottermaid, scowled darkly. "Ain't the sort of marchin' song I'd be caught singin'. Would ye like to hear a Rogue Crew song? One Skor wrote?"

Trug Bawdsley nodded affably. "Jolly nice of ye, missy. Carry on an' warble away."

Without further ado, Kite launched into the sea otter tune.

"O there's blood on the axe,
an' there's blood on the shield,
an' blood on the swordblade, too.
An' if yore a foe of our Rogue Crew,
there'll be blood all over you!
Blood blood! Blood blood—"

Corporal Welkin interrupted before Kite could sing another verse. "Oh, well done, miss. What a jolly little ditty, a right pretty paw tapper, wot!"

A nearby sea otter nodded. "Aye, it's brought a tear to many an eye, I can tell ye."

Young Flutchers chuckled. "Indeed, old chap. I'd wager it's brought more'n a bloomin' tear to some. Wot!"

Lancejack Sage, who was up in the vanguard, called out, "Scouts returnin' ahead!" Accompanied by Gil and Dreel the ottermaids, Buff Redspore loped up, saluting Rake and Skor.

"See that long ridge ahead, sah, sort of hillscape? The vermin ship has been there, anchored in the cove. But we're afraid she's gone now."

Skor scratched at his bushy beard. "Gone, which way?"

Buff answered respectfully, "Wouldn't like to make a guess, Lord. Mayhaps you'd like to judge for yourself? It ain't far."

From the ridgetop, Dreel pointed to the clear waters of the calm bay below. "It's not deep. See the mudpatch on that clean sand beneath the water? That's where they've been careenin' marsh dirt off'n their hull."

Her sister Gil explained, "That mud won't move for a day or two. Ain't much tide, water's almost still."

It was late noon when they explored the cove. Being an

expert tracker, Buff Redspore ventured her opinion. "No wheelmarks in the sand, so *Greenshroud* never left the water. Only one beast came ashore—fox, prob'ly a vixen by the prints. But see here, there was already another over by the base of the hill. Looks like an old hedgehog."

Skor stared at the tracker. "How d'ye know that?"

Buff produced a few greyish spines. "Old enough t'be losin' these. The vixen took the old un back aboard the ship with her."

Rake studied the twin tracks. "Tae get information out o' the beastie, Ah think. So, where does that leave us?"

Buff shrugged. "She hasn't gone inland, an' she's already been up north, so she must be sailin' south."

Ruggan Axehound mused, "If'n ye say the vermin wouldn't attack yore mountain again, then wot do they want down south?"

Jum Gurdy, who had stayed in the background thus far, now came forward. The big Cellardog looked worried. "D'ye think they're plannin' on havin' a go at Redwall?"

Captain Rake Nightfur stamped his paw down hard. "Och, aye! Ah'm a fool for no' thinkin' o' that mahself. But why has the Wearat no' gone inland tae do it? He has a vessel on wheels."

Jum Gurdy told him why. "Further south, twixt here an' yore mountain, there's a river runs o'er the shore, Cap'n— 'tis called the River Moss. Runs through the woodlands an' dunes, over the beach, into the sea."

Sergeant Miggory nodded. "We crossed o'er h'it on the fourth day h'outward bound, sah. I remembers it well, 'cos the water was sweet to drink, an' fresh."

Skor looked ready to march onward. He boomed impatiently, "Well, we're losin' time standin' here chinwaggin' about it. We should be marchin' south t'find this River Moss!"

Jum Gurdy interrupted. "Could I make a suggestion?"

Rake forestalled Skor by saying, "Aye, please do."

Quickly, Jum scratched out a rough map in the sand.

"This is the coastline goin' south. River Moss should be somewheres about 'ere. It flows out o' the east. Where the path to Redwall Abbey is, there's a ford o'er the water. So, if the vermin are goin' to the Abbey, this is my plan, friends. Instead o' followin' the coastline south, we should cut inland now, on a southeasterly course. That way we'll save time an' we might even spot 'em."

With a brief nod of thanks, Skor Axehound turned and began marching off, away from the sea, commenting gruffly, "Well, wot are we waitin' for? We're losin' time!"

Following his example, everybeast fell in behind him. Within a short time, they had crossed some hills and were out of sight of the cove.

In their haste, they had forgotten one of their number, Crumdun. The fat little stoat had seized his opportunity to slink away during the discussion. He squeezed in beneath some rocks at the base of the hill, pulling an old wet sack he had found over himself. He waited until there was complete silence within the cove before venturing out. Crumdun heaved a great sigh of relief. He quite liked the hares, who had fed him, treating him decently. However, he lived in mortal fear of the sea otters, convinced that with their hatred of vermin, he would be slain by them sooner or later. His new sense of freedom filled him with happiness. No more captivity or serving as a ragmop on corsair ships. Opening the sack, Crumdun found a variety of shellfish and molluscs. Later that evening he sat by a small fire roasting his supper whilst reflecting aloud.

"This ain't a bad life. I can suit meself wot I does. Funny, I allus wanted to be like me ole mate, Braggio Ironhook. But that ain't such a good idea, or I'd 'ave ended up wid me 'ead stuck atop o' *Greenshroud*'s foremast. No, I'm best off just bein' meself, liddle fat Crumdun!"

Which was indeed a fact, because not many vermin ended up being as lucky as him.

20

A stiff wind blowing easterly from across the sea buffeted *Greenshroud*'s starboard side as she ploughed southward through rising waves. From atop the mainmast, a keen-eyed searat who was lookout that day bawled out a sighting.

"I kin see a river runnin' across the shore!"

Jiboree, who was fighting to keep the tiller steady, called back, "A river, eh? Where away?"

"Mebbe a point or so to port," came the reply.

Gratefully, the weasel eased off his pressure on the long timber arm, allowing the tiller to drift *Greenshroud* landward at a southerly angle. He stopped a passing crewbeast. "Go an' tell the cap'n a river's been spotted."

Razzid Wearat wiped at his injured eye, staring at the approaching river. "Hmm, could be this River Moss. Shekra, go an' get that 'ole spikehog. He'll know."

Drogbuk Wiltud was in no fit state to walk. He staggered on deck, supported by Shekra and Mowlag. The drunken old hedgehog's head was lolling on his chest; his eyes were shut.

Grabbing him by the headspikes, Razzid yanked his head up. "Ahoy, I wants to talk with ye. Liven yoreself up, ole fool!"

Shekra cut in helpfully. "Here, Lord, let me try." She patted Drogbuk's limp, scrawny paw. "Wake up, friend, we need yore advice."

The wretched creature managed to open one eye blearily. "Eh, what . . . ? Where's grog? I need more!"

Knocking Shekra aside, the Wearat began beating Drogbuk round his head, snarling with each blow. "Ya dribblin' ole grog stopper, lookit yon river an' tell me, is that the River Moss ye told us about?"

Drogbuk made a swift recovery, trying to cringe from the vicious blunt-clawed paws. He babbled pitifully, "Aye, that'd be the Moss. But you said ye was my friend. Wot are ye hittin' me for?"

Razzid smiled wickedly as he twisted his victim's snout. "I'll hit ye if'n ye don't shape up an' tell me wot I want. Now, wot's our next move, ye drunken idjit? Talk!"

Drogbuk pointed at the stretch of clear water gushing over the beach into the sea. "Ye follows it, that's all. Just follow it east."

Loosened by age, the old hedgehog's body quills rattled to the deck as Razzid shook him violently.

"We goes east along the river. Wot then? Where's Redwall?"

Drogbuk sank to the deck whimpering. "I needs more o' that grog, I needs it bad, sir!"

Mowlag kicked him. "Then tell the cap'n the way first."

Stammering and weeping, Drogbuk explained, "O'er the shore, through the dunes an' hills, then into the woodlands. Stay wid the river 'til ye comes to a ford. There's a path either side of it. Redwall Abbey lies to the south along that path. But ye'll have ter leave yore ship at the ford an' march the rest o' the way."

Jiboree sniggered. "Hah, that's wot yew think, eh, Cap'n?"

Razzid ignored him, hauling his captive upright roughly. "Swear to me now, is that all I needs to know?"

More quills rattled to the deck as Drogbuk nodded hastily. "I've told ye true, on me oath I 'ave, Cap'n. Now can I get a taste o' yore grog, sir? Me pore 'ead's achin' somethin' awful. Just a drop o' grog to wet me sufferin' lips."

Razzid turned to watch the oncoming river. "Kill 'im!"

Shekra leaned close, murmuring, "Is that wise, Lord? Who knows wot lies ahead. We may need him yet."

The Wearat shrugged. "Then let's keep 'im awhile. But no more grog fer that un. Bind 'im t'the mast."

With the wind at her stern, *Greenshroud* entered the Moss shallows, half sailing, half rolling as the wheels were driven under full sail. It was an odd sight, the big green-sailed vessel gliding smoothly over the beach.

Jiboree managed the tiller easily, cautioning Drogbuk, whose moans were beginning to pall on him. "Quit yore whingin', y'ole grogbucket, or I'll give ye a taste—but it won't be grog, it'll be a rope's end!"

High-sided dunes formed a canyon either side of the river. The wind dropped after *Greenshroud* navigated several meandering turns, leaving the ship becalmed twixt the steep sandy slopes. All through the noontide, crewbeasts sweated as they poled away with long oars to keep the ship going.

Mowlag spat on his paw. Holding it up, he announced, "Keep goin', mates. We might catch the wind again by nightfall, mebbe once we make the woodlands."

An exhausted searat leaned on his paddle. "Huh, that's alright fer Mowlag t'say. All I'm catchin' is a pair o' sore paws from shovin' this oar."

His companion, a thin-faced weasel, complained, "It ain't right. Ships shouldn't be sailin' through places like this. The sea's the place fer a ship."

Mowlag's stern voice silenced any further complaints. "Save yore breath an' keep goin'. I'm the ship's mate, an' I'm only carryin' out Cap'n's orders. So unless ye wants me t'take the rope's end to yore backs . . ." He left the threat unfinished, knowing it would have the desired result.

Further north, the going was also arduous for Log a Log Dandy and his Guosim crew, travelling along the streams toward the River Moss. Taking only a brief rest for sleep in a side inlet turned out to be an uncomfortable mistake. They were wakened by clouds of midges. Uggo, Posy and Swiffo were forced to leap ashore, besieged by myriads of the tiny insects. The inlet, as it turned out, was a cul-de-sac choked with weeds, mud and stagnant water. Log a Log Dandy and the other shrews were not slow in following their passengers' example—they too jumped ashore and ran. The midges did not stay with them but went back to their creek, the habitat they lived in.

The entire party spent time beating out midges, which had clung to fur, spikes and clothing.

Swiffo spat out a midge. "Phwaw—that wasn't much of a place to catch a nap, was it?"

Dandy merely shrugged. "It happens now an' agin, not t'worry. When we anchored there, we weren't to know. Anyhow, 'tis a fine, bright day an' no real harm done, eh!" He ordered a fire to be lit and materials to be gathered.

Uggo, like the rest, found himself holding a bundle of dead twigs, wet grass and some greenery bound together with bur marigold stems.

Swiffo explained, "This'll drive the midges off so's we can get the logboats back out into clear runnin' water. Cover yore mouth, then light that torch in the fire."

Once the torches had taken light, the Guosim set off back to the brackish inlet in a fog of smoke. Even though Posy had her mouth covered, she soon found herself coughing and pawing at streaming eyes. However, the scheme worked well. Thick smoke soon dispersed the insect hordes, allowing Guosim paddlers to hasten the logboats out into the midstream, and fresh air. Torches sizzled as they were flung into the water.

Uggo splashed fresh water onto his face. "Ugh, I can't stand liddle crawly things!"

Around midday, the stream broadened. On the surface it looked calm, but the boats began moving faster. Little eddies appeared close to the banks.

Posy sat back and relaxed. Dappling sunlight poured through the high foliage of cedar, grey willow and wych elm, flooding the stream with patterns of light and shade. She sighed dreamily. "It's all so peaceful and pretty, isn't it?"

A Guosim paddler, who overheard her, remarked, "Won't be fer long, missy. Sit up straight an' hold on to the boatsides. . . ."

From the lead vessel, Dandy's shout confirmed what he had said. "Belay oars an' wait on my word—rapids comin'!"

Uggo felt the boat jump slightly as an underwater rock ledge scraped its keel. The little flotilla of logboats began picking up speed rapidly, some of them starting to turn sideways. Now Dandy began roaring commands.

"Port now! Back water! Keep 'em head-on to the flow!"

Rocks poked up into view, with white water foaming around them. The banksides rose steeply; ominous sounds of rushing water echoed all round. Shocked by the sudden change, Uggo and Posy clung grimly to the logboat's sides.

Swiffo, however, stood erect, balancing with the aid of his rudder. He seemed to be enjoying the situation. "Don't worry, mates. Makes no difference—sea, river or stream—no two stretches o' water's ever the bloomin' same!"

Log a Log Dandy had to bellow to be heard now. "All paws stroke deep to starboard! Make for the cove ahead. We'll have to beach an' portage!"

Uggo could tell by the urgency of Dandy's voice that they were in trouble. Some of the port shrews joined those on the other side of the boats, adding their paddle power to move across the headlong flow.

Dandy yelled, "Heavin' lines sharp, now—make a chain!"

Sinewy ropes snaked out as prowbeasts and sternbeasts skilfully caught them and tied up, forming the boats into a connected line. Posy saw the cove looming up ahead. It was an arch, scooped out by constant pushing currents. The surface was thick with floating debris—at some point a dead and broken poplar had been swept in there; its branches and shorn trunk poked out of the water.

Dandy slung a heaving line, snagging the trunk. He and two other shrews pulled hard on it, drawing the front logboat into the cove. Some of the other boats were almost swept by, but willing paws hauled on the lines, bringing them to the safety of the cove, where the water was milling in a slow circle, away from the main rushing currents.

Swiffo tied a line around his waist, joined by Uggo, Posy and four Guosim. They scaled the steep, rugged bankside. Once on top, the line was secured around the sturdy trunk of a pine. Half of the Guosim crew climbed up to the summit.

Dobble, the shrew scout, took a few paces to one side. Peering down, he pointed. "Good job we found haven there, mates. Lookit wot we would've run into. Dollrags, that's wot we woulda been ripped into!"

They stared in horror at the scene far below. Cascades of thundering water, mist and a rainbow wreathed around forbidding rocks surrounding a mighty waterfall.

Swiffo chuckled nervously. "Fancy sittin' in a boat an' shootin' down into that lot. Ye'd have no chance!"

Further speculation on what their fate would have been was interrupted by the Guosim Chieftain. "Ahoy! Are ye goin' to stand gawpin' down there all day, or are ye goin' to lend a paw t'get these logboats up?"

It was backbreaking work, hauling six logboats and provisions up to the summit. With aching limbs and paws raw from heaving on ropes, they slumped down to rest after the final boat was up.

Dandy sparked his clogs against a rock, berating them. "Wot's this, floppin' down on yore tails to take a nap? This ain't no pickernick—we got boats to portage. Up on yore hunkers, mates, look lively, now!"

Each crew lifted their logboat, upside down, over their heads. Portaging was no easy chore. With Swiffo and Dobble leading the way down the steep, wooded slope, everybeast followed, scrabbling and scrambling to carry their burden whilst keeping upright. Posy and Uggo brought up the rear, along with some older shrews, all carrying rations and paddles.

The afternoon was far advanced when they reached the bottom. Skirting the falls, they continued, with Dandy jollying them along.

"Come on, me beauties, not far now. No mutterin' from under those boats, d'ye hear!"

Dobble, who had been scouting ahead, returned with heartening news. "Stream's runnin' calm again up ahead, Chief. There's a nice shady bank where we can sit an' take a bite of vittles, aye an' may'aps a swig of shrewbeer, eh?"

Dandy shook his head. "We'll take t'the water if 'tis calm enough. Should be on the River Moss by evenin'—then ye can rest an' feed yore faces all night. So come on, mates, make an effort. Don't be showin' our guests how lazy ye are!" He broke into a song, urging them onward.

"There's always a camp at the end o' the day,
at least that's wot my ole pa used t'say.
Someplace to rest those tired-out paws,
there's noplace like the great outdoors.
Then sling off yore load when we gits there,
throw yore weary bones down any ole where,
plant yoreself there, mate, an' I'll sit 'ere,
an' we'll swig off a tankard o' nice cold beer!

"So tramp tramp tramp, onward to camp,
we'll both find somewheres t'stay,
o'er woodland an' hill keep marchin' until,
'tis the end of a long, dusty day . . . hey hey,
the end of a long, dusty day!"

Although it was a lively tune, Dandy had a dreadful voice. He sang off-key in a croaky tone.

Swiffo smiled politely. "Well, that was a lively ole song, an' no mistake!"

One of the Guosim, Rawkin, murmured out the side of his mouth, so that Dandy would not hear. "Aye, there was nothin' wrong with the song, mate—'twas the singer. Our Log a Log's a champion dancer, an' a great leader, but when he opens his mouth t'sing, it sounds like a score o' frogs bein' pelted with rocks!"

His companion, Banktail, agreed fervently. "I was goin' to say that meself, but I didn't want to 'urt the feelin's of any nearby frogs, mate!"

It was twilight when they reached the navigable section of the stream. Dandy relented, allowing them to cook a meal on the bankside.

"Get a fire goin' there, you cooks. See if'n ye can come up with some good vittles. We'll eat here, then take the stream into the River Moss an' lay up there for the night. Tomorrow we'll be on our way to the ford by dawn."

Even Uggo, who had spent his life eating Redwall fare, had to admit that Guosim cooks could serve up marvellous food. Hungry after the long day's labours, they dined on mushroom and fennel soup and flatbreads baked with cheese and flavoured with wild parsley, followed by a chestnut and acorn roll stuffed with dried plums and apple. There was pennycloud cordial to drink, or some fine pale cider.

Dobble sighed, patting his stomach. "Aaaah, that's the stuff t'feed the tribe!"

One of Dandy's clogs nudged him lightly.

"Now, don't ye think of takin' no after-vittle naps. Douse those fires, mates. All aboard the boats, quick as y'like. I wants t'be on the Moss afore midnight!" As Log a Log, Dandy Clogs brooked no arguments. Shortly thereafter, the logboats were on their way along the stream as twilight turned to dusk.

Posy dozed in the stern of the back boat, but she was aware of the little flotilla entering the main river. The boats eddied in the swirl of changing currents and gurgling waters. Downstream changed to upriver. The paddlers dug deep, though the river was not running at any great speed. They had been travelling awhile when Dandy called out orders.

"String 'em together across the river. Rawkin, Swiffo, moor the lead an' rear craft to those elms. Finished with paddles, mates. Make the most of yore shut-eye—there's another hard day t'come in the morn!"

Roped together and secured to an elm trunk on either bank, the logboats bobbed gently on the darkened river. Within moments, all that could be heard above the water-flow ripple was the snuffling and snoring of exhausted creatures. Everybeast was so wearied that they gave no thought to guards or sentries. After all, what need of keeping watch in mid-river? They slept deeply, every last creature.

Greenshroud came out of the night like a giant predator. The river was wide enough for Razzid to order full sail; she caught the wind from the sea that she had enjoyed earlier that day. The current was gentle. Mowlag was taking a turn around the deck when he discerned the glimmer of a single lantern on the water. As the big vessel closed in over the darkened river, it became clear that several small boats were moored, stem to stern, across the water. It was but the work of a moment for Mowlag to rouse his captain and the vermin crew.

The Wearat felt a shudder of evil joy run through him. This was too good an opportunity to miss, defenceless sleeping creatures with no knowledge of what was about to happen.

Greenshroud struck the rope at its centre, the force ripping both ends from the elm trunks. This left the Guosim logboats trailing both sides of the big ship, being towed upriver. Bleary-eyed shrews, still half asleep, sat up in bewilderment as Razzid Wearat gave his signal for the slaughter to begin.

21

Though he had never been a great walker, Skor Axehound marched doggedly onward alongside Rake Nightfur at the head of the column. It had been a difficult trek; Rake could hear Skor breathing heavily. Accordingly he enquired, "D'ye no' think ye need tae rest awhile, mah friend?"

The sea otter Chieftain replied gruffly, "I don't need any rest. D'you?"

The hare Captain chuckled. "Och, no. Ah'm jist fine, thank ye!"

Skor replied stubbornly, "Well, I'm fine, too, an' I can march just as good as you can, Nightfur!"

Knowing his friend was in a prickly mood, Rake changed the subject by casting a glance at the waning stars. "It'll be dawn soon, Ah'm thinkin'. We'll both rest then."

He was about to say more when Sergeant Miggory called out, "Scouts returnin', sah. May'aps now we'll find 'ow far h'off this bloomin' Moss River we h'are!"

Buff Redspore, with the sea otter trackers, Gil and Dreel, loped out of the half-light. Buff saluted.

"River's through that pine grove an' over a small rise, sah!"

Jum Gurdy nodded to Ruggan. "We'll be there in no time now, matey."

The fine golden mist of a new day touched the eastern treetops as they arrived on the broad banks of the Moss. Lieutenant Scutram inspected the scene. "No signs of comin's or goin's, I fear."

Trug Bawdsley giggled under his breath. "Ships don't often leave blinkin' tracks, do they?"

Corporal Welkin Dabbs commented tersely, "When we want your opinion, young Bawdsley, we'll jolly well ask for it, eh, wot!"

Jum Gurdy spoke his piece. "The young un's right, though, Corp. We don't know whether they've passed 'ere, though mayhaps they've not yet come this far upriver. Wot d'ye think, Skor?"

The burly sea otter leaned on his battleaxe before giving a verdict that everybeast was secretly glad to hear. "I think we should rest, camp an' eat right here. No cookin' fires, though. Then if'n they ain't sailed by us, we'll have to assume they've already passed an' are someplace ahead upriver. Does that suit ye, Rake?"

The tall, dark captain unbuckled both his blades. "Aye, that suits me grand. Ah'm fair starved!"

Jum Gurdy murmured, "If I ever meets a hare who isn't, 'twill be a rare sight. . . ."

Rake overheard the remark. He stared at the otter Cellardog. "Ye were sayin' . . . ?"

Jum replied neatly, "I was just sayin', Cap'n, we ain't had a bite to eat since last night!"

They breakfasted on a make-do assortment of bread, cheese, wild onions, some dried fruit and clear, sweet water from the river. The older creatures took a rest, sunning themselves on the bank. However, the two young sea otter trackers went straight into the water.

Skor smiled at their antics. "Just look at 'em, will ye—an' after a full night's march, wantin' to swim. There's no stoppin' those two scamps."

Dreel waved to him. "Alright if'n we takes a liddle swim upriver, Chief?"

Skor nodded. "Go on, then, but keep yore eyes peeled, an' git back here afore we march on." He turned to Sergeant Miggory. "I've got ten times their strength, but I wishes I had half their energy. Still, that's the price o' gettin' older, eh?"

Miggory gave him a crooked smile. "Yore strong as h'a bloomin' h'oak, sah. That's why yore chieftain of the 'Igh North Coast."

There was no time for him to say any more. Skor took off like an arrow when a horrified shout rang out upriver. Sergeant Miggory was knocked backward as Skor Axehound bulled past him. The chieftain roared as he plunged into the river, "That's one of our scoutmaids!"

Ruggan and a half dozen sea otters dived in after him.

Rake Nightfur called to his Long Patrol hares, "Cover them from the bankside, quick!"

Almost everybeast arrived on the scene together; it was a horrific sight. The broken stern half of a logboat had been grounded in the shallows. Lying in it was a Guosim warrior, pierced through his middle by an oversized arrow.

Skor lifted his scouts, Gil and Dreel, away from the wreckage; he touched the treelike shaft of the arrow. "So, the filthy, murderin' scum have already passed by this way. Rogue Crew, scout upriver—stay armed. Ruggan, see if ye can find anybeast still livin'."

Sergeant Miggory stared grimly at the slain shrew. "Cap'n, this is a bad business!"

Rake issued orders to his sergeant. "Take half the column to cover the otters from the bank. Go with 'em, ye may be able tae help."

By midday the bankside was littered with Guosim, both the dead and the living. Three logboats had been found damaged but intact. The haremaids, Lancejack Sage, Ferrul and Buff Redspore, were assisting Lieutenant Scutram, who had some skill in dealing with wounds. Skor's crew formed the burial detail, digging one long grave on the opposite bank and ferrying the slain across in two logboats.

Rake and Skor were listening to Tibbro, a Guosim maid, who had witnessed everything the previous night. With haunted eyes and a hollow voice, she recounted her ordeal.

"Our crews were all asleep in their boats, strung across the river, moored twixt two trees. It'd been a long, 'ard day, y'see. We was so done in that everybeast went straight t'sleep. Next thing I knows, there's noise, vermin cursin' an' roarin'. Our boats got rammed by a great big ship, one wid sails an' everythin'. I was flung into the river, but there was nothin' I could do but get t'shore. Those vermin, searats an' corsairs, an' one wid a face like a bad dream, wavin' a great fork, a trident, I thinks ye'd call it . . ." Tibbro paused, staring straight ahead, like one in a trance.

Rake had found a flask of pale cider floating on the water. He helped her to sip a few drops. "Aye, go on, lassie. Yore doin' jist fine, tell on."

She continued. "They were pullin' our boats along, either side of their ship. The murderers, stabbin' down with pikes'n'spears, an' shootin' fire arrows into the logboats. Log a Log Dandy an' our Guosim warriors tried to fight back, but they didn't stan' a chance. Three of our boats were blazin', smashed to bits, my friends floatin' facedown in the river, stuck with arrows an' spears. Then the rope holdin' our boats together snapped. The big ship went past us, sailin' upriver. I thought it was over, but then they started firin' arrows, huge things, from a giant bow at their stern end. I could hear them jokin' an' laughin' as those arrows hit our beasts who were tryin' to swim away. One buried itself in the shallows just alongside o' me. I lay flat amidst the reeds an' waited. I think I may've passed out, 'cos next time I looked up, the big ship had gone, sailed off into the night. One of yore otters, a maid called Kite, found me stuck in the mud. She rescued me. That's all I can tell ye!"

Skor Axehound wrapped Tibbro in his cloak. "Ye did well fer a young un, beauty. Rest now, an' don't fret. Those killers will cry tears o' blood when we meet up with 'em. Ye have my oath on that!"

Sergeant Miggory came to Rake's side in a crouching run, hissing a warning. "We got visitors, sah, comin' up be'ind h'us!"

Wordlessly, Rake and Skor signalled their force to spread out and intercept whoever the intruders were.

Notching a shaft to his bow, Ruggan centred on a movement behind some foliage. He was about to loose the arrow when one of the wounded Guosim called out, "Wait, they're friends! It's the Freepaws!"

The tall, silver-furred tail of Rekaby emerged from the undergrowth. The old squirrel came forward with a look of shock and concern on his aged features. "Seasons of sorrow an' disaster, what's taken place here, Axehound?"

Skor explained briefly as he followed Rekaby amongst the wounded Guosim. The old squirrel listened as he inspected the injured creatures before turning his attention to Scutram. "Have ye seen to them all yet?"

The lieutenant shook his head. "Haven't had much time, sah. Huh, ain't got much to jolly well work with either, wot!"

Rekaby nodded. "Not bad work, friend, but ye can leave this to us now. Fiddy, Frudd, Keltu, Laka, get my herbal bag an' see wot ye can do about some dressin's. Search about. I need dockleaves, woodruff, pepperwort, angelica—oh, an' some fumitory for binding an' stitching."

Rekaby addressed Captain Rake. "Have ye any more wounded?"

The tall, dark hare shook his head. "Jist what ye see here, guid sir."

The old squirrel took a quick estimate of the shrews. "It must've been a terrible slaughter. There's only just over half of the Guosim that I met with not long back. No sign of their Log a Log, Dandy Clogs, nor of the two young hogs I left in their care—"

Jum Gurdy interrupted anxiously. "Two young 'ogs, ye say? Was one of 'em called Uggo?"

Rekaby nodded. "Aye, an' his little friend, Posy. I left

226

them with the Guosim—they were goin' to take them to Redwall. Swiffo went of his own accord."

Skor strode forward. "Swiffo, that's the name my youngest son give 'imself. Ye mean he went with the Guosim?"

Dobble, the Guosim scout, sat up, nursing a shoulder wound. "Aye, sire, Swiffo was with us, an' both liddle 'ogs, but I don't see 'em anywheres round 'ere now."

Skor's hefty, gnarled paw tightened around his battleaxe. "If anythin's happened to my young un—"

Before he finished the sentence, his elder son, Ruggan, rushed into the river, brandishing his blade. "Yaylaho, Rogue Crew, let's get after those vermin!"

Hurrying to join them, Skor called to Rake, "Got to go, Nightfur—they might have my young son!"

For a moment Rake looked undecided. There were still many Guosim lying on the bankside in need of help. Rekaby motioned for him to go.

"Nothin' ye can do here, friend. My Fortunate Freepaws can deal with these shrews. Take two logboats an' pursue those evil ones. Good fortune attend ye!"

The old squirrel took Jum Gurdy's paw. "Ye'd best stay here, friend, in case yore two liddle hogs turn up. They could've escaped the attack, y'know."

Jum cast a glance at the sea otter warriors, swimming upriver swiftly, despite the weapons they carried. He saw the Long Patrol, fit young hares, battle ready, launching the two logboats. Suddenly the big Cellardog felt heavy and burdened with long seasons. He sighed. "Aye, mate, yore right. Besides, I couldn't show my face round Redwall without liddle Uggo, or at least some news of him. I'll lend a paw here."

The young squirrel, Laka, presented Jum with the mischievous babe, Wiggles, saying, "I'll start makin' dockleaf poultices. You 'ang on to this un, seein' as yore partial to 'edg'ogs."

Jum smiled at the infant, chucking her under the chin. "Well, ain't you a cute little thing!"

The babe glared up at Jum. "Ain't a cute liddle fing. I'm a Wiggles, y'ole fatty!" She bit Jum's paw, leapt down and sped off along the bank.

Laka nudged Jum. "Well, don't jus' stan' there. Git after 'er—an' be careful, or Wiggles'll bite ye agin!"

The big otter lumbered off along the bank, fervently wishing that he had gone with Skor and Rake. Wiggles shot up a sycamore trunk. She perched on a branch, just out of Jum's reach, swinging her footpaws and giggling. "Heeheehee! Can't get Wiggles, big ole fatty bottom, yore a lardy belly, that's wot yew are. Heeheehee!"

Jum Gurdy began searching for a long stick to dislodge the imp with, muttering to himself, "I've certainly got me work cut out this day!"

22

It was toward evening when the breeze died away. Mowlag glanced at the limp green sails, stating the obvious to his captain. "Wind's gone, Cap'n. We're startin' to drift astern with the current."

Razzid leaned on his trident, replying with mock surprise, "Really? Is that a fact. Wot d'ye suggest we do, bucko?"

The searat took a backward pace, answering lamely, "Break out the paddles an' get the crew t'work?"

Not dignifying the suggestion with a comment, the Wearat turned away. Brushing away a midge that was crawling close to his good eye, he stumped off wordlessly to his cabin. Mowlag sighed with relief, then began yelling out orders.

"Furl all sails an' lower 'em! Break out the oars an' git pullin' 'er upriver! Can't ye see we're drifting back'ards? C'mon, shift yore idle carcasses!"

From the mast, the keen-eyed stoat on lookout yelled down, "Ahoy, do I stop up 'ere, or do I start furlin' sail?"

Mowlag glared up at the stoat. "Git down 'ere, right now!"

With no prior warning, the stoat came down to the deck, plunging from the masthead with an arrow through his throat.

"Yaaaah!" Jiboree yelled in horror as he left the tiller, rushing to Mowlag, who stood with the dead lookout lying next to his footpaws. "Yaaaah! All paws on deck—we're under attack! All paws on deck!"

There was a confusion of vermin running about carrying long oars whilst others dropped from the half-furled sails.

Razzid Wearat stumped out on deck, brandishing his trident. "Wot'n the name o' blood'n'Hellgates is goin' on 'ere?" He turned, his face almost colliding with Jiboree as the weasel continued bawling.

"Yaaaah, did ya see that? We're bein' attacked. Lookit that! 'E's dead!"

Razzid blenched from the weasel's foul breath as he pushed him aside. "Attacked? Attacked by whom?"

He grabbed Shekra, who was looking stunned. She stammered, "I dunno, but somebeast just killed the lookout, Cap'n."

Roughly shoving the vixen from him, Razzid grabbed the unattended tiller, roaring out to both banks, "Come an' show yoreself if'n ye wants a battle!"

Thunk! A slingstone whacked him on the side of his jaw. Clapping a paw to his face, he hastened back to his cabin, dribbling blood as he spat out a broken fang. "Jiboree, git yoreself back at the tiller! Mowlag, find who's attackin' us an' rip 'em apart, d'ye hear me?"

Doing his best to look efficient, the searat tugged his ear in salute. "I'll take a party ashore, Cap'n'."

Whirling around in his cabin doorway, Razzid snarled, "Stay aboard, fool. Don't leave my ship unguarded!"

A searat named Dirgo answered, "But wot'll we do, Cap'n? Yaaaaargh!"

An arrow zipped out of the twilight, pinning Dirgo's left footpaw to the deck. The crew began milling about willy-nilly.

Razzid bellowed furiously, "Stand fast, all of ye! Mowlag, post six crew with bows'n'arrers to port an' starboard.

Shoot at anythin' that moves! The rest of ye, pick up those oars an' get us outta here! Those are my orders—now jump to 'em!"

The archers stood ready speedily, shafts nocked to bow-strings, but they were handicapped by two things, the onset of darkness and the lack of anything to direct arrows at. As the rowers began punting *Greenshroud* upriver with their long oars, a hail of slingstones rattled at them from the surrounding woodlands. A searat screamed as he was struck in the eye, another was knocked cold by a random head shot.

Mowlag grabbed a bow and arrow from a weasel corsair. "Right, where are they? Just let 'em show their faces an' I'll put a stop to 'em! Come out an' face me, if'n ye dare!"

A chunk of wet wood, a broken sycamore branch, came boomeranging out of the dusk, cracking him across the shoulders. Mowlag's bow accidentally discharged its shaft; it pierced the ear of the weasal corsair he had taken it from.

Shekra yelled at the archers, "Shoot! Loose those arrows, don't just stand there with yore bows bent!"

As the archers fired, each in a different direction, the vixen was suddenly taken with an idea.

Drogbuk Wiltud was still sitting tied to the base of the mainmast. Shekra untied him. Forming the rope into a noose, she tightened it about his neck. Throwing the other end over a jib, she hauled tight, shouting at the same time to the invisible assailants, "You out there, we've got one o' yores, a woodlander! One more arrow, slingstone or stick from ye, an' I'll hang this 'edgepig. D'ye hear?"

Drogbuk was squealing and sobbing as he teetered on tippaws, held there by the noose. "Mercy! Don't attack or they'll 'ang me—guuuuurgh!"

No more missiles came out of the darkened greenery. There was a mere rustle of foliage, then silence fell.

Shekra held on to the rope, smirking at Mowlag. "Hah, that did the trick, eh?"

Badtooth, the greasy weasel cook, ventured out of his

galley. "Aye, it worked well enough, fox. But keep heavin' on yonder rope an' ye'll finish that ole 'og off. Then where'll we be?"

Razzid took advantage of the cease-fire, coming out on deck. "Smart thinkin', Shekra. Ye did well, but Badtooth's right, ye'd best loosen the rope afore that drunken ole fool dies."

Drogbuk wheezed a gurgling sigh as his footpaws fell flat upon the deck, then he seemed to collapse in a heap.

Shekra called the cook, "Badtooth, keep an eye on this un."

The greasy weasel sat down with his back against the mast. "Huh, 'e ain't goin' noplace. Looks arf dead t'me!"

The words had scarce left his lips when Drogbuk sprang nimbly up, ducked out of the noose, and jumped overboard. He went under and never surfaced. The archers shot a volley of arrows into the river, with no results.

Rizzad snarled at them, "Don't waste shafts. The drunken ole sot's prob'ly pike food by now. Stow those weapons an' get on the oars with yore mates. When we're clear of the area, ye can rest. Shekra, Mowlag, stay alert. If'n ye spy anythin' that looks like a ford, report t'me."

Probing the broken tooth with a blunt claw, the Wearat sought his cabin.

Greenshroud moved on upriver. Spitting water and trying to shake river mud from his rattly old spikes, Drogbuk staggered upright, shielded by reeds. He shook a clenched paw as the ship vanished round a bend.

"Gurrrraaah, ye murderin' blaggards! Ye lard-gutted, stinky-bottomed, scabby-tailed, wall-eyed, dirty-lugged, misbegotten sons o' hags—"

A sturdy young paw pulled him out onto the bank. "Yore frightenin' the fishes wid language like that, Granpa. Give yore ole tongue a rest!"

Drogbuk gave Swiffo a curious stare. "Wot's a wavedog doin' round 'ere? Who are ye, eh?"

A Guosim maid passed him a pawful of dry moss to wipe

his eyes clean. "We could ask you the same question, old-spikes. Wot were you doin' aboard a vermin ship?"

Drogbuk began to explain. "I was tricked aboard. They said they was friends goin' t'visit Redwall. . . ."

He broke off to gaze around the half score of beasts surrounding him before continuing stubbornly, "But that's my bizness, not your'n. Er, ye haven't got a drop of grog about ye? Me throat's hurtin' from that rope, an' I needs grog to ease it off!"

Log a Log Dandy Clogs snorted scornfully. "Huh, I'll wager ye do, but we ain't on a picnic, so we're not carryin' grog. That ship's wot we're after, aye, an' every scurvy vermin aboard of it. Once the ship's sunk an' everybeast of its crew knockin' on the doors o' Hellgates, then ye can drink grog 'til ye don't know if'n 'tis summer or sumplace. Posy, Uggo, will ye watch out for this ole swillbelly?"

It lacked about three hours to dawn when Razzid gave the order to stow oars. At this point the River Moss flowed through a wide watermeadow. The Wearat took a good look about.

"Aye, this'll do, Shekra. No tree cover, so we can see any attack comin'. Mowlag, set two lookouts at the masthead, two on the prow, an' another two astern. Relieve 'em every hour. The rest can sleep awhile. Drop anchor!"

Jiboree sat sleeping, seated on a keg, with his head resting on the tiller. The watermeadow was a silent, fragrant area, dotted with waterlilies, bulrushes, sundew and pink flowering comfrey. Now and then the splash of a roach, or rudd, could be heard as fish flopped momentarily to the surface. Predawn birdsong trilled faintly on the still air. Jiboree snuffled, moving his head against the tiller, to seek a cosier position. The tiller arm yawled wide, leaving him sprawled on the deck. The weasel rose grumpily as the tiller came back the other way, knocking him flat once more. He grabbed the long wooden arm, expecting to steady it, but it swung loosely. Too loosely.

Mowlag growled irately as Jiboree shook him awake. "Wot is it now? Can't a beast git no rest on this ship?"

The weasel kept his voice low. "There's summat amiss wid the tiller, mate. Come an' take a look!"

Mowlag pushed the unresisting tiller back and forth, noting that the vessel did not respond. He passed it back to Jiboree.

"Keep wigglin' it back'n'forth while I takes a look." Leaning out over the stern rail, Mowlag's shouts roused the ship. "Blood'n'thunder, we ain't got a bloomin' rudder!"

Jiboree looked blankly at the mate. "Wotjer mean, we ain't got a rudder?"

Mowlag roared in Jiboree's face, covering him in spittle. "Wotjer think I mean, knot'ead? The rudder's gone, we ain't got a rudder! Ye'd better go an' tell the cap'n!"

The weasel wiped his face with a grimy paw, then laughed drily. "Not me. Yore the ship's mate—you go an' tell 'im!"

"Tell him wot?"

They both turned to see Razzid bearing down on them. Mowlag gulped nervously, stumbling over his words. "Grudder's on, I mean the rudder's gone . . . sir."

The Wearat tested the tiller before peering over the stern. "Gone? 'Ow could a rudder just go—where is it now, eh?"

"There 'tis, just off the port bow, Cap'n!" A searat called Dirgo stood on the midship rail, pointing. "Somebeast's pushin' it away—a riverdog, I think 'tis!"

As if to absolve himself, Mowlag jumped up alongside Dirgo, shielding his eyes with a paw as he sighted the rudder being pushed away through the watermeadow by Swiffo. "That ain't no waterdog, it's a wavedog!"

Razzid thundered amidships, dealing Mowlag a smack with the haft of his trident, which sent him overboard. "I don't care wot sorta beast it is—stop it makin' off with my rudder. Go on!"

He turned on the crew. "Get some bows'n'arrers. See if'n ye can't get 'im afore Mowlag does. Look sharp now!"

Swiffo was forced to abandon the rudder as arrows began raining down on the watermeadow. He dived, swimming sleekly off underwater. Having no aquatic skills whatsoever, Mowlag was forced into an awkward dog paddle.

Shekra threw him one end of a long heaving line. "Tie this to the rudder so as we can pull it aboard. Grip it in yore mouth. Go on, you can do it!"

Mowlag spluttered, spitting out water and pondweed as he gasped, "I don't know if I kin make it!"

Razzid called out a callous reply. "Either get that rudder or drown, 'cos ye ain't comin' back t'the ship without it!"

Swiffo surfaced, wading through the shallows to where his friends were waiting. Dandy and Posy helped him to the bank.

Swiffo shrugged ruefully. "I nearly made it. Still, it'll take 'em some time to get their rudder back in place. The ship's too far off for us to do anythin' at the moment."

Log a Log Dandy clenched his paws, growling, "If only I had just one good logboat an' a Guosim crew, I'd soon do somethin' about it, on me oath I would!"

Tibbro climbed up into the low branches of a grey willow. "I think they've got a rope around the rudder. I can see 'em pullin' it back to their ship. How long d'ye think it'll take 'em to fix it, Swiffo?"

The young sea otter shook his head. "Not long, matey. The rudder only slots through an iron pin. I took that out an' flung it away. Soon as they get another they'll be on their way back to the river."

Uggo gnawed on some wild ramsons that he had dug up. "No sense in us makin' a move 'til they do, I suppose."

One of the shrews, a tough-looking beast called Frabb, fanned a paw across his nose to avoid the rancid odour of wild garlic coming from Uggo's mouth. "Phwaw! If'n yew don't stop chewin' that stuff, I'll chuck ye in the water, mate!"

Old Drogbuk took the stalks from Uggo and munched on

them avidly. "Huh, yore a picknickerty sort fer a Guosim warrior. Nowt wrong wid ramsons, they're good for ye— 'ere, try some."

Everybeast moved further down the bank, distancing themselves from Uggo and Drogbuk.

Mowlag and Jiboree clung to the stern, following their captain's directions.

"Hold the rudder in place. Up a bit, now a touch port. That's it—keep it still now, right there."

He confiscated the spear that a nearby ferret was holding. Hefting the weapon, Razzid admired it. "Ain't often ye see a full metal spear. 'Tis a nice piece."

The ferret gazed anxiously at his prized spear. "Aye, Cap'n, 'tis solid bronze. Belonged to me ole father."

With a final remark, the Wearat turned his back on the ferret: "It'll make a good rudder pin."

He leaned over the stern, tapping both Mowlag and Jiboree on the head with the bronze spearbutt. "Dolts, I told ye to hold the rudder steady. Now lift up a bit. Right, press inward. . . . There!"

He slotted the spear haft neatly into place.

"Shekra, try the tiller, wave it back'n'forth."

The vixen obeyed dutifully. Razzid smiled.

"Good as new. Better, in fact—bronze don't rust in water! Git aboard, you two, an' get the sails rigged. We can't lie about here forever!"

Having unsuccessfully tried to halt *Greenshroud*'s progress, Swiffo sat on the margin of the watermeadow with Posy and the small band of Guosim. The resourceful shrews had put together a makeshift snack from whatever they could forage from the locality. Uggo and Drogbuk were temporarily banned from the company, owing to the fact they were still munching on the malodorous ramsons. Posy was nibbling on some mushrooms and young dandelion buds. When she noticed that the shrew Chieftain was not wearing his famed Dandy Clogs, she commented on this.

"What happened to your nice shoes, Dandy?"

The Log a Log answered tersely, "They weren't shoes, missy. They was proper Dandy Clogs, the sort champion dancers wears. I don't know wot 'appened to 'em for certain, an' I ain't too bothered about it. Wot grieves me is the loss of so many of my mates." His jaw tightened, and his voice shook as he spoke. "All them good Guosim warriors, ambushed, murdered, by those vermin scum. Well, I'll even the score, I tell ye. We won't rest 'til we can dance on their graves, every last mother's son o' the cowardly butchers!"

Uggo came wandering along the bank with some information. "Could see the green ship from where me'n the old un was. Looks like she's movin' off agin. Thought ye should know."

Jumping upright, Dandy scattered food left and right. He seized a Guosim rapier he had found. "Movin' off, is it? I'll show 'em there's noplace they can go without me on their tails. Come on, mates!"

"Hah, do ye think that's the right way t'go about it, me bold bucko? Ye'll end up chasin' yore own tails!"

Drogbuk had ambled up. He stood shaking his head at Dandy. "T'aint the way I'd do it."

The Guosim Log a Log brushed by Drogbuk, almost knocking him over. "Out o' me way, ole rattlespikes!"

Swiffo held up his paw, halting the shrews. "Wait, let's see wot the old un would do. Go on, mate, speak yore piece!"

One of the shrews, Banktail, muttered scornfully, "Huh, I wouldn't pay no 'eed t'that ole grogsnout."

Drogbuk drew himself up, eyeing Banktail haughtily. "Now, you lissen t'me, young blabbermouth. I'm a diff'rent 'og now. Aye, I've sworn never to drink grog ever agin. So I'm thinkin' clearer now, an' I thinks I've got a lot more seasons' wisdom about me than anybeast 'ere."

Dandy swished his rapier impatiently. "Well, out with it, Granpa, let's 'ear some o' this wisdom."

The ancient hedgehog gestured toward the vermin ship.

"That'll reach the River Moss long afore you do, 'cos it don't 'ave t'go round the long way, skirtin' this watermeadow like us. Besides, if'n ye do catch it up, wot are ye goin' t'do, eh?"

Dandy swiped at the grass with his blade. "We're goin' t'slay 'em, that's wot!"

Drogbuk chuckled drily. "Brave words, friend, but the vermin outnumber ye about a score to one. Oh, I'll grant ye could pick one or two off, like I've seen ye do. But these are corsairs'n'searats. They ain't led by a stoopid beast. If'n the mood took yon Wearat, he'd track ye down an' finish ye one by one."

Dobble, the Guosim scout, called impatiently, "You ain't told us yore plan yet, old un!"

Drogbuk snapped back at him, "Then give me a blinkin' chance, fatmouth! Lissen now, we know the vermin are goin' to try an' conquer Redwall. So, if'n we can get there afore 'em, we can warn those Redwallers an' be ready for the foebeasts when they arrive."

Swiffo could not help cutting in eagerly. "He's right, y'know! In a stone fortress, backed up by the Redwall beasts, we'd stand a much better chance o' winnin' agin the vermin. Wot d'ye say, Dandy?"

The Log a Log sighed. "Maybe so, but how are we goin' t'get to Redwall faster than them? I ain't even sure o' the way widout a logboat, an' they've got a ship on wheels."

Drogbuk winked craftily. "Ahah, but I knows the way to that Abbey, I've been there a few times in my seasons. I knows a shortcut, too, if'n yore willin' t'take the chance—"

Uggo interrupted. "W'ot's so chancey about a shortcut?"

The old hedgehog shrugged. "Nothin' if'n ye ain't scared o' snakes, toads an' lizards—aye, an' a band o' foxes."

Swiffo placed a paw about Drogbuk's shoulders, exclaiming airily, "Hah, is that all? Then lead on, ole matey!"

The very mention of snakes caused the Guosim to hesitate, for the simple reason that most shrews fear nothing more than serpents.

Dandy shook a paw in Drogbuk's face. "An' yore certain that it's a shortcut that'll get us to Redwall faster than the vermin crew?"

A few spikes rattled onto the bankside as Drogbuk nodded. "Sure, fer certain, an' that certain sure!"

Posy set an example by putting her best paw forward. "Well, that's good enough for me, sir. I'm game to try!"

Swiffo grinned at the apprehensive Guosim shrews. "I 'ope yore not goin' t'be shown up by a liddle 'ogmaid!"

Dandy trembled as if fit to burst as he roared at his warriors, "Nobeast shows up a Guosim—we're with ye. Up off yore tails, you lot. Let's march!"

They set off with Posy and Uggo either side of Drogbuk in the lead.

Uggo smiled as he whispered to his pretty friend, "Well said, Posy. That moved 'em!"

Posy answered unsmilingly, "I hope I haven't moved us into something that'll see us as snakefood!"

23

Jum Gurdy wandered amongst the injured Guosim on the streambank, looking for new arrivals. The old squirrel Rekaby and his band of Fortunate Freepaws were doing a fine job treating wounded shrews. Foober the squirrelmaid knew what Jum was looking for. She shook her head sympathetically at him.

"Yore liddle 'ogfriends ain't showed up, Mister Gurdy. I think we've seen the last of the beasts wanderin' in now."

Redwall's big old Cellardog heaved a weary sigh. "Thankee, miss. I was tryin' not t'give up hope of seein' Posy an' Uggo, but it looks like they ain't about to turn up 'ere. Where could those young uns 'ave got to?"

Foober noticed that the infant hog was no longer with Jum. She reproached him mildly. "Wot 'appened to baby Wiggles? Weren't ye in charge of 'er?"

Jum waved his rudder toward a huge sycamore. "The liddle scamp'll be up there. Who taught a hogbabe to climb like a squirrel, I'd like to know?"

Foober carried on splinting a shrew's footpaw. "Sorry. That was me." She shouted toward the sycamore, "Wiiiigggglllleeeesss! Git down 'ere right now, or I'll skelp yore behind!"

The upper branches shook, then Wiggles's head appeared amidst the foliage—she was giggling.

"Heeheehee! No, no, not 'til ole fattydog comes up t'get me!"

Jum shrugged at Foober. "The scamp knows I can't climb trees. Leave 'er. When she's hungry, she'll come down."

However, Foober was made of sterner stuff. Passing Jum a bandage, she leapt up. "You carry on bindin' this splint, Mister Gurdy. I'll see t'that cheeky wretch afore she's much older!"

With a bound, the squirrelmaid was up the sycamore trunk, vanishing into the foliage. There was a sudden rustle of leaves, followed by squeaks of dismay.

"Yeeeeek! Leggo a Wiggles! I only a likkle babe, y'know!"

In the blink of an eye, Foober dropped from the lower boughs with Wiggles firmly in her paws. She was outraged at being captured so easily.

"Leggo of Wiggles or I bite ya wiv me sharp likkle teefs!"

But Foober had other ideas. Grabbing a pawful of bandages and a splint, she went to work on Wiggles.

She liked the idea of the swing Foober rigged up for her on a low bough. But she soon began squealing when the squirrelmaid bound her to it with the bandages. Wiggles's tiny paws kicked helplessly in all directions.

"Yeeeek! 'Elp me—get Wiggles down, ole Rekbee, 'elp!"

Rekaby took an extra length of bandage, shaking it at Wiggles. "One more squeak out of ye, liddle curmudgeon, an' I'll gag ye, an' that's a promise!"

Wiggles took the threat to heart and hung there scowling darkly in silence.

Rekaby watched Jum trying to bind the splint, smiling at his efforts. "Finish off that dressin', Foober. Friend Jum's a bit lackadaisical at dressin's."

He took Jum to one side. "Can I 'ave a word with ye, mate?"

The big otter nodded. "Have as many words as ye like."

Rekaby patted Jum's back. "Good, now how's this for an idea. I know yore still hopin' that Uggo'n'Posy are still alive. So am I. So if'n they ain't turned up 'ere, they've prob'ly carried on tryin' to find their way to Redwall. Would ye agree with that?"

Jum nodded. "Aye, I would, old un, but 'ow can we do anythin' about that?"

The silver-furred squirrel explained, "Well, it looks like everybeast is bound for Redwall. Sea otters, hares, mebbe any Guosim who escaped the slaughter an' those vermin with their ship on wheels, curse their rotten 'ides! So, we've got a logboat left to us by Cap'n Rake. Why don't we travel to Redwall as well? I'll send Fiddy'n'Frudd for the rest o' my bunch, we'll rest up today an' start tomorrow. I'll load the worst-injured Guosim into the logboat an' we'll tow it from the banks."

Jum liked the idea. "Aye that'd work, an' may'aps when we gets t'the Abbey we'll find Uggo'n'Posy are already there."

Rekaby winked at Jum. "'Twouldn't surprise me."

Foober looked up from her work. "Skor Axe'ound an' Cap'n Rake might've found yore two 'ogs by now. I wonder if they've caught up with the vermins' ship yet."

At that very moment, Skor was fishing a deadbeast from the river a league or two upstream.

Lieutenant Scutram leaned out from the prow of a logboat. "Not one of ours, eh, sah?"

The sea otter Chieftain heaved the carcass up onto the bank with his axeblade, commenting gruffly, "A vermin, dead stoat. Arrowshaft clean through his neck. Wot d'ye make o' this, Ruggan?"

His eldest son inspected the arrow closely. "Guosim shrew, I'd say. Good shot, from someplace up in a tree, judging by the angle."

Rake called from the prow of his logboat, "Yonder's another, Ah'd say. Can ye reach him, Sarn't?"

Miggory trapped the second vermin with his paddle. "H'it looks like h'a searat t'me. Got no arrers in 'im, though."

Buff Redspore seized the searat's tail, hauling it round so she could view it. Buff gave a prompt verdict. "Slingstone got this villain—right through the eye, wot!" She released the tail disgustedly. "Savages! Don't they ever bury their slain comrades, wot?"

Rake chuckled mirthlessly. "Och, Ah'd like tae see mair o' the rascals floatin' round. So, et looks like we've got some Guosim allies, eh?"

Gil and Dreel, who had taken to the bankside, called out their findings. "Tracks here, Lord, looks like them."

"Aye, 'bout somewheres over half a score, mostly shrews, but there are two pair o' hedgepig prints an' one that belongs to a sea otter, sire."

Skor gave a great rough laugh. "Hohoho! That'll be my young bucko. I'd wager he was the slingstone thrower, eh, eh, hohoho!"

Rake motioned both logboats to the bank. "Buff, go with those two Rogue Crew trackers. We'll bide here awhile. Find where the tracks go an' report back tae me. Off ye go, now!"

There was not even time to sit and enjoy a snack. The trackers returned in a surprisingly short time. Buff Redspore, who was by far the superior trail reader of the trio, made a prompt report to Rake and Skor.

"Shrews must be followin' the confounded vermin ship, sah. No signs of either, but by the condition o' the ground thereabouts, I'd say there was a jolly old watermeadow not too far away. P'raps we'll catch 'em up there, wot!"

Rake helped Buff back into the logboat.

"Aye, 'tis likely we may. Time tae get underway again."

Some of the Rogue Crew took to the water, whilst others trotted along on either bank. Sergeant Miggory stretched out in the stern of a logboat, trailing his paw in the river. "This beats marchin' h'into a cocked 'at. C'mon, you layabouts, get paddlin'. Don't stray h'into rough waters, now. Stay in the nice, smooth bits."

Big Drander splashed out with his paddle, soaking the colour sergeant. He apologised, grinning from ear to ear. "I say, Sarn't, sorry about that, me jolly old paddle slipped. Didn't get too wet, did ye?"

Miggory held a paw toward Drander. "I dunno—tell me wot you think, big feller."

Drander stood awkwardly, reaching out to touch the sergeant's paw. As he did, a quick flick from Miggory toppled him into the river. Miggory watched as his comrades rescued Drander.

"Ho, sorry h'about that, young sah, me jolly h'old paw slipped. Didn't get too wet, did ye, wot?"

Drander was hauled aboard, muttering, "Couldn't get much bloomin' wetter, could I?"

Corporal Welkin Dabbs winked at the big young hare. "A lesson learned is knowledge gained, doncha know!"

They reached the watermeadow in the early evening. Trackers were sent out again as Ruggan scanned the surface. He picked up an arrow.

"This is a vermin shaft, an' here's another. Looks like they were gettin' a few shots off at the shrews."

Buff Redspore fished out a third searat arrow. "Seems they didn't have much blinkin' luck. There's no dead Guosim, or even bloodtrail on the banks. Anyhow, the *Greenshroud's* left here, carried on back to the jolly old River Moss, if ye ask me."

Skor scratched his matted beard. "Right, but where've the shrews an' that son o' mine got to?"

Rake Nightfur offered an explanation. "They're bound tae follow the ship, but with nae boats, they'll have tae go the long way around, by the bank."

Skor waded ashore. "Yore right. I say we follow 'em."

Sergeant Miggory nodded. "Good idea, sah. We might even catch up with the Guosim at the river. Then we could join forces h'an' give those vermin wot for, eh!"

It appeared to be a good plan, with both hares and otters in agreement. They set off along the watermeadow fringes, following the trail, which began to lead inland. Instead of abandoning the two logboats, they took turns to portage them.

Trug Bawdsley murmured to Flutchers, "Actually, this don't look like the way to the bloomin' river t'me, wot. Where d'ye suppose we're goin'?"

Corporal Welkin tweaked his ear from behind, reminding him sternly, "Yore bally well goin' where the officers tell ye to go, Bawdsley, so save yore blinkin' breath!"

Flutchers came to his friend's defence. "I say, steady on, Corp. All old Trug was sayin' was that if we're jolly well headin' inland, then there ain't much flamin' chance we're goin' t'bump into a bloomin' boat, now, is there, wot?"

Welkin Dabbs tweaked Flutchers's ear, though not too hard. "It's a ship, Flutchers, a ship, not a blinkin' boat. I'll tell ye somethin' else, laddie buck—it's a ship with four wheels. So why shouldn't we bump into it, eh?"

Trug came back smartly, "Because we've got three good trackers with us, an' not one of 'em's reported a single bally wheelmark, that's why!"

Captain Rake saved the corporal's face by upbraiding all three. "Och, will ye no' stop janglin' like two auld mouse biddies at a tea party? Eyes front, now, an' lips sealed, ye ken?"

Trug and Flutchers replied as one. "Sah!"

However, in the light of what Trug had said about the lack of wheeltracks, the dark-furred captain was beginning to have his doubts about the scheme.

24

It was a hot, still afternoon. The Moss was at a point where it flowed sluggishly. *Greenshroud* crewbeasts poled lethargically against the slow current. The ship was hardly moving as searats and corsairs watched a variety of water insects skimming the surface in the more tranquil areas. Lacewings, dragonflies, alderflies and pondskaters moved gracefully about.

Redtail, a corsair stoat, pointed at a big green-and-black-banded dragonfly hovering close to the prow.

"Ahoy, mates, lookit that un, 'e's a big ole thing, ain't 'e?"

Suddenly the water exploded as a huge green-gold fish powered itself out of the river, took the dragonfly in a lightning snap of its jaws and vanished swiftly back underwater.

Redtail was astounded. "Blood'n'tripes, wot was that thing?"

Dirgo, a lean searat, knew. "That's a pikefish, mate. I've 'eard 'em called the freshwater shark. Haharr! Ye wouldn't like to go swimmin' round 'ere now, would ye?"

Mowlag waved a rope's end at the talkers. "This ship ain't movin' while yew lot are blatherin' an' watchin' flies. So let's see ye puttin' a bit o' paw power into things. Come on, now, don't make me use this rope's end on ye. Push! Pull!"

The crew obeyed. *Greenshroud* inched forward, then stopped. One or two beasts were pushing so hard that their oars bent and twanged back again.

Mowlag scowled. "Well, wot is it now, eh?"

Redtail shrugged. "I dunno—the ship ain't movin, that's all."

Mowlag hailed Jiboree, who was steersbeast. "Is it that tiller agin? 'As it broke?"

The weasel tapped a paw upon the tiller arm. "Nowt wrong wid 'er tiller, mate. Why've we stopped?"

"Aye, why have we stopped?"

Razzid had come out of his cabin. Leaning on his trident, he glared from one face to the other, stopping at Mowlag. From the smouldering look in the Wearat's eye, it was obvious that no excuse would be brooked. His voice was dangerously harsh. "Go an' see why we've stopped!"

Mowlag hesitated, then went to the midship rail and peered over. "Er . . . er. . . can't see nothin' wot's stoppin' 'er, Cap'n. . . ."

The butt of Razzid's trident hit Mowlag in the back, sending him into the river.

Razzid roared, "Now take a proper look! Why ain't we movin'?"

Mowlag shot out of the water with panicked haste. He stood shivering, tugging his ear in furious salute. "Wheel, Cap'n. . . . Er, back wheel portside run afoul of underwater roots an' rocks, Cap'n—it's jammed, I think."

Crewbeasts slumped against their paddles, one murmuring wearily, "Ships wid wheels ain't no use at all."

It was a searat named Dirgo who made the remark. He suddenly found himself the object of his captain's attention.

Razzid looked him up and down, enquiring, "Do ye carry a blade?"

Dirgo touched the hilt of one which was stowed through his belt. "Just this un, Cap'n. 'Tis a dirk."

Razzid cast a glance at a ferret corsair. "Lend me that cutlass yore carryin'."

Wordlessly he accepted the heavy cutlass. His eye continued roving. "Anybeast got a good spear? Splitears, yores'll do, give it to Dirgo."

The searat took Splitears's spear and also the cutlass, which Razzid passed to him. Dirgo shook his head, a sob entering his voice. "Aaah no, Cap'n, please—not me!"

Razzid levelled the trident prongs at his throat. "Git over the side an' free that wheel."

Dirgo wailed pitifully, "But, Cap'n, there's a giant pikefish in there. I seen it meself!"

Razzid nodded, speaking reasonably. "But ye might free the wheel an' stay clear o' the pikefish. So wot'll it be, take a chance with a fish, or get my trident through yer neck for a certainty? Mowlag, Jiboree, 'elp our mate Dirgo to git 'is paws wet in the river."

The pair grabbed the hapless searat and flung him over the side. He had time for only one scream, then went under. The crew crowded the rails, watching Dirgo, who could be clearly seen underwater. Making his way to the fouled wheel, he hacked at the subterranean tree root, which had somehow become entangled with the part where axle connects with hub.

Dirgo strove at the task, cutting two deep slashes into the fibrous root before having to surface for a breath.

Redtail winked at him. "Yore doin' alright, matey, keep goin'. Ain't no sign o' the pikefish. Think it might o' gone downriver."

Dirgo felt heartened. "I'll soon git 'er free, Cap'n!"

Razzid actually smiled. "Cask o' grog for ye if'n ye do."

The searat dived back to his chore with a will.

Nobeast saw the pike arrive; it hit Dirgo like a thunderbolt. The vicious serrated rows of the predator's teeth locked fast in the back of the searat's neck. It shook him like a sodden rag. Dirgo was totally helpless in the huge fish's ferocious jaws. The crew watched the macabre scene from the rails, shouting out in horror as the water crimsoned with their messmate's blood.

Razzid however, seemed fascinated with the gory spectacle. He called to Shekra, "D'ye think that pikefish is the only one around?"

The vixen turned her face from the awful sight. "It must be. A pike that size would rule this stretch o' river, Cap'n."

Nobeast was expecting what came next. The Wearat cast off his cloak and leapt into the river, brandishing his trident, laughing wildly.

"Hahaaarrhahaharrr!"

He lunged at the pike, sending the three-pronged fork plunging into its flank. The fish released its prey, writhing madly, then went limp.

Mowlag and Jiboree were standing by to help their captain aboard. He emerged dripping, a hideous grin on his face. "Haharr, I just caught meself a monster pikefish!"

Shekra congratulated him. "Oh, well done, Lord. 'Twas a brave thing to do—no otherbeast would have dared it!"

Razzid was still laughing as he shook water from himself. "Aye, but t'do somethin' like that, ye need good bait. Ole Dirgo came in useful, didn't 'e?"

There was a shocked silence when the vermin crew realised that Razzid had deliberately sent Dirgo to his death.

Donning his cloak, the Wearat continued callously, "Nobeast but me could've done that. Mowlag, send some o' these layabouts down t'get my trident back, aye, an' tell 'em to deliver my pikefish t'the cook. I never tasted pikefish afore. 'Ave Badtooth bring it t'my cabin when it's roasted. Oh, an' get that wheel freed so we can get underway agin!"

He retired to his cabin, from where everybeast could hear him laughing and imitating Dirgo. "Ships wid wheels ain't no use at all—hahahaaarrr! Wheels or not, Dirgo, no ship's any use to ye now, mate! Hahahaaarrr! Looks like I won the keg o' grog!"

None of the crew shared the joke. They hung about on deck, casting sullen glances at the captain's cabin.

Wigsul, a corsair weasel, gnawed at a dirty pawnail. "Nobeast deserves t'die like pore Dirgo did."

Jiboree drew him to one side, whispering a caution. "Careful that Mowlag or Shekra don't 'ear ye say that, mate."

A nearby searat's lips scarcely moved as he interrupted. "Wigsul's right, though, ain't 'e? Sendin' a crewmate t'be slayed like that, just so Razzid could eat roast fish fer dinner—it ain't right, I tell ye!"

Growls of agreement came from several others who had heard the searat.

Jiboree nodded, then turned back to his tiller. "Stow it. 'Ere comes Mowlag."

The mate joined Jiboree at the tiller, remarking, "Ole Cooky's galley's scarce big enough to roast that fish. The wheel's free now. C'mon, buckoes, back t'yer paddles—there's still a bit o' daylight left."

Jiboree leaned close to Mowlag, lowering his voice. "Some o' the crew reckon 'twas a wrong thing the cap'n did to Dirgo—"

Mowlag enquired sharply, "Who were they? Wot's their names?"

Jiboree spat expertly over the rail into the river. "Couldn't tell, really. Just a general sort o' mutter."

Mowlag drew a dagger, pointing it directly at Jiboree. "Lissen t'me, bucko. We both serves Razzid Wearat, see? So if'n ye catch any o' this crew mutterin' agin 'im, then let me know sharpish, an' they'll be dealt wid as mutineers, an' ye know wot that means?"

Frowning seriously, Jiboree patted Mowlag's paw. "Don't fret, matey. I'll tell ye if'n any o' this lot even looks like they're thinkin' o' mutterin'. Leave it t'me, I'll sort 'em out!"

Mowlag stalked off, glaring about at all and sundry.

Once he was out of earshot, Jiboree nodded to Wigsul. "See wot I mean? We'll have t'watch that un!"

"Aye, if'n ye don't, you'll all end up as fishbait!"

Startled, they turned to see who had spoken. It was Shekra, who had been eavesdropping. The vixen winked knowingly at them. "Easy, mates. I won't give ye away, I don't like the cap'n any more than you do."

Wigsul breathed a sigh of relief. "Does that mean yore wid us?"

Shekra shook her head. "Don't include me in any o' yore plans. I ain't part o' no mutiny, but I ain't agin it, neither—leave me out of it. I got a few plans of my own."

Jiboree was curious. "Like wot? Tell us, Shekra."

But the Seer would not be drawn out, commenting casually, "Oh, you'll see when the time comes. Now, mind yore own schemes an' keep yore traps shut when Mowlag's around."

Slowly, ponderously, the big green-sailed vessel forged its way upriver in an atmosphere of high tension.

The monster pike was roasted to perfection. Badtooth, the fat weasel cook, had garnished the fish with fennel and wild parsley. Assisted by two crewbeasts, he bore it on a tray made from an old shield to the captain's cabin.

Razzid sniffed it appreciatively. Pouring himself a goblet of his best grog, he cut off a sizeable portion of the fish, waving the remainder away. "Take it out an' place it on the forepeak. There's plenty there for everybeast!"

Razzid appeared in high good humour. Accompanying the bearers to the forepeak, he called out to the crew, "Eat 'earty, buckoes. I'll wager there's a taste of ole Dirgo on this pikefish. Hahahaaarrrr!"

He swaggered off back to his cabin as the crew gathered around the pike. It smelled delicious until Badtooth told them, "Huh, there's more'n a taste o' Dirgo in there. I saw it meself when I 'ad t'roast the thing."

Wigsul touched the pike with a footpaw. "Well, I ain't eatin' none. It wouldn't be right!"

Several agreed in low voices.

"Nor me, I wouldn't be able to swaller it!"

"Aye, Dirgo was a good shipmate—not that it matters to that Wearat. 'E don't care for nobeast but hisself."

So the roasted pike remained untouched. Late that day, Mowlag passed the thing. It was buzzing with flies.

Razzid had his footpaws up on the cabin table as he

sipped grog and picked his teeth with a pikebone. He looked up as Shekra, Jiboree and Mowlag entered. As captain he had ordered them to attend him. He stared from one to the other.

"Well?"

He allowed the awkward silence to linger awhile before continuing. "Any news o' this ford we're supposed t'come across?"

Mowlag spread his paws wide. "Cap'n, I'm the same as yoreself. I've never been in these parts, so 'ow should I know?"

This was not an answer which pleased the Wearat. He jumped upright, then kicked aside the chair, snarling at Jiboree, "An' I suppose you've got the same excuse, eh?"

Giving the weasel no chance to answer, he turned on Shekra. "Wot've you got t'say fer yoreself—the great mumbo-jumbo Seer yore supposed t'be. Well, wot do the omens tell ye?"

The vixen bowed respectfully. "Do ye wish me to consult my omens, Lord?"

Razzid wiped his leaky eye. "Well, if'n you an' these two mudbrains can't tell me wot I wants t'know, I suppose you'd better see wot the omens have t'say."

Shekra's fertile brain was racing as she replied, "I can do it, sire, but 'tis only twixt thee an' me. The omens are not for all beasts to hear."

Razzid waved a dismissive paw at Mowlag and Jiboree. "Begone, the pair of ye!"

As they went, he added menacingly, "Go sit in the bows. I don't want yore ears pressed agin' this cabin door. Unnerstand?"

They nodded mutely and left.

Razzid would not sit. He paced the cabin impatiently. "Out with it, Seer, an' speak true if'n ye wish to live. When do we reach the ford?"

The vixen replied, using all her guile. "There is no need of casting spells to say what I know, O Great One. The ford lies ahead, how far I cannot say. Listen now, there is a far more urgent message I must deliver to ye!"

Shekra's dramatic tone caused Razzid to pause. His good eye bored into the Seer. "Speak, then!"

The vixen returned his stare, dropping her voice. "There is talk. The crew no longer want you as their captain. They say you deliberately sent Dirgo to his death and now you joke about it. They say any captain who treats his crew thus does not deserve their loyalty, sire."

There was a brief silence, then Razzid exploded. "Loyalty? I don't need loyalty from a bunch o' rakin's an' scrapin's. I'm the Wearat! I rule because they fear me. Who is it that speaks out agin' me, eh?"

Shekra shrugged. "All of them, Lord, except me an' two others."

Razzid sneered. "I ain't worried about you or two other fools. Every snake has a head until it is slain. Now, who is the leader?"

The vixen spoke confidentially. "It came to me in a dream, sire. Here is what I saw. Wigsul, the corsair weasel, was in this cabin with you. Then all went blurred an' I heard these words.

"A weasel of the *Greenshroud*'s crew,
will try to take his captain's life—
be watchful, Lord, and know this beast
is skilful with the knife."

"When my vision cleared, you were lyin' on the cabin floor with a knife in your back, sire. The weasel was shouting to the crew that he was now the captain."

Shekra held her breath, trying not to flinch under Razzid's stare. He spoke calmly.

"An' who are the two, beside yoreself, who are loyal to me? Have no fear. Ye can speak their names."

The vixen almost smiled with relief. "Mowlag an' Jiboree, sire."

Razzid resumed pacing the cabin, rubbing at his weeping eye and nodding. "Good, good. Now, I want ye to bring Wigsul to me, but make sure he suspects nothing. Can ye do that?"

Now Shekra smiled. "Leave it to me, Lord."

Mowlag, Jiboree and Wigsul were lounging on the prow, watching flies congregating on the remains of the roast pike.

Shekra joined them. "Do any of ye fancy a nice bit o' roasted pikefish?"

Jiboree ignored the vixen's remark. "Wot did ye tell the cap'n, fox?"

Shekra chuckled. "The Wearat's a law unto himself. Ye can't tell him anythin' he don't want to hear."

Wigsul swept the flyblown piece of fish overboard.

Mowlag persisted. "So wot went on in that cabin, eh?"

The vixen was hiding something alongside her paw. She stood behind Wigsul, addressing Mowlag and Jiboree. "The cap'n never mentioned you two." She patted Wigsul's back at about waist height. "Said he wanted a word with you, mate."

The weasel corsair looked bemused. "Cap'n wants t'see me?"

Shekra nodded. "Aye, you, matey. He's in a good mood, so it can't be anythin' serious. Off ye go now."

Razzid was sitting at his table with both paws concealed beneath its edge. Wigsul knocked on the cabin door and entered. Standing in front of the table, he tugged his right ear in salute.

"Ye wanted t'see me, Cap'n?"

Razzid looked up as if he had just noticed the weasel. "Are ye loyal to me, Wigsul?"

The corsair nodded, trying to keep his wits about him. "Aye, Cap'n, loyal as the day's long."

Razzid nodded. "Good! An' ye wouldn't come to my cabin t'do me any harm, would ye?"

Wigsul shook his head rapidly, wondering what he had walked into. "No, Cap'n, on me oath, I wouldn't!"

Razzid made a twirling gesture with one paw. "Turn round, right round so yore facin' me agin."

The weasel obeyed, though he was shaking nervously.

When he had completed the turn, Razzid spoke as though he was sharing a joke with the crewbeast. "Now, I want ye to take that thing out of yore belt careful like, with one paw. Do it slowly, use yore left paw, easy now. . . ."

Wigsul's face went rigid as he drew the dagger from his belt. He stammered, "H-h-how did that get there? It ain't mine, Cap'n, I swear it ain't!"

Razzid replied softly, "Now, there's a strange thing. Do me a favour, mate, put that blade on the table, right here in front o' me."

The corsair leaned over the table, placing the dagger close to his captain, still protesting his innocence. "I never seen this blade afore. Ye've got to believe me, Cap—"

Still bent forward over the table, he froze. Razzid had thrust the trident hard through the flimsy timber top, his eye meeting Wigsul's stricken gaze as he snarled, "Yore relieved o' duty aboard *Greenshroud.* Get to Hellgates!"

Pulling the trident loose, he pushed the slain weasel from him, calling aloud, "Don't go slopin' off—git in here, all three of ye. Come on, jump to it!"

Mowlag, Jiboree and Shekra shuffled in. He winked his good eye at them. "I knew ye'd be spyin' out there. Well, wot d'ye think o' this mutinous scum, eh?"

Shekra bowed. "He won't go round plottin' against ye anymore, Lord, that's for sure!"

The Wearat's piercing gaze swept over them. "Are ye loyal to me?"

Three heads bobbed in unison. "Aye, Cap'n!"

He watched in silence until they showed signs of squirming. "Then look at this un an' remember wot happens to those who ain't. Get that thing out o' my cabin."

None of the trio spoke as they dropped Wigsul's carcass over the side. Then Mowlag glared at Shekra.

"Wot was all that about, fox?"

The vixen murmured, "Keep your voice down, mate. Razzid could feel somethin' was brewin', so I gave him Wigsul. Now ain't the time for a mutiny. When Razzid conquers the red Abbey, then we'll deal with him. Between us we can outsmart him, when the time comes."

Mowlag grabbed Shekra's paw. "Yore talkin' mutiny an' murder. Wot makes ye think I wants any part in it, eh?"

The Seer withdrew her paw coolly from his grasp. "Because I've been watchin' ye. I could tell, believe me. Wigsul had a big mouth—he'd have done for us all sooner or later. Razzid thinks he's quelled any mutiny now, an' that's the way we'll keep it, until the time's ripe."

Jiboree agreed. "She's right, mate. Once the cap'n is outta the way, we'll be in charge o' everythin', that Abbey, an' all wot goes wid it!"

Mowlag looked from one to the other, then nodded. "I'm with ye!"

Shekra lowered her eyes to the deck, whispering, "Look out, he's watchin' us!"

Razzid had been standing in his cabin doorway. He began walking toward them, but a cry from the mast top brought him up short.

"The ford, Cap'n! 'Tis dead ahead as she goes. The ford!"

25

Uggo gripped Posy's paw tightly, even though they were travelling in the centre of the group. Old Drogbuk Wiltud was supposedly taking them on a shortcut to Redwall, so they could arrive ahead of *Greenshroud* and Razzid Wearat's crew. They were in a forbidding and eerie part of Mossflower, one seldom used by other travellers. The trees were enormous, their upper foliage coming together—cedar, oak, elm, sycamore, ash, beech and other varieties—blocking out the sunlight. It was a world of green gloom haunted by dark shadows. Nothing except trees and odd fern beds seemed to grow there in the all-prevailing silence. The woodland floor was deeply coated with leaf loam and dead pine needles.

Uggo chuckled nervously. "Ain't much fun strollin' through this place, is it?"

His voice echoed hollowly around the monolithic trunks. Posy squeezed his paw. "Hush, now, be quiet. Sound carries round here."

The Guosim shrew Banktail whispered furtively, "D'ye think somebeast might be lissenin'?"

Log a Log Dandy, who was bringing up the rear, pawed at his rapier hilt, putting on a show of bravado. "I don't care

who they are. They can lissen long as they like, providin'
they don't try anythin' on me. All they'll git off'n this
Guosim is a taste o' cold steel!"

Walking in the lead with Drogbuk, Swiffo had to slow
his pace to match the ancient hog. He was not best pleased
when the oldster sat down on a fallen spruce trunk.

The young sea otter held forth his paw.

"C'mon, Granpa, up ye come. Let's get goin'—I don't
like this place. Sooner we're outta here the better, eh?"

Drogbuk shook the paw off his shoulder, stating moodily,
"I don't like this place either, but a beast o' my seasons 'as
to rest. I ain't as spry as you whippersnappers."

Swiffo called a halt. "Take a short rest, mates."

Drogbuk felt inclined to argue, so he did. "A short rest is
it, eh? Lissen, wavedog, I'll rest fer as long as I likes, see?
I'm the one wot knows the way, so ye can't go anywhere
widout me to guide ye!"

Log a Log Dandy tried humouring him. "Yore right there,
ole feller. You cool yore paws awhile."

Drogbuk stuck out his snout stubbornly. "Aye, an' whilst
I'm coolin' me paws, wot about some vittles an' a drop
t'drink, or do I 'ave t'starve t'death?"

Swiffo shrugged. "Wouldn't mind a bite o' grub meself,
mate. Trouble is, we ain't got none, an' there ain't any to be
got around this place, unless anybeast wants t'go foragin'."

The Guosim scout Dobble dusted loam from his tail. "I'll
take a look around. There's got t'be somethin' a body could
eat."

Frabb, a tough-faced Guosim, volunteered himself. "I'll
go with ye, Dobble. If'n I don't git me paws on some vittles
soon, I'll start eatin' me own tail!"

As they strode off together, Log a Log Dandy called,
"Keep yore eyes skinned for trouble, mates, an' give our
Guosim cry if'n there's anythin' amiss."

After the pair had vanished into the green gloom, the
others sat resting. It was an uneasy time. A pall of silence
lay upon the whole party. Uggo and Posy moved closer to

each other, staring uneasily around, stiffening at a sound in the background.

The shrew Banktail looked rather unhappy at the situation. "See? I told ye we was bein' watched. Now they're trackin' us."

Dandy nudged him hard. "Why don't ye talk a bit louder, so that whoever it is can find us easier? Huh, wot makes ye think we're bein' tracked, eh?"

As if fearing to turn, Uggo gestured backward. "That noise just then. It sounded like somethin' slitherin' through the dry leaves, a snake maybe."

At the mention of the word *snake*, a fearful moan arose from the shrews, who were mortally afraid of serpents.

Even the Log a Log looked apprehensive; he prodded Drogbuk. "Did ye say there was snakes round here, old un?"

The ancient hog nodded. "Aye, an' I ain't in the habit o' tellin' lies. That could be the sound of a snake!"

Swiffo gathered some dried moss. With knifeblade and flint, he began conjuring up a smouldering little heap. "Ahoy, Guosim, don't sit there like crabs at a cookup, git gatherin' dry wood. Fire'll keep anybeast at bay, even snakes. C'mon, mates, show willin'!"

Nervously the Guosim set about their chore, encouraged by Dandy, who was putting on a brave face. Uggo and Posy joined in. Soon there was a sizeable stack of dead twigs and branches piled up for kindling.

Swiffo uttered a timely caution. "Don't build the fire too big. We don't want t'be faced by a forest fire."

Suddenly, Posy, who had been gathering dead ferns, hurried toward the fire. She was ashen-faced, clutching her right paw with the left.

Dandy nodded to her. "Hurt yore paw, missy? Fall, did ye?"

The pretty young hogmaid was trying to stop her teeth chattering as she stammered an answer. "Th-th-think I've b-b-been bitten!"

Uggo hurried to her side. "Bitten by what, a snake?"

Posy sat down, rocking back and forth, still clutching her paw tightly. "Th-th-think it was a s-s-s-snake!"

Uggo felt his voice go shrill with panic. "Posy's been bitten by a snake! Wot'll we do?"

"Tell 'er t'sit still, I'll take a look." Drogbuk trundled over, forcing Posy to relinquish her hold on the injured paw. He pushed his face close, inspected the mark, then sucked it and spat. Staring at the bright drop of blood that stood out, he cackled. "Heehee, it must've been a one-toothed serpent, missy. There's only one puncture, snakes make two. Where did ye get it? Point out the spot t'me."

Uggo nodded toward a fern bed. "We were t'gether, over yon."

Taking a stick from the firewood pile, Drogbuk hobbled over to the ferns. He waved the stick amongst the plants as he grumbled, "Young uns t'day wouldn't know a snakebite from a bloomin' butterfly kiss. See, here's yer snake!"

He held up a dead blackberry stem covered with prickly spines. "Ye can stop shakin', missy. Ye'll live—ouch! Gone an' stuck meself now!"

He flung the broken stem from him, almost hitting Dobble, who came marching in followed by Frabb.

"Aye aye there, Granpa, watch where yore flingin' things!"

Between them, the two Guosim were carrying the results of their foraging, bundled up in an old cloak.

Frabb emptied the contents on the ground. "Loads o' mushrooms round 'ere, some dannelion roots, last autumn's acorns, some ole chestnuts an' this thing."

Drogbuk picked up a big, brownish, wrinkled football-shaped growth and sniffed it.

"Found this stuck t'the side of a tree, didn't ye? Cauliflower fungus, they calls it—makes fine eatin' sliced up an' roasted o'er the fire—"

With no prior warning, a missile flew out of nowhere, striking the big fungus out of Drogbuk's paws. This was followed by a harsh commanding voice.

"Thieves who steal my food die!"

A very tall fox stepped out from behind a pine. He was slim but strong looking. He wore a cloak of black and green with a high collar. His pale green eyes swept over the travellers.

"I am Ketral Vane, Lord of the Hinterwoods. Leave that food here. Go now whilst ye still draw breath!"

Log a Log Dandy stepped in front of Swiffo, who was about to draw steel. The feisty Guosim Chieftain growled, "Whilst we still draw breath, eh? Fancy talk for a skinny vermin. I'm Log a Log Dandy Clogs, Chieftain o' Guosim shrews, an' I'm warnin' ye, brushtail, interfere with us whilst we're eatin' an' I'll give ye a rapier blade to chew on!"

As he spoke, Dandy drew the Guosim blade, which he was now using, and advanced on the fox.

Ketral Vane stood immobile as six other foxes stepped out of the tree cover. Each had a crossbow strung, drawn and levelled at Dandy. Ketral's cloak opened, revealing that he was similarly armed, though he had already fired the bolt at the fungus which Drogbuk had been holding.

Drogbuk stayed Swiffo's paw. "Don't try anythin', wavedog. They'll kill ye."

Ketral Vane turned his attention to the ancient hog. "Twice before ye have been through my lands, old one. Why do ye return bringing these beasts with ye?"

Drogbuk shrugged. "We're only passin' through, don't mean harm to anybeast. We was 'ungry, so the shrews rooted out some vittles. Ye wouldn't begrudge starvin' travellers a bite to eat, would ye, sire?"

One of the other foxes, an older vixen, answered, "The Lord of the Hinterwoods has spoken. Leave the food and begone, or die. Ketral Vane brooks no arguments!"

Uggo spoke out indignantly. "This ain't no 'Interwoods, 'tis all Mossflower Country!"

Drogbuk smacked the young hog's face. "Ain't ye gotten no brains? Yew was told not to argue!"

Ketral Vane, meanwhile, had been reloading a bolt into

his crossbow. He reslung it without effort. Pointing the weapon at Uggo, he pronounced sentence.

"You argued, disputed my territory and stole food. Let this be a lesson to your companions. It will be a lesson too late for you, hedgepig, for you must die!"

Posy flung herself in front of Uggo, crying out, "No! You can't just kill Uggo in cold blood. He hasn't harmed you. Let us go. We'll leave the food and travel now!"

The tall fox's pale eyes narrowed cruelly. "Move aside or die. My word is law in the Hinterwoods. The one called Uggo is to be executed!"

Posy bravely stood her ground, making an impassioned plea. "No, I will not move. Please, I beg you, don't do this!"

The fox's voice was merciless. "Then die, both of you!"

Uggo and Posy clung to each other, their eyes shut tight.

BOOK THREE

All Forward to Redwall!

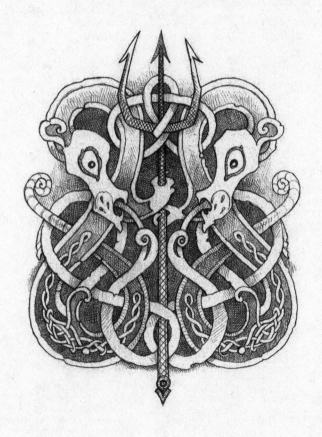

26

Time hung frozen over the awful tableau. Then one of the foxes dropped his crossbow, calling out hoarsely, "Lord Ketral, halt!"

He was held by both ears from behind by Skor Axehound, Warchief of the Rogue Crew, who was swinging his battleaxe.

"Kill the young uns an' I'll slay ye all, startin' with this bush-tailed scum!"

In the pause that followed, twin claymore blades came from behind, trapping Ketral Vane's throat. A heavy highland voice whispered in his ear, "Aye, laddie. An' ye'll be second in line at Hellgates. Wi'out a head an' all, but dinnae fret, Ah'll send that on wi' one o' yer braw beasties!"

The next voice was Sergeant Miggory, reporting, "H'all secure 'ere, sah. Just give the nod an' not one'll be left standin', sah. Drander, don't let that lance droop. Keep h'it tight by the lady's shoulderblades!"

Big Drander pressed his lance firmly against the vixen. "Beg pardon if this tickles ye, marm, but I'd stay jolly still if I were you, wot!"

Swiffo was smiling from ear to ear, shaking his head. "Pa, where'd you come from?"

Ruggan patted his head roughly. "From the High North

Coast to find ye, little brother. Hmm, got yoreself in a bit of a fix, I see."

Swiffo shook his brother's paw heartily. "Oh, 'twas nothin' I couldn't have got out of!"

Log a Log Dandy winked at Skor. "Ye'd best believe 'im, Axehound. Swiffo ain't short o' nerve when it comes to the action."

Skor passed his captive over to the bloodythirsty maid, Kite Slayer. He held out both paws.

"Come here, ye young rip, let's take a look o' ye!"

As Skor hugged his youngest son, Ruggan enquired, "Wot d'we do with these villains, sir?"

Skor replied casually, "They're vermin, ain't they? Kill 'em!"

Captain Rake was quick to countermand the order. "Och, no, ye auld savage. We're warriors, not murderers!"

The big sea otter Chieftain shook his head, sighing. "As ye wish, Nightfur, but ye'll be sorry one day. Take their weapons an' throw 'em on the fire. Let's get some vittles cookin'—I'm famished!"

Bound paw and tail to the giant tree trunks, Ketral Vane and his foxes were forced to look on as otters and hares broke out supplies and readied a meal.

Trug Bawdsley poked the flames with an unstrung crossbow. "Funny-lookin' weapons, Sarn't. Are they any good?"

The sergeant curled his lip. "Too fussy, take too long t'get ready. An' they don't fire as good as a proper yew longbow. Make decent firewood, though, don't they?"

Lancejack Sage had roasted a slice of the cauliflower fungus on a crossbow bolt. She took a dainty bite. "I say, this tastes jolly good. Wonder what it's called."

Lieutenant Scutram munched on a roasted chestnut. "Poison puffball, I should think, missy."

The lancejack smiled sweetly at him. "Lovely flavour, though, sah. Any left there, you chaps?"

Skor questioned Dandy. "Now then, old bristlebonce, y'still haven't told us what yore doin' so far off the track."

The Guosim Chieftain seemed to ignore the term *bristlebonce* for a moment, but then he came back pointedly. "Well, I'll tell ye, ole barrelbelly. We ain't so much far off the track as tryin' to get ahead o' the vermin crew. I plan on makin' it to Redwall ahead of the *Greenshroud*. That way we can warn the Redwallers, stand alongside of 'em an' face Razzid Wearat in a united group. Aye, an' from behind good, high stone walls. Drogbuk reckons he knows a shortcut that should get us to the Abbey double quick, y'see."

Skor pointed with his axehaft at the ancient hog.

"What, y'mean that ole bag o' bones an' shaky spikes? Huh, looks as though he couldn't find his snout with all four paws t'me, Dandy. You should've followed the riverbanks."

Drogbuk Wiltud waved a piece of broken crossbow at Skor. "Ahoy, bigbeast, who d'ye think yore insultin', eh? If'n I was a few seasons younger, I'd tan yore rudder with this!"

Holding up his paws in mock fear, Skor hid a grin. "'Tis a good thing I fetched some warriors to defend me. Righto, Granpa, which way is it to Redwall Abbey, then?"

Drogbuk chunnered as he tried to get his few remaining teeth around a roasted chestnut. He pointed vaguely. "Er, lemme see, that way, I think. . . ."

Log a Log Dandy threw up his paws in bewilderment. "Ye think? But you told us ye knew the way for certain!"

The old hedgehog scowled. "No, I never. All I said was I think I know a shortcut. I never said for certain. I'm old, y'know. Ye forgets things when yore old."

Ruggan shook his head in disbelief. "I think we should cut ye loose on yore own, y'ole idjit!"

Drogbuk stamped his paw down hard; there was a rattle of falling spikes. He turned on the young sea otter fiercely. "Who are yew callin' an ole idjit, eh? Lissen, fuzzface, ye'll be old yoreself one day. Hah, I 'opes they cut yew loose then, widout a crust or a drop t'drink, so there! Besides, you ain't so smart, the lot of ye, or haven't ye noticed anythin' amiss?"

Buff Redspore looked up from a beaker of pennycloud cordial. "Not really, sah. Er . . . can you see anythin' amiss, wot?"

Drogbuk employed a grimy claw to root amidst his tooth stubs. "While ye've been so busy feedin' yore faces an' tellin' me wot an ole fool I am, yore foxes 'ave escaped."

Captain Rake dashed toward the deserted tree trunks. "Why didn't ye say somethin', auld un?"

Drogbuk inspected his claw before wiping it, commenting, "'Cos ye never asked me. Besides, I've only just noticed it."

Sure enough, Ketral Vane and his six foxes had vanished, leaving behind their long black and green capes amidst a lot of severed bonds. Big Drander stared in disgust at Endar Feyblade, one of Skor's crew.

"I say, weren't you supposed t'be watchin' 'em?"

Ruggan confronted the big young hare. "No, I thought that was yore famous Long Patrol's job!"

The ottermaid Kite turned sternly on Log a Log Dandy. "We just saved you lot. The least ye could've done was to keep an eye on them foxes!"

Captain Rake had to shout to be heard over the squabbles which erupted. "Och, will ye no hauld yer whisht! We're no' gettin' anywhere yammerin' on like a lot of auld ninnies. Silence, Ah say! Those foxes slipped away like smoke. They're vermin, aye, but braw, canny beasts. So what d'we do now? Ah'm lookin' for sensible ideas, ye ken!"

"We runs fer our lives afore they come back in force!"

It was Drogbuk who had spoken.

Skor Axehound brandished his battleaxe, towering over the old hedgehog. "Not whilst I'm Warchief o' the Rogue Crew. We don't run from anybeast!"

Drogbuk sucked on a roasted acorn and chuckled. "Brave words, wavedog. I'm goin' t'run fer it. You can stay 'ere an' face a load o' toads armed with blowpipes an' poisoned darts. That Ketral comman's some snakes, too. Ye can always take a chance whether they're poison or not. Shouldn't be much trouble to fightin' beasts like yew lot."

Sergeant Miggory squatted down in front of Drogbuk. "We gets yore point, h'old feller. None of us 'ave been 'ere afore, so we wouldn't know where t'run. Where would you 'ead for, mate?"

Drogbuk tapped the side of his snout and winked. "I knows one place they stays well away from. D'ye want me to take ye there?"

Lieutenant Scutram held forth a paw, helping the old one up. "Lead on, dear chap, lead on. We're with you!"

They all moved off, with Drogbuk in the lead, assisted by Uggo and Posy lest he stumble. He took them on a twisting route through the big trees, fern beds and yielding loam. The atmosphere became distinctly gloomier.

Young Flutchers cast a worried glance at their surroundings. "I say, can't get much bloomin' murkier, can it? There's not even that sort o' green light about anymore, wot."

Corporal Welkin tweaked Flutchers's ears to silence him. "That'll be because it's nighttime, laddie buck. Now no more talking—mum's the word, wot!"

Flutchers was about to ask why when he heard Dandy the Guosim Chieftain murmuring to Ruggan. "They're on to us. We're bein' followed, listen to that."

A high-pitched yipping could be heard from some distance.

Sergeant Miggory identified it. "Fox call, h'if I h'aint mistaken. Comin' from h'off t'the left. There's a couple more fox cries, one t'the right an' two t'the rear of us someplace. D'ye 'ear 'em, sah?"

Captain Rake nodded. "Aye, Ah can that, Sarn't. Sounds tae me like they're tryin' tae trap us in a pincer movement. We'll have tae march double quick an' stay quiet."

Skor caught up with Drogbuk in the lead. "Ahoy, old un, where's this place yore takin' us to, an' how far away is it?"

Accompanied by Uggo and Posy, the ancient hog was

limping. "Can't be too far off now. Hear that runnin' water? It's over that way. Me ole footpaws aren't workin' right. I'm slowin' down, but there ain't much I can do about it."

The sea otter Chieftain summoned four burly Rogue Crew members. Lashing two shields to spear poles, they made a portable chair. Skor gave his orders.

"Carry this ole beast, an' go whichever way he tells ye."

As the sounds of running water drew closer, so did the fox calls. Captain Rake found the water source first. It was a medium-sized stream with steep banks.

Drogbuk pointed ahead. "Keep goin' this way 'til ye see the hill with a tunnel goin' into it. That's the place we want."

Lancejack Sage was heard to remark, "Well, we'd better find it jolly soon, chaps. Sounds like those bloomin' foe-beasts are right on our tails, wot!"

Skor issued a command to his best archers. "Fall back t'the rear o' the column an' pick off any enemy ye can spy. Nothin' like a good ash shaft to discourage pursuers."

Wilbee whispered to Kite Slayer, "He's enjoyin' this, ain't he?"

Fitting an arrow to her bowstring, the bloodthirsty ottermaid halted to let the rear marchers catch up. "Well, of course he is. I am, too. War is wot we're best at."

The keen eyes of Buff Redspore were first to see their goal.

"There 'tis—straight ahead, big dark openin' where the stream comes out o' the hill!"

Trug Bawdsley exclaimed, "Have we got t'go in there, Sarn't?" Sergeant Miggory pushed him forward.

"O' course we 'ave, young sir. In ye go. Let's see ye get those footpaws wet."

Everybeast splashed into the dark, icy current, pushing their way into engulfing darkness. Some of the Guosim shrews were in over their heads, but they were buoyed up by hares and otters.

Big Drander supported Uggo and Posy. "Grab on to me, young uns, but mind those spikes, please."

Skor stayed on the bank with his bowbeasts close to the entrance. He whirled a heavily loaded sling.

The sounds of pursuers drew closer as he whirled the sling faster. "Wait now . . . wait! No sense in firin' until we know we can hit 'em. One good go, then straight in after the others. Don't wait for the scum to return volleys. They'll be usin' poison darts, remember. Right, Crew, let's give 'em a warm greetin'. . . . Shoot!"

Long arrows hissed off into the woodland gloom, like a flight of angry hornets. Immediately this was followed by a scream and gurgling cries. Having hurled off his slingstones, Skor nodded with satisfaction.

"That should slow the slimy scum a bit. Right, into the tunnel with ye, hurry now!"

They went—all but one, Garrent, who was putting another shaft to his bowstring.

Skor dashed back to him. "I said into the tunnel. Now move!"

Garrent ignored the order, loosing off an arrow. "Hahah! Got 'im, big toad. I saw him comin'—uuuuunnnhh!"

He dropped like a log, pierced in over six places by long, tufted darts. Skor knew that Garrent was done for. Two darts pinged off his metal shieldplate as he threw himself into the stream, wading against the current to join the rest.

The tunnel took two bends. Skor came upon the others, waiting around the curve in the second one. He shook his big bearded head angrily.

"Lost one o' my Rogue Crew, Garrent, a great warrior, but headstrong. Wanted t'stay an' fight, just like I do. I never retreated in my life. Can't we go back an' face 'em?"

They waited in the dark silence until Lieutenant Scutram put flint and steel to a couple of torches, which he had had the foresight to make on the march.

Skor struck the rock wall with his axe, repeating his challenge. "What's the matter with ye? Come on, let's go back an' make a real fight of it. Who's with me?"

Captain Rake Nightfur shook his head. "Our task, mah friend, is tae get tae Redwall an' battle wi' the real enemy—Razzid Wearat an' his vermin crew. There'd be nay point in riskin' valuable fighters just tae show yon Ketral Vane we're no' feared o' him."

Log a Log Dandy sided with Rake. "The cap'n's right, Skor. We press on to Redwall. I've got unfinished business with that Wearat—he slew most of my clan, an' wot've you lost? One warrior?"

The sea otter Chieftain put up his battleaxe. "I'm sorry, Dandy. Yore right, I can see that. 'Tis just when the blood rises in my eyes, I can't help myself. We go to Redwall, but I warn ye now, the Wearat's mine!"

Sergeant Miggory had a salient point to make. "Beggin' yore pardon, sah, but the Wearat 'as slain some of our hares, nice beasts, young uns, too. So h'it's first there, first served, h'if I says so meself."

Skor grinned wolfishly. "Then we'll take a piece of him each!"

They continued following the flooded tunnel underground. By and by, it became shallower. A rock ledge emerged on one side. Thankfully, the Guosim and the three hedgehogs climbed onto it, some of the hares also. However, the sea otters were strong swimmers. They scorned the ledge, preferring the water. The shrew Dobble voiced a thought which had been bothering others.

"Why haven't the foxes an' their creatures followed us in here? That's wot I'd like t'know."

Posy shrugged. "So would I, but I suppose we'd better just thank our fortune an' carry on."

Ruggan swam ahead with a torch clenched in his teeth. He had not been gone long when he called back to them, "There's another tunnel up here—come an' look!"

Wading onward, Drogbuk replied, "Another tunnel. . . . Which one are we supposed t'take, eh?"

Corporal Welkin assisted the old hog along the ledge. "We'll find out when we jolly well come to it. Keep movin', sah."

The water began deepening again, and the current grew stronger. Ruggan was waiting for them around a further bend.

Skor looked puzzled. "Where's this other tunnel?"

Ruggan indicated with his blazing torch. "Above the ledge, up there in the wall, see?"

Dandy reached up from the ledge where he was standing. "Funny sort o' tunnel. Wot's it doin' that far up the wall?"

Skor looked up at the opening. "'Twill be a bit of a squeeze for me to get through that. Any volunteers to be first in there?"

Ruggan began heaving himself out of the water. "I found it, so s'pose I'd best go first."

He was almost on the ledge when his younger brother, Swiffo, denied him the chance. Bounding skilfully up onto Ruggan's shoulders, Swiffo leapt, catching hold of the entrance rim. He pulled himself up, disappearing into the dark hole. There was a momentary silence, which was cut by Skor's booming voice echoing off the tunnel walls.

"Now then, ye young scallawag, wot's it like in there?"

Swiffo's head appeared at the entrance.

"Too dark t'see anythin'. Pass me the torch, Ruggan."

Ruggan lobbed the lighted torch carefully. It described a fiery arc, but Swiffo caught it deftly. He waved and vanished again. Everybeast watched as the flickering rays diminished.

Captain Rake called out, "Dinnae get yoreself lost up there, laddie!"

More silence, then a sound began to build. It was like a gale-force wind over a grove of trees, whooshing along into a crescendo, peppered with high-pitched squeals, multitudes of them.

Sergeant Miggory had to bellow to make himself heard over the gathering tumult.

"Wot'n the name o' blood'n'thunder's that, sah?"

Swiffo came hurtling out, still grasping the smouldering torch as he hit the water and went under.

Then the huge dark shape descended on the shocked creatures.

Redwall Abbey was the picture of tranquillity in early summer dawn. Dorka Gurdy was up early, strolling the walltop, sipping a steaming beaker of comfrey and dandelion tea and nibbling on a crusty oat farl.

The rampart walks at dawn and sunset had become almost a ritual with the Abbey's otter Gatekeeper. Her constant hope was the return of her brother Jum Gurdy and Uggo Wiltud. They had been absent some considerable time now, but she never gave up hope of seeing the pair strolling home along the path which ran alongside the Abbey. Standing on the threshold above the main gate, Dorka enjoyed the quiet moments before Redwallers awakened. Far out across the flatlands a mist-shrouded horizon was being transformed by the eastern sunrise. Soft grey, faint blue and pale gold touched distant slow-drifting cloud wisps. Wood pigeons, with their constant broody chuckles, mingled with melodious blackbird and thrush serenades from the woodlands behind. The plaintive chirrup of ascending larks blended sweetly with the chorus. The Abbey Bellringer, Ding Toller, joined her.

"I was just on my way to ring the morning bells, but who needs them, with music like this, marm?"

Dorka rested her beaker on a battlement, nodding at the tall, sombre squirrel. "Aye, who indeed, sir."

Ding glanced southward down the path, then out over the flatlands. "No sign of Jum an' young Uggo?"

The big otter shook her head. "Not yet, but they'll come soon—you'll see. Though I think they'll arrive from the north. Don't know why, suppose 'tis just a feelin' I get."

Ding nodded. "Aye, ye could be right, marm. North's as

good as any place t'come from. Ye'll excuse me, but I has t'go an' see to my bells."

He was about to move off when he saw two small figures clambering up the north wallstairs.

"Will ye look at those two liddle snips! Who told 'em they could come up to these walltops alone?"

He hurried along the west rampart, followed closely by Dorka, calling out to the Dibbun pair.

"Stay where ye are, don't take another step!"

It was Alfio the shrewbabe and Guggle the tiny squirrel. They waved cheerily.

"Goo' mornin' to ee. Nice up 'ere, izzen it? We was goin' t'climb up on a wall an' look out."

Ding took Alfio by the paw. "Ho, no, you knows the rules about liddle uns wanderin' round up here alone. Now, come on down, 'tis breakfast time."

Guggle the squirrelbabe scrambled up Dorka's habit to perch on her shoulder. "I kin see everyfink from up here, Dorky—alla trees an' the path an' the big ship!"

Holding him tight, Dorka mounted the battlement top.

"Big ship? Where?"

Guggle's tiny paw shot out. "Up there onna path, see!"

There was the *Greenshroud*, far off as of yet, but quite distinct. The green sails hung limply as it trundled gently forward, propelled by its vermin crew wielding oarshafts.

Ding helped Dorka down, passing the custody of Guggle to her. "Forget the bells—marm, you watch this un. I've got t'go an' tell our Abbot about this!"

In Great Hall, Father Abbot Thibb presided over the day's first meal. He was halfway through the grace when Ding Toller burst in, his footpaws slapping the floorstones as he hurried to the Abbot's side.

Thibb gave him a reproachful stare. "Could this not wait until later?"

Panting from the run, the Bellringer tried to keep his voice down as he explained hurriedly, "Big ship with green sails comin' down the path from the north. Me'n'Dorka saw it with our own eyes, Father!"

Thibb stepped away from the table, drawing Ding close. "Carry on with breakfast in my place, and not a word to anybeast. Roogo Foremole, Sister Fisk, Fottlink, Friar Wopple, follow me, please."

27

Aboard the *Greenshroud,* all talk of mutiny was forgotten as searats and corsairs saw the long-awaited prize within sight.

Jiboree stood on the prow end, pointing his sword at the distant Abbey. "Haharr—there she is, buckoes, big an' 'andsome as ye likes!"

He summoned Shekra. "Go an' tell the cap'n we've arrived!"

The vixen tippawed into Razzid Wearat's cabin, thinking he would still be sleeping. Much to the contrary, he was sitting in his chair, wide awake, facing the door, with his trident placed within easy reach. His piercing eye was fixed on Shekra.

"What do you want, fox?"

The Seer saluted by tugging an eartip. "Lord, good news. The Abbey of Redwall has been sighted!"

Razzid did not appear unduly excited. "Where is it, and how far away are we from it?"

Expecting a happier reply, the vixen answered lamely, "Straight ahead, Lord. We should be there by noon."

Placing the trident across his lap, Razzid continued staring at Shekra. "When ye entered my cabin, I noticed ye crept in—don't deny it. I was supposed to be found lyin' asleep, eh?"

The vixen came up with a reasonable answer. "Well, sire, it is only just dawn, an' captains are allowed to sleep as they wish. I thought ye'd still be restin'."

The Wearat pointed at the deck. "Come here, stand closer to me."

Shekra obeyed hesitantly as Razzid urged her forward.

"Closer. Come on, fox, a bit nearer. That's it!"

The vixen stood trembling, not knowing what to expect next. She was so close that she could feel his breath on her muzzle. When he spoke softly, Razzid's voice had a hoarse quality.

"Is there ought your captain should know?"

Her lips quivered. "N . . . no, sire, nothin'."

Razzid wiped moisture from his bad eye slowly. "Good! You're still my Seer, ain't ye?"

Shekra nodded dumbly, aware of the single eye's intense stare.

His next enquiry came as a surprise to her. "Then, tell me, why did I not sleep well?"

The vixen relaxed slightly. "Were your old wounds troublin' ye?"

Razzid spoke but one word. "No."

She allowed a pause before speaking again. "A dream disturbed your slumbers, then, Lord."

Razzid sat back slightly. "Aye, a dream. What do ye know of a warrior who carries a flaming sword?"

Even though she was puzzled, Shekra was on more familiar territory. "This warrior, what manner of beast was he, Lord?"

His reply startled her.

"A mouse, I think."

The vixen covered her surprise by nodding, gaining time. "Sire, I will have to consult my omens. What did the mouse look like?"

As she rummaged for materials in her satchel, Razzid snapped irately, "Idiot, he looked like a mouse, in armour."

Having gained a scrap of information, Shekra cast pebbles, bones and shells. Her tone became foreboding. "The omens predict a sign of warning. Do ye fear that, sire?"

Razzid laughed scornfully. "I fear nobeast, least of all a mouse. Wot else do ye see? Tell me!"

The vixen gained confidence, resorting to flattery. "'Tis right ye fear nobeast, Great One. The creature has not been born that can defeat ye. Ignore this mouse, go forward and conquer the redstone fortress. Nought will stop ye—'tis your right to rule there!"

She awaited his reaction. The Wearat seemed buoyed up by the fact he was nearing his objective. Then his mood swung suddenly. He fixed her with a fearsome stare.

"Do ye speak truly, Seer? Well, do ye?"

Shekra adopted her mystic expression. "When did I ever lie? I always speak truly to ye, Lord."

Razzid mused aloud. "I often wonder if yore a Seer or just a Soothsayer. So, ye say truly I have nought to fear."

The vixen decided to add a cautionary word, covering herself against future events. "One thing, my Lord— beware the flames from the sword of your dream. Remember, it was fire that almost killed ye!"

The Wearat scowled darkly. "Aye, that's somethin' I won't easily forget. I'll bear these scars for life!" Razzid sat silent briefly, drumming his paw lightly on the trident haft, then startled Shekra by rising speedily, an unexpected smile on his face.

"Come on, friend, let's go and take a look at the famous Redwall, eh!"

The vixen stood to one side respectfully, but Razzid held back, making an elaborate paw gesture. "No, no, you go first. From now on, I want all my crew to go first, d'ye know why?"

Shekra shook her head. "No, Lord."

She flinched as Razzid tickled her back gently with the trident prongs, answering casually, "Because I trust only those who are in front of me."

The crew were jubilant. They cheered their captain as he strode out on deck.

"Ye did it, Cap'n, ye did it!"

"Aye, there's the easy life, dead ahead of us, an' 'twas you wot brought us 'ere, Cap'n!"

Smiling graciously, the Wearat partially mounted the rigging, so he could get a better view of the Abbey. They cheered him to the echo as he held out his trident, pointing it at their goal. Smiling benevolently, he nodded acknowledgement, noting as he did that Shekra was standing between Mowlag and Jiboree, murmuring something to them. All three turned. For a moment his single good eye was smiling straight at them, almost with a mocking expression.

Dorka Gurdy put little Guggle down on the walkway as Abbot Thibb and his followers came up the northern wallstairs to the ramparts. The Dibbun squirrel protested strongly.

"Lif' Guggle up agin, Dorky. Me wanna see da big ship!"

This caused Alfio to take up the cry. "Me too! I wanna see da big ship!"

The Abbot shook his head pointedly at Dorka, who caught on immediately. "What big ship? I didn't see no ship. Run along, now, or you'll be late for brekkist, go on!"

Paw in paw, they toddled off down the wallstairs, both minds with a single thought now. Breakfast.

"I wants 'ot scones an' hunny, wiv a big bowl of rasbee corjul!"

"Heehee, me too! I race you. One, two . . . go!"

Thibb watched them for a moment, then climbed nimbly up onto the battlements. Standing tippawed, the others peered over the walltop at the still-distant vessel. Dorka Gurdy could not resist the drama of the moment.

"So liddle Uggo Wiltud's dream 'as come true. I'll wager

when that thing gets near enough, we'll see the Wearat sign on its green sail!"

Roogo Foremole, always practical, interrupted. "Bo urr, that bee's all vurry gudd, marm, but wot's us'ns goin' t'do abowt et, Oi arsks?"

Abbot Thibb hopped neatly down to the parapet. "Good question, Foremole. We'd best come up with an answer quickly. I reckon that vessel will be alongside us around lunchtime. What d'you say, Friar?"

The weighty watervole replied sharply, "Well, they won't be gettin any lunch from my kitchens!"

Fottlink the mouse Recorder could not resist a smile. "I'm sure they won't, Friar. First thing we must do is to keep everybeast indoors, especially the Dibbuns."

Sister Fisk was still staring at *Greenshroud*. "That's a big ship, Father Abbot. Have you thought, when it draws alongside our Abbey, its mast tops will be as high as this wall? I think they could climb from there to where we are now. If they're seagoing vermin, they'll be rough, savage beasts. How'll we stop them?"

Dorka Gurdy sat down with her back against the battlements. "Wish that brother o' mine was 'ere now, Father. I wager Jum would think of an idea."

Fottlink nodded. "Aye, no doubt he would. Now, what was it that Jum told us about the Wearat? Ah, I remember. He said that Razzid Wearat had been beaten by the sea otters on the High North Coast. Weren't they supposed to have slain a lot of the ship's crew and sent it on its way in flames? Aye, that was what he said!"

Friar Wopple made a sobering statement. "All well'n'good, but we ain't no warrior sea otters."

Foremole held up a huge digging claw. "Mebbe we'm b'aint, zurr, but us'ns knows 'ow to make ee fire, hurr aye!"

Sister Fisk clenched her paws resolutely. "Then we'll make fire, lots of fire. A big blaze up here won't harm the wallstones!"

The Infirmary Sister's determination gave them heart.

"That's the way! We'll make those rascals sorry they ever thought of coming to Redwall!"

"Boi 'okey, uz'll burn thurr ship to ee cinder, hurr hurr. They'm vurrmints'll be a-scarmperin' abowt wi' thurr tails'n'bottums a-blazin'!"

Abbot Thibb held up his paws for silence. "Please, friends, let's not get carried away. I'm sure it's a sound idea, but we'll act only if they start to threaten us. Now, let's make some preparations."

Razzid Wearat had positioned himself astern. He stood leaning on the tiller, watching his crew, who were all for'ard. As far away from him as they could get, the three conspirators, Shekra, Mowlag and Jiboree, stood on the bow peak.

Mowlag muttered angrily at the vixen, "How d'ye know he suspects anythin', eh?"

Shekra cast a swift glance back at Razzid. "I told ye wot he said. Why d'ye think he's stayin' astern? He knows, I tell ye. Razzid Wearat ain't stupid!"

Jiboree had his eyes fixed on Redwall. "Wot d'ye say we rush 'im? We could slay Razzid an' take the ship. After all, 'e's only one beast, ain't 'e?"

Mowlag curled his lip. "Well, you carry on, mate. I won't be with ye. I know Razzid. He'd either kill one or all of us. Right?"

Shekra was forced to agree. "Right, an' another thing, the crew are all set on gettin' the prize—that place an' all the good life wot goes with it." The vixen was getting more disenchanted with the idea of a mutiny since her interview with the Wearat. "I think we'd be best forgettin' any of our plans until after that place is taken. We need Razzid for that."

Mowlag was inclined to agree with her. "Aye, the cap'n's the one to have on yore side in a battle."

The impulsive Jiboree was not happy, but he was forced to agree. "So be it, then, we wait. But lissen, mates, once we're inside that Redwall Abbey or wotever ye calls it, then our cap'n's a deadbeast. Right?"

On the walltop, Abbey creatures were carrying wood up from below. Ding Toller and Dorka Gurdy were piling it at the northwest gable whilst keeping an eye upon the ship's progress. Roogo Foremole and his crew arrived with a pile of old barrel staves from the wine cellars, which they placed on a heap of dried moss, dead grasses, withered branches and other combustibles. Roogo dusted off his huge paws, winking at Dorka.

"They'm barrel stavers makes gurt flames. Yurr, b'aint ee vurmint boat arrived yet, marm?"

The otter judged the distance from *Greenshroud* to the Abbey. "Nay, sir, 'twill be some time a-comin' yet. When do we light the fire, I wonder?"

Milda, a helpful young volemaid, tossed a bundle of dried bracken onto the pile. "Not yet, marm. Abbot said he'd do it when the time comes."

Sister Fisk called down the wallstairs, "Has anybeast seen Abbot Thibb?"

Friar Wopple was hauling a large cauldron up the steps, assisted by some of her kitchen helpers. "I've seen him not long ago. Excuse me, but would some of you lend a paw with this thing? It's very heavy."

Willing volunteers hurried to help with the cauldron. Having delivered her contribution, the tubby watervole sat on the top step, mopping her brow with a dockleaf.

"I saw Father Abbot not long ago. He was standing in front of Martin the Warrior's tapestry, so I thought it best not to disturb him. I expect he'll return here when he's ready."

Sister Fisk sniffed the contents of the cauldron. "Phew, that smells a bit ripe. What is it, Friar?"

Wopple explained. "That's some waste vegetable cooking oil. I find it excellent for lighting fires—it burns for quite a while. Be careful how you use it, Dorka."

Morning wore on toward midday* as the tension increased. Trundling along at an unhurried pace, the big green-sailed ship drew closer to the Abbey. It was clearly visible now, a very threatening sight. Searats and corsairs lined the rails and forepeak, armed with a fearsome array of weapons, ready and eager to use them. Razzid Wearat held his position at the tiller, with Mowlag and Shekra attending nearby, at his command.

He sized up the huge, red sandstone building, nodding in admiration. "Well, I ain't never seen nothin' like this. Wot d'ye say, Mowlag, do we attack?"

Confused that he should be consulted, the searat mate merely lowered his eyes. "I'm here t'do wotever ye say, Cap'n."

Razzid turned to Shekra. "An' you, fox, wot do you say, eh?"

The Seer had been expecting this. She had a ready reply. "Lord, if ye are set on attackin', I cannot stop ye."

Razzid raised one scarred eyebrow. "But?"

The Seer chose her words carefully. "But I would counsel caution, sire. This is a big stronghold and unknown to us. What number creatures wait behind its walls? Mayhaps if we were to sound them out first, talk to their leaders, let them know who ye are. We might not have to fight, once they know yore name an' reputation."

Razzid stared pointedly at Mowlag. "A wise decision, I think. Wot d'ye say, Mowlag?"

The searat maintained his humble attitude. "Like ye say, Cap'n, a wise decision."

The Wearat stamped his trident butt on the deck. "Good! we'll halt within hailin' distance o' the wall."

In the Abbot's absence, Ding Toller had taken charge at the walltop. Roogo Foremole levered himself up, noting how close *Greenshroud* was.

"Hurr, Ding, they'm almost yurr. Do ee loight ee fire naow?"

The gaunt squirrel drew in a deep, nervous breath. "Aye, I think 'tis about time, but where's the Abbot got to?"

Friar Wopple dipped a tankard in the cauldron, then spread oil over the waiting heap of kindling. "I don't know, friend, but we'd better do somethin' fast!"

Dorka Gurdy lit a fir twig from a lantern. At that moment, the top of a mainsail drew level with the wall.

Redtail, the corsair stoat lookout, climbed into view. Grinning nastily, he swept off his battered hat, addressing them. "Good day to ye, gennelbeasts—"

As the words left his mouth, Dorka touched the lighted twig to the pile and flames shot up with a whoosh.

Redtail yelled out in shock, falling backward. His footpaw caught in the rigging, and he hung there upside down.

Fear gripped Razzid at the sight of the sudden blaze. Memories of his blazing ship at the High North Coast flooded back. He roared at the crew.

"Take 'er back! Back, I say, take 'er back!"

The vermin on the poles shoved hard, reversing the course as the vessel rolled back from the inferno on the walltop. The Wearat ran the length of his ship, heart pounding. He made it to the prow, followed by Mowlag and Shekra.

The vixen stared up at the flames. "Just as well we never attacked right off, Lord. They have a stone fortress, but we've only got a wooden ship!"

Jiboree pointed to the battlements. "Lookit there!"

Razzid stared, wiping moisture from his injured eye, dumbfounded at the sight which confronted them.

Standing astride the battlements was the mouse warrior from his dreams. He was wearing armour and holding forth a flaming sword.

28

Startled by the sudden invasion, Long Patrol, Rogue Crew, Guosim and hedgehogs ducked into the water. The very air above them thrummed with noise and ear-splitting squeaks. Gasping for air, Swiffo broke the surface, still holding the smouldering torch. Dimly he could make out masses of black shapes wheeling and swooping everywhere. He struck out with the dead torch, left and right, trying to defend himself. However, he hit only empty air, no matter how hard he tried.

Skor Axehound came up for air. Swiftly sensing what was going on, he grabbed the torch from his young son.

"Don't harm 'em—stay still!"

Hugging himself and closing both eyes tight, Swiffo obeyed. One by one, the others emerged from the water, with Skor still calling the same advice to them. Everybeast stood stock-still, some covering their ears to shut out the deafening sounds. Then as suddenly as it started, all was normal again. They were left standing waist deep in the watery, dark tunnel. Fresh torches blossomed into light, bringing relief to the gloom.

Lancejack Sage shook herself. "I say, what'n the name o' blinkin', blitherin' seasons was that, wot?"

Skor lifted her onto the ledge with a single huge paw.

"That was bats, missy. Hundreds, nay, thousands o' the things. They must roost up there inside yon hole."

Captain Rake chuckled. "Och, 'tis nae wonder our foebeasts didnae pursue us. They're affrighted o' the beasties!"

Big Drander exclaimed, "Well, I don't bloomin' well blame 'em. They gave me a few nasty moments, I tell ye."

Sergeant Miggory agreed. "Aye, me too, h'I must confess, but those batbeasts 'ave gone now. Let 'em go an' frighten the rascals who were shootin' poison darts h'at us."

Lieutenant Scutram mounted the ledge. "Indeed! There certainly were a lot o' bat blighters. How many would ye say, sah?"

Rake Nightfur scratched an ear. "Och, as many as ye like. Mahself, Ah wasnae countin', just wonderin' how we're goin' tae get oot o' this place!"

Buff Redspore pointed up to the hole. "I'd say by that route, sah. The stream'll only take us underground, an' we ain't otters. What if it goes deeper, maybe up to the tunnel roof? There'd be no room for us to breathe. I vote we go up through the hole. It's drier, an' there ain't no bats up there right now, wot!"

Skor shouldered his great battleaxe. "We're with ye. Sounds like a sensible idea. Huh, that's if'n a beast like me will fit through that hole."

Ruggan patted his father's ample midriff. "Right, you go last. If ye get stuck, we can always pull ye through, ole wavedog!"

Skor pawed his axe, nodding at his son. "You ain't so big I can't clip yore rudder a touch. Now, move! Shrews, hogs'n'hares first, Rogue Crew t'the rear!"

Sergeant Miggory went first, setting a torch in a crack as he helped Uggo and Posy through into the dark, silent hole. Ever practical, the tough colour sergeant found some thick dead roots protruding overhead. These he pulled out, making more torches. Soon they were all assembled, even Skor, who had managed to bull his thick body through after two tries.

Buff Redspore, along with Gil and Dreel, the young otter scouts, went ahead whilst the others took a short rest.

Log a Log Dandy rubbed his paws together, shuddering. "Gloomy flippin' place, ain't it? Sort of eerie, eh!"

Captain Rake looked around at the thick-packed earth and rock, with roots dangling from the low ceiling. "Ah'm no' verra fond o' it mahself. We'll move on soon, before the bats come back."

Old Drogbuk, who had remained quiet so far, began grumbling. "Huh, stuck unnerground without a thing to eat or sup, an' my rheumatiz is playin' me up after sloppin' through that stream. Wish I'd never come 'ere."

Skor waggled his axe under Drogbuk's snout. "Well, yore here now, ole pincushion, so stop moanin' or I'll land ye a smack that'll knock all those spines out!"

The trackers returned. Buff Redspore threw Skor and Rake a quick salute. "Got to report more bats ahead, though they ain't in our way. They're in a sort of chamber off to one side."

Captain Rake drew his claymores. "Right, let's go an' see. Try not tae make much noise, mah bonny beasties."

Uggo grasped Posy's paw. "Oh, no, more bats. I ain't too fond o' bats!"

Posy pulled him along with the others. "Oh, Uggo, they're only creatures, same as us, an' they haven't done us any harm so far. Trust Cap'n Rake."

The side chamber was off to the left of the winding uphill passage. Holding up a torch, Rake peered in. "Och, nothin' tae fret aboot in there. 'Tis full o' babes an' a few auld bat-wives, all hangin' upside doon."

Swiffo pushed past him. "Can I take a look?"

Skor dragged him back by his rudder. "Leave them alone an' get back with the Crew."

Swiffo mumbled, "Huh, only wanted a quick peep."

The bats began setting up a feeble clamour of squeaks.

Skor shook his head at his young son. "See wot ye've done, upset the creatures, ye scamp!"

Sergeant Miggory held up a paw for silence. "It ain't Swiffo wot's h'upset 'em, sah. H'it's a snake."

Skor stepped back from the chamber. "Wot makes ye say that, Sar'nt?"

Miggory confirmed his suspicion. "That smell, that sound, h'I'd know h'it anywhere. There's a serpent in there, stalkin' the bat babes."

Lieutenant Scutram waggled his ears. "Hmm, stands to reason, I'd say. Just the place for those confounded reptiles, a ready-made larder o' vittles. Could ye say what type o' snake the blighter is, Sarn't?"

Miggory drew closer to the chamber, sniffing the air. "A h'adder, sah. I'd stake me scut h'on it!"

Skor made to march onward. "Well, let's hope there's no more ahead, eh!"

Rake Nightfur confronted him. "Ye cannae just march off an' leave the babbies t'be eaten by a snake. 'Tain't right, Skor!"

The Rogue Crew Chieftain stared oddly at Rake. "Then wot d'ye propose we do? Adders can kill with a single strike—poisonfangs, we call 'em. Best left alone, eh?"

The hare captain turned away, throwing a nod in Miggory's direction. "Right, Sarn't, we'll deal with this."

Miggory's craggy features broke into a grin. "D'ye mean a quick decoy an' the ole one-two, sah?"

Rake winked at him. "Aye, that should do the job, Ah ken!"

The word went round like wildfire.

"Surely they ain't goin' t'take on a bloomin' adder, wot?"

"They must be mad—us Guosim stays away from adders!"

"Well, come on, buckoes, we've got t'see this!"

Lieutenant Scutram gave an order. "You beasts, stay away from the chamber. Ye can watch, but stay still an' quiet. Cap'n Rake an' the sarn't can deal with an adder. I've seen 'em do it before. So stand clear!"

It was indeed an adder, a fully grown female complete

with black chevrons decorating its scales. Slowly, it was making its way up the chamber wall toward the tiny hanging bats. The older batwives were squeaking piteously, unable to deter the snake from its purpose. Unaware of the peril, the little ones squeaked along with their elders.

With sinister, unhurried grace, the predator slithered up the wall, latching on to outcrops for support. Rake sheathed one of his blades, arming himself with the other and a torch. He nodded to the sergeant.

"Are ye fit'n'ready, mah friend?"

Miggory was balanced lightly, both paws clenched. "Aye, let's h'open the ball, sah!"

He dropped to one side of the snake as Rake inched forward and touched its tail tip with the lighted torch.

Then things happened with a speed which amazed the onlookers. The snake spun around, jaws open, fangs exposed. Captain Rake thrust the claymore blade edge-on at it. Instinctively, the reptile struck, clamping its mouth on the blade edge. Before it could let go, Sergeant Miggory slipped in beneath it. With lightning rapidity, he delivered two stunning uppercuts, right under the adder's jaws.

Bang! Whack!

Rake watched the snake slide off his blade, senseless. "Mah thanks t'ye, Sarn't. Ah think two blows is enough."

Miggory picked up the snake, checking its fangs. "Never needed more'n two blows to break h'a sarpint's fangs, sah. That'n won't be a-feedin' off baby bats no more!" He tossed the unconscious adder to one side and was immediately surrounded by young hares and sea otters.

"Blood'n'thunder, Sarge, how did ye do that? I never seen anythin' so fast in all me life!"

One of the Rogue Crew seemed a bit cynical. "'Twas all some sort o' trick, wasn't it, Sergeant?"

Miggory's fisted paws wove a dazzling pattern around the otter's face. He leaned back against the tunnel wall, awestruck. The tough veteran hare chuckled lightly.

"Allus remember, young sah, the quickness o' the paw can deceive the eye—h'an' like h'as not, blacken h'it!"

Lieutenant Scutram gave the order to move on. "Right, chaps, let's leave the batbabes t'their nap an' the serpent to a jolly sore mouth when it wakens. Fall in by the right, straighten up, but mind your nut on the ceilin', especially you, Drander!"

No sooner were they on the march again than old Drogbuk started complaining. "I'm starvin' t'death. Don't we even get a mizzuble bite to eat?"

Skor trod on the back of his footpaw, making him stumble. "Give yore tongue a rest, y'ole famine-faced nuisance. There ain't vittles nor drink for any of us, so quit moanin' about it. Just shut up an' keep up!"

Trug Bawdsley was startled by an ominous rumble. "What's goin' on chaps? Is the blinkin' tunnel collapsin', wot?"

Big Drander answered mournfully, "'Tis this flippin' stomach o' mine, it won't stop grumblin'."

A loud gurgling groan confirmed this. Drander smiled wanly. "See, I told ye. The jolly old tum's got a mind of its own!"

Corporal Welkin Dabbs glared at the culprit. "Keep that up, bucko, an' I'll put your stomach on a charge!"

Drander raised his voice over his protesting abdomen. "I say, steady on, Corp. That ain't fair!"

Captain Rake stifled a chuckle. "If ye can sing a bonny tune, I'll drop all charges on ye, Drander."

The big hare promptly broke into song.

"Here I'm sittin' in the guardhouse,
wot a sad old sight to see,
so take warnin' by my story, chaps,
an' lissen carefully. . . .
Oh, don't let your stomach rule your life,
don't let your gut decide your fate,

you'll regret it in the end, so hearken to me, friend,
a glutton doesn't have a single mate. . . .
Oh, noooooooo!

Drander had long been voted the worst singer in the
Long Patrol. There was general laughter as Captain Rake
called out to him, "Och, that's enough, bonny lad. Ah've
changed mah mind—Ah'll put ye on a charge if ye continue
singin'!"

Corporal Welkin Dabbs chuckled. "I say, Drander old
lad, why not let your jolly old tum give us a verse or two,
wot? It'd sound a lot better'n that voice o' yours!"

The tunnel ceiling became gradually lower. All the taller
beasts had to duck their heads or bend. Skor Axehound's
grunts echoed around the gloomy passageway.

"Flamin' hard t'catch breath down here, an' my back's
startin' to bother me. Shall we take a rest, eh?"

Captain Rake was in agreement with the sea otter Chieftain. "Aye, a wee rest'll nae harm us. Buff, take yon two wee
otterscouts an' see what lies ahead."

Everybeast sat down gratefully, backs to the tunnel wall.
Posy cupped a paw around one ear, listening. "Hark, I can
hear noises from behind us, a bit faint yet."

Lieutenant Scutram's long ears stood up. "Aye, I hear it
too, missy. Sounds like those bats returnin'. Keep y'voices
down, chaps, we can do without a visit from them."

Uggo murmured unhappily, "I don't like it down here.
We could be goin' anywhere or nowhere, could even be lost
forever!"

Young Wilbee was equally miserable. "I say, imagine never
seein' flippin' daylight again, wot. Dyin' of hunger'n'thirst
miles underground!"

Sergeant Miggory raised his voice sternly. "H'attention,
now, ye can stow that kind h'o' talk. We'll get h'out of 'ere
sooner or later, right, sah?"

Rake nodded. "Right, Sarn't. Och, here's the scouts

returnin'. They've no' been gone long. What's tae report, Buff?"

The haremaid saluted. "Not very good news, I'm afraid, sah. Just round the next bend there's a whoppin' great hole in the tunnel floor blockin' the flippin' path. There ain't no way around it. Come an' take a look, sah!"

Rake, Skor and a small party went to investigate. Buff Redspore led the way, holding forth her torch as they came to the spot.

The floor fell sharply away, leaving them on the edge of a gaping abyss, which threw up a pale green light.

Ruggan edged to the rim, peered down, then stepped back. "Blood'n'bones, it makes ye dizzy just lookin' at it!"

Sergeant Miggory chanced a peep. "Aye, 'tis h'a long way down. There must be water at the bottom—that's wot's makin' the green light."

Rake stared across to the other side of the huge hole. "Och, only a bird could cross that!"

Taking a lighted torch, he swung it to gain momentum, then flung it. The torch twirled in a blazing arc, landing on the far side in a shower of sparks.

Skor shook his grizzled head. "Ye can see the tunnel continues over there. Steel an' hellfire, how do we get across that distance?"

Buff Redspore answered, "We can't, sah. Without ropes or planks, it looks like we're blinkin' stuck here!"

They faced the disappointing fact in silence.

Then trouble piled upon trouble when the remainder of the company came running. Behind them the whirr and squeak of bats rose to a deafening crescendo as Uggo yelled, "The bats are comin', thousands of 'em!"

Then the dark horde broke over them like a tidal wave.

Protecting *Greenshroud* from the menace of fire, Razzid Wearat ordered his ship to retreat from the bonfire on Redwall's northwest walltop. Amidst the cheers of Redwallers,

Abbot Thibb maintained his stance on the battlements, holding high the flaming sword of Martin the Warrior.

Foremole Roogo stared at him in admiration. "Boi 'okey, zurr, you'm looken gurtly brave oop thurr. Oi thought et wurr Marthen ee Wurrier cummed back to save us'ns frum they vurrmints!"

Not returning the trusty mole's glance, Thibb spoke out of the side of his mouth as he held his pose. "I'm hoping that's what the vermin think also, Roogo. D'you think I'll have to stay up here for long? My paw is tired from holding up the sword, and I don't want the burning oil to drip down on me."

Fottlink, the mouse Recorder, nodded toward the enemy ship. "I think you and our bonfire warned them off, Father. Come on down and tell us, what gave you the idea of dressing up?"

Ding Toller and the Foremole helped Thibb down onto the parapet. He put aside the flaming sword gratefully. "Whew, I could feel the heat from that blade!"

Friar Wopple removed Thibb's helmet, chuckling. "My copper trifle mould suited you well, Father."

Accepting a beaker of cold pear cordial, the Abbot removed the rest of his disguise. "Thank you, Friar, the trifle mould was indeed yours, just as the sword belonged to Martin. As for the rest, this red cloak is my bedcover, the gauntlets are a pair of oven mitts which one of your kitchen helpers loaned to me. The idea must belong to Martin the Warrior. I stood in front of his tapestry long enough, wonderin' what to do. Then I sat down on the floor—I must have dropped off for a while. Suddenly, I knew exactly what I must do, so I took his sword, disguised myself as him and came straight up here. Just in time, too, so we've got our Abbey Warrior to thank."

Dorka Gurdy spoke, dampening the victorious mood slightly. "No matter what we do, I think those rascals are goin' to attack sooner or later."

*

Aboard the *Greenshroud*, Razzid had been putting his mind to the problem. He had not come this far to see himself turned away from his aim. Having reached a decision, he called the crew together.

"Well, buckoes, one thing's for sure, they ain't goin' to attack us. Those woodlanders'll sit tight behind their big stone walls. So, we're safe enough here, eh?"

"So wot d'ye say, Cap'n, are we goin' to take that place, or 'ang about 'ere 'til we grows old?"

The voice, which came from a group amidships, was that of Jiboree.

Giving no clue that he knew this, Razzid answered, "Dig the dirt outta yore lugs an' I'll tell ye. I wants a good gang of ye to go into that forest. Yore to chop down about six good-sized trees—pines or firs should do, good straight ones. When ye've done that, bring 'em back 'ere, an' I'll tell ye the rest o' my plan."

The crew stood in silence, as if unsure of the next move.

Razzid wiped moisture from his bad eye. "Mowlag, Jiboree, yore in charge o' the tree-choppin' gang. Pick twoscore crewbeasts an' get to it. Vixen, I wants a word with ye. Come t'my cabin!"

As the searat and the corsair weasel chose their party, Razzid jabbed his trident toward the cabin. "You go first, fox."

Filled with trepidation, Shekra entered the cabin. Razzid closed the door behind him. Leaning on his trident haft, he fixed the vixen with a piercing stare, stating flatly, "Ye know the penalty for mutiny agin yore cap'n, I suppose?"

With a sob in her voice, Shekra protested, "Sire, I have always been loyal to you, I swear!"

He knocked her flat with a swift kick, hissing viciously, "D'ye take me for an idiot? I know wot's been goin' on twixt you an' those other two, Mowlag'n'Jiboree. Speak just one more lie an' I'll rip yore throat out with this trident. Tell the truth an' I'll let ye live. So?"

Shekra had no option but to confess, though with a little twist of her own. "Lord, they threatened to kill me if I didn't go along with 'em. They were going to murder you as we sailed up the River Moss, but I talked them out of it. I said wait until we conquer Redwall first. I was playing for time, you see. I was going to warn you, believe me, sire."

Razzid nodded. "I see, an' were the crew with them, too?"

The vixen sensed a further opportunity. "They wouldn't tell me, sire. Some were, some weren't. But leave it to me. I'll discover who was in on it with them."

The Wearat leaned forward, his breath tickling her nostrils. "Leave that to me, an' heed wot I say now. Nobeast, not Mowlag, Jiboree or any o' the crew must know of this—not a single word, d'ye hear me?"

Shekra gulped. "My lips are sealed, Cap'n!"

Razzid's searching eye never left her for a moment. "They'll be sealed for good if'n ye play me false. Get up!"

The vixen staggered up on shaking limbs as Razzid pointed to the bulkhead wall. "Stand there an' raise yore right paw. Go on, fox, do it. I ain't goin' to kill ye. Just raise that paw an' swear to serve me truly."

Gaining a little confidence, Shekra spoke up. "I give my oath I'll always serve you truly, sire!"

Razzid struck like lightning.

Thud! The trident's middle prong went right through the vixen's paw into the wall behind. She gave an agonised screech, which was stifled by Razzid's paw across her mouth. Smiling savagely at Shekra, he explained his cruel act. "Said I wouldn't kill ye, didn't I? That didn't mean ye weren't to be punished for plottin' agin me."

Shekra gave vent to a long-stifled moan as he twisted the trident, withdrawing it. Razzid shoved her contemptuously toward the door. "Yore still alive, ain't ye? Stop whinin' an' git out o' my cabin. Yore gettin' blood everywhere!" With her face a drawn mask of pain, the Seer reeled out on deck, clasping her paw tightly to stanch the wound.

Razzid put his head out, calling to the cook, "Badtooth,

bring me some decent food an' a jug o' the best grog. Move yoreself, I'm famished!"

Badtooth, the fat greasy weasel, watched as Razzid divided a roast wood pigeon into two portions and placed beakers of grog on the table. Razzid winked. "Join me, my ole shipmate—ye did well."

Badtooth gnawed on the meat, then slopped down some grog. "Thankee, Cap'n. Anythin' else ye need me t'find out for ye?"

Razzid clinked beakers with his spy. "Just keep yore eyes'n'ears open when ye mix with the crew."

The fat weasel cackled. "Heeheehee! That'll be easy. Oh, I sent me liddle nephew Twangee out wid the tree-choppin' gang. Young Twangee's got a sharp pair of ears on 'im fer a wee galley weasel."

Razzid nodded. "Good! When ye dish up vittles t'night, give the crew an extra ration o' grog, eh!"

The cook's huge stomach wobbled as he laughed. "Heehee, ain't nothin' like extra grog t'set their tongues loose an' waggin'. I'll give 'em plenty! Well, Cap'n, here's t'the death of yore enemies an' a victory over that Abbey!"

Razzid winked his good eye at Badtooth. "I'll drink to that, shipmate!"

Dusk was falling as Sister Fisk and Milda the volemaid supervised the Dibbuns' bedtime. It was difficult, as there was an air of excitement amongst the Abbeybabes. No sooner were they put into their truckle beds than they wriggled out and scurried to the dormitory windows. The Sister stamped her footpaw firmly down.

"Back in those beds immediately. Right now, d'ye hear me?"

The squirrelbabe Guggle yelled as Milda prised her paws from the windowsill.

"Lemmego, Mildy, wanna see da big naughtybeast ship!"

Sister Fisk tried not to raise her voice. "There's nothing to see—it's dark outside. Now go to bed!"

Alfio, the Dibbun shrew, wrinkled his nose cheekily as he encouraged the others to set up a chant. "Dab! Dab! Dab!"

Milda sighed. "They're starting the Dibbuns Against Bedtime chant, Sister. What'll we do?"

Ever resourceful, Fisk emptied the contents of a small vial into a jug of warm plum cordial. This she poured into small beakers, coaxing the Dibbuns into their beds with it.

"Last one in bed doesn't get any plum cordial—hurry now!"

There was a mass scramble to be first under the covers. As Fisk and Milda distributed the drinks, the little ones kept up a constant chatter, each question demanding a reply.

"Will the bad naughtybeasts go away, Mildy?"

"Oh, yes, I expect they will, when Father Abbot has a word with them. Careful with that drink now."

"Hurr hurr, ee h'Abbot choppen they tails off with Marthen's gurt sword—they'm wull soon go 'way!"

Sister Fisk smiled at the molebabe. "Indeed he will, and you'll be next if you're not asleep soon."

Alfio the shrewbabe sat up, shaking his head decisively. "Alfio can't go t'sleep wivout a song!"

Milda gently eased him back down. "All close your eyes, then I'll sing for you."

The young volemaid had a warm, soothing voice. She sang a lullaby as Sister Fisk moved quietly about, collecting the beakers.

"When all the trees stand silent,
this is the time I love best,
after old daylight's faded,
when the sun has sunk to rest.
Off midst the tranquil darkness,
a nightingale sings to the moon,
butterflies close their eyes,
they'll be a-slumb'ring soon.
Lullaby, hush you now,
after your busy day,

298

even bees on nights like these,
cease bumbling away.
Deep streams go quietly murm'ring,
faintly small breezes sigh.
Hush now . . . hush now . . . lullaaaaby."

Sister Fisk patted Milda's paw. "Oh, well done, miss. Now come away carefully, we don't want to disturb them."

Outside the dormitory door, Milda remarked, "The little ones were asleep before I'd finished, Sister, but I usually have to sing the lullaby twice."

Fisk held up the small vial, chuckling. "My last few drops of marjoram oil—pure and harmless, the best slumber medicine I know. I shouldn't say this, but I wish the Dibbuns would sleep through all of this ill fortune which has descended on us. Mark my words, young un, there's trouble ahead for our Abbey. Big trouble!"

29

In the close confines of the tunnel, countless bats filled the limited space. There were so many of the dark-winged creatures that the hares, otters and the three hedgehogs had to crouch so low they were almost flat with the ground.

Sergeant Miggory covered Posy with his paws. "H'are you alright, missy?"

The young hogmaid replied, "I'm fine, thank you, Sergeant. There's so many bats, but I haven't been touched by one yet."

Lancejack Sage added. "Neither have I. Jolly odd, ain't it?"

Skor had overheard them. He called out from nearby, "We're swamped by bats, but all ye can feel is the breeze from their wings as they fly by."

As quickly as it had started, all bat activity ceased.

Captain Rake stood up cautiously, gazing around as he picked up a fallen torch. "Ah dinnae know what's happenin' now. Look, the things are hangin' upside doon everywhere. Ah wonder what they want." As far back as the eye could see, covering the ceiling over the void and massed on the far side, the bats had stationed themselves.

Everybeast stood up slowly, with old Drogbuk hissing

a warning. "Keep a close eye on the brutes. I think they're goin' to attack. Hah, I never trusted bats in me life!"

A bunch of quills rattled as Ruggan gave Drogbuk's rear a light kick. "Silence, y'ole fool. If'n they were goin' to attack us, they'd have done it by now. Cap'n Rake, look!"

A convoy of bats came looming toward them, headed by one larger than the rest. Between them a line of bats were carrying the writhing form of the adder which had been hunting their young. All that could be heard was the hissing of the injured reptile. Silently the bats bore it out, over the deep abyss, holding it there until the big bat motioned with one wing. They dropped the snake, and it fell, down, down, finally disappearing from sight into the waters far below. The big bat gave a piercing squeak to the others gathered on the opposite side of the chasm. In a group they winged soundlessly back, bearing a long, rough cable of woven root and vine.

The big bat spoke in a low whisper to Sergeant Miggory. "I am Hiposir, Bigwing of this tribe . . . this tribe. You are Stonepaw . . . Stonepaw . . . saviour of our babes and old ones . . . old ones. With one blow, Stonepaw . . . one blow . . . you rid us of the great Poisontooth . . . Poisontooth. Hiposir thanks you. I go now . . . go now. Follow the sweet smell . . . the sweet smell. Long may ye live . . . live . . . live."

Hiposir glided off, followed by all his tribe, in a rush of wing noise and squeaking.

Uggo Wiltud was first to break the uncanny silence which followed the bats' departure. He winked roguishly at Sergeant Miggory. "Good ole Stonepaw the serpent stunner, eh!"

Miggory picked up the loose cable end. "That'll be h'enough out o' you, young un. Me name's Miggory, Colour Sarn't Nubbs Miggory, h'in fact. Beggin' yore pardon, Cap'n, but wot are we supposed t'do with this, h'a bloomin' tightrope walk?"

Rake took the cable from the sergeant. He gave it a tug.

"Ah think 'tis tied to somethin' over yonder. Here, mah bonnies, lend a few wee paws an' we'll see, eh?"

Willing paws heaved on the thick cable, stowing it behind as it payed out.

Old Drogbuk roared excitedly, "Lookit, 'ere she comes . . . lookit lookit!"

It was a curious affair which they heaved across the rift. A wide, primitive-looking net, woven from roots, fibres and branches.

Posy clapped her paws. "It's a bridge. I wonder who made it."

Lieutenant Scutram shook his ears happily. "We'll never know, miss, but a jolly good vote o' thanks to 'em, whoever they flippin' well were. Come on, chaps, take firm hold. We don't want the bally thing fallin' down that confounded hole, wot!"

They hauled away until the structure was taut. Skor grabbed the original single cable, securing it several times around the bulky taproots of some woodland giant whose ends penetrated the tunnel ceiling. "Right, who's goin' to try it, eh?"

Even before he had finished speaking, Swiffo was out on the crude network, picking his way nimbly across.

Skor roared after his youngest son, "Go easy, ye young rip. Slow down or ye'll fall!"

Balancing on his rudder, Swiffo swayed playfully, halfway across the abyss. He was followed by the equally nimble Log a Log Dandy.

Swiffo shouted to his father, "Yore next, Pa—but stow yore axe lest ye trip on it!"

Skor's huge, booming laughter echoed around as he gave Corporal Welkin Dabbs a pat on the back, which almost sent him sprawling. "Impudent young blood pudden. Wouldn't ye just love to have a son like 'im, eh?"

Swiffo reached the other side and danced a little jig. "C'mon, mates, let's go an' find a sweet smell to follow!"

Skor stepped gingerly out onto the raftlike network over

the chasm. He crouched there wobbling and calling out, "Never mind dancin' around over there, ye scallawag. Get back here an' help me across this contraption!" Fortunately the frame held whilst everybeast made his way across, with Dandy shouting advice.

"Don't look down or shut yore eyes, mates, just keep starin' straight ahead at this side. Ahoy there, Drander, you'll have to tote ole Drogbuk across on yore back, or he'll hang around there 'til next season!"

The ancient hedgehog put up a struggle as Drander heaved him up onto his back. "Lemme go, ye great omadorm—I ain't goin', I tell ye!"

The big young hare held Drogbuk firmly and started out. "Oh, yes, you are, sah, so hold on now. Phew! When was the last time you took a bloomin' bath?"

They gathered on the other side at the continuation of the tunnel. Corporal Welkin Dabbs checked everybeast out quickly. "They're all present an' correct, sah, everyone safe over!"

Captain Rake saluted. "Thank ye, Dabbs. Right, Sergeant, form these bonny lads up an' let's be on our way."

With torches flaring, they marched off down the gloomy passage, kicking up dust as they went.

Lancejack Sage wiped a paw across her mouth. "I'm absoballylutely dyin' of the thirst, wot!"

Corporal Dabbs, a bit of an old campaigner, gave her some timeworn advice. "Try suckin' a pebble, miss. That should help, wot."

Sage was in no mood for old remedies. "Oh, go an' boil your blinkin' head, Corp. All that gives you is a dusty mouth. I've tried it."

Captain Rake spoke out so everybeast could hear. "Och, did Ah hear insubordination an' insult to a corporal? We'll have less o' that, wee lassie. There's no drink or vittles until we're out o' here, is that clear? So if'n ye quit jawin' an' start pawin', mebbe we'll get closer tae guid nourishment!"

This quickened the pace, which after a while became difficult. Young Wilbee complained, "I seem t'be goin' slower. Huh, must be the air in this confounded place, or the lack of it."

Buff Redspore knew the reason. "It's because we're marchin' uphill. Can't ye feel it?"

Though Skor Axehound was gasping for breath, he sounded happy. "Must mean we're gettin' somewhere. Not much further t'go, eh! Gil, Dreel, go ahead with the Long Patrol tracker. See wot ye can find an' report back. I've got t'have a rest, Rake."

The captain ordered a short halt.

This time it was Log a Log Dandy who began to go on about food. He started up an old Guosim river ditty. Nobeast tried to stop him, in fact, one or two joined in. It seemed to lighten the mood in all that gloom.

"My oh my oh my,
what would I give for a pie,
just like me dear old granny used to bake,
stuffed full o' juicy plums, an' to lubricate me gums,
enough good ale to fill a forest lake!

"Why oh why oh why,
doesn't somebeast hear my cry,
an' toss me just a hunk o' bread'n'cheese,
with a pot o' cold mint tea, I could sup not fussily,
go tell the cook that I ain't hard to please!

"Dear oh dear oh dear,
I'm so close t'death, I fear,
who's goin' to grant a poor ole beast's last wish?
If ye sit me in a seat an' let me eat an' eat an' eat,
I'll lick the pattern off the flamin' dish!"

The trackers returned. Buff was behind Gil and Dreel, who reported jointly.

"The way's pretty safe up ahead."

"Aye, but the tunnel splits off two ways."

"Er, so we weren't sure which is the right un to take."

Ambling up, Buff threw a casual salute. "'Cos they never stayed long enough t'jolly well find out, sah. The tunnel we follow is the one with the sweet scent."

Dandy wrinkled his snout. "Sweet scent, wot sweet scent?"

Buff Redspore allowed herself a huge smile as she explained, "Fresh air, m'friend. What smells sweeter than that after wanderin' about these musty old tunnels, wot!"

The news caused a joyous uproar. Creatures leapt up and made to run off and find the exit tunnel. It was Skor Axehound's booming shouts which stopped them in their tracks.

"Stand steady, there. You ain't had orders t'move off! Try an' behave like warriors—an' that goes for you hogs, too."

Posy retorted sharply, "Oh, does it really. Well, where have your young scouts run off to, eh?"

Log a Log Dandy chuckled. "Aye, barrelbelly, ye should see to yore Rogue Crew afore shoutin' at others. Where've Gil an' Dreel gone, pray tell?"

The big chieftain's head swivelled this way and that as he enquired of his crew, "Where've those two liddle rips gone?"

Ruggan shrugged. "Prob'ly dashed off to smell the air. Let's hope they take the right tunnel this time. Don't worry about 'em. They'll be waitin' for us out in the open."

Skor slammed his rudder down hard. "Them young uns are my responsibility. Take yore brother, Swiffo, an' get after 'em afore they come to some harm!"

Ruggan and Swiffo sped off along the tunnel.

After a while, the rest followed at a steady pace, following the upward sloping passage. Young Ferrul was the first to smell anything, even before they reached the junction where the tunnels split. She twiddled her ears with anticipation.

"Oh, I say, chaps, can ye sniff it? Fresh air, it's better'n a fresh strawberry'n'plum fruit salad. Mmmmm!"

At the junction, one tunnel began to slope downward but the other continued to rise. From the latter, there was a summer breeze wafting in.

Sergeant Miggory breathed deeply. "Seasons h'of flowers'n'ferns, sah, h'aint it nice!"

Captain Rake sniffed appreciatively. "Och, 'tis like a wee butterfly kissin' mah nose!" He was almost bowled over by the return of Ruggan and Swiffo, who hurtled down on him, waving their paws for silence.

Skor Axehound scowled at the pair. "Well, did ye find Gil'n'Dreel?"

Keeping his voice low, Ruggan appeared to be stifling laughter. "Aye, sir, they been captured by vermin!"

The sea otter Chieftain waved his battleaxe. "They've what? Been captured by vermin, an' ye think 'tis funny?"

Swiffo stood in his father's path, hastening to explain. "Steady on, Pa. There's only about a score of 'em, runty stoats an' rats. We followed 'em to their camp. It ain't far off, an' guess wot? They're havin' a feast!"

Skor glanced from one to the other. "Ye weren't seen by the vermin, were ye?"

Ruggan smiled cannily. "Of course not, sir. A feast!"

His father caught the irony of the situation. He grinned slyly and licked his axeblade. "I'll wager they'll welcome guests to their feast, eh? Are ye ready, Rake an' Dandy? Come on, let's eat!"

There were actually about thirty vermin, mostly stoats and rats, with a few ferrets. Their camp was on the bank of a stream; both Gil and Dreel were bound to a willow trunk. The young otters did not seem unduly put out, as they had seen Ruggan and Swiffo spying on their captors. A cauldron was bubbling over a fire whilst the brigand vermin prepared food. Some were grilling trout on green twigs; others placed flatbreads on hot stones, whilst some broached a keg of nettle beer. Their leader, a patch-eyed overweight ferret, was discussing his prisoners with an old rat.

"Theez muz be der ones Lord Ketral was chasin' after, ya!"

The old rat bared toothless gums. "Ayarr, but uz catchered dem, so worra we do, Viglat? Give dem ter Ketral, or roast 'em inta vikkles? I ain't never et riverdog, 'ave yew?"

Viglat the patch-eyed ferret grinned. "Ketral won't mizz two liddle uns like dem, wotja t'ink?"

The old rat sniggered. "Riverdogs fer brekkist tamorrer!"

"Ahem!"

The sound got the pair's attention. They turned to see Sergeant Miggory leaning against a beech tree. He was unarmed and smiling rather simply.

"H'excuse me, friends, but could h'either of ye tell me the way to Redwall Abbey? I'm lost, y'see."

A quick nod from Viglat brought the closest six vermin to surround Miggory. The patch-eyed ferret drew a rusty dirk from his waist sash, swaggering around the sergeant. "Lookit 'ere, mates. We got uz a rabbet!"

The old rat nodded eagerly. "I et rabbet once—'twas nize!"

To their surprise, Miggory showed no fear, but joined in amicably. "H'I don't think ye'd like me, though. H'I'm a hare, not a rabbit. We're tough, y'see."

A nearby stoat poked him in the back. "Tough, eh? 'Ow tough?"

Rounding on the stoat, the sergeant knocked him out cold with a thunderous straight left. "H'is that tough h'enough for ye, scumnose?"

Viglat was about to thrust his dirk into the hare's back when a commanding shout rang out. "Drop that frogsticker or yer a deadbeast!"

Sea otters, Long Patrol hares and Guosim shrews emerged from the trees on the streambank. Now that the position was reversed, Viglat found that he and his crew were surrounded.

As Skor Axehound was releasing Gil and Dreel with a few slashes of his axeblade, he consulted Lieutenant Scutram. "Have ye got a head count o' these rascals?"

Scutram confirmed his total. "Aye, sah—thirty-two, all told."

Skor nodded. "Right. Read 'em the rules, Lieutenant."

The astonished Viglat was about to protest when Captain Rake kicked his rear end sharply. "Hauld yer wheesht an' dinnae speak 'til you're told. Carry on, Lieutenant."

Scutram laid out the rules of engagement to the vermin. "Listen up now, you scabby bunch! This is a contest—we'll match you beast for beast, wot. Now, all into the stream, quick as y'like. Come on, move y'selves, you idle vermin!"

Viglat and his followers were ushered roughly into the water by some sea otters as Scutram continued, "It's t'be a jolly old scrap, a fight, actually. Thirty-two of our chaps'll face ye in the water. Winner takes the feast. No rules, really—winnin's the thing, eh, wot!"

Viglat finally spoke, in indignant protest. "Dem's our vikkles—diz ain't right!"

Captain Rake waved a dismissive paw. "Och, away with ye an' quit whinin'. Ah'll tell ye what. If ye defeat us, we'll surrender to ye. That's fair, ain't it? Och, Ah'm fed up arguin' with ye. Go to it, braw beasties!"

The thirty-two consisted of fourteen sea otters, an equal number of hares and four Guosim shrews, who were in the minority. Without further ado, they charged the vermin, roaring their war cries.

"Yaaaylahooo!"

"Eulaliiiiiaaaa!"

"Logalogaloooooog!"

Startled by the fury of the onslaught, most of the vermin scrambled deeper into the water and swam off downstream. The rest threw away their weapons, flinging up their paws in surrender. Sitting on the bank, Skor lifted up the keg of nettle beer and took a deep draught. He shook his great bearded head in disgust.

"Ah, 'tis a sad ole life, Rake, after havin' to run away from vermin, we finally get the chance to fight 'em. Hah, an' wot d'they do? Turn tail an' run away! It ain't fair!"

The hare captain sipped glumly at a beaker of nettle beer. "Aye, just so mah friend. Hoho, what's this Ah see?"

It was Gil and Dreel lugging the patch-eyed ferret between them. He was groaning as they kicked his tail.

Skor chuckled. "Wot d'ye want with that worthless bag o' fat, young uns?"

The answers came alternately from the young scouts. "We never caught him, Lord. The sergeant did."

"But he gave this rascal to us—we're allowed to punish him."

"Aye, 'cos he was goin' to roast us for brekkist tomorrow."

Shaking water from himself, Miggory came out of the stream. "That un's their chief, sah. I think 'e might know the way to Redwall, seein' h'as ole Drogbuk don't."

The vermin feast was less than adequate for hungry creatures. The fish were golloped down by Skor's Rogue Crew, whilst hares and shrews shared the flatbreads. Uggo sampled a sip of the bubbling liquid from the cauldron. "Hmm, tastes like vegetable soup with some watershrimps thrown in."

"Watershrimp, y'say!" Skor was swiftly at the cauldron. Rummaging in his belt pouch, he found a packet of reddish powder. This he tipped into the mixture. "Ahoy, Crew, anybeast for watershrimp'n'hotroot soup?"

The Rogue Crew descended on the cauldron eagerly. Shrimp'n'hotroot soup is a great favourite amongst otters, particularly sea otters from the High North Coast, who are partial to a fiendish blend of hotroot pepper.

"Wo hoa, buckoes, this is the stuff t'serve the Crew!"

"Hahaarr, I can feel it curlin' me rudder!"

Trug Bawdsley tried a spoonful; the result sent him dashing to the stream for huge mouthfuls of water. With eyes streaming and burning lips, he exclaimed, "Great flippin' flames, I thought somebeast had lit a bloomin' fire in me mouth, wot!"

The Rogue Crew otters roared with laughter at his discomfort. Sergeant Miggory had an idea, which he whispered to Skor.

The sea otter Chieftain listened, then replied, "Let's give it a try, though I think 'tis a shameful waste o' good vittles. Right, bring the villain to me."

Viglat the patch-eyed vermin leader was hauled forward by Gil and Dreel. Sergeant Miggory put the question to him. "Ye might recall me h'askin' you before, could ye tell me the way to Redwall h'Abbey?"

Viglat answered sullenly, "Dunno no Redwall Abbeyz, never 'eard of it in me life."

Young Dreel kicked his tail. "Don't lie t'the sergeant!"

Skor smiled at the patch-eyed ferret in a kindly way. "Oh, leave the pore beast alone. Maybe he's just forgotten the way to Redwall. Sergeant, d'ye think a nice drop o' soup will cure him, jog his memory a bit, eh?"

Viglat was seized by two brawny otters. He watched Miggory filling a bowl with soup from the cauldron.

The ferret grinned impudently. "Zoop, eh? Viglat likes zoop!"

Sergeant Miggory blew steam from the bowl, holding it to the vermin's mouth. "Well, h'I'm sure yore goin' to love this. C'mon now, bucko, sup up hearty!"

The first sip was enough. Feeling the ferocious heat of the hotroot ingredient, Viglat spluttered, trying to spit it out. "Bulagggh! Itza burn me mouf off!"

Skor registered mock surprise. "Don't talk rubbish. We brings our babes up on that—'tis good for ye. Give him some more, Sarge, lots more!"

Viglat began blubbering as he was fed another mouthful. "Wahaaah! No more, no more—wanna drinka water!"

Miggory continued pouring mercilessly. "Sup up. There's more'n arf a cauldron t'go yet. You'll get water when ye tell h'us about Redwall. Where is h'it?"

Slopping liquid down his ragged shirt, the ferret wailed, "I tell ya, I tell ya. Wahaaah! No more zoop . . . please!"

The sergeant kept pouring as he consulted Rake. "Wot d'ye think, sah?"

The captain looked up from cleaning his pawnails on the tip of one of his claymores. "Och, he looks a truthful wee sort. Let him speak his piece."

The brawny sea otters held Viglat, keeping him from scrambling to the stream for water. He was making unmentionable noises, trying to cover his mouth, massage his throat and rub his stomach all at the same time.

Miggory filled the soup bowl, holding it forth threateningly. "H'if'n h'I was you h'I'd speak."

In a hoarse strangled rasp, the ferret talked. "Foller dis stream 'til it bendz east, den look out fer da t'ree-topped oak, it'z due south o' there!"

Drogbuk hiccuped loudly. "I could've told ye that!" With that, he fell flat on his back, drunk.

Young Wilbee giggled. "I say, sah, the old sot's been at that nettle beer. He's stinko!"

Grabbing Viglat by the scruff of his neck, Skor marched him into the stream, ducking his head. "Drink up, scumface, so ye can lead the way. Aye, an' ye'll be carryin' Drogbuk on yore back. Ruggan, fix up a rope harness an' tie that ole fool to the vermin's back!"

Rake chuckled. "Ah'd let yon ferret come up for air afore ye drown him, Skor!"

They marched east along the streambank as evening shades fell gently over the land. The haremaid Ferrul picked a yellow iris and set it behind her ear as she waxed lyrical about a summer eve.

"Ain't it pretty, the end of a summer day, wot? Have you noticed how a calm settles over the woodlands? The stream quietly murmurin', birdsong in the distance, hardly a blinkin' breeze to stir the weary oak leaves. . . ."

Viglat's stomach bubbled aloud; he groaned pitifully.

Drogbuk swayed on his back, hiccupping and belching.

Corporal Welkin Dabbs sniffed the iris, murmuring in Ferrul's ear, "Ain't it all jolly pretty, miss?"

She glared frostily at him. "Yah, go an' boil your bloomin' head. You've got no finer flamin' feelin's!"

As darkness fell over the woodlands, Log a Log Dandy caught up with Viglat. "Ahoy, mudguts, how far is this three-topped oak?"

The ferret muttered, "Gudd way yet, I t'ink."

Skor, who had overheard, sat down on a felled spruce trunk. "Well, I ain't trailin' round behind a vermin all night. I vote we camp here 'til daylight."

Waving a paw to halt the column, Rake joined him. "Ah'll say aye tae that. Och, there's always the morrow."

Viglat turned, letting them see Drogbuk. "Izzent nobeast gunna ged this stinky 'og offen me back?"

Lieutenant Scutram wrinkled his nose in distaste. "Good grief, old lad. Fancy you callin' anybeast stinky. The pair of ye smell like a blinkin' mess midden on a flippin' midsummer midday, wot!"

Skor nodded. "Aye, they're a ripe ole pair, sure enough. Here, Endar Feyblade, Kite Slayer, take those two into the stream an' see they get a good scrubbin'. I want t'see them come out smellin' like daisies!"

The cold streamwater swiftly wakened Drogbuk from his drunken slumber. Both he and Viglat began screeching unmercifully as the two powerful sea otters went to work on them with vim and gusto.

"Owowyeek! Stoppit, ye'll have all me spikes off!"

"Ohhouchaaargh! I'm bein' murdered t'death!"

Endar had the ferret firmly by his ears. She scrubbed away remorselessly. "Oh, shuttup, ye great baby. A rubdown with dockleaves an' banksand never killed anybeast!"

Amidst hoots of merriment from the bankside, big Drander rubbed his stomach. "One cob o' flatbread an' a drop o' soup that near burnt the ears off me, that's all I've eaten today, mates. Flamin' rotten, ain't it?"

Sergeant Miggory was about to reply when a sturdy hog-wife emerged from the shrubbery close by. She was laughing so hard, the tears ran down her cheeks.

"Whoohoohahaha! Oh, good grief, I'll wager that's the first decent bath Drogbuk Wiltud's ever had. Oh, dearie me, haha!"

The sergeant sprang up, facing her. "Beggin' yore pardon, marm, but who might you be?"

Taking a blue spotted kerchief from her beautifully embroidered apron pocket, she wiped her eyes and sniffed. "Never mind me—this is my land. So who might you be, eh?"

The grizzled veteran saluted courteously. "H'I'm Colour Sergeant Nubbs Miggory of the Long Patrol, from Salamandastron, marm!"

The hogwife performed a mock curtsy. "Ho, graciousness, that's fancy talk for a rabbet. Well, I'm Pinny Wiltud, an' that's one o' my clan yore takin' the hide off in the water. Huh, not that he doesn't need it, filthy ole rattlespikes!"

Big Drander saw an opportuntity. He smiled winningly at her. "'Scuse me, O lovely one, but d'ye know where there might be a bit o' food t'be found hereabouts, wot?"

She considered this a moment, then nodded. "I've been watchin' you lot all day. Saw you scare those vermin off downstream, a job well done, I'd say. Now, do ye like proper, thick woodland stew?" She held up a paw before Drander could reply. "I mean real Woodland Stew, made to an ole Wiltud recipe. With every veggible ye could shake a stick at chopped up into it. Aye, an' full o' chestnut'n'acorn dumplin's."

Overcome by emotion, tears sprang to Drander's eyes. "Chestnut'n'acorn dumplin's, marm, it makes me weak just thinkin' about 'em. Oh, my giddy granddad, where is it, marm?"

She silenced him with a glance. "If ye build a fire an' lend a paw, I can make it ready for service just afore midnight—oh! Ooooh! Cover him up! Ooooh!"

Her kinbeast Drogbuk Wiltud had emerged from the

stream without a single quill on his scrawny frame. They had either fallen or been scrubbed off by the vigorous bathing he had received. Pinny had meanwhile thrown her voluminous flowered apron up over her face.

Drogbuk hobbled about on the bank, not knowing where to hide himself. He was ranting, "See wot ye did? Great clumsy-pawed sea otters, how'm I goin' to last out the winter like this? Plank-tailed oafs!"

Captain Rake grabbed the cloak which the ferret Viglat had discarded. He tossed it to the naked old hog. "Here, cover yersel' up, ye auld sack o' wrinkles. Och, ah've seen some sights that'd frit a duck, but never anythin' like this!"

Skor grinned, shaking his huge, bearded head. "He looks like an ole pink cattypillar that never turned into a butterfly. Hahaha, I hope yore cloak fits him, ferret . . . ferret! Where's that vermin got to?"

A hasty search revealed that Viglat was missing. Swiffo shrugged. "Must've slipped off durin' all that din ole Drogbuk was makin'. Hope we can still find Redwall."

Pinny Wiltud scoffed. "Find Redwall? Huh, I know the way to the Abbey like the back o' my paw. But let's get ye fed first. Some of ye get a fire goin', the rest follow me."

It was dark by the time Pinny's woodland stew was ready. Everybeast had worked hard to help with it. True to her boast, the hogwife's recipe worked superbly—it was rich, fragrant and delicious. They sat round the campfire on the streambank, each filling a bowl several times from the sizeable cauldron.

Drogbuk sat apart, wrapped in an old blanket, whilst Pinny busied herself, cutting and sewing the ferret's cloak into a suitable garb for him. Posy and Uggo sat with her, gratefully downing the stew.

Pinny stared at Posy awhile, then shook her head. "You ain't a Wiltud, missy. I can tell—yore too pretty. But that un"—she pointed her needle at Uggo—"huh, he's got Wiltud written all over 'im. Sharp nose, greedy face an' twinkly eyes. Who was yore mum'n'dad?"

Uggo fished around after a dumpling. "Never knew 'em, marm. I was brought up at Redwall by Dorka Gurdy an' her brother, Jum. Did ye say that you were at the Abbey? Did ye live there?"

Pinny looked up from her tailoring. "Aye, I did for a while when I was younger, but I left."

Posy asked, "Why did you leave, marm?"

Pinny seemed suddenly out of temper as she snapped, "I wasn't stayin' anywhere that they accused me o' bein' a vittle robber. Hah, I never scoffed their hefty fruitcake. The nerve o' that lot—anyway there wasn't many plums in it!"

Uggo could not resist giggling. "There was in the one I ate!"

Pinny patted his head fondly. "Wiltud by name an' Wiltud by nature. I 'ope ye wolfed every crumb of it. Here, Drogbuk, try this on for size."

She tossed the finished garment to the ancient hog, who vanished into the bushes with it. A moment later, he strutted out wearing what was in effect a one-piece smock.

"Well, wot d'ye think? Kin I join yore Long Patrol as a rabbet?"

Sergeant Miggory donated an old sword belt. "H'I should say not, sah. Try this belt round yore waist. It'll make ye look h'a liddle better'n a sack o' firewood."

Kite Slayer nodded in mock admiration. "Oh, ain't you the smart beast!"

Drogbuk topped up his stew bowl. "I ain't talkin' to you ever agin. Yore the savage who scrubbed all me pore spines off!"

Pinny put aside her sewing kit. "Pore ole Redwall Abbey, sez I. They're about to have three Wiltuds to visit."

Skor's battleaxe thudded into the ground near to her. "There'll be no vittle thieves whilst we're at the Abbey. Just let me hear o' one crust goin' missin', an' the next pot o' woodland stew'll have you in it as dumplin's!"

Pinny glared fiercely at the sea otter Chieftain. "Yew wouldn't!"

315

Kite Slayer tapped the hogwife's paw. "Oh, yes, he would, marm—ye can take it from me!"

Lieutenant Scutram wiped his bowl clean, saluting Pinny Wiltud. "Excellent supper, marm, thankee kindly. Right, chaps, finish messin' an' turn in. Big day tomorrow, wot. We're goin' to the jolly old Abbey o' Redwall!"

30

With its sails furled, *Greenshroud* looked like a bird of ill omen resting on the path north of the Abbey. It was a clear night, with a silver white moon presiding over a star-scattered sky. Razzid Wearat stood alone on the afterdeck, leaning on the tiller, staring at Redwall. Still burning bright on the northwest walltop corner, the bonfire silhouetted creatures guarding the battlements.

Razzid gritted his fangs. So near, yet so far from his dream of conquest. Now, having seen the magnificent Abbey, he was consumed with the desire to make it his own. However, mere yearning would accomplish nothing. It was planning and swift action which would win the day for him, and Razzid's fertile brain had provided the solution. He knew what he must do. Treachery by Mowlag and Jiboree could wait until later. Once he was inside, ruling Redwall, he would mete out punishments to the pair, which would make his name feared amongst searats and corsairs.

A sound disturbed his train of thought. He turned and saw a scrawny young weasel climbing over the stern gallery. Immediately the Wearat's trident was a whisker away

317

from the intruder's face. The weasel held out his paws to show he was unarmed.

"Cap'n, I'm Twangee. Me uncle Badtooth's the cook—told yer about me, didn't 'e?"

Razzid lowered the trident. "Aye, he did. Well, wot's to report? Have ye been watchin' Mowlag an' Jiboree?"

Twangee winked slyly. "I kep' me eyes on 'em, Cap'n, an' I been a-lissenin', too. Yore safe fer now. They don't plan on makin' no moves 'til we take the Abbey. They've carried out yore orders, they chopped down six trees, all pines, good'n'straight. Lissen, I can 'ear 'em comin' along the path now. I'll git outta the way, lest they sees me talkin' to yer, Cap'n."

Razzid nodded approvingly. "Aye, you do that, Twangee. Tell yore uncle t'give ye the best o' grog'n'vittles. Ye did well tonight."

The Wearat watched the young weasel scuttle off, then leaned over the stern rail.

Mowlag was heading the party, who were rolling the six pine trunks along with them. "Here y'are, Cap'n, six o' the best from the woodlands."

Razzid's keen eye scanned the other crewbeasts, noting that Jiboree was bringing up the rear.

"Move those trunks so they're bridgin' that ditch alongside this path, then lash 'em together so they won't roll apart. Look sharp—I don't want t'be here after dawn."

Once the trunks had been bound in place to form a bridge over the ditch, Razzid gave orders for the entire crew to haul his ship over onto the flatlands beyond. The sails were set, and soon, with the gentle night breeze, *Greenshroud* trundled slowly off westward. The pine-trunk bridge had been dismantled; it went with the vessel, three logs bound to either side of the hull. The Wearat assembled his crew amidships and faced them.

"Good work, mates, now ye can go to the galley. There's skilly'n'duff, aye, an' enough grog to keep ye happy!"

The crew were about to move off when a searat called out, "But I thought we was goin' to conquer that Abbey place, Cap'n."

Razzid smiled. "So we are, shipmate, so we are. But we does it accordin' to my plan. Go an' get yore supper. I'll come t'the galley an' tell ye how 'tis t'be done."

He beckoned Shekra to his side. The vixen came warily, nursing a heavily bandaged paw. "Lord?"

Razzid kept his voice low. "When I go t'the galley, I want ye behind me, watchin' my back. Arm yoreself with a good dagger. Can I trust ye, fox?"

She answered earnestly. "Aye, Lord, I swear ye can trust me."

The Wearat left it some time before he went to speak with the crew. Meanwhile, they were crowded into the galley and the adjoining messdeck. On his captain's orders, Badtooth had done them proud. There was as much grog flowing as anybeast could want. The mood was quite jovial; Badtooth even requested a song when a corsair stoat dug out his melodeon. "Cummon, Jibbo, give us an ole ditty!"

Jiboree the bosun went straight into a popular ditty.

"Ho, the *Scabby Frog*'s a floatin' shame,
we've had no grub for weeks,
there ain't a veggible in sight,
but the ship is full o' leaks!

"I've said it once an' said it twice,
an' I'll say a third time yet,
the weevils in the biscuits, mates,
is all the meat you'll get!

"Last night the cook baked up a pie,
he said it tasted great,
we've searched the ship from stem t'stern,
an' still ain't found the mate!

"There's mutiny on the *Scabby Frog*,
I knew that this would happen,
the crew have planned a master feast,
we're goin' to roast the cap'n!"

Jiboree faltered on the final line of the song as Razzid entered the galley. The melodeon squawked to a finish, and an awkward silence fell over the crew.

Razzid gave his bad eye a long, slow wipe, his good one darting back and forth. "Wot sort o' song d'ye call that? Mutiny aboard a ship, endin' up with the crew roastin' the cap'n—makes ye think, don't it, mates, eh?"

Jiboree lowered his eyes, murmuring, "'Twas only a joke song, Cap'n, a bit o' fun." His footpaws trembled as the Wearat edged closer to him.

Razzid's voice took on a lighter tone. "Not a very good line, though, is it? 'We're goin' to roast the cap'n.' You ain't a cap'n, are ye?"

The weasel shook his head, relaxing slightly. "No, Cap'n, I'm a bosun."

Razzid kept advancing, forcing the bosun to step backward until he was almost against the galley stove, with the big cauldron of skilly'n'duff bubbling on it. Razzid smiled.

"Let me give ye a better line. How about 'we're goin' to boil the bosun'? That sounds better, don't it?"

Jiboree nodded several times. "Aye, it does, Cap'n!"

Some of the cauldron contents bubbled over, landing on the weasel's tail. He yelped, but Razzid did not move away to release him from his position. The Wearat winked broadly at Mowlag the mate, remarking almost casually, "Like Jiboree said, just a bit o' fun, eh? A bosun couldn't roast a cap'n, but a cap'n could boil a bosun, or even a mate, ain't that right?"

Mowlag tugged his ear in salute, "Aye, right, Cap'n!"

Razzid seemed to lose interest in the confrontation with the pair. He moved to one side, freeing Jiboree. Turning, he addressed the crew. "Hearken now—this is the plan. We're movin' westward across these flatlands until we're out o' sight. I ain't standin' by, near to that Redwall place, to watch me ship catch flame from their big fire. Right, mates, 'ere's wot we do. Let 'em think we've run away to try our luck somewhere else. They'll get fed up o' burnin' all the wood an' let the fires die away. So, we waits out yonder, for a night, mebbe even two or three nights. But when the winds blows strong at our stern an' 'tis dark, then the *Greenshroud* strikes! Gatherin' speed, with all sails set, we flies o'er the flatlands like an arrow out of a bow, straight for the big front Abbey gates. Those woodlanders'll be tucked up an' snorin'. They won't know wot's hit 'em. We'll knock those gates flat with a single blow an' be inside afore they're awake. So, ain't that a good plan, eh?"

Young Twangee piped up. "But we gotta get back over that ditch, Cap'n. How'll we manage that, without stoppin' to build the pine trunks across it?"

Razzid chuckled. "Yore a smart young un, but ye ain't as clever as Razzid Wearat. I've already thought o' that. We're carryin' the logs with us, so afore we sets off, we lashes 'em back into position an' stands 'em on the bows. At the right moment, we lets 'em flat, right across the ditch without losin' speed. Then it's over the ditch an' bang! *Greenshroud*'ll knock only once on those doors, an' they'll fall flat."

He turned to Shekra. "An' ye know wot happens then?" Without waiting for a reply, he raised his voice into a harsh shout, waving the trident on high. "Then we conquers Redwall Abbey, shipmates! Slaves to wait on us, loot to share, soft berths an' the best o' vittles. Now, 'ow does that sound to ye?"

A roar went up from the assembled corsairs and searats. "Razzid! Razzid! Razzid Wearaaaaaaat!"

Captain Rake had been sleeping peacefully on the stream-bank, wrapped in his cloak but with his two claymores lying close to paw. It was not any woodland sound that wakened him, but a scent. A tantalising aroma of hot mint tea and fresh-baked coltsfoot and rosehip scones. It was still dark as he made his way to the glowing embers of the previous night's campfire. Pinny Wiltud was already awake, readying breakfast.

Rake made an elegant leg. "Guid mornin' tae ye, marm. Up an' aboot early, eh!"

Busy with her work, the hogwife hardly gave him a glance. "I was wonderin' when somebeast would sniff my breakfast. Sit ye down, Cap'n. You can be first served."

She ladled out a beaker of the tea from her cauldron and placed four scones on a dockleaf.

"Careful now, the tea an' scones are still hot."

Rake sampled a nibble of scone and a sip of tea. He nodded admiringly at Pinny. "Marm, you're a real treasure! Ah havenae tasted scones like these since mah auld granny used tae bake 'em. Rosehip an' coltsfoot, right? Wi' just a wee touch o' dandelion bud. Och, a real taste o' mah young seasons!"

Just then several voices echoed from the bank.

"Ahah! Brekkist, just lead me to it, mates!"

"Huh, lead your flippin' self, planktail. I'm so jolly hungry I could scoff the bloomin' bark off a dead tree!"

"Aye, well go an' find yoreself h'a dead tree, young sah. I'm h'all for some proper vittles. Move over, Drander!"

"I say, Sarge, watch who yore jolly well shovin, wot!"

Pinny Wiltud was no shy young blossom. She got order with paw raps from her stout beechwood ladle. "Back off, ye famine-gobbed beasts! There's enough to go round, so form a line! Here, young Posy wotsyername, come t'the front."

Trug Bawdsley protested. "I say, marm, I was here before her!"

Skor Axehound lifted Trug bodily and placed him to the back. "You 'eard Miz Wiltud. Now behave yoreself. I'm next after liddle Posy. Ahoy, Feyblade, stop pushin' or ye'll feel my footpaw round yore stern!"

Order was restored, and everybeast was served in turn.

Uggo picked scone crumbs from his pawspikes. "Much further to Redwall, is it, marm?"

Pinny wrapped a spare scone in a dockleaf, slipping it to Posy, who was rapidly becoming her favourite. "If we sets a good pace, we should make it after evenin'! Make the most o' these vittles, 'cos I ain't stoppin' t'cook anymore today. Now, who's the best climber amongst ye?"

Log a Log Dandy stepped smartly forward. "That'll be me, darlin'. Where d'ye want me to climb?"

She pointed out a stately elm. "Try that un. Get as high as y'can, then shout down wot ye see to the east an' a bit south'ard."

The Guosim Chieftain was a nimble-pawed shrew. He shot up the elm trunk and was soon lost amidst the leafy canopy. There was a moment's silence, then he yelled down, "Hah, 'tis a three-topped oak. A real ole giant!"

Captain Rake strapped on his twin blades. "So, away we go, eh, Sergeant?"

The grizzled veteran bellowed out in good parade-ground style, "Fall h'in, ye lollop-eared, bang-tailed, spiky-'eaded rabble! H'on the double, now, look smart, look smart! Chins in, chests out, shoulders back, paws swingin', h'eyes front! Quick—wait for it, Miss Ferrul—quick march!"

Away they went, hares, otters, shrews and hedgehogs, with Lancejack Sage, who had a sweet strong voice, singing out.

"If I had no fine boat to sail,
then I'd walk all the way,
an' if nobeast would carry me,
I'd march the livelong day,
hey, up the hill an' down the grade,
with comrades true each one.
Ten! Twenty! Thirty leagues!
From Sala manda stron!
Go t'your left, left right, it's a long way 'til tonight!

"So keep the vittles warm for me,
an' serve me more not less,
an' shed a tear, O Sergeant dear,
for Cooky in the mess,
he's dishin' double helpin's
to all who haven't gone.
Ten! Twenty! Thirty leagues!
From Sala manda stron!
Go t'your left, left right, it's a long way 'til tonight!"

Tramping alongside Ferrul, the ottermaid Kite Slayer felt her feelings warming to Long Patrol hares. She mentioned this blithely to the haremaid. "I'm gettin to like this, y'know? All walkin' along t'gether, singin' songs an' such. Aye, it'll do me fine!"

Sergeant Miggory, who was nearby, on the left flank, had a word or two to say on the subject and let her know in no uncertain terms (as regimental colour sergeants invariably do). "Likes it, do ye, missy? Well, h'I am pleased for ye. Aye, h'an I'd like h'it, too, if'n ye could march properly. Wot h'is it about h'otters—'ave ye h'all got two left footpaws, h'an a tail wot keeps gettin' h'in the way?"

Ferrul fluttered her eyelashes at Miggory. "Oh, I say, Sarge, don't be too hard on Kite. She's tryin' jolly hard to keep step, ain't ye, Kite?"

The tough sea ottermaid scowled. "I'm in perfect step. 'Tis all the rest who aren't!"

Miggory raised his eyes imploringly skyward and fell silent.

It was just past high noon when they reached the ancient three-topped oak, a massive woodland giant with a treble crown of foliage. They rested in its shade whilst Drogbuk questioned Pinny.

"Which way now, ole miz fussy apron?"

She treated him to a glare that would have wilted daisies. "Listen, you scrawny-peeled Wiltud. Anybeast that looks like you shouldn't dare to try and make fun of others!"

Captain Rake interrupted. "Mah sentiments exactly, marm, but could ye ignore that auld misery an' tell us the route tae the Abbey, please?"

The hogwife pointed south, across the stream. "Certainly, Captain. It's that way. The next tall tree we come across, our Guosim Chief should be able to view Redwall's belltower roof in the distance."

Rake saluted. "Thankee, marm. Right, rest up awhile. Those who are thirsty can take a drink at the stream."

Posy enquired, "Can we cool our footpaws in the water?"

Skor Axehound huffed. "Aye, miss, as long as ye do it downstream from where I'm drinkin'."

Droghuk grumbled, "I'm too old an' tired t'go further."

Lieutenant Scutram, who knew that Drogbuk was only hoping for volunteers to carry him, answered, "Why, to be sure, old lad, if you're too jolly tired to march with us, then you can flippin' well stay here an' catch up with us when you're recovered an' fit t'walk, wot!"

The ancient fraud groaned pitifully. "S'pose I'd better cool me footpaws in the stream if yore forcin' a beast o' my seasons t'march!"

Kite Slayer advanced on him, smiling maliciously. "Pore ole creature, d'ye think another good hard scrub would help ye? I'm willin' t'do it!"

Drogbuk fled down the bank. "Yew keep away from me, ye young murderer!"

When they set off again, Captain Rake noticed Buff Redspore looking back over her shoulder, sometimes stopping and listening. Keeping his voice down, he walked alongside her. "Is anythin' wrong, bonny miss?"

She shot a swift glance at the surrounding woodland. "Actually, I'm not sure, sah, but now an' again I feel we're being followed. Not too certain, though."

Rake persisted. "How many d'ye think there is—one or a group?"

She shook her head. "No more'n one, sah, but whoever it jolly well is knows somethin' about shadowin'."

Rake nodded. "Ah'll take the other side o' the column an' keep mah eyes'n'ears peeled."

Noon shades were lengthening when Pinny Wiltud pointed out a very tall, slender ash tree, which towered over its neighbours.

"Now, if'n ye was to climb that un an' look south, the top o' the Abbey buildin's can be seen clear from there."

Log a Log Dandy spat on his paws, peering upward. "Looks like a fair ole climb t'me."

Young Swiffo laughed. "You ain't scared o' heights, are ye? Bet I could climb t'the top quicker'n you."

Dandy called back as he raced for the ash trunk, "Yore welcome to try, ye young pup!"

Swiffo bounded to the ash behind Dandy. As the Guosim Chieftain placed his paws on the trunk, the young sea otter bounded up his back, jumped on Dandy's head and went away up the tree with a great turn of speed. Dandy was right after him, slightly behind but doing his best to catch up. Everybeast on the ground began cheering them onward.

"Hoho, go on, Chief, you can beat 'im!"

"Come on, Swiffo mate, don't stop t'look back!"

"Try the other side o' the trunk, Dandy—there's more holds!"

"Stick at it, Swiffo, yore winnin'!"

As good as Dandy was, Swiffo had youth and fleetness of limb on his side. He vanished for a moment into the high, spreading foliage, then emerged on top of the tree. Leaning dangerously out, the young otter shouted, "Yore right, Pinny, I can see the belltower roof!"

On a slightly lower bough, Dandy clung to the trunk. "Aye, me too, an' I can see the weather vane stickin' up!" What happened next was not clear, but Dandy, who was looking down, suddenly yelled, "Look out, Swiffo, there he is—look out!"

Swiffo clutched his throat, gave a gurgling groan, then plunged headlong from his high perch. Dandy was scrambling down behind him, roaring, "It's that fox, off t'the right! Grab 'im. Stop the fox!"

Buff Redspore spotted the shadowy form slinking off amidst the trees. She pointed. "There he goes!"

She raced off, with Ruggan Axehound at her side. Skor was bellowing like a stricken beast. "Yaaahaaarrr! My son, my liddle young son!"

Swiffo lay in a heap at the base of the ash trunk. Sergeant Miggory had reached him first. He plucked a long, tufted dart from the young otter's throat. One look from him to Captain Rake confirmed the worst.

Miggory shook his head sadly. "H'afraid 'e's gone, sah!"

Skor picked his dead son up tenderly. Tears were streaming down his huge beard. Then he seemed to go rigid. Endar Feyblade and Kite Slayer took Swiffo from his paws.

Skor Axehound threw back his head, howling like a wildbeast. "Heeeeylaaaahooooh!" Swinging his big battleaxe, he crashed off into the shrubbery like a runaway boulder.

Captain Rake grabbed Miggory's paw. "Come on, Sergeant, we'll have tae stop him hurting hisself!"

Lieutenant Scutram cast about, coming up with a very long, hollow reed and two more of the tufted darts. "This confounded thing could shoot further than a bloomin' arrow, accurately, too. Poor young blighter didn't stand a chance. These darts are poisoned."

Posy was sitting holding Swiffo's head in both paws. She was weeping, rocking him back and forth. "But why, what was the reason, why did he have to die?"

Lancejack Sage patted the hogmaid's paw. "Who can say what's in a vermin's mind."

In his wrath, Skor had stumbled, thudding his head against an elm trunk. He dropped his battleaxe, kneeling with his head shaking. That was how Rake and Miggory came across him. Without a thought for their own safety, they threw themselves on the burly chieftain, restraining him. Skor struggled, weakly.

"Free me or I'll slay ye both, friend or foe, it don't matter t'me. I've got to catch my son's killer!"

Captain Rake's body was bobbing up and down as he tried to hold the big beast in a headlock. "Och, ye couldnae outrun a fox, mah friend. Those days are lang gone, ye ken!"

Sergeant Miggory was blinking—a huge footpaw had kicked him in one eye. He clung grimly on to Skor. "Lookit, sah, 'ere comes Redspore. Hi, Buff, h'over 'ere!"

The Long Patrol tracker, seeing the situation, leaned over Skor, shouting, "Be still, sah. Ruggan caught up with the fox!"

Skor straightened, shrugging off his two captors with a couple of shakes. Forgetting the bark-splintered bruise which stood out from his forehead, he spoke in a dazed mutter. "Ruggan caught the fox? Where is he?"

"Right here, Lord, an' I brought this with me!"

The fox's head bounced dully off the elm trunk.

Ruggan strode up, still gripping his axe. "I spread the rest of the murderer out amongst the trees, vittles for the carrion. See who 'e was, Cap'n?"

Rake held the head up by its ears, gazing into the half-open eyes. "Ach, 'tis Ketral Vane, Laird o' the Hinterwoods. Though Ah dinnae think he'll rule anymore, eh!"

Buff Redspore could not take her eyes off the grisly trophy. "But how did he find us?"

Ruggan pointed back the way he had come. "He was with another one—that ferret Viglat, who got away from us. Their paths must've crossed, an' Viglat told him which way we were headed. Hah, he didn't escape a second time, I'll tell ye. That un's fishbait now!"

Back at the ash tree, there was an air of sadness over everything. Skor wrapped Swiffo in his cloak, binding him in tight. "We'll lay 'im t'rest in Redwall Abbey."

He straightened up, wiped his eyes and addressed everybeast. "You lost a good comrade. I lost my youngest son. Now, 'tis hard I know, but we must go on an' rid this land o' the Wearat and his vermin afore they do serious damage to Redwall Abbey. That's always been our task, an' our friends, the Long Patrol Hares and Guosim Shrew warriors, are needed to protect Mossflower an' its coasts. If we sat about weepin' an' didn't carry out our vows, how d'ye suppose Swiffo would feel? What would he say, eh?"

Captain Rake drew his twin blades. "Ah'm with ye. We'll do it in honour o' your son!"

Suddenly sea otters, hares, Guosim shrews and hedgehogs were up on their paws, waving weapons as they yelled, "For Swiffo! For Swiffo!"

Ruggan swung his bloodstained axe overhead until the air thrummed. "On to Redwall, mates, paw an' heart!"

They broke camp, thundering across the stream, splashing out into the woodlands on the far side. The pace stepped up, faces were set grim, weapons grasped tight. On to the Abbey of Redwall, and bad fortune to any foebeasts who dared stand in the way of such warriors!

31

On the Abbey's walltop, the fire was still burning a red-gold warning against the night sky. However, it was a somewhat diminished blaze, owing to Ding Toller's rationing of wood. Foremole Roogo had his back to the comforting warmth.

Dorka Gurdy noted the blissful look on his face. "Wot'll ye do when winter comes, huh, a-warmin' yore back agin' that fire on a warm summer night?"

Foremole wrinkled his velvety snout, chuckling. "Hurr-hurrhurr, Oi do loike a foire ennytoime, marm, be it warmish or cold. Boi 'okey, 'tis a gurt feelin'!"

Fottlink had been dozing against a battlement. His head drooped forward, bumping against stone. He righted himself quickly, remembering he was on guard duty, then peered north up the path. The mouse Recorder became instantly alert. "Look, the vermin ship's moving!"

Abbot Thibb, who had been resting on the north steps, came running. "Moving, did you say? Which way?"

Those on guard, the Abbot included, hurried to see. Dorka Gurdy shielded her eyes against the firelight. "Well, I never. They must've built some sort o' bridge, 'cos the vermin are pushin' it o'er the ditch!"

Ding Toller hissed, "Get down, everybeast down! We don't want 'em t'know we can see wot they're doin'!"

Everybeast crouched below the wall, leaving Ding to spy on *Greenshroud*.

"The ship's over on the western flatlands now. They're hoistin' the sails. Wot d'ye think, Father, are they goin' away?"

Abbot Thibb scratched his ears. "I hope they are, friend, but who can tell? What are they doing now?"

The tall, sombre squirrel reported. "So that's how they got over the ditch—six logs made into a bridge. Now they're bindin' 'em t'the ship's sides an' takin' 'em along. All the vermin are back aboard. I can see that Wearat at the tiller. I tell ye, it does look odd t'see a ship sailin' along on wheels."

Dorka Gurdy prodded Ding's back. "We know that! Which way's the ship bound?"

Ding pointed. "Straight into the west. She's only goin' along slowlike. There's nought but a breeze to help 'er. But there she goes. It's safe enough now. See for yoreselves."

Heads popped up all along the west walltop. Foremole Roogo shook a clenched paw after the vessel. "Goo orn, away with ee, durty ole vermints. Burr aye, an' doan't ee cumm back yurr no more!"

Friar Wopple came trundling up the stairs; the old vole was in a panic. Thibb helped her onto the ramparts. "Friar, what is it?"

The good cook was quite out of breath, but she did the best she could to explain. "I . . . I . . . was out in my liddle 'erb patch behind the Abbey, pickin' some fresh mint for brekkist tea, y'see. Then I 'ears noises from outside. There's creatures in the woodlands at the east wallgate, Father!"

Dorka thumped her rudder hard on the stones. "I knowed those rascals was up to somethin'. I could feel it in me whiskers, I swear I could!"

Fottlink grabbed her paw. "What d'ye mean, marm?"

The ottermum snorted, "A trap, a trick, that's wot I mean. That great scummy Wearat was tryin' to makes us think he'd sailed off. But he's split his crew. I wager there's a gang

331

o' the murderin' scoundrels tryin' to break in the back o' the Abbey whilst we're all watchin' the front wall!"

Ding Toller looked grim. "Aye, that makes sense. Good job ye heard 'em, Friar. I'll sound the bells an' raise our creatures!"

Abbot Thibb halted him. "No, wait. Our bell sound carries a long way. The Wearat could hear it. Knowing we're wise to his plan, he'd come back and attack us, maybe at the south wall, where there isn't a fire burning."

Fottlink waved his paws in agitation. "Oh, dear, what'll we do?"

Thibb did not hesitate. "We'll sneak over to the east wall and see how many vermin there are. Once we know that, I'll be able to put some sort of plan into action. Come along, all of you, but go quietly as you can."

They crept off in a bunch along the north walltop. As they neared the northeast gable, Fottlink gave a squeak of alarm. "There's somebeast on the battlements yonder—a rat, I think!"

An indignant voice hailed them. "Rat yoreself, old mouseyface! Don't ye know a Guosim Log a Log when ye see one?"

Dandy Clogs hopped nimbly from the battlements and swaggered up to meet them. "Has everybeast at Redwall got moss in their ears? We've been knockin' on that liddle wallgate for long enough!"

Chuckling with relief and joy, Thibb held out a welcoming paw. "Guosim! Thank the good seasons for that. Do ye have some of your warriors with you, Log a Log?"

Dandy clasped the outstretched paw warmly. "Oh, I've got a couple o' Guosim with me, but our bunch is mainly a load o' Long Patrol hares an' Rogue Crew sea otters. They've only come along 'cos they've heard o' Redwall's fine vittles, so ye'd best warn yore cook. Right now ye'd do well to open that small wallgate, afore Skor Axehound decides to take his battleaxe to it!"

Abbot Thibb was ecstatic as he saw the warriors crowd-

332

ing in through the wickergate. Captain Rake performed a smart salute with his blades. "Ah'm Captain Rake Nightfur, commandin' a score o' Long Patrol fighters frae Salamandastron. This is mah companion, Skor Axehound, Chieftain o' the Rogue Crew from the High North Coast. We're at your service, mah friend!"

Thibb waved his paws excitedly. "Let's not stand on ceremony, Captain. I'm Thibb, Father Abbot of Redwall, but I'm sure we'll all become acquainted soon enough. Right now I'm sure you'd much sooner be enjoying our hospitality at supper. How does that sound?"

Any reply Rake made was drowned by enthusiastic cheers. Abbot Thibb found himself hoisted onto the brawny shoulders of Ruggan and Big Drander, who bore him swiftly forward.

"Point the way, Father, an' send somebeast to warn the cook!"

Dorka Gurdy spotted Uggo. She ignored his spikes, giving him a fond hug. "Well, well, look wot the wind blew in. Have ye brought my brother Jum back with ye, Uggo?"

The young hedgehog shook his head. "No, marm, but last time I saw Mister Jum 'e was well enough. I 'spect he'll turn up sooner or later. This is my friend Posy, but she ain't a Wiltud."

Dorka smiled. "She's far too pretty for that. Yore a lucky young beast, Uggo. Well, come along. I 'spect yore all ready to take a bite o' supper."

All the Redwallers, even the Dibbuns, who had been wakened by the din, flooded into Great Hall to mingle with the new arrivals. Extra help was brought into the kitchens, and more trestle tables were laid out.

Rogue Crew and Long Patrollers, who were experiencing their first visit to the Abbey, were overwhelmed by the sheer size and grandeur of the place. Friar Wopple soon had helpers scurrying out, filling the boards with food from their trolleys. Everything was in a glorious state of organised chaos.

Abbot Thibb had a quiet word with Ding Toller, who carried the cloak-wrapped form of young Swiffo off to rest temporarily in the entrance chamber of the belltower. Thibb seated himself in the Abbot's chair, with Rake and Skor sitting either side. Silence fell over the gathering as Thibb rose and recited a special grace.

"Welcome to this table, friends,
our greetings to you all,
who offer paws and hearts so brave,
in service to Redwall.
But ere pale dawn lights up the earth,
come, eat and drink for all you're worth!"

Skor raised a tankard of best October Ale. "Thankee, Father, I'll drink to that!"

Then supper commenced in earnest.

Huge summer salad, garnished with hazelnut and chestnut cheese, sage- and thyme-crusted bread, leek and onion soup, mushroom and carrot pasties in gravy. Followed by plumcake and sweet arrowroot pudding with blackberry sauce, latticed apple tarts, mixed fruit turnover and meadowcream. All was washed down with a variety of drinks. October Ale, hot mint tea, dandelion and burdock cordial or rosehip and elderflower water.

Whilst they dined, the Abbot listened to their journey account, then brought them up to strength on the latest news of Razzid Wearat and the *Greenshroud*.

Rake held a short conference with Skor, then issued orders. "Sergeant Miggory, Ruggan Axehound, Ah'd be obliged if ye would take a score of our braw lads tae guard the walls. They'll be relieved throughout the night. Ah want ye tae pay special attention tae the westward plain. Let us know if the vermin ship is sighted anywhere aboot!"

Thibb placed his paw on Skor's huge mitt. "I was sorry to hear about your young son, Lord. Is there anything we can do to aid you in this matter? Please don't take offence at our simple offer."

The sea otter Chieftain stared at the tabletop. "No offence taken, Father—I'm grateful to ye. My son was more a creature of peace than war, but Swiffo was a fine young un. Is there a place to bury his body within your Abbey walls, somewhere quiet?"

Thibb nodded. "Indeed there is. Just behind the belltower there's a peaceful spot shaded by an old yew tree. I'll make arrangements with our bellringer for tomorrow."

Some of the Dibbuns were curious as to who old Drogbuk Wiltud was. He pointedly ignored them as he stuffed his face with food. Guggle the squirrelbabe was trying to peer inside the garb which Pinny had tailored from the vermin cloak.

"Pardin' me, but wot sorta h'aminal are you?"

Drogbuk pulled his outfit closer to his spineless frame. "Go 'way, ye nosey liddle wretch!"

Murty molebabe chuckled, wrinkling his snout at Drogbuk. "Oi'm thinken you'm a blizzard or ee toadybeast, zurr!!"

Kite Slayer took Murty on her lap, allowing him to nibble at her plumcake. "Nay, liddle un, he's only a daft ole 'og wot's lost his spines, ain't ye, Drogbuk?"

The ancient hog was reaching for a tankard of October Ale when Fottlink rescued it, pushing a beaker of cordial forward. "Drogbuk, eh? I recall that name—you'd be a Wiltud, the one who's been banished twice from Redwall."

Dorka Gurdy wagged a paw at Drogbuk. "I thought I recognised ye, old un. Well, ye can stay, but keep yore rovin' paws off vittles that ain't yores an' no ale or strong wine, either. I'll be watchin' ye!" Dorka turned her wagging paw upon Pinny. "An' you too, marm. Yore a Wiltud. One false move whilst yore at our Abbey an' out ye'll go!"

Posy smiled winningly at the big ottermum. "Oh, Dorka, don't shout at Miz Pinny, please. She's a nice, kind Wiltud."

Dorka sniffed. "Aye, missy. Well, she's yore responsibility from hereon. Keep 'er out of trouble, y'hear!"

Friar Wopple was called from the kitchens, shuffling her footpaws. She took a bow amidst the rapturous applause afforded her by the new supper guests.

"I say, marm, well done. Top-hole vittles, wot!"

"Aye, we ain't got scoff anythin' like this up on the coast!"

"Indeed, marm, any chance o' givvin' us some of your recipes, 'specially the one for that jolly nice pasty with the gravy? That'd perk up some o' the lads back at the mess in Salamandastron, eh, wot!"

Wopple smiled shyly. "Wait'll ye taste my breakfast tomorrow. 'Twill be a treat for hearty eaters like yoreselves."

This prompted further cheers from the trencherbeasts.

Later that night, when the guests had been shown to Cavern Hole, which was to be their sleeping quarters, a conference was held by those still at table.

Lieutenant Scutram allowed the Abbot to replenish his tankard. "So, what d'ye make of all this kerfuffle with the Wearat an' his vermin, eh, Father?"

Thibb pondered the question before answering, "Well, as I've already told you, I think my disguise as Martin the Warrior, plus the bonfire we built on the walltops, was enough to put the vermin off attacking us. Now, earlier tonight, they went away, out across the flatlands. We're rather hoping they've left for good. But I'm sure you know more about the ways of vermin, so I'd value your opinion, friends."

Skor Axehound growled flatly. "They'll be back!"

Captain Rake nodded his agreement. "Aye, Ah doubt ye've seen the last of them, Father. Razzid Wearat didnae come all this way tae turn tail an' run awa'. Skor's right, he'll be back!"

Fottlink licked his lips nervously. "But when?"

Sergeant Miggory replied, "When yore least h'expectin' it, sah—that's the way with vermin murderers. We've h'already seen 'is work at Salamandastron."

Rake gripped his beaker so tightly that the earthenware cracked. "Aye, an' we're lookin' forward tae the return engagement, Father, so Ah'd be grateful if ye'd leave the business of bloodshed tae me an' Skor!" He said it with such a coldness in his voice that the Abbot felt his fur tingle.

Thibb nodded. "Just as you say, Captain, but my Redwallers will be here to offer you any help you require."

Skor patted his back fondly, knocking the wind from Thibb. "Thankee, Father, but you look after yore liddle uns an' keep our beasts in drink'n'vittles—that's all we ask of ye!"

Dawn broke calmly, with ascending larks trilling beneath a sky awash with pale pastel hues. Out on the flatlands, grasshoppers set up their rusty chirruping as varicoloured butterflies flitted silently around the soft blue forget-me-not, bright gold tormentil and pinky cranberry blossoms skirting the ditchside.

Lancejack Sage viewed it all from the threshold battlements, commenting dreamily, "Jolly pretty, ain't it, wot!"

A stern voice in her ear startled her to attention. "You h'aint up 'ere to sniff the flowers, missy. Yore supposed t'be on watch for vermin. Now git those lovely eyes workin'. Do yore duty an' don't let me catch ye nappin' agin, or yore on a fizzer!"

Not daring to turn and look at Sergeant Miggory, Sage sprang to attention, saluted with her javelin and set her gaze on the horizon. "Indeed, Sergeant, 'twon't happen again, I jolly well promise ye, sah!"

Miggory nodded to four kitchen helpers, who carried a trolley up the wallstairs to the top. He beckoned the guard with a wave of his ears.

"Wilbee, Drander, Bawdsley an' you, Lancejack, come an' take a bite o' brekkist, compliments o' Friar Wopple. But eyes front whilst yore h'eatin', d'ye hear?" He stalked off along the ramparts, still issuing orders. "When ye've h'eaten, these goodbeasts will take yore place for h'a while. Go straight back to the billet h'an spruce h'up. We'll all be on parade shortly, to bury Lord Axe'ound's young un. So look smart, best be'aviour, h'an' the time'll be slow march, with bowed 'eads. H'unnerstood?"

After breakfast, the sea otters and Long Patrol hares formed up in ranks of four. At their centre, Skor, Ruggan, Rake and Scutram bore the body, still bound in his father's cloak, to the burying spot. Ding Toller rang both Matthias and Methusaleh, the two Abbey bells, to keep pace with the solemn, slow march.

At the graveside, Skor watched the bundle being lowered. Wiping a paw across both his eyes, he enquired gruffly, "I'm not good with words at a time like this. Anybeast got a song to sing or a line to say?"

Kite Slayer was weeping openly. She shook her head. "Only songs or lines I know are all about blood'n'war. Swiffo was a gentle creature. 'Twouldn't suit him."

Buff Redspore made a suggestion. "Beg pardon, sah, I'm a pretty hopeless singer m'self, but I've heard Lancejack Sage singin' a jolly nice song. I say, Lance, you know the one—somethin' about a dove's wing. D'ye recall the ditty, wot?"

Lancejack Sage pondered briefly. "Hmm, a dove's wing . . . Oh, yes, it's a lovely song. I say, Lord Axehound, would you like me to sing it for Swiffo?"

Skor nodded his huge bearded head. "Aye, miss, I'd be beholden if'n ye did, please."

Everybeast was moved to tears by the beauty of Sage's voice and the heartfelt way in which she sang.

"When sunlight wanes and evening shadows fall,
old weary earth in dusky silence lies,
a small lost dove doth mournful call,
its lone lament to darkling skies.

"Hark to its cry, poor little thing,
it rests with head beneath one wing,

and breeze that wends through woodland fair,
passes it by with ne'er a care.

"Throughout the night in trembling fear and dread,
until the welcome light of gentle morn,
the little dove lifts up its downy head,
and soars into the heav'nly dawn."

The sea otters and Long Patrol hares walked away then, leaving Skor and Ruggan alone to complete the burial.

Roogo Foremole broke the oppressive silence by calling from the walltop, "Yurr, zurrs, Oi bee's a-seein' summat yonder!"

Relieved to be doing something, Captain Rake sprinted up the wallstairs with a crowd of warriors at his heels.

Roogo was standing on the western threshold, with both paws shading his eyes, peering off to the horizon. "Moi ole eyes b'aint vurry gudd these days, zurr, but see far yonder? Wot do ee think that'n is?"

Rake's keen gaze found the object. "'Tis the vermin ship, mah friend, nae doubt o' that. Corporal Dabbs, can ye no' see what they're aboot?"

Welkin Dabbs, who was noted for exceptional clarity of vision, watched the distant vessel intently. "Some kind o' maneuver, I'd say, Cap'n. She's piled on all sail. Comin' this way, if'n I ain't mistaken. No, wait . . . now they're tackin' south an' west. Can't see much else, I'm afraid. She's vanished o'er the horizon."

"Testin' the wind, that's wot the vermin are up to!" It was the sea ottermaid Kite Slayer who had spoken. Rake continued staring at the horizon.

"How d'ye know, bonny lass?"

Kite leaned back against the battlements. "We've seen it lots o' times, up on the High North Coast. Ships'll do that if'n they want to sail in fast an' launch an attack. They stands off, doin' little trial runs, until the wind's just right an' strong enough. That's when they come in, hopin' to raid us. Hah, our scouts have seen 'em long since, an' the Rogue Crew's waitin' for 'em. Lord Skor gives 'em blood'n'steel. They never come back for more, usually 'cos they're all fishfood by the time we get done with 'em!"

Kite licked her paw, dabbing it on both eartips. She turned this way, then that. "Ain't much wind today—it's gentle an' sou'west."

Sergeant Miggory nodded grimly. "Ye know wot that means, sah!"

The captain nodded. "Aye, yon Wearat an' his crew'll be payin' us a wee visit soon, eh?"

All talk stopped momentarily as Ruggan and Skor strode up the gatehouse wallsteps. There was something about the presence of the sea otter Chieftain which engendered silence. He began honing the blade of his mighty battleaxe on the side of a battlement, looking up to stare bleakly out to the western horizon. His voice was a bitter snarl. "Oh, Razzid Wearat'll be comin', sure enough. Sometime after midnight, I reckon."

Lancejack Sage looked dubious. "Beg pardon, m'Lord, but what makes ye say that?"

Testing his axe edge on a paw, Skor gave her a rare smile. "Ye've got a wonderful voice, Miz Sage, an' ye sang my young son peacefully to his rest. I thank ye. I'll tell ye why I'm so sure the vermin'll attack late tonight. I've lived all my life on the High North Coast, an' I know all about sea, wind an' weather. That liddle breeze ye feel is a sou'wester, but by noon 'twill be startin' to blow from the due west. By dark we'll get rain, more as the night progresses. There'll be clouds hidin' wot moon there is. That's when they'll come."

Abbot Thibb looked to Captain Rake, who nodded, confirming Skor's words.

Thibb heaved a sigh. "I was hoping we'd seen the last of the vermin ship."

Skor chuckled humorlessly. "Just wot ye'd expect a peaceful Abbeybeast to think, Father—no offence meant, o' course. Rake, my friend, would ye like to tell him how they'll come at this place?"

Drawing one of his claymores, the Long Patrol captain pointed straight out across the threshold.

"From yonder, with full speed, under all sail, right at us. Ah mean, Father, what better way tae do it, eh? A dark, moonless night, runnin' with a west wind at his stern an' thinkin' ye'll all be tucked up in your beds. Wearat could nae charge stone walls with fire blazin' atop o' them, so he'll sail full tilt at Redwall's front gates. They're made o' wood, d'ye see. Aye, a real surprise ambush, ye ken!"

Skor could not resist a smile of grim satisfaction. "Right enough, Father, but wot Razzid don't know is that we're here now, ready an' waitin' to welcome him an' his crew. I won't miss him a second time, I swear it!"

Recorder Fottlink had a question. "But if he rams Redwall's gates, he'll ruin his own ship, won't he? Doesn't seem to make sense."

Lieutenant Scutram answered, "Put y'self in his position, old lad. What'd you sooner have, a ship or Redwall Abbey? I know what I'd jolly well prefer, wot!"

Skor patted the mouse Recorder's head. "Don't worry, old un. He won't ruin either ship or gates, 'cos we'll leave the gates unlocked for him, eh, Rake?"

The captain sheathed his claymore. "Aye, so we will. Ah want Razzid an' his crew in here. We'll lock the gates behind him an' trap 'em within these walls. Now that's what Ah call a canny plan!"

Abbot Thibb seemed quite upset with the wild scheme. "What, here inside my Abbey, a ship and its vermin crew? I . . . I've never heard of such a preposterous thing!"

Sergeant Miggory threw a friendly paw around Thibb's shoulder. "Don't ye fret, sah. We'll take care h'of h'everything. Er, by the way, wot's for lunch today, sah?"

Abbot Thibb looked totally bemused. "Lunch? You can speak of lunch at such a time as this?"

Big Drander coughed politely to gain Thibb's attention.

"Beg pardon, Father old chap, but every bloomin' Patrol an' Crewbeast is lookin' forward to a spot o' the famous Redwall vittles—at a time like this, or any flippin' time y'care to mention, wot!"

The Abbot took a glance at the hulking hares and burly otters, all young, and all ready to eat at the drop of a crust. It was difficult not to smile.

"How about a big extended picnic luncheon in the orchard? I could have our good Friar run it on into afternoon tea."

Big Drander's ears waggled with anticipation as he added, "Mayhaps it could carry on through dinner, then into supper."

Thibb chortled as he waved them down the wallsteps. "Aye, why not indeed, as long as you keep eating!"

Captain Rake patted Thibb's paw sympathetically. "Och, ye braw mousey, Ah think ye'll regret those words afore the day's out, mah friend. These walkin' stomachs will be eatin' as lang as yer Friar keeps sendin' more."

Thibb shrugged. "That's because they're young and full of life. Don't fret, Captain. We'll feed 'em like heroes—'tis the least Redwall can do for those who'll be defending our Abbey."

Uggo Wiltud overheard Thibb. He piped up boldly, "Does that include me, Father?"

The Abbot shook his head. "No, I have other plans for you."

The orchard lunch was up to Redwall standards—in a word, delicious! Sister Fisk sat sharing some apple and blackberry flan with Skor. The sea otter Chieftain interested her, and she plied him with questions as he did full justice to the lunch.

"Pardon my asking, sir, but doesn't it put you off food, knowing that you'll be fighting a war with the vermin soon?"

The big beast took a long draught of October Ale. "Why

should it, marm? Warriors never give such things much thought."

Fisk topped up his tankard. "Forgive me. I'm not a warrior, so I wouldn't know."

Reaching for bread and cheese, Skor touched her paw lightly. "Let me tell ye somethin' about warriors, Sister. We always eat well and never worry, because tomorrow we may be hungry, or dead. It doesn't do to dwell on the past or the future. Take me, now. Today I laid my young son to rest. 'Twas a sad an' hard thing t'do. But I'm a chieftain—my Crew look to me. I can't sit round for a season, mopin', weepin' an' tendin' a grave. There's others to think of, my other son, an' the Rogue Crew, an' my friend Captain Rake, with his Long Patrol, d'ye understand?"

The Sister nodded. "Indeed I do, sir, but I just wish there was something us Redwallers could do to help you."

Skor chuckled gruffly. "Feedin' this lot is a big help, marm, but I'll tell ye wot else ye can do. When the action starts, 'twould help if'n the Abbeybeasts stays out of our way. Lock yoreselves up in Cavern Hole, take care o' yore babes an' Dibbuns. Then after the battle's end, ye can serve us with yore healin' knowledge. I'm told yore good at bandagin' an' salvin', eh?"

Sister Fisk smiled modestly. "So I'm told, sir. Thank you for your advice, and now perhaps you'd best take care of that great appetite, before your otters and those hares clear the board of every crumb!"

The feasting continued until early evening, when Sergeant Miggory whispered in Abbot Thibb's ear. "H'it's startin' t'cloud over, Father. Captain Rake says the breeze is freshenin' from westward, an' ole Drogbuk's just felt a spot o' rain. No panic, Father. Get yore Redwallers inside, h'in a h'orderly manner."

In a short time the Abbeybeasts had gone from the orchard, leaving only the Rogue Crew, Shrews and the Long Patrol.

Rake drew his twin blades. "Which d'ye choose, Axe-hound, the main gates, or walltops?"

Flexing both paws, Skor gripped his battleaxe haft. "We'll come to the walltop with ye. Then when the vermin ship is sighted, I'll take my crew down t'the gate. Agreed?"

Rake felt raindrops beginning to patter on the rising wind. "Agreed, mah bonny friend. Let's get tae it!"

32

Out at the western horizon, Razzid Wearat had kept all the *Greenshroud*'s canvas furled. Leaning on the tiller, he wiped his injured eye, watching night descend amidst dark, heavy cloudbanks rolling overhead. Rain hissed against the stern timbers, as further west lightning flared briefly, followed by a distant roll of thunder. Shekra stood sheltered beneath the aft stairway. She hurried forward as Razzid beckoned her with his trident. The vixen quailed as Razzid reached out, drawing her close. "So then, my Seer, shall I tell ye what ye see?"

Without waiting for a reply he continued, "A night for storm! For swift sailing! For blood an' slaughter! For death! For victory! For Redwall Abbey, which will be mine by morning light! Is that what ye see?" His voice rose to a harsh roar; he shook Shekra until the teeth in her head rattled and her limbs did a crazy jig. "Is that what ye see? Tell meeeeee!"

The vixen could hear herself wailing in terror as the Wearat's grip tightened on her throat. "Aye, Lord, aye! 'Tis as ye say, truly it is, Lord!"

With a burst of insane laughter, he cast her aside. Pointing the trident at his crew, who were gathered, rain drenched, amidships, Razzid bellowed, "Haul in the anchor cable! Put

345

on all sail from stem to stern, every stitch o' canvas! Let's hear the storm singin' through the ratlines! Jump to it, ye rakin's an' scrapin's o' Hellgates!"

Corsairs and searats clambered aloft, loosing all sail. Ropes were swiftly hauled through blocks and made fast to cleats and bollards. As the last vermin slid to the decks, a mighty gust of wind smote the vessel's stern. *Greenshroud* lurched forward, sent on her voyage of evil by a mighty thunderclap and a sheet of lightning.

Razzid pointed his trident at Mowlag and Jiboree. "Haharr, attend yore cap'n, messmates!"

The pair approached him warily, saluting.

"Aye aye, Cap'n!"

He could see fear stamped on both their faces. Leering wickedly, he snarled, "Come here an' stand by me!" Enjoying the distress he was causing them, Razzid tapped the tiller arm. "Git yore paws on this, both of ye!"

As their trembling paws rested on the tiller, the Wearat's mood changed abruptly. He winked roguishly at them. "Stay true to yore ship an' trust yore cap'n, mateys. Will ye do that for me, eh?"

The relief was so great that they babbled readily.

"Aye, Cap'n, we'll stay true t'the *Greenshroud*!"

"We'd trust ye with our lives, Cap'n, we swear it!"

He grinned, nodding his head cheerfully. "That's the spirit, mateys. Now you hold 'er on course, dead east. Hahaarrr, this time tomorrer we'll be livin' like lords inside Redwall. Waited on paw'n'tail, the finest o' vittles, barrels o' grog an' soft beds to lay our heads on. Wot d'ye say t'that, mates?"

Together with the rest of the crew, Mowlag and Jiboree took up the cry. "Razzid! Razzid! Razzid!"

As the chant continued, Razzid strode for'ard, acknowledging their shouts by waving his trident.

Mowlag blew rainwater from his snout, exchanging looks with Jiboree. "The scabby-eyed fool don't suspect a thing, I'm sure of it!"

Jiboree spat over the side bitterly. "Puttin' the fear in us like that. Hah, just wait'll that Abbey's ours. He won't live to enjoy it!"

Mowlag glared hatred at Razzid Wearat through the storm-swept night. "Aye, the length o' my blade through 'is gizzard is all our cap'n will get from me!"

Razzid had reached the big bow set up on the forward peak. He turned, leaning against it, staring back at the two grasping the tiller, his good eye unblinking, regardless of the wind-driven downpour.

As though fearing to be overheard, Jiboree muttered to Mowlag, "Keep chantin', mate, 'e's watchin' us."

As the mate and the bosun resumed chanting, Shekra, who was still crouching nearby, slid off silently. She had heard all that went on between her one-time conspirators.

Now *Greenshroud*'s sails were stretched tight, thunder boomed as lightning flashed overhead. The wheeled vessel sped east like a juggernaut, jouncing and lurching over tussock and hollow, timbers groaning, rain sheeting along its length as it clattered over the flatlands, straight for Redwall Abbey. Razzid ordered crewbeasts to load the big bow on the peak.

He crouched behind it, peering along the huge arrowshaft, murmuring to himself, "This'll be a good way to knock on their door, though I don't suppose there'll be anybeast there to answer it. They'll all be snorin' in their nice liddle beds!"

Twangee, the young weasel nephew of the cook Badtooth, clambered nimbly down from the crow's nest, where he had been posted as lookout. His paws slapped the deck wetly as he hastened to Razzid's side to tell him the news. "Cap'n, Cap'n, I seen it, I seen the Redwall place!"

Razzid stared down at the bedraggled young weasel. "Are ye sure?"

Twangee waved his paws excitedly. "Sure, I'm sure, Cap'n—ye'll see it for yerself soon. There's liddle gold lights, like stars. That'll be from some o' the rooms upstairs, an' if'n ye look 'ard enough, ye can just about make out its shape!"

The Wearat patted Twangee's head. "Ye did well. Now find Redtail an' send 'im t'me."

Redtail the stoat was the ship's official lookout; he had keener sight than most. Razzid ordered him up to the crow's nest.

"I wants ye to take a good look around, then come back down an' report t'me. Look sharp, now!"

Sensing the urgency of his captain, Redtail performed his task smartly, clambering swiftly back to the deck. "'Tis the Abbey, Cap'n, we're on a course right for it. If'n this weather keeps up, we'll be there in about three hours by my reckonin'."

The Wearat was trembling eagerly. "I wants this ship to hit those Abbey gates dead centre. Git back up there an' make sure we stays on course, Redtail. I'll take over the tiller, so there'll be no mistake!"

Mowlag and Jiboree were glad to be relieved of the tiller. They were soaked and wind battered from trying to hold the vessel on its wild, careering course. Tugging their snouts in salute, they slunk off toward the galley, where there was warmth and grog to be had. However, before they had gone a few paces, Razzid's voice halted them.

"Ahoy, mates, I've got a job for ye both up on the for'ard peak. Bein' as yore such trusty beasts, ye can stand by, ready to throw that log bridge o'er the ditch when we reaches it. Git ye up on that forepeak now, cullies!"

He watched them being driven for'ard by the gale, both cursing under their breath at the perilous task they had been allocated. One false slip at the crucial moment of bridging the ditch was a virtual death sentence. The Wearat laughed callously as he urged them on.

"Jump to it, me lucky friends! Show our crew 'ow true to me ye are. Haharr, I wouldn't trust nobeast to do it, except me ole shipmates Mowlag an' Jiboree!" Casting a swift glance over the crew, he called four hulking ferrets to him, issuing them with orders. "Hearken t'me, bullies, go an' arm yoreselves with long pikes. If'n Mowlag or Jiboree don't stand fast an' carry out my biddin', then kill 'em an' take their place!"

The brawniest of the ferrets, a corsair named Lugsnout, narrowed his eyes viciously. "Leave it to us, Cap'n. If'n they moves a paw back'ards, they're both worm meat!"

As they went to get pikes, Razzid reached behind him, dragging Shekra forward by her tail.

"An' you, my Seer, you'll be watchin' the watchers. If'n anythin' goes amiss, the job o' bridgin' the ditch'll be yores. Unnerstand?"

The vixen protested, "But, Lord, I've got a ruined paw. I couldn't lift those pine trunks on my own!"

Razzid winked at her. "You'd be surprised at wot ye can do if'n I comes behind ye with my trident. Go on with ye!"

Whilst all this had been going on, *Greenshroud* had been rattling forward over the flatlands. Razzid pulled himself up on the tiller, peering ahead. He was rewarded by the sight of Redwall Abbey in the distance, its monumental bulk highlighted by twinkling lantern lights from dormitory windows. The Wearat shuddered with unholy joy.

"I see ye now. Ye can't run or hide from ole Razzid. I'm comin'—there's nought ye can do to stop me!"

Howling gale-force winds drove battering rain at the main door of the Abbey building. Fortunately, almost all the Redwallers were dry and warm inside. Friar Wopple and her helpers busied themselves in the kitchens, baking, cooking and preparing for the valiant defenders on the outer walltops. Sister Fisk and her assistants were hard at it in the Infirmary, readying supplies of bandages, poultices and healing remedies for the inevitable casualties of the coming conflict. However, the proudest creature in the Abbey was Uggo Wiltud, who had been ordered by the Abbot to guard the door against all comers. Armed with the sword of Martin the Warrior, the young hedgehog stood sentinel behind the huge oaken door. This was the greatest honour ever bestowed on him, and live or die, Uggo was determined to see it through.

Outside on the ramparts, it was difficult to distinguish anything on the western flatlands. Corporal Welkin Dabbs and Kite Slayer, two of the keener-sighted beasts, were on lookout. Skor Axehound and Captain Rake Nightfur stood alongside them in an effort to keep watch. Blustering winds and driving rain, plus the heavily clouded darkness of the night skies, limited their vision drastically. Captain Rake turned his head aside, dashing rain from his eyes. "Och, can ye nae see anythin' out yonder?"

Welkin Dabbs blew water from his nosetip. "Alas, sah, not a bloomin' thing, I'm afraid. What about you, miss? Your eyes are jolly much younger'n mine, wot?"

Kite Slayer shielded her vision with a dripping paw. "Huh, waste o' time tryin' t'spot anythin' in this foul lot!"

Skor patted her back. "Keep lookin', young Kite."

The other hares and otters sat below the walltops with their backs against the battlements, crouching hooded and cloaked on the lee side of the storm.

Buff Redspore tugged the hem of Rake's cloak. "Beg pardon, but might I take a peep, sah?"

Sergeant Miggory shot her a reproving glance. "You'll h'obey h'orders, miz. Keep yore 'ead down, like you've been told to!"

Lieutenant Scutram cast an eye over the waiting warriors, dispensing some sound advice. "Steady in the ranks, chaps. Stoppin' where you are gives us the element of surprise, y'see. I'm sure you'd all like t'be up on watch, but that'd let the vermin spot us. Don't jolly well want that, do we? By the left, we don't—it'd lose us the blinkin' edge. Right, Cap'n?"

Rake nodded. "Aye, that's mah plan. Though if anybeast has a canny idea tae suggest, Ah'm ready tae listen."

A Guosim shrew piped up eagerly, "Wot about sendin' up a pile of fire arrows? Then we'd be able to see the vermin."

Log a Log Dandy stared scathingly at the unfortunate

shrew. "Fire arrows? How long d'ye suppose a flamin' shaft'd last in this storm? Huh, the way the wind is blowin', it'd come straight back at us. Fire arrows! Are ye crazy?"

The Guosim ducked back under his cloak, murmuring, "Sorry, Chief. 'Twas just a thought."

Dandy softened his tone. "Never mind, mate, we're all on edge."

Everybeast gave a start as a thunderous blast boomed out directly overhead. Then a prolonged flash of chain lightning ripped its way across the sky for several seconds.

Corporal Welkin Dabbs pointed, roaring out frantically, "The ship! There they are! I saw the ship, sah!"

Rake hastened to the corporal's side. "Ye saw it? Where away?"

Dabbs kept his paw pointing out into the storm-torn night. "Right there, sah, midway twixt us an' the horizon, comin' this way, sah!"

Another fitful flash of lightning lit the land briefly. It was enough. All four lookouts saw *Greenshroud* clearly.

Nothing could have stopped the vermin vessel. It was stampeding madly forward, every stitch of sail canvas stretched almost to bursting. Timbers cracked and groaned; rigging whistled a dirge in the gale. The four wheels jounced and banged over every hillock and rut as the ship careered toward the Abbey at an alarming rate.

Skor was in his element. Bounding up onto the battlements, he whirled his huge battleaxe. "Come on, wavescum! I'm the Axehound, Warchief o' the Rogue Crew! Come an' take our name to Hellgates with ye. Come on!"

The lightning that crackled over the scene also allowed the vermin a plain view of Redwall. Perched high on the masthead, the stoat lookout took a swift bearing on their target. Scrambling to the deck, he informed Razzid, "Cap'n, I kin see that Abbey plain as a pikestaff. 'Tis dead ahead, an' we're bound to hit the door plumb centre afore too long!"

The Wearat seized a stout coil of line, skilfully lashing the tiller into a fixed position. He grabbed his trident. "Thankee, Redtail. Let's go up for'ard—I don't want to miss any o' this!"

The searats and corsairs toward the prow were knocked roughly aside as Razzid bulled his way up to the forepeak.

Shekra followed close on his paws, waving and gesturing. "Sire, we won't need those pine trunks, at the rate she's goin'—*Greenshroud* will jump that ditch at a go!"

Pawing Mowlag and Jiboree aside, the Wearat stood out on the prow, grasping at staylines to steady himself.

"Aye, nothin' can stop us now. Mowlag, Jiboree, git yoreselves on that big bow. As soon as ye see that main gate clear, then loose one o' those shafts at it, an' don't miss!"

Relieved from a virtual death sentence of their former task, both beasts sprang smartly to obey the new order.

Corporal Welkin Dabbs joined Skor and Rake on the threshold, waving and pointing. "I say, lookit the speed o' that bloomin' ship! Well, chaps, 'twon't be long before they arrive here, eh, wot!"

Skor bared his teeth savagely. "Hah, the gates ain't locked. 'Tis only good manners to open the doors to visitors, eh, Rake!"

The tall, dark hare drew both his blades. "Aye, let 'em come. But Ah'd no' be surprised if yon ship doesnae get stuck in that gateway. Looks tae me like it might, d'ye think?"

The big sea otter scratched his matted beard. "Mayhap 'twill, but they'll still have to face us. Right, let's get down there an' form a welcomin' committee." Swinging his battleaxe, he roared out over the storm, "Rogue Crew, all down to the gates. Yaylahoooooo!"

Skor's warriors needed no urging. They rushed to the wallsteps yelling bloodcurdling war cries.

Long Patrol hares and Guosim shrews arose, ready to follow, until Log a Log Dandy shouted sternly, "Hold yore positions. Ye ain't been told t'move yet!" They stared from the ramparts, spellbound, as *Greenshroud* burst out of the storm-tossed night. The vessel's rattling wheels could be plainly heard now.

Rake watched it come, calling to his warriors, "Hauld tight here until she strikes the gates!" He commented aside to Scutram, "Then Ah'll know best what move tae make."

Young Kite Slayer was easily the swiftest of paw in the crew. The ottermaid was first down the wallsteps, arriving in the curved stone alcove of the main gates. Brandishing spear and buckler, she called to her comrades, who were still coming down the steps. "There'll be a lot more notches on this shield rim afore the night's out. Come on, ye stinkin' vermin, we're wait—"

Her words were cut off as the giant arrow hit the gates dead centre. Both gates fell open, and the big shaft whizzed through, slaying Kite and whizzing on across the lawns. The Abbey's main door shook under the impact as the shaft buried its point in the stout oak timbers.

On the walltop, Sergeant Miggory bawled out a warning to the Rogue Crew as the *Greenshroud* shot over the narrow ditch. "Stan' aside beloooooooow!"

The otters hurled themselves to both sides of the long sandstone arch as the enemy vessel arrived.

Thrust onward by the immense gale force, the ship rammed into the open gateway. Both gates were ripped from their hinges, carrying on with the momentum as they were cleaved to the sides of the foebeasts' craft. With a cracking and snapping of timber, the masts hit the main arch, breaking like twigs as they struck the stonework. Some vermin were killed amidst the wreckage, crushed under falling timbers and rigging. Yet still the *Greenshroud* continued its wild rush forward.

With the awful din singing in his ears, Razzid Wearat had fallen flat on the bowsprit. His good eye stared wildly about as he scrambled upright. Seeing the gateway wide open in his wake, he felt the ship still rolling across the Abbey lawns. Razzid grabbed his trident, bellowing jubilantly, "Ahoy, mates, we're in! Now for the slaughter. Yahaaaaaar!"

33

The defenders on the walltop above the gates felt the rampart stonework shudder as the big ship was forced, under the storm's momentum, right through into the Abbey. Skor and his Rogue Crew were already racing in pursuit of *Greenshroud* as it rattled over the lawns.

Captain Rake hastily ordered the hares and shrews, "On the double now, down intae the grounds!"

Inside, the Abbey walls became a scene of wild and stormy chaos. However, the only positive action of the moment came from Skor's son Ruggan. Speedily he caught up with the ship's stern, grabbing hold of a line, which trailed after it. With his sword clenched in his teeth, Ruggan hauled himself nimbly upward, finding holds for his footpaws as he went. The ship was on its set course, heading for the main Abbey door. The daring young otter had already noticed this. With a bound, he vaulted over the stern rail, almost bumping into a startled searat, whom he despatched with a swift sword thrust.

Ruggan slashed the lashings, which had been holding *Greenshroud* on course. Gale-force winds caught the rudder, causing the tiller to swing loose so the vessel yawed, running off course. It heeled broadside on to the storm, slamming hard into a huge, ancient elm, which brought the ship to a shuddering halt. The crew were knocked flat but quickly recovered as Razzid hurried amongst them. He bellowed orders through the sheeting rain.

"Loose the riggin'! Throw all ropes over the side—use 'em to abandon ship. Quick now!"

Searats and corsairs promptly obeyed, swarming down over the lines to the saturated lawns below. Skor Axehound and his Rogue Crew charged to meet the foebeast. They were far outnumbered by enemies, but Skor was of the opinion that one good sea otter was worth any five vermin.

The Wearat, garbed in his iron-spiked helmet and a thick red cloak, stood at the centre of his crew as they fought to repel the otters.

Rake sized the situation up before he threw his fighters into the fray. He formed a swift strategy. "Most o' the vermin got off on the side which wasnae hit by the tree. So we'll circle aroond an' board the ship on the other side, eh, Dandy!"

Log a Log Dandy smiled grimly. "Good idea, Cap'n. 'Twill put us up on deck so we can come down behind 'em! There ain't too many came down on our side—about two to one, I'd say. Come on, me buckoes, let's give the scum some steel!"

It was no easy task, as the vermin had their backs to the ship's side, facing Rake's warriors. Hares and shrews knew enough not to warn the rest of *Greenshroud*'s vermin, so they fought without war cries, in savage silence.

Rake went at it with twin claymores flailing. Behind him came Sergeant Miggory, who had picked up a fallen spear. Log a Log Dandy and Lieutenant Scutram attacked from both sides, fore and aft, with rapier and sabre flashing. Churned up by rain and fighters, the lawn around them became a welter of mud. Both sides battled for their very lives, with no quarter given as steel clashed upon steel.

Lancejack Sage became surrounded by four of the foe. She took a knife throw in her shoulder as they closed in on her. A corsair ferret raised a scimitar as he leaned over the young hare. He snarled wickedly, "Haharr, time ta die, rabbet!"

He was about to slash down at Sage with the broad curved blade when a long oarshaft swept across, breaking his skull. Ruggan Axehound, leaning over the ship's side, swung the oar again, wiping out the life of a searat. Big Drander and Buff Redspore fought their way to the lancejack's side. As Buff stanched the wound in Sage's shoulder, Drander leaned over, shielding them both with his body. He winked at Sage.

"Steady on, old gel. We'll soon have ye up'n'about, wot!"

The breath was knocked from both haremaids when Drander suddenly slumped on top of them, a spear embedded deep between his shoulders.

Lieutenant Scutram slew the spear thrower with a hefty sabre slash. The ferocity of Long Patrol hares and Guosim shrews was so swift and ruthless that the vermin fled willy-nilly.

The shrew Chieftain chased after a corsair stoat; he despatched his quarry and divested him of his footwear, chuckling grimly. "Hahah! So this is the villain who stole my clogs!" Donning them, he skipped back to the ship, clicking both heels and sending sparks about.

"Ahoy, Rake, lookit me! I'm Log a Log Dandy Clogs agin!"

The tall Captain smiled momentarily. "Och, an' so ye are, bonny lad. Right, all aboard, buckoes!"

On the other side of the vessel, Skor Axehound and his warriors found themselves outnumbered and hard pressed. Razzid Wearat stood at the centre of his crew, urging them forward in a bid to wipe out the otters and gain entry to the Abbey building.

Skor battled stoically on, ignoring minor wounds, the red light of Bloodwrath blazing in his eyes. Being outnumbered had never bothered the Warchief of the High North Coast. From where he stood, Razzid could see Skor. He was not anxious to cross steel with the big sea otter, so he drove the vermin hard, feeling that they could soon overwhelm the defenders. By then the heroic chieftain, wielding his mighty battleaxe amidst the storm-rent night, would doubtless be wounded many times.

Razzid sneered as he imagined himself finishing Skor off slowly with the trident. However, the sight of his mortal enemy seemed to send Skor into a frenzy. He beckoned with his axe, bellowing, "Don't hide there in the middle of yore crew, dribblesnout! Come an' get yore ugly head chopped off. I'll stick it on that ole pitchfork ye call a weapon. How'll that do ye, eh?"

Bloodwrath kept welling up in Skor Axehound's eyes. He hurled himself into the vermin ranks, regardless of the wounds he was taking in his attempts to reach Razzid. The sight brought fear to the Wearat; he started retreating through his crew. He was almost at the rear when Shekra appeared at his side, urgently tugging his cloak.

"Lord, look behind you!"

"Eulaliiiaaaaa!"

"Logalogalogaloooooog!"

Long Patrol hares and Guosim swarmed down *Greenshroud*'s side, cutting off any escape. Razzid's cunning now came to the fore. He scanned the gale-swept night, finding a way out. Grabbing a burly ferret corsair, he gave him his helmet and cloak. "Here, mate, put these on. Lead our crew forward. I've got a plan that'll win this battle for us. I'll reward ye special like when Redwall's ours!"

Led by Rake and Dandy, the fighters fell upon the rear vermin ranks. Razzid tore himself loose from Shekra. Crouching down, he scuttled off toward the shelter of the orchard. The vixen stumbled and fell. Looking up, she found herself staring into the wrathful face of Trug Bawdsley.

Throwing away her blade, she pleaded, whining piteously, "Mercy, sire, mercy. Can't ye see I'm unarmed?"

Trug swung his sword, gritting out the words. "Aye, I'll show ye mercy, just as ye did to my young sister an' her friends the night ye murdered them!"

The young hare's words echoed in the Seer's head. It was the last voice she ever heard.

Skor, Dandy and Rake were in a racing fight to reach the cloaked and helmeted figure who was now at the centre of the melee. The disguised corsair panicked at the sight of the battleaxe-wielding sea otter closing in on him. He turned, meeting Captain Rake, who was swinging his twin claymores like a drum major—it was a fatal mistake. The corsair dropped like a log under the whirling blades.

At the sight of the legendary Wearat going down, all fighting ceased for a brief instant. The iron-spiked war helmet rolled off onto the sodden grass as Log a Log Dandy bounded up to crouch over the fallen one.

"Blood'n'whiskers! This un ain't no Wearat. We've been fooled!"

Mowlag took advantage of the lull. He grabbed Jiboree, not having heard what Dandy had said.

"Well, that saved us a job, mate. Quick now, we'll split up an' conquer the Abbey between us. Keep out the way o' those madbeasts if'n ye can. Let's scatter an' regroup later."

Vermin fled in all directions. The defenders gathered round the dead corsair.

Skor was whirling about in baffled rage. "Wot d'ye mean, not the Wearat? I saw Rake slay him!"

Dandy stood aside from the limp carcass. "Take a look for yoreself, bigbeast. That ain't Razzid!"

Skor thudded his battleaxe blade deep in the wet earth. "Then where's the bilge-blighted scum got to, eh?"

Lieutenant Scutram ignored him, calling out orders. "Get after the vermin! Stop 'em gangin' up again before they try to break into the bloomin' Abbey! Sergeant, take charge, will ye!"

Miggory bawled out commands in true parade-ground style. "Yew 'eard the h'officah—git movin'! Patrol, follow Cap'n Rake, h'otters go with yore chieftain. Guosim, go with yore Log a Log. Quick as y'like, now!"

Hearing the din of warfare outside, the screams of wounded and dying beasts, mingled with barbarous war cries, did not boost the composure of young Uggo Wiltud.

He paced back and forth, guarding the Abbey's main door, trying hard to look fearless. Martin the Warrior's great sword quivered in his paws, seeming too heavy to hold much longer. He was letting the blade lag when a light tap on his back caused him to jump. However, it was only his friend, the pretty hogmaid.

Uggo berated her shrilly. "Posy, you ain't supposed t'be up here. Get back down to Cavern Hole with the Redwallers!"

Posy pushed him aside. Putting her eye to the door, she tried to peer through a crack near the hinges. "I only wanted to see what's going on out there. Are we winning, Uggo?"

He pulled her from the door, his voice shaking as he tried to be stern. "You've got no business bein' here. Guardin' this Abbey door's my job. Abbot Thibb left me in charge!"

Posy rapped the imposing oak timbers with her paw. "Well, there's not much danger of vermin getting past this. What about the other doors an' windows? Are they all locked up tight and secured? You should check."

Uggo turned to continue his sentry duty and almost tripped over the blade of his sword. "Guard the door—that's all Father Abbot said."

Posy shook her head impatiently. "Well, I'm sure he never meant just this door. There's lots more side doors and shuttered windows to this Abbey, Uggo. If they broke in anywhere else, you'd look pretty silly marching up and down in one place. Come on!"

Trying to maintain his dignity, Uggo strode off in an effort to outpace Posy. "Huh, suppose I'd better just take a look around."

They were crossing the floor of Great Hall when Milda the volemaid came hurrying toward them. "Oh, sir, you'd best make 'aste. I think there's somebeast tryin' to break in. Come an' see for yoreself!" She ran off, with Uggo and Posy close behind her.

The gale-force wind slackened off, and rain slowed to a fine drizzle as Razzid Wearat made his way through the dark orchard. Hearing the sounds of an affray, he threw himself down beside an overturned wheelbarrow. A fleeing group of about a dozen vermin had been overtaken by Ruggan and some Rogue Crew otters who had outrun them. They were dealing out retribution.

Though the vermin fought desperately, they were no match for their ferocious adversaries. Razzid watched as the otters backed their foes up against a bramble hedge. Battering his swordblade against his shield, Ruggan howled like a madbeast, "Bloody yore blades an' send 'em to Hellgates, mates! Yaylahoooooo!"

Seething with rage, Razzid watched as his crewbeasts were slaughtered, though some escaped by crashing through the hedge. They fled off into the grounds, with sea otters hard on their tails, thirsting for vermin blood.

When they had gone, Razzid was about to rise, but somebeast flopped down beside him. He whirled his trident to deal with the intruder.

"Yaagh, don't 'urt me, Cap'n—'tis only ole Badtooth!"

Razzid grounded the trident, staring at *Greenshroud*'s cook. "I thought you'd ha' been long dead."

The fat weasel gave a gap-fanged grin.

"Not me, Cap'n. I might be fat, but I'm too quick an' greasy t'get meself slayed. I thought you was a goner. Wotcher doin' round 'ere, stealin' apples?"

Razzid ignored the joke, nodding toward the Abbey. "I'm lookin' for a way to git in there. Any ideas?"

Badtooth shrugged. "Who, me? I wouldn't know where t'start, Cap'n. Wait up, kin ye smell somethin'?"

Razzid sniffed the air as Badtooth answered his own question. "Cookin', I kin smell cookin'. Smells nice, too."

The Wearat nodded. "Yore right, the kitchens must be somewhere about. They must have a kitchen window or a door. That'll be it—come with me, matey."

Avoiding one or two other skirmishes between defenders and crewbeasts, they crossed the vegetable plots. Redwall Abbey loomed large through the damp night.

Razzid pointed with his trident at a thin, pale shaft of golden light piercing the darkness at about waist height. "There, see? Let's take a look, mate."

It was a shuttered window. Badtooth put his nose to the crack, sniffing blissfully. "New-baked bread, an' scones, too, if'n I ain't mistook. Mmmmm, they certainly knows about cookin' in there, Cap'n."

Razzid pulled him from the window, flinging him to the ground. "Shut yer slobberin' gob an' stay outta my way!" Inserting the prongs of his trident into the gap between shutter and stonework, he pried it silently wider.

Crouching, he put his good eye to the gap.

Badtooth sat up eagerly. "Can ye see anythin', Cap'n?"

Razzid murmured, almost to himself, "Not much, just some sacks an' a stone wall. There's stuff hangin' from nails. Herbs an' veggibles, I s'pose. No, wait, hush, somebeast's comin'."

Friar Wopple could be heard calling out, "Bring some onions, an' a bunch of parsley, too, Brugg."

A moment later a mole appeared, answering, "Bunions an' parsee, marm, roight away." Taking the vegetables, the mole went away.

Razzid whispered to Badtooth, "It's a storeroom leadin' out into the kitchen. Ye couldn't find a better place to break in, eh, mate?"

The fat cook looked distinctly nervous. "Cap'n, mightn't it be better if'n I waited out 'ere? I ain't never done no breakin' in—"

The Wearat's claw actually pierced Badtooth's ear as he dragged him close, gritting the words out. "You gotta choice, lardtub—either come inside with me or stay outside here, after I slit yore throat."

The weasel cook gulped. "I'm with ye, Cap'n!"

Jamming the trident prongs under the gap between sill and shutter, Razzid began trying to pry it outward. It was a heavy oaken shutter and refused to budge. The Wearat had several attempts at the shutter, even having Badtooth prying with him, but it was a futile task. Removing the trident, he leaned on it, breathing heavily as he surveyed the window as a whole.

Badtooth was immensely relieved. "Ye'll break yore trident on that shutter, Cap'n. Let's go back to that orchard place. We could lie low an' eat all sorts o' fruit'n'berries."

The trident butt struck him hard in the stomach, bending him double. Razzid hissed fiercely, "I'm goin' to split that shutter through its middle. So stand clear, an' keep yore slobberin' trap shut!"

The trident prongs thudded into the shutter's centre. Razzid began wresting it free, giving Badtooth an order. "Look through that crack at the bottom after I strike it. Tell me if'n the coast's still clear, right?"

Badtooth peered beneath the gap. "Nobeast must've 'eard anythin'. All clear, Cap'n."

Razzid battered the shutter with his trident points several times. The wood began to splinter and crack.

Next time Badtooth went to look, he had something to report. "Hold on, Cap'n. One o' those mouse things, a vole, I think, has just come in. I think it musta heard ye. . . . No, wait, now it's gone away. All clear agin!"

Razzid dealt the shutter another shuddering blow, then crouched down to look for himself. He chuckled wickedly. "There's a whole pile of 'em come to see wot the noise is about. Huh, cooks an' kitchen skivvies, they look scared out o' their wits. I'll give 'em somethin' t'be scared of. You keep an eye out for any wavedogs or rabbets!"

He attacked the shutter with renewed vigour, causing further damage as the old timber creaked and splintered.

Friar Wopple stopped her workers from crowding into the storeroom.

The mole Brugg looked anxiously to the Friar. "Hurr, wot'll uz do, marm?"

Never having been faced with a vermin attack, Wopple

was frightened. However, she tried to stay calm and reassure her helpers. "Stay back, please. I've sent Milda to bring a warrior who can deal with this. Oh, dear, look at that!"

The shutter trembled as it was struck again. This time three sharp metal prongs burst through.

Razzid went at it in a frenzy. *Thud! Whump! Bang! Crash!*

Between blows, he issued instructions to the fat cook. "When the shutter bursts, you get right in there. Kill the nearest one, then jump to one side. I'll be straight in behind ye. Unnerstand?"

Badtooth saluted miserably. "Aye aye, Cap'n!"

Two more thunderous strikes, and the shutter collapsed, falling inward and leaving the window open to the night drizzle, with both vermin waiting outside. Razzid prodded Badtooth with the trident.

"Right, mate, in ye go!"

34

As the two young hogs followed the volemaid into the kitchens, Posy was throwing questions at Milda. "You say there's vermin trying to get in. How?"

Milda waved her paws in agitation. "Through the store-room window, miss. They're bangin' on it really loud. I'm sure 'tis vermin!"

Uggo was trying hard to feel like a warrior. He growled, trying to stem the fear welling up in his throat. "How many of the scum d'ye think there are?"

Milda looked distracted. "Couldn't say, sir, but there's more'n one makin' all that din. Could be a gang of 'em!"

Everybeast crammed into the storeroom doorway moved out of Uggo's way as with sinking heart he heard the hammering racket on the window and saw the shutter disintegrating in a shower of splinters and timber chips.

Behind him, Milda was shouting, "Leave it to the warrior! He's carryin' Martin's sword. Stand clear an' give him room!"

Even as the words left her lips, the entire shutter burst inward. Uggo was inching hesitantly forward when the big fat weasel, Badtooth, came bounding in. Martin's blade slashed his throat as he landed on top of the young hog.

The sword went flying from Uggo's faltering grasp, clattering against the far wall.

Then the Wearat scrambled over the windowsill, wielding his trident. He stepped on Badtooth, cursing as he stumbled.

"Serves ya right, ye fat idiot!"

At the sight of Razzid, kitchen staff fled screaming. It was like seeing a living nightmare. Uggo lay stunned beneath the slain cook, his head having been banged on the floor when Badtooth landed on him. The Wearat kicked Badtooth aside, exposing Uggo lying there.

Razzid wiped at his leaky eye, staring down at him. "Hah, the liddle 'edgepig who escaped from my ship. Well, yore runnin' days are done!"

He stabbed down with the trident, spearing Uggo's footpaw. Uggo screeched out in agony as Razzid pushed the weapon hard. The Wearat taunted him cruelly. "Now, 'old out yore other footpaw. I likes t'make sure o' my work. Hahaaarhaar! This is gonna hurt ye!"

"You leave him alone, you dirty old Wearat!"

Razzid let go of his trident, which was still stuck in his victim's footpaw. He turned, surprised that any kitchen lackey would challenge him.

Posy put her whole weight behind Martin's sword. She lunged, with both eyes tight shut.

Razzid seemed to lose the power of speech. He stood stock-still, looking down at the venerable blade which had impaled his stomach. Time stood still in the frozen tableau. Uggo lying on the floor with his footpaw transfixed by the trident; Posy with a shocked expression on her face; the Wearat, glaring with his good eye at the sword of Martin the Warrior protruding from his midriff.

Then Razzid gave out with a wild roar. "Hayaaaar! Do ye think ye can kill me? I'm Razzid Wearat!" He staggered to one side, grabbing the trident out of Uggo's footpaw. Still with the sword in him, he lurched at Posy, snarling, "Die, liddle spikepig . . . die!"

There was a deep bellow from behind him.

"Redwaaaaaalllll!"

Despite his age, size and weight, Jum Gurdy bounded through the open window, swinging his hefty stave. Before Razzid could turn, the Redwall otter dealt him a blow which broke both the stave and his skull. Razzid Wearat collapsed in a limp heap.

This time there was no doubt about it—the Wearat had been truly slain.

Uggo hauled himself into a sitting position. "Mister Gurdy, where'd you come from?"

Jum withdrew the sword from his enemy's body. "My ole uncle Wullow can rest easy now. Eh, wot's that ye say, young Wiltud?"

Posy repeated the question. "He asked where did you come from, sir?"

Jum wiped the blade clean on Razzid's carcass. "I couldn't travel as fast as you, bein' in charge of the wounded shrews. We fetched up at the Abbey gates just a few moments back. Seein' the state Redwall was in, I left those Guosim out on the path an' came right in. Ran straight into a searat—huh, he dashed off. Well, I gave chase, an' as I was comin' by the kitchen window, I heard that Wearat roarin' an' shoutin', so I came to investigate. Hah, just as well I did fer you two, eh? Seen ought of my sister Dorka? She should be pleased t'see her ole brother."

Jum hefted the sword of Martin admiringly. "Hoho! I likes the feel o' this blade. Tell Dorka, if'n ye see her, that I'm lendin' a paw t'clear our Abbey of those vermin scum. Breakin' into Redwall an' leavin' their ship on our property—the bloomin' nerve o' them!"

Brandishing the sword, he scrambled out of the storeroom window, roaring, "Look out, vermin. Jum Gurdy's come 'ome!"

Both leaders of the remaining *Greenshroud* crew, Mowlag and Jiboree, found themselves deserted. Losing heart at the ferocity of Long Patrol hares and sea otters, the vermin

367

had fled in all directions. Most found the open main gates and dashed out onto the flatlands. Faced with Skor Axehound and Captain Rake, the pair were backed up against the Abbey pond. They made one last mad charge, hoping to get by their enemies, but to no avail. Skor's battleaxe and Rake's twin claymores made short work of Mowlag and Jiboree. The pond crimsoned in the night drizzle over the place where they had sunk beneath the waters.

Dawn arrived, misty at first but clearing into a bright sunlit morn. Abbot Thibb threw open the Abbey door, allowing relief to the gallant defenders. Sister Fisk and her helpers went to assist the wounded whilst Friar Wopple sent out kitchen workers pushing trolleys laden with breakfast. However, there were other things to attend to.

Sergeant Miggory called briskly, "Form up in rank, Patrol, smartly now, no gossipin', Miz Ferrul. Vittles later, young Flutchers, git in line!"

The Rogue Crew of Skor did likewise. All activity ceased as the lists were taken.

Corporal Welkin Dabbs reported, "Sah, Drander an' Wilbee have fallen, I regret to say. Lancejack Sage, Trug Bawdsley an' Lieutenant Scutram all sustained wounds, sah, but they'll recover, I'm told. The rest o' the column are all present an' correct . . . sah!"

Ruggan Axehound saluted his father. "Rogue Crew lost Kite Slayer an' Endar Feyblade. I ain't counted the wounded yet, but there's not many. Er, permission to go after the vermin who escaped out the west gates, Chief?"

Sister Fisk stamped a paw down angrily, her voice shrill. "Haven't you had enough of killing! Kindly take yourselves into the orchard so we can dress your injuries and feed you!"

Skor was about to speak when Rake interrupted him. "Och, the Sister's right, ye bloodthirsty auld beastie. We're all guests o' the Father Abbot an' these good creatures, so let's abide by their rules!"

Thibb bowed solemnly to Rake. "My thanks to you, Captain. Please feel free to avail yourselves of anything Redwall has to offer."

There was a moment's silence, then Skor yawned, leaning on his axe haft. "Fair enough, so be it. I'm tired an' hungry, too. Crew, put up yore weapons!"

Dorka Gurdy had a request. "When yore all fed an' bandaged, mayhaps ye'd like to shove that filthy ole boat out of our Abbey. It don't look nice, sittin' there!"

Amidst general laughter, the warriors of the Long Patrol and the sea otters of the Rogue Crew went off to the orchard followed by a crowd of cheering Redwallers.

35

In her forge chamber at the mountain of Salamandastron, the Badger Lady Violet Wildstripe sat reading. She loved going back through the archives of her legendary fortress. It was early morning. She was sipping a beaker of coltsfoot and burdock tea, perusing the yellowed scrolls and volumes of past scribes. Lady Wildstripe looked up as a gentle tap sounded on her door.

It was Major Felton Fforbes. He eased himself into the chamber quietly. "Ahem, sorry to disturb ye, Milady."

Putting aside her reading materials, she rose. "Bit of a chill on the air these last few days, Major. May I offer you some hot tea?"

Fforbes twitched his neat grey moustache, accepting the tea. This had almost developed into a morning ritual, as the two mulled over Salamandastron affairs.

The Badger Lady drifted across to the long window, which stood open to the outdoors. There was still a sea mist out on the western horizon. She inhaled deeply, leaning out slightly as she surveyed the mountainside. The major joined her, waiting politely to see what Lady Wildstripe had to say.

Breathing deeply once more, she exhaled slowly with a sigh. "Autumn days have a charm of their own, the aroma of heather and sea milkwort, enchanting!"

Fforbes gave a perfunctory sniff, nodding. "As ye say, Milady, nice scent of autumn, wot!"

She pointed to the lower slopes of the southern face. "And those mountain ash trees, see how they've become changed? All the leaves are red and golden brown."

Fforbes took a quick glance at the rowans, which he had already seen several times since dawn. "Ahem, yes, indeed. Charmin'."

They stood in silence, the major knowing what Lady Wildstripe's question would be.

After a while she spoke. "No news of Captain Nightfur and his column today?"

The major drained his beaker, dabbing his moustache with the back of a paw. "No, Milady, 'fraid not. They've been gone for some time now, don't know what the deuce is keepin' 'em!" He humphed slightly. "Y'd think a simple mission to Lord Axehound on the High North Coast wouldn't take 'em this long. Autumn's almost a quarter gone. Let's hope they make it back by winter, wot, wot?"

Lady Violet watched as the sea mist began evaporating into the soft warm day. "Do you think we should put out a search party, Major?"

Felton Fforbes placed his beaker firmly on the stone windowsill. "Search party, marm? What'n the name o' blitherin' seasons for? We've got up'ards of a score o' Gallopers out on the dunes an' across the northern shores. You'll know immediately if they're sighted. No need of search parties. None at all, I should say not!"

Lady Wildstripe felt rather nonplussed. "Why not?"

The major explained, with a hint of vehemence in his tone, "Rake Nightfur, Lieutenant Scutram, Corporal Dabbs an' Colour Sarn't Miggory, that's why! How d'ye think warriors an' veterans like them would feel? Havin' t'be fetched back home by some bunch o' shave-scutted leverets? They'd never live down the blinkin' shame, Milady!"

Lady Violet spoke softly. "Forgive me, Major. I never thought of that. It's just as well I have you to advise me."

Felton Fforbes poured her another beaker of tea, his brusque manner vanishing. "Ahem, I wouldn't fret over such things, Milady. Tell ye what, though, how'd you like t'go out on a patrol yourself?"

She looked puzzled momentarily. "Me, out on patrol? Whatever for, Major?"

The Long Patrol officer smiled briefly. "Call it a sort of jolly old exercise, wot! You an' I, an' the relief Gallopers, we could all go. That way you could see the lay o' the land. Who knows, marm, ye might even spot Cap'n Nightfur an' his column. As for the young Gallopers, they'd see it as some sort o' test. Y'know they're always out to impress their Badger Lady."

Violet Wildstripe expressed surprise. "Oh, dear me, I never realised they felt that way."

The Major chuckled. "Still learnin', eh, Milady? Shall we say you'll meet us all shortly on the foreshore? 'Twould be a pity t'waste such a glorious day—great hikin' weather, wot!"

Lady Wildstripe was delighted at the prospect. "Right, then, I'll be down in two ticks!"

Old Colonel Bletgore was seated on a smooth sun-warmed rock, leaning his chin on a long knob-handled stick. He accosted a passing Galloper. "I say there, young ripscut, where's everybeast off to, eh, wot? Speak up!"

The Galloper saluted. She was bright eyed, bushy tailed and eager not to stop and gossip with the ancient colonel. But courtesy to a senior officer bade her reply. "It's the Second Season Gallopers, sah, we're to escort Lady Wildstripe on a patrol of the area, sah!"

Bletgore waved his stick at the young hare as she hurried off to join the ranks. "What'n the name o' blitherin' boulders would she want t'go on a confounded patrol for, eh ... wot ... wot?"

Thirty of the young hares stood lined up on the foreshore, every one brushed, combed, rigged out in light green tunics and fully armed. Lady Wildstripe paced alongside the major as he inspected them. She kept silent, letting Felton Fforbes comment.

"Ah, young Folderum, got Right Markers post, eh? Very good, your pa'd be proud of ye, laddie buck!"

Folderum saluted with his father's sabre, which was still a trifle too large for him.

"Thankee, Major sah. The patrol are well armed, all carryin' blades, ten with lances an' the rest with bows an' shafts . . . sah!"

The major nodded, moving on down the ranks. "Chin up, Miz Peasblossom. Tuck that tummy in, Grumby. Hold that lance upright, Twilby—don't want to stab any of your messmates. Is that a top button I see undone, Frubbs Minor? Do it up, bucko, that's the style!"

He turned to Lady Wildstripe, barking out briskly, "Parade all correct, Milady!"

She gave him a gracious smile. "Thank you, Major. Give the order to lead off. Perhaps with a good marching tune, please."

Major Felton Fforbes made a small circle in the air with his swagger stick. "Patrol will lead off to the left—aye, an' give us a lively song. How about 'General Billyoh's Rant.' Right, off y'go, now, quick march!"

Every hare knew the marching song by heart. They roared it out with gusto into the clear autumn morn.

"Now, here's a rule or two for you,
as outward bound ye stroll,
you've got to prove so true'n'blue,
to join the Long Patrol.
An' here's a tip, stiff upper lip,
when facin' vermin foe,
give 'em lots o' blood'n'vinegar
an' General Billyoh!
Aye, General Billyoh, me lads, General Billyoh!
No quarter, no surrender, strike 'em hard an' lay 'em
low!

"Eulalia is our battle cry,
so shout it long an' loud,
Ye hail from Salamandastron
an' don't it make ye proud,
so when they see ye chargin'
hear the enemy wail 'oh, no,'
we're in for steel'n'slaughter
an' General Billyoh!
'Tis General Billyoh they'll get, General Billyoh,
throw open wide the Hellgates, an' we'll show 'em
    where t'go!"

Stamping their pawprints in the damp sand, the column marched north along the beach. The sea was in floodtide, creating a din as it rolled in, with white-combed rollers booming as they broke on the coast. This, combined with the raucous calls of seabirds, vied with the song the young hares were singing.

With a twinkle in his eye, the major called out, baiting the patrol, "Is that the flippin' best ye can do, wot? Lady Wildstripe an' meself can hardly hear a word from any of ye!"

The Badger Lady caught on to what he was doing and joined in the fun, shouting aloud, "It must be the sound of the waves and those gulls squawking. I think 'tis drowning our singers out, Major. Mayhaps they could try a little harder, eh?"

The patrol began singing with renewed vigour, increasing their volume. Necks straining and ears flat back, they yelled out the song with all their power.

Major Fforbes shook his head sadly. "I tell ye, Milady, in my young Galloper seasons, I could've probably drowned 'em all out with my voice. Young Foghorn Fforbes, they used to call me, wot!"

Lady Wildstripe hid a chuckle. "Oh, I don't doubt it, Major. Perhaps they haven't reached full volume yet. Maybe if they sing it once more, we'll hear them loud and clear."

It was some time before the young hares realised what was going on. By then they had sung themselves hoarse.

Peasblossom fluttered her eyelids at the officer. "It's no good, sah. We'll never be as jolly good as you were. I say, d'you think you could sing out an' show us how?"

Major Felton Fforbes touched his throat, uttering a cough. "Ahem, ahem. . . . Wish I could, missy, but I've got this sore throat, d'ye see. Not possible, I'm afraid. Column, left wheel, let's try a hike into the dunes, wot!"

They halted at midday in a sheltered hollow between four sandhills. Provisions were broached whilst they sat down to relax. Scones, dried fruit and elderflower cordial were passed around.

Lady Wildstripe remarked to Folderum, who was sitting nearby, "Well, young sir, are you enjoying our little foray?"

Folderum nodded enthusiastically. "Oh yes, Milady, it's absolutely top hole out here, wot!"

The Badger Lady gazed up at the warm blue sky. "I agree. It's so long since I've been away from the mountain. How would you like to spend the night out here? Would you like to camp down on the heathland?"

She was met with an overwhelming reply from the patrol.

"Oh, I say, that'd be bloomin' splendid, wot!"

"Rather—a full night out under the blinkin' stars!"

"Oh, marm, say we can, please. It'd be jolly good fun!"

Lady Wildstripe looked to Felton Fforbes. "What do you think, Major?"

Fforbes chewed on a candied chestnut. "Hmm, I doubt whether Colonel Bletgore'd approve."

Young Grumby was heard to murmur, "Don't suppose he'd even miss us, he sleeps so bloomin' much, the old fogey."

The major fixed Grumby with a severe look, which dissolved into a grin. "No, I don't suppose he would, an' if you're lucky enough t'reach his age, you wouldn't either, Grumby. Anyhow, 'twould be gone dark by the time we got back to Salamandastron. So if a night out in the open'd agree with ye, Milady, then I'm all for it, wot!"

The remainder of that fine day was spent happily. Leaving the dunes, they trekked off onto the heathland, singing and joking with one another. The Badger Lady was still young enough to enjoy herself with the Gallopers and sang out as loud as anybeast. In the early evening, the major spotted a suitable campsite.

"Over yonder—twixt that flat-sided hummock an' those gorse bushes. We'll be protected on two sides, eh!"

Folderum's ears twitched; he held up a paw. "Quiet, you chaps. I think I can hear runnin' water. Maybe there's a brook hereabouts, wot?"

The major tapped him with his swagger stick. "Well done, laddie buck, very observant of ye!"

Peasblossom sniggered, whispering to Lady Wildstripe, "Very observant, my left paw, Milady. He's Galloped round here before—I know he has, the flippin' fraud!"

Darkness fell on a scene of contentment. A fire had been built from dead gorse, water was bubbling to make dandelion tea, and the hares were toasting scones on their swordpoints. Major Fforbes relented and rendered a song. The young Gallopers were surprised at the richness of his fine baritone voice, none of them having heard him sing before. He made the heathlands echo, his tones ringing up into the velvet star-strewn night.

"My friends, now let us pause,
survey these great outdoors,
they're here for me, they're here for you,
all pals an' comrades good an' true.
I must say who could ask for more,
the sky's our roof, the earth's our floor,
out in the great outdoors!
Kind season, treat us right,
don't let it rain this night,
forbid that gales blow fierce,

or frost our hides to pierce,
pay heed an' help our cause,
out in the great outdoors!
But havin' said all that,
just look at where we're at,
with a roarin' fire to toast our paws,
I'll warm mine, an' you warm yours,
whilst happily we sing an' shout,
out out out out, out out out out!
Out in the great outdoors!"

There were further campfire songs, riddles, jokes and poems. The patrol were totally at their ease. Lady Wildstripe lay back, surveying the starry night sky, with its huge, white moon shedding pale, silent light over all.

Young Peasblossom gave a gusty sigh. "Ain't it jolly good, Milady, I mean, bein' out here an' all that? Wish we could stay out here all season, wot!"

Ruffling the haremaid's ears, Lady Wildstripe smiled. "Indeed, it's very enjoyable. D'you know, I've decided that we're going to do this a lot more in the future."

The major interrupted with his customary briskness. "Beg pardon, Milady, but I think it's about shut-eye time for these young uns. Folderum, take Grumby an' Frubbs Minor. Mount a movin' sentry. Keep circlin' the area outside o' the camp. No need to march, but stay movin'—stop ye noddin' off. Both eyes peeled, all around at all times. I'll send a relief after midnight."

Folderum saluted. "Understood, sah!"

The rest of the patrol settled down after banking up the fire. Within moments, the calm autumn night had worked its spell. Everybeast was slumbering peacefully.

From where he was walking, Folderum could make out Frubbs Minor's back. Every now and then, he would turn to catch sight of Grumby, some way behind him. They had been circling the camp for a while when Grumby broke off and walked away.

Folderum saw this. Catching Grumby up, he tapped his back. "Beg pardon, but where d'ye think you're off to, eh?"

Grumby wiped a paw across his mouth. "I'm flippin' well parched, old lad. Just nippin' back t'camp to see if there's a drop o' that dandelion tea."

Being responsible for the sentry walk, Folderum turned Grumby around. "Oh, no, you're not, bucko. Y'don't do that sort o' thing when you're guardin' our comrades. There'll be plenty o' time for bloomin' tea once we're relieved."

Grumby went dutifully back to his task, though Frubbs Minor had already passed. Folderum strode off, keeping him in sight. This left Grumby pacing along behind Folderum. They continued without further incident, though Frubbs Minor slowed his pace.

Turning, he whispered aloud to Folderum, "I say, we've been trudgin' round out here for blinkin' ages. When's that relief comin', wot?"

Folderum waved him on. "They'll come when the major sends 'em. You just carry on patrollin', m'laddo. Er, what are ye starin' at, pray?"

Frubbs Minor was looking past Folderum. "Where's Grumby got to?"

There was a muffled squeak from behind the hill.

Folderum narrowed his eyes meaningly. "I told him he couldn't go to the camp for tea. I know where he'll be at, though. He'll be gluggin' water, round at that brook. Come on!"

No sooner were they in sight of the brook than Folderum spotted Grumby—he was struggling to break free from a gang of dark figures.

Folderum drew his sword. "Hurry, Frubbs, get back t'the major, tell him we're bein' ambushed. Looks like vermin t'me. Go!"

Frubbs Minor scooted off whilst Folderum dashed to Grumby's aid. Though he was outrageously outnumbered, the brave young hare charged in, waving his sabre and roaring, "Eulaliiiiaaaaa!"

Suddenly taken aback, the foebeasts paused momentarily. That was enough for Grumby. He wriggled free, dashing to his companion's side. He had lost his weapons, so he armed himself with a rock, brandishing it as he echoed the cry.

"Eulaliiiaaaa!"

The enemies were vermin, a villainous-looking bunch about a score in number. Now over their initial surprise, they swiftly recovered and advanced snarling on the two young Patrollers. Then the night air reverberated with the Salamandastron war cry, bellowed forth by the rest of the patrol and a tall badger with a thunderous yell. "Eulaliiiiiaaaaa!"

The villains fled south, but Major Fforbes shouted orders when he saw which way they were heading.

"Don't chase 'em yet! Cut 'em off—they mustn't go that way. Come on, Gallopers! Milady, you take some t'the left, an' I'll go right with the rest. Outpace the blighters an' get behind 'em! They mustn't reach Salamandastron!"

The Badger Lady took off, calling to her creatures, "Come on, let's show them how Long Patrol Gallopers run!"

The vermin were left slack-jawed as the hares raced by them, skidded to a halt, then turned to face them. Still armed with only a piece of rock, Grumby screeched, "Yahaaarrr, give 'em blood'n'vinegar!"

This time the vermin ran back into the heathland, their paws pounding with renewed speed, the speed of panic. None wanted to stand and face the huge badger and her hares.

Young Twilby was already dashing after them when the major neatly tripped him.

"Stand fast until you're ordered to charge, laddie buck. Steady in the ranks, there!"

Every hare was trembling with anticipation, weapons ready.

Major Felton Fforbes brought them back to earth with a bump. "I said stand fast! Now, anybeast injured or slain?"

He looked about to assure himself. "All present an' correct, eh? Good! Patrol awaitin' your orders, Milady!"

Not quite certain of her next move, Lady Wildstripe paused before addressing them.

"Er, quite. . . . You all did very well tonight, particularly you, Folderum, and thank you, Major, for your quick thinking. As for those vermin, well, I really don't know. If we chased them, it might be dawn before we caught up, eh, Major?"

Felton Fforbes knew that she was seeking his experienced advice. He nodded, putting up his blade. "As y'say, Milady, they've got a good head start. We'd be runnin' all night to catch the rascals up. I think we should go back to camp, marm, get a good night's rest, wot!"

The crestfallen young hares dragged their paws on the way back to camp. The major jollied them along. "We'll keep a sharp lookout at dawn. If they're determined t'come back this way, they'll have to get past us first. Then we'll show 'em fur'n'slaughter, wot!" The patrol arrived back at camp in high spirits.

"Huh, vermin, did ye see the way they tucked in their tails an' ran off?"

"Aye, truth is, they didn't fancy facin' Long Patrol warriors!"

The major murmured to Lady Wildstripe, "Hope I did the right thing, Milady. These young uns ain't been in a killin' an' slayin' fight yet."

She patted his paw. "Thank you, Major, you did right. By the way, you don't think they'll return this way, do you?"

Felton Fforbes chuckled. "Not if I'm any judge o' vermin. We're not babes an' old uns—we train fighters, Milady." Throwing more fuel on the fire, he settled down. "Folderum, change the sentry, will ye, there's a good beast. The rest of ye, stop chatterin' an' get some sleep."

Dawn's first light was heralded by Peasblossom, who was on sentry, racing into the camp. "Sah! Milady! They're comin' back, those flamin' vermin!"

To seek a better view, all three climbed to the hilltop behind the camp. News spread quickly; soon almost all the Patrol were up beside them. Having exceptionally good sight, Lady Wildstripe soon picked out the vermin on the heathland. "Hmm, it's a bit misty out there, but that might be them, eh, Major?"

Felton Fforbes shielded his eyes as sunlight turned the mist into a blanket of golden tendrils. "Looks like 'em, Milady, about the same number I'd say. But they fled from us last night, so why are they runnin' back toward us in such a blinkin' hurry? They're not even tryin' to sneak up on us, like vermin do. Very strange, marm!"

The reason became startlingly clear a moment later. Folderum shouted wildly, "It's the ship! Look . . . the ship!"

The vessel *Greenshroud* emerged, riding a breeze, which was dispersing the mist lazily. Amongst the young hares speculation ran rife.

"Are they showin' their crew where we are?"

"Looks like we've got a real battle t'face now, chaps!"

"Well, stand by, buckoes—true blue an' never fail, wot!"

The major rapped out an order. "Everybeast down below this hilltop. Don't dare show an eartip until I see what's goin' on. Smartly now!"

They obeyed with alacrity, but not without comment.

"I say, aren't we goin' to fight 'em, sah?"

"Not like warrior hares, hidin' from a jolly old scrap, eh?"

Lady Wildstripe's voice silenced further speculation. "It's not a matter of hiding from a fight. Do as the major says. The way they're running, it looks like the ship may be chasing them. It could be some sort of mutiny amongst the crew, vermin fighting vermin."

Peasblossom chuckled. "Oh, I say, wouldn't that save us a blinkin' job, wot. It'd cut the odds down a bit, Milady."

The badger nodded. "Perhaps it would. Let's wait and see."

The major interrupted. "That ship had a large crew last time it visited Salamandastron. Even if they slew those vermin who are runnin', we'd still be well outnumbered. Milady, the best thing we could do is retreat to our mountain. 'Twould give us more of a fightin' chance."

The Badger Lady lay flat, peering over the hilltop. "You're right, of course, Major, but I'd like to see the outcome of this incident first. They're closer now—it's the gang who were here last night, sure enough."

Overcome by curiosity, the major and the rest of the contingent joined her to watch. Like all young hares, they kept up a commentary.

"Hah, those runners are slowin' down. Must be winded, wot!"

"Oh, look, a band have jumped from the ship. They're after 'em like Billyoh!"

"Haha, so they are! C'mon, you rascals, give those other rascals a spot o' blood'n'vinegar. Get 'em!"

Lady Wildstripe stood up abruptly, in full view. "Those beasts that came from the ship—they're not vermin, they're otters . . . and hares, too!"

The screams of falling vermin mixed on the breeze with fierce ringing war cries.

"Yaylahooooh!"

"Eulaliiiiaaaaa!"

Drawing his sword, the major ran toward the conflict. "That's Cap'n Rake. I'd know those twin claymores anywhere! Aye, an' there's Sarn't Miggory. Eulaliiiiaaaa, you chaps!"

The Patrol drew blades and lances, dashing along with him. "Eulaliiiiaaaa! Eulaliiiiaaaaa!"

Skor Axehound despatched the last vermin with a mighty sweep of his battleaxe. He leaned on the haft, nodding at the approaching patrol. "Looks like some o' yore young bucks, Rake, tryin' to make a name for themselves. A bit late I'd say, eh?"

Rake Nightfur wiped his blades on a slain corsair before sheathing them across his back.

"Aye, Ah reckernise Major Fforbes by his war cry. Och,

he's a braw singer, the noo. But Ah cannae help wonderin' what they're doin' sae far frae Salamandastron."

Sergeant Miggory shook his head in disapproval. "Chargin' off like h'a load o' bees to brekkist, h'an leavin' their lady h'on 'er own. Bad form, sah!"

Lady Wildstripe could be seen descending the hill with slow dignity. Rake called out, "Bawdsley, Fletchers, Miz Ferrul, hop tae it an' provide escort for Lady Wildstripe!"

Skor nudged his son Ruggan. "You go, too, an' mind yore manners. She's a Mountain Lord . . . er, Lady!"

He signalled to the vessel. "Ahoy, bring 'er for'ard an' help the Badger Lady aboard when ye reach her. We'll take her back to Salamandastron in style!"

EPILOGUE

Herein is an extract from the journal of Lady Violet Wildstripe.

Reunions are often a source of both sorrow and joy. Sorrow for the fallen, those valiant ones who gave their lives that their mission should succeed. Joy in welcoming back our Long Patrol comrades. Also the making of new friends, the mighty Skor Axehound and his formidable Rogue Crew. Sea otters are not only brave, fearless beasts, but jolly good company.

The ride back home on a wheeled ship was a wonderful experience. Major Fforbes sent two of his fastest Gallopers ahead to announce our arrival. We rolled smoothly up to Salamandastron—it was a tremendous reception. Even old Colonel Bletgore forsook his noontide nap, appearing resplendent in full dress uniform, bedecked in medals and ribbons from neck-band to midriff. Our hares lined the shore and rock slopes, cheering the warriors' return.

Such a feast we had on that day. In the main mess hall, I learned something about sea otters, too—they could eat and drink as much as any of my hares. Skor could become a living legend for his massive appetite! The festivities lasted three full days, during which time I learned of the mission I had sent them on, the marches, skirmishes and the strange beasts they encountered. I listened with rapt attention to the report of that final battle on the grounds of Redwall Abbey. Thank the fates and seasons, they emerged victorious.

Both Rake and Skor were slightly crestfallen not to have triumphed against the evil Razzid Wearat. To my surprise, I learned that he was slain by a young hogmaid and an old otter Cellarkeeper. Once the enemy was vanquished, everybeast set to work repairing the vermin ship, as Skor and Rake had plans for it. Fortunately, it is a sturdy craft, and Redwall carpenters volunteered their skills to the task. The vessel was soon restored to its former state. It needs only two things to be altered, the hated mainsail, with its wicked twin eyes peering through the trident prongs, and the dreaded name *Greenshroud*. However, these will soon be done.

But to get back to the report given. Once the ship was both seaworthy and landworthy, the Rogue Crew and Long Patrol took their leave of the Abbey. They set course for Salamandastron whilst pursuing those searats and corsairs who had deserted the battle at Redwall. Everybeast agreed that such hardened, murderous vermin could not be left alive to terrorise and slay any innocent creatures they came across. Even though their quarry had a long head start, they needed to forage for food and halt to rest, unlike the great wheeled ship, which could travel both night and day. They dealt summarily with quite a number of vermin. Their last encounter was with the band who had attempted to ambush us the previous night. I stood on a hilltop, witnessing it all. No quarter was given, no surrender permitted. The last of that barbarous crew paid the final price for their vile ways.

So, Captain Rake's mission has been accomplished. We are all looking ahead, planning for the future. I have formed an alliance with Skor Axehound between Salamandastron and the High North Coast. We are to share the ownership of the wheeled ship, which will be renamed the *Posy Gurdy*. This is in honour of the young hogmaid and the old otter who rid the earth of that vile Razzid Wearat. A new mainsail has been designed; it will be white canvas with a depiction of two paws grasped in friendship, that of a sea otter and a Long Patrol hare. Now our seas and shores will be fully protected.

The arrangement will run thus: a joint band of hares and otters will crew the *Posy Gurdy*. Captain Ruggan Axehound will command at sea whilst Captain Nubbs Miggory, who was elected unanimously to the post, will run the vessel on land. I am looking forward to next summer, when I will be making my first-ever visit to Redwall Abbey, under sail of course. Perhaps we'll meet, if you are there, my friends. Well, I'll finish my writing for now, but here is something I almost overlooked. It is a letter from Abbot Thibb, given to me by young Lancejack Sage, when I met the Patrol on their return.

(The letter from Abbot Thibb is enclosed here.)

Lady Wildstripe,

I have not yet had the pleasure of meeting you, but be assured that Redwall is forever indebted to you. I include Skor Axehound and his Rogue Crew. Redwallers all have many valiant warriors to thank for delivering us from the Wearat and his barbarians. After the hares and otters left, Log a Log Dandy and his Guosim shrews stayed on at the Abbey. What faithful and trusty creatures they are, helping with repairing battle damage and the raising of our new main wallgates. They are welcome to stay as long as they desire, as are you and your courageous Long Patrol. Also, I would dearly like to meet up again with Skor and his Rogue Crew. Would you all consider coming here, even if only for a visit? Redwall is always open, its tables laden, to you and any of good heart.

I send this message in the hope that you may honour us with your presence someday.

Thibb, Father Abbot of Redwall Abbey in
Mossflower Country